THE WORKS OF TOBIAS SMOLLETT

The Devil upon Crutches

THE WORKS OF TOBIAS SMOLLETT

Alexander Pettit, General Editor
University of North Texas

O M Brack, Jr., Textual Editor
Arizona State University

*This edition includes all of the works by which Tobias Smollett was best known
in his own day and by which he most deserves to be remembered.
The edition conforms to the highest standards of textual and editorial scholarship.
Individual volumes provide carefully prepared texts together with biographical
and historical introductions and extensive explanatory notes.*

Don Cleofas Breaks the Vial and Releases Asmodeus. (Sterling Library, Yale University.)

The Devil upon Crutches

By ALAIN RENÉ LE SAGE

Translated by

TOBIAS SMOLLETT

Edited by

O M BRACK, JR.

and

LESLIE A. CHILTON

The University of Georgia Press

Athens and London

Paperback edition, 2014

© 2005 by the University of Georgia Press

Athens, Georgia 30602

www.ugapress.org

Set in Janson Text by Graphic Composition Inc.

Most University of Georgia Press titles are
available from popular e-book vendors.

Printed digitally

The Library of Congress has cataloged the hardcover
edition of this book as follows:
Le Sage, Alain René , 1668–1747.
[Diable boiteux. English]
The devil upon crutches / by Alain René Le Sage ;
translated by Tobias Smollett ; edited by O M Brack, Jr.
and Leslie A. Chilton.
xxviii, 283 p. : ill. ; 24 cm. — (The works of Tobias Smollett)
Includes biographical references and index.
ISBN 0-8203-2053-6 (hardcover : alk. paper)
I. Brack, O M. II. Chilton, Leslie A. III. Title.
IV. Series: Smollett, T. (Tobias), 1721–1771. Works. 1988.
PQ1997.D5E5 2005
823'.6—dc22   2004013914

Paperback ISBN 978-0-8203-4605-2

British Library Cataloging-in-Publication Data available

CONTENTS

ILLUSTRATIONS

The title pages and illustrations, except for the frontispiece to volume 1, are from the second edition of *The Devil upon Crutches* in the Sterling Library, Yale University. The frontispiece for volume 1 is from the second edition in the William Andrews Clark Memorial Library, UCLA. The receipt for payment for correcting the second edition of *The Devil upon Crutches* is from the Bodleian Library, Oxford University.

PREFACE

This is the first reprinting since the eighteenth century and the first scholarly edition of Tobias Smollett's translation of Alain René Le Sage's *Le Diable boiteux*. Numerous signs of haste appear in the first edition (1750) of the translation: run-on sentences, faulty syntax, and ambiguous pronoun references. When Smollett revised a copy of the first edition to serve as printers' copy for the second edition (1759), many but not all of these anomalies were corrected. The second edition also introduced a few new errors. Nevertheless, the second edition, revised by Smollett and perhaps corrected by him for the press, represents what the translator wished the public to read; it has therefore been chosen as copy-text for this edition. The present edition preserves the text of the second edition, except when the second edition is manifestly in error or when sense is affected to the extent that the reader might be confused. Any impulse to co-author the translation by guessing at what Smollett would have done had he had another opportunity to revise and correct the text has been firmly resisted.

This new edition of *The Devil upon Crutches* is the first to provide a carefully edited text, with historical annotation and notes on the translation. The edition has not been prepared as though Smollett's *Devil* were an original composition. That is to say, no attempt has been made to annotate Le Sage's narrative. Rather, Smollett's translation itself is the focus of the notes, which are generally confined to explanations of unfamiliar terms, definitions of obsolete English words, citation of archaic English usages, and identification of substantive or otherwise significant departures from the French text. Smollett regularly varies from the French by the omission or, more frequently, the addition of words, phrases, or clauses; a representative selection of such variations, including all the important instances of them, is given in the notes. Other substantive changes, including alterations of the meaning or the narrative progression of Le Sage's work, are indicated by quotations from the French, allowing the reader to make comparisons.

Le Sage's text is filled with references to Greek gods; authors and literature; personages; places and events in Spain, Portugal, and North Africa; demons; and pharmaceuticals, all of which seem to demand annotation. Again, however, it is not Le Sage's narrative but Smollett's translation that must remain the focus. The frequent references to specific sites in Spain and the surrounding area, for example, have been added by Le Sage for the sake of local color and authenticity and rarely have additional significance. With the exceptions of Cinquellos, Corita, Melorido, Vieso de Mediana, and Zebroso, all sites, towns, rivers, and mountains in Spain, the Baleric Isles, and North Africa can be easily found on appropriate maps. Le Sage's references to Asmodeus, demons, and demonology are a slightly more complex issue, although even here the brief mentions of demons are made largely to enhance the satiric quality of the work. Pharmaceuticals, however, require more attention and special handling. Since Smollett studied medicine and served as a surgeon's mate in the navy, he takes a personal interest in the references to medicinal treatments found in Le Sage's work. Indeed, on occasion Smollett revises

Le Sage's preparations and ingredients. Therefore, it seemed useful to provide the reader with information on medicinal matters in a separate appendix.

Le Diable boiteux, initially published in 1707, was extensively revised by Le Sage for the 1726 edition. Although at least eight editions of the French text appeared between 1726 and the date of Smollett's translation, a careful examination of these editions has failed to establish the one he might have used as the basis of his translation. Hence, for purposes of comparison and citation in the notes, the editors have used a copy of the 1737 edition (Paris, 2 vols.) held by the Bibliothèque nationale, Paris. The second edition of Smollett's translation in the Sterling Library, Yale University, has been compared with the Bibliothèque nationale copy (shelfmark Y2 11257–11258): "LE | DIABLE | BOITEUX. | *Par Monsieur* LE SAGE. | NOUVELLE ÉDITION, | *Corrigée, refondue, augmentée d'un volume par* | *l'Auteur, & ornée de Figures,* | *AVEC* | LES ENTRETIENS SERIEUX, | & Comiques des Cheminées de Madrid, | ET | LES BEQUILLES DUDIT DIABLE. | *Par Monsieur* *** | . . . | A PARIS, | Chez PRAULT pere, Quai de Gêvres, | au Paradis. | M.DCC.XXXVII. | *Avec Approbation & Privelege du Roi.*" Quotations in the notes retain the spelling and accents of this French edition.

For definitions of words the *Oxford English Dictionary (OED)* has been consulted, supplemented by the *Concise Scots Dictionary* (Aberdeen: Aberdeen University Press, 1985) and *A Dictionary of the Older Scottish Tongue* (Aberdeen: Aberdeen University Press, 1931–), especially for Scotticisms. References to Milton are to the *Complete Poems and Major Prose*, edited by Merritt Y. Hughes (New York: Odyssey Press, 1957). Works used in compiling the guide to pharmaceuticals are identified in the headnote to that guide.

The introduction places *The Devil upon Crutches* in the context of Smollett's career as a writer; discusses the publication, popularity, and influence of the French original; reviews the evidence supporting attribution of the translation to Smollett; assesses the translation itself; and concludes by tracing the history of its composition, printing, and reception.

ACKNOWLEDGMENTS

No bibliographical and textual study can be completed without the assistance of librarians; we wish to thank especially the staffs of the William Andrews Clark Memorial Library at UCLA, the Henry E. Huntington Library, the University of Virginia Library, and the Sterling Library at Yale University. We wish to thank David Foster for providing suggestions and directions for untangling Spanish references; Lisa Rengo George for assistance with Greek references; Thomas Kaminski for assistance with classical allusions; John Mulryan for advice on medieval and Renaissance matters; and David L. Vander Meulen for bibliographical information. We also wish to thank Huidi Tang for early work with collation and proofreading; Jonathan Drnjevic for always answering a request for assistance, no matter what the task; Sydney L. Chilton for translating some of the Spanish-language resources; and William and Josephine Jackson in Bramley, Surrey, for providing a home for Leslie while she was working at the British Library.

Thanks as well to Alex Pettit, general editor of the Georgia Smollett; to his assistants, Rima Abunasser and Ashley B. Bender; and to the chair of his department, James T. F. Tanner.

INTRODUCTION

The *General Advertiser* for 1 February 1750 and the *Whitehall Evening Post* for 1–3 February announced the forthcoming publication of a new translation of Alain René Le Sage's *Le Diable boiteux* (1707; revised edition 1726); it was published, according to these same newspapers, on 27 February. This new translation of the 1726 version, titled *The Devil upon Crutches*, appeared one year after a successful translation of Le Sage's greatest work, *L'Histoire de Gil Blas de Santillane* (1715–35). Neither work carried the name of its translator, Tobias Smollett; this was not unusual in the eighteenth century, when the book trade viewed translating recent and vernacular works as largely the province of the Grub Street hack. But the translations provided money for Smollett; and *Gil Blas*'s picaresque form, filled with comic and satiric characters and episodes like *Le Diable boiteux*'s satiric delving into the recesses of human duplicity, were well suited to Smollett's talent and temperament and suggested new directions to the struggling author.

BIOGRAPHICAL BACKGROUND

Smollett's career as a translator was one of expediency rather than deliberation. His first translation, *L'Histoire de Gil Blas de Santillane*, was published in 1748, within months of the publication of his highly successful first novel, *The Adventures of Roderick Random* (1748). *Gil Blas* proved equally successful, and in a letter of 14 February 1749 to Alexander Carlyle, Smollett boasts that of "three thousand Copies that were printed, scarce 400 remain unsold."[1] *Roderick Random* and *Gil Blas* were, however, isolated successes during the difficult years between 1747 and 1750, when Smollett was struggling unsuccessfully to establish himself as a surgeon and a dramatist. His calculated moves to Downing Street, to Chapel Street in Mayfair, to Beaufort Street (near Somerset House), and then to Old Chelsea, all made in the hope of attracting patients to his surgical practice, did not pay off; the London medical establishment refused admission to the transplanted Scot, and he was too proud to resort to the kind of quackery by which others made their fortunes.[2] His relentless pursuit of theater managers and his many attempts to secure patronage on behalf of his tragedy, *The Regicide*, could not bring the play to the stage. An opera, *Alceste*, with lyrics by Smollett and music by George Frederick Handel, and a comedy, *The Absent Man*, similarly failed.[3]

Smollett fictionalized his frustrations over *The Regicide* in the Melopoyn episode of *Roderick Random* (chapters 61–63). Melopoyn, after failing to have his tragedy produced, is driven to peddle his genius on Grub Street: "I was . . . persuaded to offer myself as a translator, and accordingly repaired myself to a person, who was said to entertain numbers of that class in his pay."[4] Turned away even after reducing his rate of pay to an intolerable half guinea per sheet, Melopoyn is forced to the even more desperate step of writing half-penny ballads. Smollett proved more fortunate in obtaining work as a translator than Melopoyn did; nevertheless, Melopoyn's story surely reflects Smollett's original reluctance to turn to the much-maligned task of translating. Before Smollett boasted of *Gil Blas*'s sales in his letter to Carlyle, he declared, "Gil Blas was actually translated by me, tho' as it was a Bookseller's Job, done in a hurry, I did not choose to put my name to it."[5]

However disparaging his comments, Smollett's success with *Gil Blas* must have demonstrated to him that translation was a ready source of income, even if it were not the best way to establish one's reputation. In any case, he immediately sought work of this sort and, in 1749 or early 1750, completed *The Devil upon Crutches*. Smollett soon achieved far greater success than his fictional counterpart in *Roderick Random*, but he apparently continued to regard certain kinds of translators with disgust, as revealed in *The Adventures of Peregrine Pickle* (1751), a novel that he seems to have begun about the time he completed *The Devil upon Crutches*. In chapter 102 the destitute Peregrine, trying to make his way in the London literary world, attends a meeting of a "college" and views the humiliation of a hack translator: "[S]oon as his design took air, the proprietors of those miserable translations had endeavored to prejudice his work, by industrious insinuations, contrary to truth and fair dealing, importing, that he did not understand one word of the language which he pretended to translate."[6]

Nevertheless, the success of *Gil Blas* was satisfying, and *The Devil upon Crutches*, while not as successful as *Gil Blas*, further demonstrated the expediency of translation. Smollett would pursue such projects for the next six years. Indeed, until he established his successful *Critical Review* (1756) and wrote *The Complete History of England* (1757–58), translating seems to have been a consistent source of income for him. In 1748, as he was working on *The Devil upon Crutches*, he also began his most ambitious translation, *Don Quixote*.[7] And the translation of Cervantes overlapped Smollett's translations of three works by Voltaire, ultimately published in one volume as *Micromegas: A Comic Romance. Being a Severe Satire upon the Philosophy, Ignorance, and Self Conceit of Mankind. Together with a Detail of the Crusades; and a New Plan for the History of the Human Mind* (1752).[8] In 1754 he completed the clearly commercial *Select Essays on Commerce, Agriculture, Mines, Fisheries, and other Useful Subjects*.[9] In 1755 Smollett finally completed *Don Quixote*.[10] After this, perhaps discouraged by the difficulty of translating, he forsook such work to concentrate on criticism, editing, and political writing. He would produce one more translation—of François de Salignac de la Mothe-Fénelon's *Les Aventures de Télémaque*—in the 1760s, when he was ill and in need of money.[11] Although the quantity and quality of his translations are impressive, and his translations in many ways influenced his own work, Smollett, it seems clear, pursued translation mostly for its financial rewards.

LE SAGE AND *LE DIABLE BOITEUX*

In Le Sage's *Le Diable boiteux* the student, Don Cleofas Leandro Peréz Zambullo, fleeing for his life from an interrupted love affair, finds safety in a necromancer's study, in which he meets and releases from his bottle the lame yet personable devil, Asmodeus. In reward, the "devil upon crutches" carries the student over the rooftops of Madrid, allowing him to peek into houses, prisons, palaces, and even tombs and, more fundamentally, to examine the various motivations of the human hearts residing within them.

The combination of comedy, fantasy, realism, romance, satire, sentiment, sexual intrigue, and moral admonition clearly had an appeal to the cynical French audiences in
the declining years of the ancien régime.

Le Sage (1668–1747) and his translator had, to a degree, parallel lives and literary careers. Both were born far from the capital cities in which they would eventually live and
gain fame. Middle class, ambitious, hardworking, and stubborn, they undertook professional careers and then abandoned them for writing, supporting themselves and their
families with their pens. Above all, their popular productions helped to define their literary age.

Le Sage was born in Bretagne and, when a student, left for Paris to study law. He practiced as an *avocat*, married in 1694, and about the same time left the law and entered literature. Le Sage's first notable success came with his 1700 translation of two Spanish
comedies, *Le Traître puni* by Francisco de Rojas Zorrilla and *Garder et se garder* by Lope
de Vega. In 1702 Le Sage made his debut at the Théâtre-Française with *Le Point d'honneur*, a translation of another play by Rojas. Two years later he published a popular translation of Alonso Fernández de Avellaneda of Tordesillas's spurious continuation of *Don
Quixote* (1614). Finally, in 1707 his apprenticeship as an author ended when he achieved
success as both a dramatist and a novelist: his comedy, *Crispin, rival de son maître*, was
quickly followed by his first version of *Le Diable boiteux*. *Turcaret*, his theatrical master-
piece, appeared in 1709. Then in 1715 the first two volumes of his *L'Histoire de Gil Blas
de Santillane* were published. Described by Le Sage as his "favorite child," *Gil Blas* grew
over the years, with volume 3 appearing in 1724 and volume 4 in 1735. He published
three other picaresque novels—*Don Guzman d'Alfarache* (1732), *Estevanille Gonzales*
(1734), and *Le Bachelier de Salamanque* (1736)—that, like *Le Diable boiteux* and *Gil Blas*,
were inspired by Spanish literature.

This literature, which had already captured the popular and intellectual imagination
of France, gave Le Sage ideas and direction. From the great romances to their satiric
counterpart in *Don Quixote*, Spanish literature had been admired, copied, and adapted.
During the reign of Louis XIV—who was married to the Spanish infanta, Marie-
Thérèse—Pierre Corneille (1606–84), the leading dramatist of the period, borrowed
from Spanish plays, and Spanish farces often provided models for French comedies. By
the late seventeenth century, political interests had increased literary borrowings; the
War of the Spanish Succession produced nonfictional works of correspondence, jour-
nals, relations, notes, and memoirs.[12]

It was the lighter, more popular vein of Spanish literature that most influenced Le
Sage. *Le Diable boiteux* has as its starting point *El diablo cojuelo* (1641) by Luis Vélez de
Guevara. In his preface Le Sage states that he had "made a new work based upon the
same foundation" as the earlier work.[13] In fact, he borrows the title and the characters
of Don Cleofas and Asmodeus, and for a chapter or two he follows the plan and the language of *El diablo cojuelo*. But after the opening chapters Le Sage abandons his source
and writes a tale with original characterization, incidents, and style.

Le Sage's narrative, at least according to one critic, nominates the author "to be
counted among the first creators of the modern novel."[14] Labeling any work of prose fic-
tion in the eighteenth century a novel is likely to provoke debate about the essential features of the genre, but *Le Diable boiteux* seems a particularly difficult work to categorize.

The satirical portraits and episodes in *Le Diable boiteux*, for example, recall *Les Carac-tères* (1688) of Jean de La Bruyère (1645–96). Le Sage's relaxed and uncluttered prose recalls Paul Scarron (1610–60), who had rebelled against the artificiality and preciosity of fashionable literature. The tale of a witty devil carrying a student through a sinful city blends fantasy, realism, and morality in the manner of the fables of Jean de La Fontaine (1621–95) and Charles Perrault (1628–1703). Transforming Asmodeus into Cupid and making several classical allusions, mocking and serious, Le Sage addresses the "quer-relle des anciens et des modernes" that, famously, had concerned Jonathan Swift in *The Battle of the Books* (1697; published 1704). Finally, he borrows character types from Molière (1622–73) and Charles-Rivière Dufresny (1648–1724).

Twentieth-century scholars of French literature have accorded *Le Diable boiteux* high praise. English Showalter, for example, regards it as "a serious novel, despite its fantas-tic frame," while Geoffrey Brereton considers it a "novel of manners."[15] Arthur Tilley similarly describes it as a "series of observations on society . . . [given the] form either of portraits, characters, or anecdotes."[16] Roger Laufer, editor of the most recent edition of *Le Diable boiteux* (1970), characterizes Le Sage as a stylist whose work is a triumph of the rococo literary style, which challenged the baroque excesses of seventeenth-century literature: "His manner is his message; and [*Le Diable boiteux*] is the first masterpiece of rococo style and of the Age of Reason." He proclaims the work "close to the *Lettres per-sanes* [of Montesquieu], the tales of Voltaire, and the works of Diderot, all of which find their value from a mixture of romance, criticism, imagination, reflection, sensibility, and reason."[17]

The mercurial shifting in *Le Diable boiteux* from high to low, brutality to sentimen-tality, and cuckoldry to pure love softens an essentially harsh story about two Peeping Toms. Le Sage's simple, unaffected phrasing further alleviates any potential grimness. Above all, the message is ironic: despite his multitude of experiences, his encounters with the frequently sordid motives for many actions, young Don Cleofas learns only that he should never take anything seriously. A woman's smile may cover a deceptive heart; a man's solicitude for his fellow creatures may well be a matter of a failing mind. The secular humanist wisdom taught by *Le Diable boiteux* is all the more ironic for being taught by a mere scamp of a demon.

Indeed, *Le Diable boiteux* may be viewed as a distant and mocking relative of the de-monology manuals published in the sixteenth and seventeenth centuries, when fear of the supernatural reached an unfortunate high. Works such as Agrippa von Nettesheim's *De Occulta Philosophia* (1531), Pierre Binsfield's *De Maleficis* (1589), and Sebastien Michaelis's *The Admirable History of the Possession of and Conversion of a Penitent Woman* (1612) named and ranked demons according to formulas and vocabularies known only to the authors. Le Sage's titular hero, Asmodeus, provides an interesting example. Bins-field declared Asmodeus "demon-patron of lechery"; Michaelis ranked Asmodeus as one of the seraphim and "Prince of Wantons."[18] Agrippa, in contrast, regarded him as leader of the fourth order of angels, the "revengers of evil."[19]

Le Sage orders and assigns duties to his demons—Belphegor, Beelzebub, Griffael, Leviathan, Lucifer, Palliardoc—in a similarly haphazard fashion, perhaps to satirize such elaborate and arbitrary ranking systems. His own Asmodeus is cut from the whole cloth of demonology. A creature derived from Jewish folklore and his imagination, Le Sage's Asmodeus is a likable trickster and a revealer of the baser designs of humanity. He describes himself as the Cupid of Greek fame and, therefore, the inventor of the philosopher's stone and the demon-patron of pleasure, passion, luxury, and lust. He oversees ridiculous and improper matches between partners of all ages and wealth. A dandy, he is the father of fads and fashions, yet he is also a scholar and a philosopher. Le Sage makes his Asmodeus small, homely, and crippled rather than casting him as the handsome, energetic, and slightly limping figure of other sources. In fact, Maximilian Rudwin in *The Devil in Legend and Literature* references *Le Diable boiteux* as a source of material on the likable demon, whom he describes as "an excellent critic of men and morals, and a splendid satirist of the follies and foibles of the human family."[20]

However modern critics may define *Le Diable boiteux* (romance, fable, novel of manners, comic philosophical tale, or amalgam), there can be no doubt that the formula was immediately successful. Laufer reports that seven editions appeared between June and December 1707: four by Veuve Barbin in Paris, a counterfeit of the second Barbin edition, and two printed in Lyon and Amsterdam. Laufer reports that "between 15,000 and 20,000 copies" of *Le Diable boiteux* were printed.[21] The most famous anecdote about the work's popularity was reported by the *Journal de Verdun:* "Two lords of the court carried swords in hand to the shop of Barbin to have the latest offering from the edition."[22]

In 1726 Le Sage revised *Le Diable boiteux*, a process that he described as "correcting, reforming, and augmenting."[23] The new edition was more lavish than its predecessor, for the enlarged text was framed by Le Sage's dedication to Vélez de Guevara, author of the original *El diablo cojuelo*, and by "Asmodeus's Crutches," a lighthearted defense of *Le Diable boiteux* by Abbé Laurent Bordelon (1653–1730). The text was followed by Le Sage's "Dialogues between Two Chimnies of Madrid," in which the chimneys make a series of observations on the people surrounding their hearths. *Le Diable boiteux* itself was notably altered. Leaving the first four chapters intact, Le Sage transposed episodes, repositioned the Comte de Belflor novella, and moved up the scene in which Don Cleofas has revenge upon his duplicitous mistress. Le Sage added the story of Seraphina, her rescue from fire by the demon disguised as Don Cleofas, and her meeting with the real Don Cleofas, who has been given her hand in reward for his seeming rescue. New anecdotes were added; as Le Sage declared in his preface to his 1726 revision, "[T]he folly of humankind furnishes examples easily to me."[24] In all, the text grew from fifty-eight thousand to ninety-three thousand words. The most striking difference between the two versions is that Asmodeus changes from a malignant if friendly guide into a guardian angel and even a marriage broker to Don Cleofas and Seraphina. As Laufer observes in the introduction to his edition, "In 1707 [Le Sage] had followed Guevara's *Diablo cojuelo;* in 1726 he demarcated *Diable boiteux* into its own work."[25]

English readers enjoyed the adventures of *Le Diable boiteux* in both its original and revised versions. In 1708 an unknown translator produced an English version; by 1718 at least four editions of this version had been printed. This same version was revised to reflect Le Sage's changes and was issued in a new edition in 1729 (though lacking "Asmodeus's Crutches" and "Chimnies of Madrid"). Smollett's translation of 1749 was followed in 1770 by a third version, issued several times, by an unknown translator.

His translation and his later revisions suggest that Smollett enjoyed *Le Diable boiteux*, but a seriousness of purpose in his life and works during this period was not alleviated by Le Sage's sparkling outrageousness. Even so, we can see that in *Peregrine Pickle*, completed by 1751, Smollett was affected by *The Devil upon Crutches*. Roderick Random, like Gil Blas, is thrust upon the world to make his way; but Peregrine, like Don Cleofas, has money and is out to have some fun. There is, moreover, in *Peregrine Pickle* a hardness, even a viciousness, not present in *Roderick Random*. Peregrine has a crueler nature than either Roderick Random or Don Cleofas, but he delights in playing tricks, both upon the foolish and the innocent, much in the manner of Asmodeus.

Peregrine Pickle also resembles *Le Diable boiteux* in the insertion of a romance into the midst of the action. "Memoirs of a Lady of Quality" resembles Le Sage's entertaining but somewhat intrusive tale of Comte de Belflor in book 1, chapters 4–5 of *Le Diable boiteux*, as well as "The Power of Friendship" in book 2, chapter 2. All these stories address the cruelties of love, comically and then tragically, among the rich and powerful. Perhaps the closest resemblance among them is their exposure of the corrupt motives and desires of the upper classes. Indeed, Peregrine Pickle's elaborate fortune-telling scheme (chapters 90–91) is a more realistic version of Asmodeus's lifting of roofs to peer at the deceptions beneath.

ATTRIBUTION OF *THE DEVIL UPON CRUTCHES* TO SMOLLETT

The one piece of external evidence for attributing *The Devil upon Crutches* to Smollett is the receipt for correcting the first edition signed by him:

London, Jan. 5, 1759
Received of Mr. A. Millar Seven Guineas and a half,
an Account of Correcting the Devil on Crutches by me
Ts. Smollett[26]

Andrew Millar had purchased three of the one-quarter shares of the copyright of the work at the bankruptcy sale of John Osborn's "books in quires, and copies" on 19 November 1751.[27] Millar, a fellow Scot but a bookseller with whom Smollett did not normally publish, undoubtedly discovered the identity of the translator and turned to him when it was time to publish a new edition, allowing him to say truthfully on the title page, "The Second Edition, corrected."

The announcement of publication for *The Devil upon Crutches* in the 1 February issues of the *General Advertiser* and the *Whitehall Evening Post* failed to mention Smollett. The following announcement appeared in the *General Advertiser*:

In a few Days will be publish'd, Elegantly printed on a new Elzevir Letter and superfine Dutch Paper, adorned with a new Set of Cuts, in Two Pocket Volumes, Price bound in Calf 4s.

THE DEVIL upon CRUTCHES: From the *Diable Boiteux* of Mr. LE SAGE. A New Translation. To which are now first added, *Asmodeus's Crutches*, A Critical Letter upon the Work: And Dialogues between Two Chimnies of Madrid.

Printed for J. Osborn, at the Golden Ball in Pater-noster-row.

Where may be had, printed on the same Letter and Paper, and translated from the same Author. The Adventures of GIL BLAS of *Santillane*, adorned with 33 Cuts, neatly engrav'd, in 4 vols. Price in Sheets 6s. sew'd in Boards and Marble Paper 7s. bound in Calf 8s.

Above this announcement is an advertisement for *Gil Blas*:

In a few Days will be publish'd, Beautifully printed on a new large Pica Letter, and superfine Paper, in Four Volumes, Twelves, Price bound 12s.

THE ADVENTURES of GIL BLAS of SANTILLANE. A New Translation. *By the* AUTHOR *of* RODERICK RANDOM.

The Second Edition, corrected; with the Addition of some Notes by the Translator. Adorned with 33 Cuts, neatly engrav'd.

Printed for J. Osborn at the Golden Ball on Pater-noster-Row.
                    Where may be had,
The First Edition, elegantly printed on a new Elzevir letter, in Four small Pocket Volumes, Price bound 8s.

After the success of the first edition of *Gil Blas*, Smollett allowed his bookseller, John Osborn, to identify him as the translator on the title page of the second edition with the declaration, "By the Author of *Roderick Random*." Unsure of the success of his second "Bookseller's Job," Smollett apparently wished to remain anonymous. Not to be out-done by such reticence, Osborn appears to have tried to make readers associate the author of *Roderick Random* and the translator of *Gil Blas* with *The Devil upon Crutches*. Announcements of the publication of the first edition of *The Devil upon Crutches* also appeared in the *Gentleman's Magazine*, the *London Magazine*, and the *Scots Magazine* without identifying the translator.[28] Much later, in 1794, an anonymous author in the *Biographical Magazine* listed *The Devil upon Crutches* as among Smollett's translations, although giving it the more popular title "The Devil on Two Sticks": "It would be difficult to enumerate all his literary labours. He translated Gil Blas, The Devil on Two Sticks, and Telemachus."[29]

No scholarly tradition opposes the attribution of the translation to Smollett, as was the case with his translation of *The Adventures of Telemachus*.[30] Biographers and critics have, instead, ignored the work. The contributor to the *Biographical Magazine* is the only biographer of the eighteenth or nineteenth century who even mentions the work, much less attributes it to Smollett. Even John P. Anderson of the British Museum, who made the first carefully compiled bibliography of Smollett's works for David Hannay's *Life of Tobias George Smollett* (1887), failed to list it. The lack of mention, even if to question its legitimacy, suggests that biographers were unaware of the work or unsure that it existed.

In 1932 Lewis M. Knapp took a step toward openly restoring *The Devil upon Crutches* to Smollett's canon when he uncovered and published the receipt for the 1759 edition. In an argument that he reviewed in his 1949 biography of Smollett, Knapp points out that the alterations of the 1759 edition are familiar: "Like [Smollett's] manuscript corrections" of the *Travels through France and Italy* (1766), he notes, "the emendations illustrate his fondness for precise diction and his scrupulous care in syntax."[31] Nevertheless, despite the discovery of the receipt and the plausibility of Knapp's argument, *The Devil upon Crutches* has continued to be overlooked by scholars of Smollett.[32]

Some doubt about Smollett's hand in *The Devil upon Crutches* is understandable. After all, Smollett's name does not appear on the title page. Even when Smollett was identified as translator on a title page, as in the case of *Gil Blas* and *The Adventures of Telemachus*, doubts arose, because in the eighteenth century famous names were commonly used by unscrupulous booksellers to sell works written, translated, or compiled by others.[33] As a result, by the end of the eighteenth century both titles were considered booksellers' editions to which his name had been attached.[34] The one piece of external evidence connecting *The Devil upon Crutches* with Smollett only confirms that he corrected the work rather than translating it.

True, Smollett did not identify himself as the translator, either on the work or in his extant correspondence, but then neither does he refer in his letters to *The History and Adventures of an Atom*, *The Expedition of Humphry Clinker*, or *Telemachus*. Besides, the slightly more than one hundred letters that have survived must be only a fraction of those he wrote; had we more letters, we might have acknowledgments of all these works. *The Devil upon Crutches*, designed by Smollett or John Osborn as a companion piece to *Gil Blas*, was a work of Smollett's early career, when he was apparently loath to identify himself as a translator. Considering the popularity of his translation of *Gil Blas*, it would be only natural that he was hired or nominated himself to translate another one of Le Sage's popular works. A careful examination of the translation and the revisions to it places *The Devil upon Crutches* firmly in Smollett's canon.

SMOLLETT'S TRANSLATION OF *LE DIABLE BOITEUX*

In his edition of Smollett's version of *Don Quixote*, Carlos Fuentes asserts that "sometimes translation is an act of homage; sometimes an *auto da fe*. On the few occasions when it really works it is almost always a serendipity; a clash between one great writer and another in which a foreign, a *strange* language becomes the authentic vernacular version."[35] Fuentes finds Smollett's Cervantes to be such a "clash." Although *Le Diable boiteux* cannot reasonably be compared with *Don Quixote* as a work of art, Smollett may be said to have had a similar degree of success as a translator of both works. Of the three known English translations of the eighteenth century, his is undoubtedly the best. Smollett's version is not only complete, accurate, and highly readable, but it also matches Le Sage's irony. Comparison with an earlier translation reveals that Smollett used a technique found helpful by other translators: the reliance on predecessors for a borrowed word or phrase to lend assistance with difficult passages.[36] But, for the most part, his translation of *Le Diable boiteux* is fresh, new, and more nearly possessed of the spirit and flavor of the original than its anonymous predecessor.

Prior to the nineteenth century, translation was conducted in a near vacuum of theory and methods; its general goal was to reproduce the ideas and spirit of the original as faithfully as possible while avoiding both extremes of word-for-word mimeticism and overfree adaptation. Though admirable, these vague standards, which can be traced to John Dryden in the seventeenth century, were undermined by the high marketability of translated books: "The utility of translation is universally felt," wrote Alexander Tytler Fraser in his *Essay on the Principles of Translation* (1791), and this "continuous demand . . . has thrown the practice into mean and mercenary hands."[37]

Smollett cannot be called "mean and mercenary," but he was a translator of his time in his beliefs and methods. As he observed later in the "Translator's Note" to *Don Quixote*, "[I have] endeavored to retain the spirit and ideas, without servilely adhering to the literal expression, of the original."[38] Yet it would be wrong to assume that such an attitude made Smollett careless about his translations. Even his most commercial works reveal attention to accuracy and neat expression; and Smollett brought to *Le Diable boiteux* a ready knowledge of French, both formal and idiomatic, probably learned at school in Dumbarton but polished through his recent work on *Gil Blas*.

A comparison of the French and English versions reveals that in *The Devil upon Crutches* Smollett did not introduce any extensive changes into Le Sage's original story. But although Smollett remains close to the text of *Le Diable boiteux*, he freely imposes his own style on the work. Examples of Smollett's fondness for Latinate diction appear frequently in the text; this sometimes increases the irony and other times seems inappropriately or unnecessarily heavy handed for a text noted for its elegantly simple prose. Le Sage's exposure of hypocrisy, so dear to Smollett's heart, seems to elevate him to new heights of inventive rephrasing. But, for the most part, Smollett limited himself to his usual methods of combining sentences, reversing word order, employing idiomatic words and phrases, and adding short phrases for color and detail.

Above all, Smollett was sensitive to the tone of *Le Diable boiteux*. The chief and most endearing virtue of his translation is his attempt to re-create Le Sage's irony and dry humor, as when rendering Le Sage's observation on two steadfast lovers encountering additional troubles—"mais la fortune avec qui ces amans n'étaient pas encore bien reconciliés"—as "but fortune, with whom these two lovers were not yet quite good friends" (144). Smollett's attempts to re-create Le Sage's humor frequently accounted for his more inventive moments. In his anecdote of a miserable poet, Le Sage describes one of his meager furnishings as "une table." In Smollett's hands, this becomes the more expressive "something that resembles a table" (22). In the scene where the "ancient" poet quarrels with the "modern" playwright, the giddy poet's claim, "Je viens d'enfanter des Vers," becomes, in Smollett's invention, "I am just now brought to bed of twins; of most beautiful couplets" (127). When the two writers resort to fisticuffs to settle their argument, Smollett takes delight in embellishing the description of the fight, making it even more ludicrous (116–17, 130–32).

Smollett's hand is most clear in the translation with his use of nautical and pharmaceutical language. When Le Sage describes a ship simply as a "tartane," Smollett refers to it specifically as a "sloop" (126). In another instance he translates "à se rendre pour Alger" as "strike to" rather than "yield to" (133). Later he translates "*Arrive, arrive*" as "*strike, strike*" (137). When translating pharmaceutical terms, Smollett, drawing on his surgical experience, embellishes Le Sage's account by adding "syrup of spit-wort" (52).

However, Smollett sometimes decides against re-creating Le Sage's phrasing, perhaps thinking that it did not properly suit a given character. This leads to some of his most inventive moments, revealing his distinctive style. For example, when describing an aged man who is paying court to a young woman, Le Sage terms him "un soupirant," which simply translates to "suitor." Smollett preferred the more colorful though less ironic phrase "fribbling fumbler" (38). In another instance, Le Sage very simply describes the joy of a young man upon being freed from slavery in North Africa: "[I]l est charmé." Smollett is much more visual: "He huggs himself" (168). A prisoner, released after a long term of slavery, has "une barbe rousse rend affroyable à voir," which Smollett renders far more vividly as "clotted, red beard" (168). When Le Sage describes a proud but impoverished nobleman who has just purchased new clothes as "il tranchoit du Seigneur," Smollett says "he strutted with the utmost insolence" (169).

On other occasions, Smollett's Latinisms unnecessarily overwhelm Le Sage's graceful diction. Le Sage's phrase "mais ce malin esprit y ajoûtoit toujours quelque trait satyrique. Il leur donnoit à chacun son lardon" becomes overblown: "in giving of which, this evil spirit, following the biass of his own diabolical nature, always intermixed some satyrical stroke, not much to the honour of these great personages" (163). Elsewhere, Le Sage's "lui donne un beau rang dans la societé civil" becomes "which enables him now to stand a distinguished publican at the receipt of custom" (162).

Smollett's corrections of his 1750 text, incorporated into the 1759 second edition, reflect his usual methods and goals for emendation. As had been the case in his correcting of *Roderick Random*, Smollett's chief goal was to refine the style in rough portions of the text. For example, "it is far from being the same in" is revised to "the case is not the same in," and "in this other street, this racket?" is changed to "that racket in the other street?" (21, 25). Smollett also sought to refine obvious examples of his Scottish diction, such as his use of "got."[39] In 1750 his "got to ship" was emended to "reached the ship" (145). In a more striking example, "got in with" was revised to "insinuated herself into the good graces of" (24). This last example also points to another of Smollett's consistent emendations, attempts to smooth what he must have considered roughness in his diction: "round which went" becomes "surrounded by," and "as poets say" becomes "according to the poets" (16, 17). Also, "I shall be able to get myself clear of" is revised to "by these means I shall be able to extricate myself from" (34). Yet another consistent emendation is Smollett's sharpening of his sentences by means of an additional noun or verb: "but that gave" is emended to "that reflection gave," and "witness upon it" becomes "witness my protestations" (40, 41). A striking example is the simple pronoun "them" elaborated to "these convenient ladies" (51). Perhaps the most Smollettian quality of all is that the energetic substantive emending of the first few chapters soon gives way to mere orthographical corrections and to the filled-out abbreviations found in all chapters and commonly considered compositorial.

COMPOSITION, PRINTING, AND RECEPTION

We can only speculate about precisely when Smollett prepared his translation of *Le Diable boiteux*. The first edition of *Roderick Random* had been published on 21 January 1748, and the money he received for a first novel could not have been substantial. A revised second edition was published on 7 April 1748, and, even if Smollett received additional money for revising and correcting the text, his take could not have been more than a few pounds.[40] Soon he must have been in need of financial support. At some time in the late winter, spring, or summer of 1748 he was at work on his translation of *Gil Blas*, published on 14 October 1748.[41] Probably after it was clear that *Gil Blas* was a success, John Osborn approached Smollett, or Smollett approached his bookseller, about the translation of a second Le Sage work. In the letter of 14 February 1749 to Carlyle, observing the success of the publication of the first edition of *Gil Blas*, no mention is made of a translation of *Le Diable boiteux*, perhaps suggesting that Smollett began the translation after that date. This would have him working on the translation of *Le Diable boiteux* at any time in the spring, summer, or autumn of 1749 or even in the early winter of 1749 and 1750. Since the translation, like most of Smollett's early work, shows signs of haste, he may have translated it quickly in the autumn or early winter. During the same period he found time to revise and correct a copy of the first edition of *Gil Blas* for a second edition that would be published at about the same time as the first edition of *The Devil upon Crutches*. Encouraged by the sales of *Roderick Random* and *Gil Blas*, Osborn had the work printed in an edition of two thousand copies.[42]

When *The Devil upon Crutches* was published—on 28 February 1750, according to the *General Advertiser*—it seems not to have attracted any attention; apart from the announcements of its publication, no notices have been discovered in the periodical press. On 14 November 1751, the first day of the sale of John Osborn's stock, more than twenty months after the publication of *The Devil upon Crutches*, 654 of the 2,000 copies remained.[43] A second, and final, edition did not appear until 1759.

Smollett had almost certainly been paid, as was usually done, on the completion of the translation, so the modest sale of *The Devil upon Crutches*, compared to that of *Roderick Random* and *Gil Blas*, could not have hurt him financially. The endeavor could not have hurt his reputation either, as he had chosen not to acknowledge his work on the title page. In the end, the public had a good translation of a popular literary work of the period, Smollett had his money, and we have an example of how one of the best professional authors of the eighteenth century maintained his artistic integrity in the face of financial difficulties to produce the best English translation of a masterpiece of eighteenth-century French literature.

Notes

1. Lewis M. Knapp, ed., *The Letters of Tobias Smollett* (Oxford: Clarendon Press, 1970), 10.
2. See Lewis Mansfield Knapp, *Tobias Smollett: Doctor of Men and Manners* (Princeton, N.J.: Princeton University Press, 1949), 74.
3. See Tobias Smollett, *Poems, Plays, and "The Briton,"* ed. Byron Gassman (Athens: University of Georgia Press, 1993), 76–77, 78, 80. For *The Absent Man*, see Patricia Hernlund, "Three Bankruptcies in the London Book Trade, 1746–61: Rivington, Knapton, and Osborn," in O M Brack, Jr., ed., *Writers, Books, and Trade: An Eighteenth-Century English Miscellany for William B. Todd* (New York: AMS Press, 1994), 106–7.
4. Tobias Smollett, *The Adventures of Roderick Random*, ed. Paul-Gabriel Boucé (Oxford: Oxford University Press, 1979), 384.

5. Knapp, ed., *Letters*, 10.

6. Tobias Smollett, *The Adventures of Peregrine Pickle*, ed. James L. Clifford (Oxford: Oxford University Press, 1964), 645.

7. On 7 June 1748 Smollett wrote to Carlyle, "I have contracted with two Booksellers to translate Don Quixote from the Spanish Language, which I have studied some time. This perhaps you will look upon as a very Desperate Undertaking, there being no fewer than four Translations of the same Book already extant, but I am fairly engaged and cannot recede" (Knapp, ed., *Letters*, 8).

8. For *Micromegas*, see Louis L. Martz, *The Later Career of Tobias Smollett* (New Haven, Conn.: Yale University Press, 1942), 92, and Knapp, *Tobias Smollett*, 151. The volume was noticed in *Monthly Review* 7 (November 1752), a copy of which, annotated by Ralph Griffith, is held by the Bodleian Library, Oxford, and includes the note "translated by Dr. Smollett" at the bottom of the first page of the review (376).

9. For *Select Essays*, see Smollett's letter of 1 March 1754 to John Moore (Knapp, ed., *Letters*, 32).

10. On 11 December 1754 Smollett wrote to George Macaulay, "Nay, I am put to very great straits for present subsistence as I have done nothing all the last summer but worked upon Don Quixotte, for which I was paid five years ago" (Knapp, ed., *Letters*, 41).

11. See the introduction to Tobias Smollett, trans., *The Adventures of Telemachus, the Son of Ulysses*, ed. Leslie A. Chilton (Athens: University of Georgia Press, 1997), xvii–xxxi.

12. See Arthur Tilley, *The Decline of the Age of Louis XIV, or French Literature, 1687-1715* (1929; reprint, New York: Barnes and Noble, 1968), 107.

13. Alain René Le Sage, *Le Diable boiteux*, ed. Roger Laufer (The Hague: Mouton, 1970), 83. Translations from the French are by the editors.

14. Geoffrey Brereton, *A Short History of French Literature*, 2nd ed. (Harmondsworth: Penguin, 1976), 111.

15. English Showalter, *The Evolution of the French Novel, 1641–1782* (Princeton, N.J.: Princeton University Press, 1972), 125; Brereton, *A Short History*, 111.

16. Tilley, *The Decline of the Age of Louis XIV*, 108.

17. Roger Laufer, *Lesage ou le métier de romancier* (Paris: Gallimard, 1971), 180. Translations from the French are by the editors.

18. Demons have been cataloged, ranked, and classified since the early centuries of the Christian Era. Johann Weyer, in *Pseudo-Monarchy of Demons* (1568), devised the most complex hierarchy, estimating that there were 7,405,926 demons serving under 72 princes. See Rosemary Ellen Guiley, *The Encyclopedia of Witches and Witchcraft* (New York: Facts on File, 1989), 94.

19. See, for example, the book of Tobit (3:8–17). *The Testament of Solomon*, written early in the Christian Era, lists "the names and functions of various Hebrew, Greek, Assyrian, Babylonian, Egyptian and perhaps Persian demons." In this work, Asmodeus tricks Solomon out of a magic ring that he uses to command demons; thus empowered, he sets himself up as king. When Asmodeus throws the ring into the sea, Solomon recovers it from a fish's belly and restores himself to his throne. He then imprisons Asmodeus in a jar. See Guiley, *The Encyclopedia*, 94, 181–82.

20. Maximilian Rudwin, *The Devil in Legend and Literature* (1931; reprint, New York: AMS Press, 1970), 90. An interest in diabolism is evident in English literature after *Le Diable boiteux*'s first appearance. See, for example, *The Devil upon Two Sticks: or the Town until'd* (1708); *The Devil upon Crutches in England, or Night Scenes in London* (1755); and, later, William Combe, *The Devil upon Two Sticks in England: being a continuation of Le Diable Boiteux of Lesage* (1790).

21. Laufer, *Lesage*, 196.

22. Laufer, *Lesage*, 189.

23. Le Sage, *Le Diable boiteux*, ed. Laufer, 84.

24. Le Sage, *Le Diable boiteux*, ed. Laufer, 84.

25. Laufer, introduction to Le Sage, *Le Diable boiteux*, ed. Laufer, 11.

26. See Lewis M. Knapp, "Smollett and Lesage's *The Devil upon Crutches,*" *Modern Language Notes* 47 (1932): 91–93; and Knapp, *Tobias Smollett*, 105. The following is written, in another hand, on the verso of the receipt:

> D Smollett's rect for
> correcting
> Devil on Crutches
> 5 Janry 1759   7.7.16

27. See Hernlund, "Three Bankruptcies," 105.

28. See the February 1750 issues of the *Gentleman's Magazine* 20 (1750): 96; *London Magazine* 19 (1750): 96; and *Scots Magazine* 12 (1750): 104.

29. Quoted in Knapp, *Tobias Smollett*, 104. Two translations, the first completed in 1708 and the second completed in 1770, were entitled *Devil on Two Sticks*.

30. See the introduction to Smollett, trans., *The Adventures of Telemachus*, ed. Chilton, xxiv–xxvii.

31. Knapp, *Tobias Smollett*, 105.

32. In his discussion of Smollett's translations, Paul-Gabriel Boucé discusses only *Don Quixote* and *Gil Blas*; see Boucé, *The Novels of Tobias Smollett* (London: Longman, 1976), chap. 3.

33. Smollett condemned the practice of authors lending their names to booksellers in his letter to Richard Smith of 8 May 1763: "I am much mortified," he wrote, "to find it is believed in America that I have lent my name to Booksellers; that is a species of Prostitution of which I am altogether incapable" (Knapp, ed., *Letters*, 113).

34. Smollett's responsibility for the translation of *Gil Blas* was disputed when claims surfaced that he directed the works of others. These claims were challenged in 1801, when the *Philadelphia Portfolio* published Smollett's letter to Richard Smith of 8 May 1763 in which, among the items in a "genuine List of my Productions," he includes "A translation of Gil Blas" (see Knapp, ed., *Letters*, 113). But even so, doubts about *Gil Blas* persisted for years. Henry Malkin, in the separately published "Advertisement" for his own 1809 translation of the work, contrasted its "More easy and spirited transcript" with the translation "published under the name of Smollett." Smollett's *Gil Blas* survived such doubts, and numerous editions published in the nineteenth century bore his name. In a touch of irony, the title pages of some editions of Malkin's translation attribute the work to Smollett.

35. Carlos Fuentes, introduction to Tobias Smollett, trans., *The Adventures of Don Quixote de la Mancha* (New York: Farrar, Straus and Giroux, 1986), xiii.

36. The 1708 translation reads: "Leonora cast down her eyes and blushing own'd she had no Aversion for him." Smollett's version reads: "She cast down her eyes, and blushing, owned she had no aversion to him" (30).

37. Alexander Tytler Fraser, Lord Woodhouselee, *Essay on the Principles of Translation* (1791; reprint, Amsterdam: John Behamins, 1978), 7–8; John Dryden, "Life of Lucian," in *Prose 1691–1698*, ed. A. E. Wallace Maurer and George R. Guffey (Berkeley: University of California Press, 1989), 226–27. On the influence of Dryden, see John W. Draper, "The Theory of Translation in the Eighteenth Century," *Neophilologus* 6 (1921): 241–54. See also Martin C. Battestin on Smollett as translator in Tobias Smollett, trans., *The History and Adventures of the Renowned Don Quixote*, introduction and notes by Martin C. Battestin (Athens: University of Georgia Press, 2003), xxv–xxvi.

38. Smollett, trans., *Don Quixote*, 20.

39. See O M Brack, Jr., and James B. Davis, "Smollett's Revisions of *Roderick Random*," *Papers of the Bibliographical Society of America* 64 (1970): 295–97. Smollett eliminated the use of "got" in the 1755 fourth edition of *Roderick Random*.

40. Brack and Davis, "Smollett's Revisions," 296, 300.

41. Knapp, *Tobias Smollett*, 103.

42. See the textual commentary, p. 237, below.

43. See Hernlund, "Three Bankruptcies," 105–6.

The Devil upon Crutches

VOLUME ONE

THE
DEVIL upon CRUTCHES:
FROM THE
DIABLE BOITEUX
OF
Mr. LE SAGE.
A
NEW TRANSLATION.

To which are now first added,

ASMODEUS's CRUTCHES,
A CRITICAL LETTER upon the WORK;

And DIALOGUES between Two CHIMNEYS
of MADRID.

Adorned with CUTS.

Michael from Adam's Eyes the Film remov'd
---Then purg'd with Euphrafy and Rue
The vifual Nei…, for he had much to fee.　　MILT.

The SECOND EDITION, corrected.

IN TWO VOLUMES.
VOL. I.

LONDON:
Printed for T. OSBORN, A. MILLAR, R. BALDWIN,
S. CROWDER, J. RIVINGTON and J. FLETCHER,
and I. POTTINGER.

MDCCLIX.

The AUTHOR's
DEDICATION
To the ILLUSTRIOUS
DON LEWIS VELEZ DE GUEVARA.[1]

To you, Signior Guevara, I dedicated this work at its first publication; and as I thought it my duty then to pay you that mark of respect, I think still that I am now bound to re-new it. I have already declared, and do now again declare to the world, that to your Di-ablo Cojuelo, I owe the title and plan of this work; so that I yield to you the honour of being the inventor, without giving myself the trouble, as I have said to you before, of searching whether there be any Greek, Latin, or Italian author that can justly dispute your claim.

And I must farther own, that if the reader looks narrowly into some of the passages of this performance, he will find I have adopted several of your thoughts. I wish, from my soul, he could find more, and that the necessity I was under of accommodating my writ-ings to the genius of my own country, had not prevented me from copying you exactly; I should have been proud of being your translator, but have been obliged to depart from the text, or to speak more properly, write a new book upon the same plan.

In the dress it now appears in, as I have sent it into the world, it has undergone in France I don't know how many different editions; and we have both shared in the hon-our redounding from its success; but I ought not to say that we have shared, for at Paris I have only passed for your copier, and what reputation I have got, has been at second hand. It is true, indeed to make some amends, the copy has been re-translated into Spanish at Madrid, and has there been considered as an original.

I am now publishing a new edition, and once more I inscribe this performance to you, Signior Luis Velez. But to render it more fit for making its appearance again in the world, after a space of nineteen years, there was a necessity to touch it up anew, and give it a dress, if I may say so, agreeable to the mode. For though the world in general be still the same, there are so many original characters daily succeeding one another, that they seem to make some change in the whole.

I have not only corrected, but new-modelled it; and have added a second volume, for which the foibles of mankind easily supplied me with materials. They are a never-failing source for endless volumes, but I have not attempted to exhaust the subject. I leave that immense undertaking for some one of those laborious writers, who think a long life well spent, if their works extend a whole fathom on the shelves of a library. As for me, who have no farther ambition than to enliven and make my readers merry for a few hours, I have been contented to present them with the manners of the age in miniature. Having now acknowledged Signior de Guevara, the obligations that my demon must always lie under to yours, I must proceed in the discharge of my conscience, and farther own, that I have borrowed some verses and some thoughts from Francisco Santo, author of a book entitled, *Dia y Noche de Madrid.* Though it be but a petty larceny, I hereby make confession of it, lest some satyrical wag might take into his head to compare me with those thieves, who when they steal a piece of plate, take out the arms, that they may vend it with more safety.

I wish the public may receive this edition as favourably as it has accepted the former; an indulgence which I dare hardly flatter myself with the hopes of, even though the work in general be more correct, and I have done every thing in my power to give my readers a new relish for it.

THE
CONTENTS
OF THE
FIRST VOLUME.

ASMODEUS'S
CRUTCHES.

SIR,

I take this opportunity of acquainting you, that there is published a new edition of The Devil upon Crutches. Notwithstanding the antipathy that all mankind have conceived, ever since the original sin of Adam, against the race of fallen angels, every body loves Asmodeus. He is read, he is caressed; never was devil so fondled. True it is he might have appeared to Cleofas under a somewhat more gracious figure; such as the poets represent him, when he is introduced under the specious appellation of Cupid. But he scorned to use any disguise to his deliverer, and shewed himself, therefore, in all his original ugliness, as a proof he had a mind to deal sincerely with him; and an instance of sincerity it was, not very common; for how many lovers are there, who never had once an opportunity of beholding the faces of their mistresses only in their native, and without borrowed charms? And after all, such as we see him, he appears more like the god of pleasure, than in all those beauties and graces the ancients have bestowed upon him, when they equip him, as the god of love; and his mantle, with its ingenious emblems, becomes him better than the fillet, the gilded wings, and the sounding quiver.

In other respects, the fine moral character he sustains, and the vast sense and discernment he shews in the course of his observations, do more than compensate for the deformity of his person. He acquits himself religiously of the promise he made Don Cleofas, does him most important service, and discovers nothing of that falshood and deceit, for which the inhabitants of his country are rendered so justly infamous. In point of sense and discernment, he supports nobly the reputation of his brother-demons; he shews as much discretion as one could well expect from the whole society together; of which there needs be no other proof than what he says on the subject of his own quarrel with Palliardoc. After which, says he, our friends reconciled us, we embraced, and have cherished a mortal hatred against each other ever since. This hint leaves more to the imagination than can be expressed by words; and you will find an hundred such other instances in the remarks he makes on the folly and vices of mankind.

Can the foibles of men be exposed with more sense or more force of ridicule than he has expressed? No, his paintings are all finished. When I represent to myself this demon halting on his crutches, I cannot help considering those sensible and satyrical strokes of ridicule, with which he every now and then lashes the follies and vices of mankind, as so many pats of the crutches, which he bestows on such as he thinks deserve them; and, notwithstanding the careless air he puts on, as if seemingly he intended only amusement, he never misses, or strikes in the wrong place: his arrows are sure, and hit the mark.

Doubtless the young gentleman improved more in one night from the instructions of Asmodeus, than he had done all his life before from the lectures of the doctors of Alcala. These people, by their eternal jargon, instil into the minds of youth a distaste of morality and virtue. Instead of which Zambullo found in Asmodeus an artful and able master, who could find the way to his pupil's heart, and whilst he entertained him with agreeable scenes of pleasurable amusement, conveyed instruction at the same time, exposing the foibles of human nature, and teaching the young student how to correct them, without disgusting him by tedious and insipid prelections.

I am not therefore at all surprised, that this demon should be well received upon his coming among us. For how can any man in France refuse his approbation to a work, that, under the appearance of a trifling amusement, contains such a happy assemblage of wit, delicacy, sense, and politeness? The minds of men are naturally prejudiced against the dryness of dogmatic precepts; they want to be entertained with something agreeable and pleasant; but, along with that, they expect reason and sense. In a word, we are a rational people, and Signior Asmodeus has exactly suited himself to the genius of Frenchmen. He certainly must have conceived a previous affection to our nation; though I cannot but wonder at his generosity in having taken so long a journey to make us wiser, against his own interest, and against the interest of the society in general, who, I dare say, give him no thanks for his pains.

Is there any man, Sir, who does not envy the situation of Zambullo, on those towers of speculation, where Asmodeus pitched him? As for me, I fly along with him, on the wings of fancy, to the top of St. Salvador; and behold, in his company, with infinite pleasure, the objects that are represented to his consideration. A super-annuated coquette, who leaves upon her toilet her hair, her eye-brows, and her teeth, before she goes to bed; a beau of threescore, who takes off, with his own hands, one eye, and a pair of whiskers, waiting for his valet to help him off with his wooden arm and wooden leg, that he may go to bed with the rest; and the sister of this lovely Adonis, who, by means of artificial hips and bubbies, passes for a lady of twenty-five: I cannot, I say, forbear laughing, with Zambullo, at the thoughts of three such lodgers all in the same house.

Shifting the scene, I see with pleasure my good old Zanubio pierced to the heart with the cries of his wife in labour, and the undisturbed repose of the footman, who is the cause of all the pains she endures; and I greatly commend the diligence of that physician, who is dressing in such a hurry to visit the bishop, who has coughed above three times since he went to bed.

Exalted in that airy garret methinks I see the ingenious author, who compiles a system of all social and civil virtues, and copies all the praises and commendations that have ever been bestowed on any man, for his personal merit, or the fame of his ancestors; which he puts into a dedication; and though he has not as yet any patron particularly in view, keeps them ready for market to any one that will bid for them. There are many authors to be sure, who eat the bread of flattery; but I am surprized at the court-lady, who thinking the dedication made to her not sufficient, drew up one herself, and sent it to the author to have it printed.

Was I to pass the streets with my companions, I should certainly bewail the hard fate of the faithful Castilian, shivering under a window, and pouring forth his love-complaints; while his mistress bewails to the soft airs of his guittar, the absence of his rival. And in the other large house I perceive, greatly to my edification, a banker, stung with remorse of conscience, resolving to found a monastery out of the unjust gains he has made. He is certainly in the high road to salvation; for having once performed this vow, he thinks all his sins are forgiven. Nor am I less pleased with the scruples of that lady in her grand climacterick, who marries a boy of seventeen, that she may have what she wants, without remorse of conscience; and I think her nuptials, upon that account, ought to have been celebrated with a more decent concert of musick than basons, kettles, and frying-pans.

The demon having shewed Don Cleofas several other entertaining objects, that he might not clog him with too much variety, stops short to make him observe the appearances of joy and satisfaction in a great hotel, and relates to him particularly, from beginning to end, the affair of Leonora de Cespides. We must allow, Sir, that Asmodeus tells a story well. The incidents of this romance are entertaining, the winding up natural and interesting, and a moral runs thro' the whole. The innocence and credulity of Leonora, the love and ambition of Belflor, the artifices of Marcella, the rage and indignation of Don Lewis, and every other character there introduced, are represented according to the truth of nature; for Asmodeus was certainly well acquainted with the various passions and emotions of the human mind.

After the recital of this history I return with fresh pleasure, to partake of the new variety of scenes Asmodeus opens to his pupil, and which he comments upon with great judgment and penetration. In that hotel lives a booby of a lord, who, forsooth, would pass for a Mæcenas. In order to acquire the character of a patron of men of learning, he gives the use of one of his garrets to a dictionary-maker. Some doors beyond him, lives an experienced dealer in her way, a woman who is agent for a society of rich widows, and keeps a kind of register-office, containing an account of all strangers, who successively come to Madrid; their parentage, their country, their age, their shape, and complexion. Of these she gives in a list to her customers, who peruse this roll, and pitch upon whom they like; and then this lady sets about procuring an interview.

In another house you see the devotees, who are in such a hurry and alarm about the sick inquisitor, a scene extremely diverting; one is preparing slops, and another sits at his pillow, taking care to keep warm his head and breast; these two are no doubt favourites of the holy father. The anti-chamber is crouded with other penitents, who bring him different sorts of remedies, every one praising his own in particular, and slipping a ducat into the hand of his servant, begs of him, Laurence, my dear Laurence, recommend my bottle to your master above the others. To make Cleofas sensible of the happy condition of an inquisitor, Asmodeus adds, Was I not a demon, I would be an inquisitor.

Let us, Sir, accompany Zambullo to the prisons to which he desired the demon to convey him; and what think you pray, of that gallant, who being caught as he was mounting by a ladder into a balcony, runs the risk of being hanged for a house-breaker, rather than save his life at the expence of his mistress's honour, by owning the intrigue? He will be, perhaps, the first and last martyr of this kind, and I am satisfied won't find a man in France to imitate his example. I heartily pity that other innocent person, the unhappy groom of the chambers, who lies there accused unjustly of having stolen a diamond, and could have wished, as Don Cleofas, that Asmodeus had set him at liberty; but I am mightily pleased with the reason he gives, why it is not in his power, when he tells him, that was he himself in prison, he could not escape the hands of justice, without pay-ing his ransom. Mentioning another robbery, for which the man who committed it lies likewise in prison, he seems to strike the judges pretty hard. Zambullo asked him, if the man who lost the pistoles has had them returned to him? Not at all, says Asmodeus; they are so many proofs of the fact, and such witnesses they never part with; nor, indeed, does he shew more regard to the holy inquisition, only that he speaks of that reverend tribu-nal in a very low voice.

The dismal prospects of the prisons are succeeded by scenes more pleasant. What do you think of the distinguished piety of Sanguisuela, that rancorous vulture, who took six hundred ducats premium for the loan of three hundred and forty; but would not tell the money, till he had first been at mass, and heard a sermon. The sleeping lady, who mis-took her lover for her footman, must have been in great confusion at the discovery; and that coolness of behaviour her gallant shewed upon the occasion, is admirable. He met the happy valet upon the head of the stairs; Ambrose, said he to him, do not go in, your mistress desires you will let her rest a little longer.

We shift the scene once more, and come to an hospital for the reception of people who are lunatick, or mad. How many different kinds of madness do we there find pro-ceeding from as various causes? That Castilian news-monger had his brain disturbed by a paragraph in the news-papers, giving an account that twenty-five Spaniards were beaten by fifty Portuguese. Don Blas is gone mad, for being obliged to give back the dowry of his deceased wife; and that poor schoolmaster has crack'd his brain in re-searches after the *paulo post futurum*[1] of a Greek verb. You see women, too, confined here; the wife of a country justice, who ran mad at being called a cit,[2] by a woman of quality. And the wife of the treasurer of the council of the Indies, who has undergone the same fate, at being obliged, in a narrow passage, to make her coach go back, to give way to a dutchess.

Asmodeus then shews the student a number of people who deserve to have a place in Bedlam, as much as they who are confined. As that rich widow of a master-builder, who bequeaths all she has to grandees, merely on account of their titles, and will leave noth-ing to a man, who, she acknowledges, has done her very great service, for fear his name should be a disgrace to her last will and testament; and I am hugely pleased with that gallant cavalier of threescore, who recounts the adventures of his youth to a young lady he is in love with, and expects she will regard him for what he has been. I moreover like that good dean, who buys up jewels, trinkets, and all sorts of rich furniture, that, after his death, they may embellish the catalogue of his inventory. You may judge of the other fools from these instances.

Asmodeus extends his observations even to the dead. He carries Zambullo to a church full of sepulchral monuments, and gives him an account of the persons for whom they are erected. Sometimes he gives a very short character of the deceased, or only mentions the manner of their death. This is the tomb of a general officer, who at his re-turn home, like Agamemnon, found an Ægisthus in his house. In another lies a courtier, who never troubled himself about any thing but attending the levee. And a little farther lies an old director of the Indies and his young wife, strangely mingled together. An apoplexy seized him just as he was going to disinherit two children he had by a former marriage; and his wife died the next day, out of vexation that her husband did not live three days longer.

The demon, by the power he possessed, makes Zambullo see the departed spirits of the dead, and among the rest, three famous actresses, whose exit was pretty extraordinary. One died of a surfeit after a debauch; a second of envy at the applauses given another actress at her first appearance upon the stage; and the third of a miscarriage, after she had been acting in the character of a vestal. I question much if the physicians greatly like those pieces of representation, that Asmodeus shews the student upon the wings of death; and a man must have a diabolic imagination, to suppose young graduates in physic making their appearance there in the presence of death, who confers upon them their degrees. I would not advise a man of a sickly constitution to speak of doctors so disrespectfully.

Observe, Sir, how artfully Asmodeus changes the subject; and, to efface from the mind of his friend the melancholy impressions occasioned by the sight of death, and the ghosts of the dead, introduces a history founded on the effects of the strength of friendship. It is equally well told as the story of Count Belflor; though, on account of the tragical catastrophe, I am not ill-pleased to find it immediately followed by the chapter of dreams, which the demon unfolds very often in a manner that approaches to reality. The dreams, for example, of the attorney and his wife, do not much deviate from truth. The man dreams he is going to see a client in the infirmary, and to supply him with some of his own money; and the woman is possessed with the imagination that her husband is driving out of his house a strong stout fellow of a clerk, of whom he is become jealous; and the dream of that lady, who fancies that Jupiter is fallen in love with her, and endeavours to win her, under the appearance of a handsome page, is not, perhaps altogether chimerical.

I will not say any thing, Sir, upon the observations you will find on the several people who pass in the day-time thro' the streets of Madrid, nor on the subject of the redeemed captives. It is still the same Asmodeus who speaks, and continues his remarks, with the same sense and penetration. The work is finished in the manner in which it was begun, and the judicious reader will find, to the last, strokes of the crutches, which he may improve to his advantage and edification.

I am, Sir, &c.

THE

DEVIL

UPON

CRUTCHES.

CHAPTER I.

Which shews what sort of a devil this same devil upon crutches was; where and by what accident Don Cleofas Leandro Perez de Zambullo became acquainted with him.

It was in the month of October, one dark and cloudy night, at a time when the people being retired to their respective homes, had left the streets of Madrid free for the serenades of lovers, some of whom sung their success, while others, to the soft airs of the guittar, tuned their mournful plaints, alarming the jealous husband and anxious parent.—It was now almost the hour of midnight, when Don Cleofas Leandro Perez Zambullo, a student of Alcala, sallied suddenly through the window of a house where a love-affair had engaged him, to get clear of a set of ruffians, who closely pursued him, with a design to force him to marry a woman they had surprised him with, or take away his life.

Although he was single against three or four of them, he valiantly defended himself, and would not have had recourse to flight, but that in the scuffle he was disarmed. They followed him for some time over the tops of the houses; but by the favour of the night he escaped their pursuit, and made the best of his way towards a light, which, though faint and glimmering, served as a beacon to direct him how to steer in this perilous course. After having been often in danger of breaking his neck, at last he got to the place whence it proceeded; where, entering through a window, he was as much rejoiced as a pilot, who from the dangers of shipwreck sees his vessel sail safely into port.

The first thing he did was to consider attentively every thing about this apartment he had entered, and which, upon examination, he found to be very singular. There was a copper lamp that hung from the cieling, with books and papers in confusion upon the table, a sphere and compass in one corner, and vials and quadrants[1] in another; all which made him conclude there lived below some astrologer, who in this musæum[2] made his learned observations. He was reflecting upon the danger he had fortunately escaped, and considering with himself whether he had better stay there till morning, or take some other course, when he was all on a sudden surprized with a deep groan issuing from something that was near him. At first he took it for a phantome of his own disturbed imagination, some illusion of the night; and therefore disregarding it, continued his reflections; but hearing the same thing repeated, he no longer doubted of the reality of it, and perceiving no body in the room with him, immediately cried, Who the devil makes this groaning here? He was immediately answered, in a very extraordinary voice, Signor student, 'tis I, who have been for above these six months corked up in one of these vials. The fellow that lives in this house is a great astrologer, and magician into the bargain;[3] and by the power of his cursed art keeps me plugged up[4] here in this manner. What, you are a spirit then? answered Don Cleofas, somewhat surprized at the oddity of this adventure. I am a devil, (replied the voice) and you come most opportunely to set me at liberty; for I languish here under a state of inactivity, being, in my own nature, of all the devils in hell, perhaps the most alert and industrious.

These words, not a little startled Signor Zambullo; but, as he was naturally bold, he soon recovered himself, and with a resolute tone made answer, I desire (says he) your devilship will please to inform me what rank you hold in your own country; do you sit in the house of peers, or are you only a plebeian?[5] Sir, (answered the voice) I am a demon of high rank, and of the greatest character of all, both in this and the other world. Perhaps then you are Lucifer: (says Cleofas). No, no, (replied the voice) he is concerned only with mountebanks. Are you then Uriel? (answered the other). O fye, Sir! (answered the voice hastily) he has nothing to do but with taylors, bakers, butchers, and all scrub sort of fellows.

I fancy then you must be Belzebub, (says Leandro). You jest surely, (says the other) he is the demon of grooms and governantes.[6] That surprizes me; (continues Leandro) for I always took him to be one of the principal of all your fraternity. So far from it, (replies the demon) that he is one of the very lowest among us. I find, Sir, you know nothing at all of hell.

Who a plague are you then?[7] (continues the student). Are you Leviathan, Belphegor, or Ashtaroth? Oh! as for these three, (said the voice) there you touch upon spirits of the first order; they all belong to the court, enter into the counsels of princes, inspire ministers, form leagues, plan conspiracies, and light the flambeaux of war. They are none of your petty-fogging rascals, such as before you mentioned. I pray tell me, (says the student) what are the functions of Flagel? He presides over the inns of court,[8] is the soul of chicane, and the spirit of the bar, (replies the other). He furnishes bailiffs and attornies with cases, precedents, and reports, dictates to special pleaders, suggests hints to counsel, and now and then makes the circuit with the judges.

As for me, my function is different from all these, my province being to make matches between old dotards and young girls, masters and their maids, and to couple young ladies of small fortunes with passionate lovers that are not worth a groat.[9] It was I that first introduced into the world luxury, debauch, gaming-tables, and the philosopher's stone. I claim the honour likewise of having first brought into vogue dancing, music, farce, revelling, drums, routs, beatups,[10] and all the other fashionable modes of France. In a word, Sir, my name is Asmodeus, alias, The devil upon crutches.

Lord! (cries Don Cleofas) are you the celebrated Asmodeus, of whom so honourable mention is made by Agrippa,[11] and in the talmud of Solomon?[12] If it is so, you have not told me all the qualifications you possess, but have passed over the very best of them. If I am not much mistaken, you amuse yourself now and then in giving some of your assistance to unhappy lovers: by the same token, I fancy it was by your help a friend of mine, a young fellow in the town of Alcala, about a year ago, found ways and means to insinuate himself into the good graces of a lady, the wife of one of our doctors of the university. Why, that is even true enough; (says the spirit) I did not mention that talent of mine to you;[13] I kept it to the last, as being the most valuable of all my qualifications. I am the demon of luxury, or to speak more honourably of myself, the god Cupid; for the poets have given me that pretty name, and have been pleased to make such descriptions of me, as if I was the loveliest babe in the world.[14] If you take their words for it, I am equipt[15] with gilded wings, a fillet over my eyes, a quiver full of arrows rattling on my shoulder, and am a child of passing beauty. You shall immediately see how far all this is true, if you will only set me free from my prison.

Signior Asmodeus, (replies Leandro Perez) you know 'tis a long time since I have been entirely your votary, witness the danger I have just now escaped; and I should be proud of any opportunity to serve you; but as the vessel you have got rammed into[16] is doubtless enchanted, I shall never be able to disengage you from it; so that I see no way possible for me to get you out.[17] Besides, I really am not much used to exploits of this kind; and to be plain with you,[18] if a devil of your vast abilities and address cannot extricate yourself from these dilemmas, it would be a kind of presumption,[19] I think, for a weak mortal like me to attempt it. Men have a power to effect such things: (replied the demon). This vial I am corked up in may be as easily broken as any other common glass bottle. If you take it only and dash it against the ground, you will immediately see me appear in a human shape. If that is the case, (says our student) the affair is more easily managed than I imagined. Come, let me know then in which of these bottles you have taken up your residence, for there are a number of them so like one another, that I cannot possibly distinguish you. I am the fourth from the window; (replies the spirit) and though there be a magic seal upon the cork, yet the vial will go to pieces for all that.

I am satisfied; (says Don Cleofas) and am now ready to do what you desire of me; there remains only one small difficulty: when I have done you this piece of service, perhaps I may have the broken bottle to pay for my pains. There shall no evil happen to you on my account; (replies the demon) on the contrary, you will be quite satisfied with my gratitude. I'll instruct you in whatever you desire to know. I'll let you into every thing that passes in the world, and discover to you the foibles of mankind. I will be your tutelar demon, and a much more able one than the familiar of Socrates;[20] for I take upon me to make you more wise and knowing than that philosopher. In short, I make a tender of myself to you,[21] with all my good and bad qualities, and both will be equally serviceable to you.

Why faith, you promise very fair, Mr. Devil, (said the student) but gentlemen of your cloth[22] are not the most famous for always strictly observing promises. I own (replies Asmodeus) there is a good deal of truth in what you say; my brethren do all of them very often fail of performing what they have promised: but as to me, the case is quite otherwise; for not only the service you are to do me is what I can never sufficiently requite, but I am besides naturally a slave to my word; and I swear to you by every thing that can make an oath binding, I will not deceive you; you may fully depend on the assurances I give you. And what ought still to be more agreeable to you, I engage, that before this night be at an end, you shall be amply revenged upon Donna Thomasa, that perfidious woman, who had concealed these four assassins to surprise you, and oblige you to marry her.

Young Zambullo was particularly tickled[23] with this last declaration: to hasten the acomplishment of it, he immediately laid hold of the vial the demon had pointed out to him, and without more hesitation of what might be the consequence, dashed it against the floor. It broke into a thousand pieces, and covered the ground with a blackish kind of liquor, which evaporating by degrees,[24] formed a cloud, that disappearing all at once, presented to the view of the astonished Leandro Perez the figure of a man in a cloak, of about two foot and an half high, supported on two crutches. This little, deformed monster had the legs of a goat, a long visage, a sharp chin, a flat snub nose, with a complexion somewhat between black and yellow; his eyes, which were extremely small, resembled two burning coals; his mouth excessively wide was garnished with a pair of lips that could scarce be matched, and feathered with red moustachos.

This sweet little Cupid had upon his head a kind of turban of red crape, crested with a plume of cock's and peacock's feathers. Round his neck he wore a kind of scarf,[25] on which was drawn several models of necklaces and earings. He was clothed in a short, satin vest, surrounded by a broad belt of white parchment,[26] marked with cabalistick characters.[27] On that were represented divers patterns of stays for the ladies, all contrived to set off the neck and bosom to advantage; scarfs, various coloured aprons, and new-fashioned caps, every one more extraordinary than another.

But all this was nothing in comparison to his cloak, the ground of which was likewise of white satin. On it were represented with China ink,[28] an infinite number of various figures, with such an amazing force of pencil, and such strength of expression, as shewed plainly some demon must have had an hand in the performance. In one part was a Spanish lady in her veil, enticing a stranger to take a walk with her; in another a French coquette practising new airs at her glass, which she was to make trial of before a young Abbé, who attended at her chamber-door with patches and paints. Here Italian cavaliers sung and played on the guittar, under the balconies of their mistresses; and there you might see a set of Germans, open-breasted, in horrible confusion,[29] all roaring drunk, spewing round a table, and stinking more of tobacco, than a Parisian petit-maitre[30] smells of perfume. In another place you might see a mussulman lord coming out of the bath, attended by the women of his seraglio, who, every one more officious than another, pressed round him to offer their service. And among other things was represented, in most lively colours, an English gentleman, who with excessive politeness, and with all the airs of a gallant, was tendering to his mistress a quart pot and a pipe of tobacco.

There were likewise intermixed gamesters of all sorts, wonderfully well represented; some, under the sensations of the most lively transports, were filling their hats with gold and bank-notes; and others, who had been quite stript, were uttering most horrid blasphemies, and hurling defiance toward the vault of heaven. In a word, there were represented on this robe as many wonderful phænomena, as on that shield which Vulcan made at the request of Thetis; but with this difference, that the figures of the buckler bore no manner of allusion to the exploits of Achilles; whereas the figures on Asmodeus's mantle were so many lively images of all that passes in the world by his instigation.

CHAPTER II.

Continuation of the deliverance of Asmodeus.

This demon easily perceiving that his outward mein was no great recommendation in his favour, said, with a smile, Well, Signior Don Cleofas Leandro Perez Zambullo, you see the charming god of love, this sovereign master of hearts. What do you think of my air and beauty? Are you not of opinion the poets are excellent painters? Why, upon my soul, I think, to speak freely, they rather flatter a little, (replied Cleofas). I fancy you did not chuse this form when you appeared before Psyche. No, thank you, Sir, (replied he) I knew better; I appeared before her in the figure of a French marquis, to do the quicker execution.[1] Vice must put on an agreeable outside, otherwise it would not take; and I can assume all shapes I please, and could have shewn myself to you in any fantastical figure; but as I am entirely devoted to your service, and want to disguise nothing from you, I thought it best you should see me under a form the most suitable to the opinion people have of my person and function.

I do not at all wonder (answered Leandro) you should be so confoundedly ugly;[2] (I beg pardon for the expression, Sir, only the situation we are in at present requires we should not use ceremony) your features exactly agree with the idea I formed of you, only I should be glad to know how you come to be lame.

It happened to me in France (answered Asmodeus) in a fray I had with Palliardoc, the demon of usurers. A young squire from the country came to Paris to make his fortune. As he was an excellent subject, a youth of most promising parts, we very briskly disputed the possession of him, and fought in the nether[3] region of the air; when Palliardoc, being stronger than I, threw me down to the earth, as Jupiter erst served Vulcan, according to the poets. From the resemblance of our adventures my companions called me The devil upon crutches; and in their mirth fixed this nick-name upon me. However, lame as I am, I can make shift[4] to go a good pace; you shall presently have a proof of my agility.

But (continued he) let us finish this conversation, and make haste to get out of this place. The magician will be here by and by, to settle the affairs of a beautiful sylphid,[5] who comes here every night to meet him. Should he catch us, he would certainly not fail to bottle me up again, and it would be odds but he provided for you in the same manner;[6] and therefore let us throw the bits of broken glass out of the window, that this necromancer[7] may not perceive my escape.

Suppose (says Zambullo) he should perceive it after we are gone, what should be the consequence? What would be the consequence? (replied the demon) I suppose, by asking that question, you have never read the book on Restrictions:[8] Should I fly to the mansions destined for the burning salamanders, or seek for shelter in the solitary recesses of the desert: were I to wing my flight to the regions of the Gnomes, or plunge into the fathomless abysses of the sea; none of these could protect me from the power of his resentment. He would make such horrible exorcisms as would awaken hell thro' its inmost caverns. It would be in vain for me to resist his will. I should be obliged, do what I could, to appear before him, and submit to what punishment he should think proper to inflict on me.

If that is the case, (answered Cleofas) I am under some doubts that our correspondence will be but of short duration. This tremendous magician will undoubtedly find out that you have escaped. That I cannot pretend to determine; (answered the spirit) for we are ignorant as to the secrets of futurity.[9] How, (replied the other) are demons kept in the dark as to what shall happen hereafter? Assuredly, (answered Asmodeus). The people who trust to us on that account are all bubbled.[10] And hence it is that all your fortune-tellers talk such absurdities to ladies of quality, when they consult them on future events. We know nothing but the past and the present; and therefore I am ignorant whether the magician will discover my escape or not. I only hope he will not; and that as there are several vials of the same kind with that which was my apartment, he will not perceive it to be missing: and I have further to say, that I was among his apparatus, as a law-book in a counsellor's study. He hardly ever thought of me; and if he did, he never honoured me so far as to take the least notice of me. He is the most insolent of all the necromancers I know; for during the time I was in his custody, he never vouchsafed so much as once to speak to me.

What a fellow this must be! (answered the student) but what have you done thus to draw upon you his resentment? I thwarted him in one of his designs, (replied the demon). A place happened to be vacant in a certain university, which he had a mind to dispose of in favour of his friend; and I supported the interests of another candidate.[11] The magician made a talisman composed of several cabalistick characters, and I got my friend into the service of a great minister, whose interest was too prevalent for the conjurations[12] of the other.

After this Asmodeus picking up all the bits of the broken vial, threw them out of the window, and addressing himself to the student, Signior Zambullo, (says he) let us make our escape as quick as we can; take fast hold of the skirts of my cloak, and fear nothing. Tho' this appeared to Don Cleofas a very perilous expedient, he thought it preferable to running the risk[13] of the magician's resentment, and therefore clung as close as he could to the demon, who winged him off in an instant.

CHAPTER III.

To what place the demon carried Don Cleofas, and what scenes he first presented to his view.

It was not without reason Asmodeus boasted of his agility. He cut the air swift as the flight of an arrow, and perched on the pinnacle of the church of St. Salvador.[1] When he had fixed himself there, he said to his companion, Well, (Signior Leandro) what do you think? when people meet with a bad coachman, they say he is the devil of a driver, are they not in the wrong? Very much so, (answers Leandro) and I can bear witness to it. I assure you, Sir, your vehicle is smoother than a litter, and makes so much speed that one can hardly be tired on the road.

Well, Sir, (answers the demon) you don't know why I have pitch'd you here.[2] I intend to shew you every thing that now passes in Madrid; and as I am to begin with this part of it, I could not find any spot more proper than this for my purpose. In consequence of the power I possess as a demon, I will strip off the tops of all the houses of this great city; and notwithstanding the shades of the night, you shall see what passes within them, as clearly as if it were noon-day.[3] After saying this, he stretched out his right hand, and instantaneously the tops of the houses vanished from their sight. Immediately upon this the student of Alcala had a full view of all the different apartments. He saw them, to use the words of Louis Velez de Guevara,[4] as a man sees what is in a pye when the upper crust is taken off.

Such a scene opened to his view as was too interesting not to command all his attention. He cast his eyes every where, and the variety of objects that presented themselves to his sight, afforded him abundant matter to employ his curiosity. Signior Don Cleofas, (says the demon) this variety of objects that forces your attention[5] is doubtless a very amusing scene of contemplation, but is amusement only. I want to render it useful to you; and by giving you a perfect insight into the characters of the different persons, to explain those parts they are now acting on this stage of your world;[6] and by discovering the most inward and hidden motives,[7] disclose the true and real sources of human actions.

And to begin: observe first that old man in the house upon your right hand, you see him counting over his money. He is a city miser.[8] His coach, which he had for almost nothing, in the distress of a seizure,[9] is scarcely dragged along by two jades of horses, whom he feeds according to the laws of the twelve tables: that is to say, he allows them a pound of oats a day, and deals by them as the Romans did by their slaves. * It is now

---

* Monsieur Le Sage seems to be indebted for the learning in this remark to his friend M. Dacier,[10] who in his commentary upon the passage of Horace,

Rogabat

Denique cur unquam fugisset, cui satis una
Farris libra foret,[11]

two years since he returned from the Indies with a vast sum of gold in ingots, which he has turned into specie. Observe the old rogue, with what a glee he feasts his eyes in looking upon his money: he can never have enough of it; but at the same time cast your eyes upon what passes in a little parlour just by him; don't you see there two young fellows and an old woman? Yes I do (says Cleofas); I suppose they are his children. No, they are not (replies the demon); they are his nephews, who are to be his heirs; and so impatient are they to share his spoils, that they have sent for that old hag of a fortune-teller, to inform them how soon he will die.

In the next house I perceive two pretty odd figures; one a superannuated coquette, who is gone to bed, after having discumbered herself of her hair, eye-brows, and teeth, which she has placed with the other implements of her toilet. The other a beau of three-score, who is come home quite warm from an intrigue.[12] He has undressed himself without help, as far as one eye and his whiskers, and a wig that covers a bald pate; but waits for his servant to take off his arm and his wooden leg, and then he'll go to bed with what remains.

If I can trust my eyes (says Zambullo) I see in the same house an exquisitely fine young lady of a graceful stature: what a delicate air she has! That beauteous damsel you are so smit with, (replies Asmodeus) is no other than the eldest sister of the beau that is now going to bed; she exactly matches the old coquette who lodges with her. That graceful stature you so much admire, is owing to a machine which is the utmost effort and perfection[13] of all mechanics. Her breasts and hips are artificial; and it is not a great while ago that she went to celebrate high mass, and had the misfortune to drop her backside at the altar. However, as she assumes the airs of a young lady, there are two gentlemen have disputed their pretensions to her so warmly,[14] that they have even, upon her account, fought a duel. I give them joy with all my heart.[15] Methinks I see two dogs worrying one another for a bare bone.

Come and divert yourself with me at this concert of musick here in the house of a citizen. They are a-singing cantatas. The subject of the song is the love-sick passion of an alderman; the words are made by a city-beau, who composes for his own amusement, and the plague of his neighbours, and set to music by a grave counsellor. The instrumental musick consists of a spinnet and a bagpipe. A great lath-backed fellow from the choir of one of the cathedrals sings the treble, and a hoarse young girl warbles out the

---

says the *libra farris* was the common allowance to the slaves, and quotes the authority of the twelve tables, *qui eum vinctum habebit, libras farris indies dato.*[16] But I am afraid there is a small literary mistake both in the foresaid M. Dacier's commentary, and consequently in our author, who takes it upon his word; as this pound of oats seems to have been allotted by the decemviri, as the groats in our jails,[17] for the maintenance of the Nexi, or confined debtors, which the creditors were obliged to give them: And I shall for the comfort and edification of my readers, transcribe the fragment of that ancient and venerable record.

Æris confessei rebusque joure joudicatis, triginta dies justi sunto: postidea manus endo jactio esto: in jous ducito. Nei joudicatum facit, aut quips endo joure em vindicit, secum ducito, vincito aut nervo, aut comped-ibus quindecim pondo, ne minore: aut si volet majore vincito. Seu volet, suo vivito, nei suo vivit, qui em vinc-tum habebit libras farris endo dies dato; sei volet, plus dato.

base. What a delightful entertainment of musick this is! (says Don Cleofas laughing) if one were to exhibit a ridicule upon all concerts, it could not be done so successfully.

Turn your eyes towards that magnificent hotel, (continues the demon) and you will perceive a man of quality lying in a rich apartment: he has by him a box full of billet-doux, which he is reading over to procure him soft slumbers; for they are from a nymph whom his soul adores, and who has already taken so much care of his finances, that he must by and by see to get himself transported to some government.[18]

But if every thing in this great house is hushed in repose, the case is not the same in this other on our left hand. You distinguish, don't you, a woman in a damask bed? she is a lady of quality: her name is Donna Fabula. She has this moment sent for a midwife, and is going to compliment her husband, Don Torribio,[19] whom you see by her bed-side, with a son and heir. Are not you delighted with the great good-nature of her spouse? The cries of his dear rib quite pierce him to the heart,[20] and he suffers as much as she does. With what officious earnestness he hurries up and down to fetch things for her.[21] Upon my word, (says Leandro) the man seems in a great deal of agitation; but I see another person in the house who seems to sleep snug, without any concern about what passes. Ay, but he is in the wrong, (says Asmodeus) for he is a footman in the family, and is the true cause of all this good lady's pain and distress.

Look a little farther, and observe that hypocrite in a parlour, who is larding himself with hogs-grease, in order to go to a society of wizards, who are to hold an assembly this night, in a place between St. Sebastian's and Fontarabia. I would take you there imme-diately, and entertain you with a sight of the community, but am afraid of being known by the demon who presides over that congregation.

I suppose then, (says Cleofas) this demon and you are not quite good friends. No, by God: 'tis the same Palliardoc whom I have before mentioned to you. That rascal would betray me; he would not fail to give notice to the magician of my escape. There has been a fresh quarrel then between you and this same Palliardoc? (says Cleofas). You are in the right, (replied Asmodeus). It is about two years ago that we differed about a young Parisian, who was a-going to begin the world.[22] Each of us wanted to have the disposal of him. Palliardoc wanted to have made him an attorney. I intended him for a beau; and our friends, to end the dispute, made him a monk;[23] and after that they reconciled us. We shook hands and have ever since been at mortal enmity with each other.

Come (says Don Cleofas) let us leave these sorcerers; I have no inclination to make one with them. We'll examine a little more these objects we have now in view. What is the meaning of those sparks of fire that come out of that cellar? This is one of the most foolish pursuits men ever engaged in, (replies the demon). The man you see hard by the flaming furnace is a chymist, and that fire gradually consumes his fortune; nor will he ever find out what he is in search of. To tell you the truth, the philosopher's stone is nothing else but a chimerical bubble[24] I myself invented as a mockery upon human un-derstanding, which is always endeavouring to pass the bounds nature has prescribed it.

This subterraneous student[25] has for his neighbour a very good kind of a man, an apothecary, who is not yet gone to bed: see how he works in his shop, with an old woman his wife, and that boy his apprentice. You don't know what they are busied about; the apothecary is making a prolifick bolus[26] for an old barrister that is to be married to-

morrow; the boy is mixing a laxative potion, and the old woman is very busy about astringent pills.[27]

In that house over-against the apothecary, (says Zambullo) I see a man who, in a great
hurry, is got out of bed and dressing himself. Pshaw! (said the demon) 'tis a physician
they have called, upon a very pressing occasion truly: a fat bishop[28] has happened to
cough two or three times since he went to bed, and this doctor of physick has been sent
for in a great hurry, to prescribe for him.

But come, look this way and take a peep into that garret. You see a man walking up
and down this apartment in nothing but his shirt, and his room lighted by a lamp that
scarcely burns. I do observe him, (answers the student) and think I can make an inventory of his moveables, a flock-bed,[29] a joint-stool,[30] and something that resembles a
table;[31] and the walls of the room seem to be daubed with black. This same personage,
who has taken up his residence so near the skies, (replies the spirit) is a poet; and those
daubings of black are tragick verses of his own composing, with which he hangs his
chamber instead of tapestry; for being disappointed in paper he is fain to have recourse
to the walls.

What strange faces the man makes! (says Cleofas) how he skips and twists himself as
he walks![32] surely he must be big with some work of mighty import. You are not mistaken in your conjecture: (replied Asmodeus) it was but yesterday he finished a new
tragedy, entitled, The Universal Deluge: and notwithstanding the extent of his subject,
he cannot be reproached for breaking the unity of place, for the whole scene is confined
to Noah's ark.

In good truth it is a most excellent piece. Not a four-footed beast in it but speaks like
a learned doctor. He intends a dedication for this rare performance;[33] and as he designs
to find a patron, has been working on the dedication for above these six hours, and is, at
this instant, subscribing himself with proper epithets: and one may venture to affirm,
that of all dedications which have ever yet appeared, this is the master-piece. No one
virtue, civil or moral; no commendations whatsoever, that can be claimed by any man,
either for his own or the atchievements of the most illustrious ancestors, have, in this
epistle dedicatory been omitted: never did any other offer incense of praise so liberally.
On what illustrious patron (said the student) has he bestowed this high elogium? That
he don't know yet (replied the demon) he has left a blank for the name, and intends to
look out sharp for some noble lord that may be less close-fisted than those who stand at
the head of his former works. In reality, there are but few people now a-days that give
any tolerable price for a dedication. Great men have got the better of their foibles in this
respect; and it must be owned, that in so doing they have rendered an infinite service to
the publick, which was quite pestered with such a deluge of trash[34] as no age had ever
laboured under; for the most part of all their books were writ with no other view than
of what they were in hopes to touch from the dedication.

A propos, (continues the demon) now we are upon the chapter of dedications, I'll tell
you a merry story enough. A lady belonging to the court gave leave for a dedication, but
would see it before it was printed; and upon reading it over, judged that there was not
enough said; upon which she was so good as to write a dedication herself, and sent it to
the author to put to the press.

I think (cries Leandro) I see some people entering into a house thro' a balcony; I fancy they are thieves. You are in the right, (says Asmodeus) they are; and are now going into a banker's shop. Let us see what they are about; they are now got into the compter,[35] and are rummaging every place: but this prudent cash-monger has bit them.[36] Last night he went off for Holland with all the money he had.

I see another of these gentlemen, (says Zambullo) he is scaling a balcony by a silk ladder. No (says Asmodeus) he is no house-breaker, he is a marquis, who wants to get into the bed-chamber of a maiden lady, who has hitherto preserved her virginity, but now wants to get clear of the incumbrance.[37] He has made her some slight promises of marriage, and she has very easily swallowed them; for in love-traffick these marquisses are a set of people that can command mighty credit upon their bare word.

I am vastly curious (says the student) to know who this man is, I see writing in his gown and night-cap. He appears mighty eager about his business, and there is a little black fellow by him, who seems as if he guided his hand. The man who writes (answers the demon) is an attorney, who, to oblige a very grateful guardian, is altering a deed made in favour of an orphan; and that little black devil is Griffael, to whose charge is committed all attornies. But this Griffael (answers Cleofas) must only act by way of deputy; for as Flagel presides over the inns of court, I fancy these gentlemen belong to his office. No they don't, (replies the demon). After much debate it was carried that the attornies should have one entirely for themselves; and upon my soul he has enough to do.

Observe (says Asmodeus) in that merchant's house next the attorney's, a young lady who lodges in the first floor; her husband is dead, and the man hard by her is her uncle, who lodges in the apartments above her. How modest this widow is! she won't so much as touch her smock in the presence of her uncle, but chastely retires into a closet, for her gallant to put it on, whom she has there concealed.

There lives with the attorney one of his relations, a fat, jolly batchelor,[38] who is a nonpareil for mirth and buffoonry: Volumnius, *[39] whom Cicero talks so much of, for smartness and repartee, was a fool to him: he is called in Madrid by way of pre-eminence, the batchelor Donoso,[40] and is courted by people of all ranks and conditions, whose tables are ever open to him, and where he is always welcome. He has a most happy talent at making a company merry, and is the joy of an entertainment; so that every day in his life he repairs to some house of good cheer, and generally stays till about two in the morning. To-day he dined with the marquis of Alcanizas, which happened by chance. How by chance? (says Leandro). I will explain my meaning to you (says Asmodeus) this day at noon there were at his door five or six coaches from different noblemen, to invite him to dinner. He brought all their lacqueys into one room, and taking a pack of cards, As I cannot (says he) have the honour of waiting upon all your masters at

---

* This Volumnius was in his day, it seems a great joker: and Cicero had in that way a great opinion of him; for in a letter he writes him, (ep. 32. lib. 7. ad familiares) he desires they may preserve *urbanitatis possessionem, in qua*, says he, *te unum metuo, contemno cæteros;*[41] though, by the way, it appears from the same epistle, that he thought himself in point of wit and repartee, superior to Volumnius, and every man breathing.

once, and won't presume to prefer any one to the rest, you shall cut for me: I dine with the king of clubs.

What can that man mean, (says Cleofas) in the next street, who sits upon the threshold of a door? does he wait till some Abigail comes to let him in? No, no, (says Asmodeus) he has no such hopes.[42] He is a young Castilian; the very essence of romantick love.[43] Out of pure gallantry, and to imitate the ancients *, he lies whole nights at his mistress's door, thrumming upon the guittar passionate airs of his own composition; but his Dulcinea,[44] who lodges in the second story, passes the night in sighs for the absence of his rival.

Let us pass to this new building, which is divided into two parts. One of them is inhabited by the owner, who is an old cavalier, whom you see walking up and down his room, and every now and then dropping into his great chair. I fancy (says Zambullo) he is big with some mighty project;[45] who is he? if one were to judge of him from the richness of the furniture that is in his house, he seems to be a nobleman of the first distinction. He is only a money-scrivener,[46] for all that, (says Asmodeus). This fellow has grown grey-headed in different lucrative employments, and is now worth a brace of plums:[47] and as he is not without some scruples in regard to the ways and means he has used in amassing this great fortune, and finds himself drawing near the period when he must make up his accounts in the other world, his conscience is a little touched. He intends to build a monastery; and flatters himself that by this religious act, he shall be able to make a compensation for his former iniquities.[48] He has already obtained a permission to found a religious house; but as he is at present determined to fill it only with such as are chaste, sober, and humble, he is greatly puzzled whom he shall fix upon.

In the other part of this building dwells a handsome woman, who, after having bathed in milk, is just going to bed. This fine lady is the widow of a knight of St. Jago,[49] who left her nothing but a title; but she has luckily insinuated herself into the good graces of two gentlemen of the council of Castile, who club for the expence of her family.

My God! says the student, what cries and lamentations do I hear? the very air rings with them; has any terrible misfortune happened? I'll tell you the occasion of it, says Asmodeus: two young gentlemen were engaged at cards, at that gaming-house where you see such a number of lamps and tapers; they quarrelled, and immediately drew, and wounded each other mortally. The eldest is married, and the youngest is an only child. Both at this instant are expiring; and the father of the one, and the wife of the other, hearing of this fatal accident, are come to the spot here, and fill the air with their cries. Unhappy boy! (cries the aged father, addressing himself to his son, who now no longer

---

* These nocturnal pains (if we may be allowed the expression) occasioned by the ladies to their lovers, is not modern, or the invention of Castilians.—

Me tuo longas pereunte noctes Lydia dormis,[50]

was an old complaint. Horace has given us a compleat specimen of these nightly dittys, in the 10th ode of his 3d book, and in the opinion of the learned, examples of these *portal hymns*,[51] these ἄωρα κλαυσίθυρα; (as the *Greeks* of old called them) may be seen and perused by the young student in the 3d and 23d Idyll of Theocritus.

hears him) how often have I warned you of the dangerous consequence of play? how often have I told you it would one day or other cost you your life. Witness heaven! it is not my fault you perish thus miserably. The poor lady is likewise distracted: tho' her husband had squandered at play the whole fortune she brought him, and had made away not only with her jewels, but every thing she had, even to her wearing apparel, she is inconsolable for the loss of him; and in the bitter anguish of her soul curses cards and those who invented them, curses the gaming table, and all that belong to it.

I much pity those unhappy men (says Cleofas) who have a passion for play; they must of necessity be often in a horrible situation; thank God, I have no itch that way. Ay, but you have an itch after something else quite as bad (replies the demon). Is the passion of following courtezans, think you, a bit more reasonable? was not your life this very night in danger of falling a victim to it, by the hands of four ruffians? I love you mortals for that: your own particular failings you see in miniature, but look upon the foibles of your fellow-creatures thro' a magnifying glass.

I must shew you some more melancholy spectacles. Look upon that fat man, stretched upon his bed, in a house hard by; this is an unhappy Levite,[52] who is just now fallen into an apoplexy; his nephew and niece, far from affording him any help, leave him there to die, and are busy packing up every thing that is most valuable, to carry them to a proper house, where they will have time to bewail and lament their deceased uncle.[53]

You see likewise two men whom they are burying: they are brothers, and were both sick of the same disease, but followed different methods of cure; one had a confidence in his physician, and the other left all to nature. They both died, one for taking every thing the doctor prescribed, and the other for taking nothing at all. This is very hard (says Leandro). What must a poor man do that is sick? That I cannot inform you of (says the demon). One thing I know, that there are very good medicines; but I will not answer that there are as good physicians.

Come, let us change this scene (continues Asmodeus). I will entertain you with some more diverting objects. Do you hear that racket in the other street? a widow of sixty has this day married a young fellow of seventeen. All the wags of the neighbourhood have bestirred themselves to send them a braying concert of basons, kettles, and frying-pans. You told me, (says the student) that all sorts of ridiculous marriages were under your direction; tho' you could have no hand in this. No, really, (replies the demon) I could not well meddle in this, as I was not at my liberty: but if I had been at large, I should not have concerned myself in this affair. This lady is a woman of piety, she married only for conscience sake, that she might have, without remorse, what she so much longed for; and these are things out of my province; I chuse rather to sting than quiet people's consciences.

Notwithstanding the noise of this burlesque serenade, I hear another which drowns the din of the former. That other which drowns the noise of the charivari, proceeds from a tavern, where a fat Dutch captain, a French chorister, and a German officer, bawl in *trio*. They have been drinking bumpers since eight in the morning, and every one of them thinks the honour of his country concerned in making the others drunk.

View that house which stands by itself over-against the canons, and you will perceive three famous Gallician women deep in revels with as many gentlemen belonging to the court. Ah! how pretty they are! (cries Cleofas) no wonder people of fashion should covet their company. And how fond the pretty creatures are of their lovers; certainly the ladies are desperately in love with them! What a simpleton you are![54] (says Asmodeus) it seems you know these sort of ladies well indeed: their hearts are falser than their faces. Whatever shew they may make, they don't value these great men one farthing.[55] They want the protection of one, and the other two they intend to trick out of a settlement. This is the way of all coquettes. 'Tis the greatest folly imaginable for men to be at any expence with them, for they love them not a whit the more for that: every man that bleeds freely is the husband for the time being.[56] This rule I have myself established in all love-intrigues. But we will leave those gentlemen in the possession of the pleasures they buy so dear; while their footmen wait for them in the streets, and hug themselves in the hopes of coming in for the second course at free cost.[57]

For God's sake (says Leandro Perez) let me know the meaning of this other scene I see; every body seems to be yet on foot in this great house upon the left hand; whence proceeds all this mirth, some laughing, others dancing? doubtless they celebrate some high festival. These are nuptial joys: (replies the demon) all the domesticks are making merry; and 'tis not above three days since every one in this same house was in the utmost grief and affliction. I have a great mind to recite the particulars; the story is indeed somewhat long, but I hope, will entertain you. The demon then began.

CHAPTER IV.

The history of the amours of the Count de Belflor and Leonora de Cespides.

Count Belflor, one of the greatest lords about court, was passionately in love with a young lady, Leonora de Cespides; but he had no intention to make her his wife: the daughter of a private gentleman did not seem to him a match of sufficient dignity: he wanted only to make her his mistress.

With this view and no other, he embraced every opportunity of making her sensible of his passion, but never was able to come to an interview, or convey her a billet, so narrowly was she watched by a strict and vigilant governante, whose name was Marcella. Though he was on the brink of despair, and found his love increased by the difficulties that attended it, he studied all the means he could think of to deceive this watchful Argus that guarded his Io.

On the other hand, Leonora, who perceived the count's passion by his looks,[1] could not guard herself against the same for him, and instantly conceived an affection for his person, which in the end became very violent, even without my interfering in any shape to increase it: the magician, who then had me in his clutches, put a stop to the activity of all my functions; but nature, in this case, had a proper effect: it is often as effectual as my skill, and the only difference is, that the former makes but a slow progress, and needs my help to quicken the operation.[2]

Affairs were in this situation, when one morning Leonora and this eternal governante going to church, were met by an old woman, who was counting[3] a rosary of the largest beads hypocrisy had ever yet invented. She came up to them with a smiling countenance, and addressing herself to the duena, Heavens preserve you! (said she) may the peace of God ever rest upon you. May I be so bold as to ask, if you are not Madam Marcella, the chaste widow of the deceased Signior Martin Rozeta? Upon which the other answered immediately that she was. Then I meet you in a happy hour, (said the old woman) to inform you, there is a relation of mine now at my house who wants to speak with you. He is just arrived from Flanders, and was an acquaintance, a most intimate acquaintance of your worthy husband, and has some matters of the last consequence to communicate to you. He would have waited upon you himself, if he had not been taken so very ill; but alas! the poor man has received extreme unction.[4] I live but just by, do take the trouble to step along with me.

The old governante, who was a sensible, discerning woman, was staggered at this, and being afraid of taking some wrong step, was doubtful what to do; which the old woman perceiving, and suspecting the reason, said, Madam Marcella, you may without any scruple or hesitation trust to me; my name is la Chicona. The rector Marcos de Figueroa, and the curate Mira de Mesqua, will answer for me, as they would for their own grandmothers. The reason of my desiring you to go with me is, that my kinsman designs to make you restitution of a certain sum of money he once borrowed of your deceased husband. That word restitution immediately cleared dame Marcella's doubts.[5] Come, child, (says she to Leonora) let us go see this good woman's friend. It is an act of charity, and recommended by the church, to visit the sick.

They were at the house of Chicona, who conducted them into a room, where they saw a man in bed with a grey beard,[6] who either was, or appeared to be in the last extremity. Here, cousin, says Chicona introducing the governante, this is dame Marcella, the virtuous and chaste widow of your once much respected friend Signior Martin Rozeta. At these words this ancient man, raising up his head, bowed to the duena, and making a sign for her to sit down, as she sat by his bed-side, spoke to her in a feeble voice: My dear Madam Marcella, I return thanks to heaven for having been graciously pleased to spare my life 'till this moment, the only thing I earnestly wished for on this side of time.[7] I was anxious lest I should die before I could have the satisfaction of seeing you, and repaying into your own hands the hundred ducats which my intimate friend your husband lent me at Bruges, to discharge a debt of honour I stood engaged for. Did he, never, good Madam, speak to you about such an affair?

Never in his life,[8] replied the widow, never so much as once mentioned one word about it. O he was the most generous creature! may his soul ever find rest in the presence of God! he forgot the services he did his friends, and, far from being of the same disposition with those pitiful fellows who make a merit of their good works, I declare, that 'till this present moment, I never had a hint that in the whole course of his life he had ever been of the least service to any of his fellow-creatures. He must have undoubtedly had a noble soul, says the old man, and I ought to be of all men the most sensible of it; and to convince you I am so, I must inform you of the circumstances of my situation at the time he so generously relieved me: but as I have things of the last consequence to mention, that regards the memory of the defunct, I should be very glad to mention them only before his chaste and discreet widow.

Well then, says Chicona, you may be alone with Madam Marcella; and in the mean while this young lady and I will retire into my closet. In so saying she left the governante with the sick man, and carried Leonora into another chamber, and without going about the bush,[9] told her at once, My pretty Leonora, the present moments are too precious to be lost without employing them as they should be. You know Count Belflor by sight: he has been passionately fond of you a long while, and desired nothing so eagerly as an opportunity of making to you such a declaration: but the vigilance and strictness of your governess has never till now allowed him an opportunity. Being driven to despair, he has had recourse to me, and I have exerted my abilities in order to serve him. That old man you have been with is the count's valet de chambre; and every thing I have been about is only a trick to deceive Marcella, and get you here.

As she ended these words, Count Belflor, who was concealed behind the hangings, ran up to Leonora, and casting himself at her feet,[10] Madam, said he, forgive this artifice of a lover, who can live no longer without you. If the obliging Chicona had not found out this method of procuring an interview, I should have abandoned myself to despair. These words, pronounced in a most tender manner by a man she no ways disliked, made a sensible impression on the mind of Leonora.[11] She remained for some time in suspence what answer she should make, but at last recovering herself, answered the count with looks of anger and disdain: You imagine yourself no doubt extremely obliged to this lady for her officious service, which she has dexterously performed: but know, that you will reap no advantage from it.

As she spoke this, she retired back some steps towards the room she had come from, but the count prevented her: Stay, lovely Leonora, and vouchsafe to hear me one moment; my passion is so pure that it needs not alarm the most perfect virtue.[12] I must own indeed, the method I have taken to procure this interview may justly awaken your suspicions, but have not I attempted in vain every other means to speak with you?[13] for above these six months have I constantly followed you to the church, the park, and the play. In vain have I sought for every opportunity to tell you how much I am your slave. That cruel, that relentless governante has always been the bane of my happiness. Alas! instead of blaming me for what I have done, pity rather the cruel necessity which has obliged me to have recourse to stratagem, and which has made me undergo these tortures of absence and expectation: judge from the consciousness of your own charms, what mortal agonies I must have suffered.

Belflor did not fail to heighten this pathetick expostulation with all the airs of tenderness possible, which these sparks have always at command: he even dropped some tears. Leonora was extremely moved: she could not help feeling the sentiments of tenderness and compassion: but far from yielding to such emotions, the more she found herself inclinable to relent, with so much more eagerness she press'd to get away. Count, said she, all your fine speeches are to no purpose, and I will hear no more of them. Don't offer to keep me here any longer: quit me, and let me go out of a house where my honour is in danger, or I will immediately call out, and make the whole neighbourhood witness to the insolence of your behaviour. She pronounced these words with so resolute a tone of voice, that Madam Chicona, who for divers and weighty reasons declined appearing before a justice, begged Count Belflor not to carry the thing any farther. He gave over and pressed Leonora no more,[14] who went out, that which had never happened to any woman before, as much a virgin as she had come in.

She immediately rejoined her governess; Come, my good mother, said she, let us leave this sham conversation, 'tis all a trick; get out of this dangerous house. What is the matter, my child? says Marcella with astonishment, what makes you want to go in so great a hurry? I will tell you immediately, replied Leonora, but we must be gone: every moment I stay here gives me fresh uneasiness. How eager soever the governante was to know the reason of all this, she was obliged to defer her curiosity, and yield to the pressing instances of this young lady. They both quitted the house directly, and left the count, his valet de chambre, and la Chicona, as much disconcerted as a set of players, when the first representation of a piece is saluted with hisses from the pit and gallery.[15]

As soon as Leonora was in the street, she began, all in a flutter,[16] to give her duena an account of what had passed in the apartment of la Chicona. Dame Marcella listened with great attention, and when they were got home, I protest, said she, I am extremely shocked at what you tell me: how could I be the dupe of this old hag? 'Tis true indeed, I did at first make some difficulty, but why did not I hold out? I ought to have distrusted her demure and sanctified looks: I protest I have been guilty of a folly not to be forgiven in one of my experience. Why did not you tell me of it when we were in the house of that abominable woman? I would have torn her eyes out: I would have spoke to Count Belflor as he deserved: and as for that pretended old fellow with the beard, who amused me with these sham stories, I would have pulled his ears[17] for him. However, I must immediately go back and return the money they gave me as a real debt; and if I meet with them, they shall lose nothing for having waited so long. So saying she took up her mantle, and immediately set out for the house of la Chicona.

The count was there still, in despair for the bad success of his enterprize: any other man would have given up the suit; but he was not quite discouraged. Count Belflor, amidst a thousand good qualities, was very blameable in one thing: he allowed himself to be too much led aside by his passion for women; and when in love with any one, was so warm in his pursuits, that tho' naturally, in other respects, a man of strict honour, yet on these occasions he was capable of violating the most sacred rights of mankind, to accomplish his ends. He was sensible he could do nothing in this affair without the assistance of Marcella; and however strict and severe her morals might be, he fancy'd she would melt at the sight of a handsome present; and he judged rightly. The fidelity of governesses is owing to want of money, or want of generosity, in those who solicit their interest.[18]

The moment Marcella got there, and saw them all three together, she began to open as loud as ten fish-women.[19] She called Chicona and the count all the names she could think of, and made the hundred ducats fly at the head of his valet de chambre. The count endeavoured to lay this storm,[20] and falling on his knees before her, to make the scene more moving, begged of her to take back the ducats, and offered her a thousand pistoles more, conjuring her to take pity on him. As she had never met with such a powerful argument before to move her pity, she found herself inclinable to sentiments of compassion. She left off scolding, and balancing in her own mind the thousand pistoles with the sum she expected from Lewis de Cespides, she found, by calculation, it was better to seduce her ward, than to preserve her virtue; and after some affected difficulties, she took back the purse of ducats, agreed for the thousand pistoles, engaged to serve Count Belflor in his amour, and went off immediately to set about fulfilling her promise.

As she knew Leonora to be a virtuous young lady, she was upon her guard, to conceal from her every thing that might have given the least suspicion of any intelligence between her and the count, for fear of her discovering it to her father; she determined to compleat her ruin more artfully, and spoke to her in this manner: Leonora, says she, I have had my revenge; I found them all three together, they were quite confounded with your resolute behaviour. I threatened Chicona with your father's resentment, and with bringing her to justice, and said to Count Belflor every thing that my passion could suggest. I hope that young lord will be cured of making any more such attempts, and that we shall have no more trouble from that quarter. Heavens be praised! that your virtue has got the better of the snare laid for you. I cannot help crying for joy. How I rejoice that he has not succeeded in his wicked artifice! for these great men make nothing of seducing young women: even those who pique themselves upon honour in other respects, make no scruple in this; as if the ruin of families was no dishonest or disgraceful action. Though I do not positively say that this is the case with the count, or that he had an intention to ruin you. No, we must not always judge uncharitably of our neighbour: perhaps his intentions were honourable. Tho' his rank and fortune may indeed intitle him to the greatest match in the kingdom, yet who knows what effect your beauty may have upon him?[21] and I reflect that in the answers he made to my reproaches, he dropped some hints of that.

How do you mean, (replies Leonora) if he had intended any such thing, he certainly would have asked me of my father, who doubtless would have readily agreed to such a proposal. You are perfectly in the right, replied this governante, and I am entirely of your opinion: his conduct is far from being clear, and his designs cannot be honourable. I have a great mind to go back again, and scold him afresh.[22] No, says Leonora, 'tis much better to forget what's past, and shew our resentment by contempt. You are right again, replies the other, that is surely the best way; you certainly judge of things better than I: but then I would beg to observe, that even notwithstanding this, we perhaps still judge too harshly of him. Supposing this conduct of his the effect of delicacy, and that before he would make any proposals to Don Lewis, he had a mind, by long services, to merit your esteem, and be assured of your love, that your mutual happiness may be more compleat; and if that is really the case, do you think, my dear, it would be wrong to listen to him? come tell me your thoughts; my tender concern is well known to you. Have you any inclination for the person of Count Belflor? or would it be any violence upon your inclination to be made his wife?[23]

This artful question had its effect upon young Leonora, whose heart was open, and suspected nothing;[24] she cast down her eyes, and blushing, owned she had no aversion to him. Her virgin modesty would not allow her to say more; but the duena pressed her to speak her mind without reserve; and made such good use of her pretended affection, that the young lady opened to her all her mind without reserve. Since you would have me speak freely, said she, I own that Belflor deserves the love of any woman.[25] His person appears to me so graceful, and I have heard so many things spoke to his advantage, that I have not been able to preserve myself from being sensibly moved with his addresses to me. Those constant pains you have taken to guard against them, have caused me often much uneasiness; and I will even confess to you, that I sometimes in secret bewailed the sighs your watchful diligence has made him suffer: and to say more, at this moment, instead of hating him for this wild attempt, my heart, in spite of me, pleads in his behalf,[26] and is willing to throw the blame of it upon your too great severity.

My dear child, says Marcella, since I find his addresses are not disagreeable to you, I warrant you I will manage him. I am but too sensible, replies Leonora sighing, of the service you are willing to do me. Was Count Belflor not the great lord he is; was he only a private gentleman, my heart would give him the preference to all men; but we must not feed ourselves with such hopes. Count Belflor is a man of the first distinction, and his birth entitles him to one of the greatest matches in the kingdom. We must not expect that he will stoop to the daughter of Don Lewis,[27] who can bring him but a very small fortune. No, no; added she, he can have no such thoughts: he does not look upon me as one worthy to bear his name; and if I should flatter myself with any such hopes, it would be only making myself more miserable.[28]

Why so? replies the governante, why will you imagine he does not love you enough to make you his wife? love works greater wonders than that every day. To hear you speak, one would imagine that there is an infinite difference between the count and you: do yourself more justice; his marrying you would be no disgrace to his rank; you are descended of an ancient and good family, nor need he at all blush at such an alliance; and since you own an inclination for him, I'll go speak to him, and see to get at the bottom of his intentions;[29] and if they are such as I approve of, I will give him some hopes. Take care how you act in this; cries Leonora, I am quite against your going to him; for if he should but suspect that I was in the least privy to it, he could not avoid holding me cheap.[30] Oh! I know how to manage such matters better than you imagine, says Marcella. I'll begin by reproaching him with having a design upon your virtue; he will instantly endeavour to justify himself; so I shall hear what he says, and make him come to an explanation. Let me alone; I will be as tender of your honour as I would of my own.

The duenna went out in the dark of the evening, and found the count near Don Lewis's house; to whom she gave an account of what passed between her and her young mistress; and did not fail to insist upon her own address in discovering that he was not indifferent to Leonora.[31] As nothing could give him greater satisfaction than this discovery, he thanked Marcella in the most lively terms; that is, he promised to deliver into her hands by to-morrow the thousand pistoles; for he looked upon his enterprize as good as finished, well knowing, that when once a young lady's affections are engaged, she is already half undone; so that they parted extremely well satisfied with one another, and the duenna returned home.

Leonora, who impatiently waited, asked her what news she had brought? The best in the world, replied Marcella. I have seen Count Belflor, and can assure you, his intentions are no ways dishonourable. He has no other design but that of marrying you. This he has sworn to me by every thing that is sacred. However, you may believe I did not rest satisfied with that. If it is so said I, why did you not speak to her father? Ah! my dear Madam, (said he, without being at all disconcerted with the question), would you approve that, without knowing the inclinations of Leonora, and following only the dictates of a blind passion, I should reduce her to the cruel necessity of obeying the orders of a tyrannical father? No, I would sacrifice my passion to her repose; and am more a gentleman than to run the risque of being the occasion of her perpetual unhappiness.

As he spoke in this manner I observed him with the greatest attention, and made use of all my skill, to see if I could read in his eyes, whether he was really smit with this violent passion as he pretended; and it plainly appeared to me his love was real and unfeigned, which gave me such joy as I was scarcely able to conceal. However, I was fully persuaded of his sincerity; and to fix a lover of his importance, I thought it adviseable to give him some light into your sentiments. My lord, said I, Leonora has no aversion to your person; on the contrary, she has conceived an esteem for you; and if I am able to judge of her sentiments, your addresses will not be disagreeable.[32] O heavens! cries the count, in a transport of joy, what do I hear! does Leonora, the amiable Leonora, entertain favourable sentiments of me? what am I not indebted to you, kind Marcella, for having relieved me from such a long state of uncertainty? and it adds to my joy that you are the messenger of such good news; you, who, far from assisting my love, have occasioned me such cruel anxieties: but end what you have begun; complete my happiness, by letting me have an interview with the divine Leonora. I want to pledge my faith to her, and in your presence, to swear an eternal fidelity.[33]

To these expressions, continued the governante, he added others yet more passionate; and, in a word, pressed so much to procure him a secret interview, that I could not get off promising him. How! (cries Leonora, with some emotion) why did you make him such a promise, when you yourself have told me a hundred times, that a discreet young lady ought, upon no account, to trust herself to such conversations, since they must always endanger her virtue? I have done so to be sure, replied Marcella, and it is an excellent maxim, tho' you are not under a necessity of following it upon this occasion, as you may look upon the count as your husband. But he is not my husband yet, replies Leonora; and I ought not to see him 'till my father has given his consent.

At that instant Marcella repented having brought up Leonora so strictly, whose virtue she found so difficult to conquer: but being determined, at all events, to accomplish her designs,[34] she replied, My dearest Leonora, I greatly commend your being so scrupulous: happy effect of my labour! I see how you have improved by every lesson of virtue I inculcated in your mind.[35] I rejoice in the work of my own hands. But, my child, you are too delicate, you have refined upon my precepts; and your virtue is rather too rigid. Tho' I pique myself on being severe in every thing that concerns a lady's honour, yet I do not require such a severe reserve, as arms itself equally against guilt and innocence. A lady may hearken to her lover even consistently with the purest virtue,[36] when she is assured he means honourably; and it is then no more criminal in her to answer his love than it was before to be sensible of it. Depend upon me, Leonora, I have too much experience, and am too much in your interest to advise you to any step that might be attended with bad consequence.[37]

But in what place, says Leonora, do you intend then I should see him? In your own apartment, replies the other; that of all others is the safest; I'll introduce him to-morrow before it is light. You don't reflect on what you say, replies the young lady; what, shall I allow a man—Yes, yes, there is nothing in it, replies the governante, 'tis no such extraordinary matter as you imagine: 'tis what happens every day; and I would to God, all the ladies who receive such visits were as pure in their intentions as you are. Besides, what have you to fear? shall not I be with you? But if my father should come and surprize us? says Leonora. Don't be uneasy about that, replies the other; your father is in no pain as to your conduct, he knows my fidelity, and has a full confidence in that. This young lady, pressed so warmly by her governess, and prompted by her own secret inclinations, could not resist any longer, and at last agreed to what the duenna proposed.

Count Belflor was soon informed of this, and was so overjoyed, that he gave Marcella instantly a purse of five hundred pistoles, and a ring of the same value; and she, on the other hand, finding he kept so well to his word, was resolved to be no less punctual in what she had promised. The night following, when she supposed every body was gone to bed, she fixed a ladder of silk cord, the count had given her, to the balcony, and by that introduced him into the chamber of her mistress.

In the mean time, Leonora abandoned herself to reflections that cruelly agitated her mind. Tho' she loved Count Belflor, yet notwithstanding all her governess had been able to say to her, she could not be satisfied but that the easiness with which she had consented to this visit was a breach of her duty; nor could the consciousness of the innocence of her intentions remove her scruples.[38] To receive a man into her chamber in the night, without the consent of her father, and without being thoroughly satisfied of the honour of his designs,[39] appeared to her not only criminal, but what ought even to expose her to the contempt of her gallant. This last reflection gave her the greatest pain, and she was full of it, when the count entered her chamber.

He immediately threw himself at her feet, to thank her for the favour she had done him. He seemed full of love and gratitude, and assured her he designed to make her his wife. However, as he did not enlarge upon that head[40] so much as she expected, she said, Count, tho' I am extremely willing to believe you have no other views, yet whatever assurances you can give me, I must always suspect them, 'till they have received the sanction of my father's approbation. Madam, answered the count, I would have asked that long ago, had it not been from a tender regard to your peace and quiet. I don't upbraid you for not having done it hitherto, replied Leonora, I rather approve of your delicacy in that point; but as all these reasons are now removed, I must insist upon your speaking immediately to my father Don Lewis, or resolve never to see me more.

How so, my adorable Leonora, says the count, why never see you more? Ah! how insensible you are to the sweets of love! did you feel them as I do, it would heighten our joys, for you to receive my addresses in private, and conceal our amours, at least for some time, from the knowledge of your father. What charms would two souls, strictly united in love, find from such a sweet correspondence! It may be so to you, replied Leonora; but as for me, it would be a source of continual uneasiness:[41] These delicate refinements of gallantry but ill suit with a woman of virtue. Don't talk to me of the charms of a criminal correspondence. Had you that regard for me you ought to entertain,[42] you never would make such a proposal; and if your intentions are such as you would make me believe they are, you ought, in your mind, to despise me for not shewing a proper resentment at such treatment. But alas! continued she, dropping some tears, 'tis to my own weakness I owe such an insult: I have deserved it from what I have done upon your account.

My charming Leonora, cried Count Belflor, 'tis you who do me a cruel injustice; your too scrupulous virtue takes false alarms. What, because I have been so happy as not to appear indifferent in your eyes,[43] would you from thence infer, that I should abate in my esteem for you? can any thing be more cruel, or more unjust![44] No, Madam, I set a just value upon your goodness to me: that cannot lessen you in my esteem, and I am ready to do every thing you require of me. To-morrow I will speak to Don Lewis. I will do every thing in my power to procure his consent to crown my happiness; but I must at the same time tell you, I see but little appearance of success. What do you say, answered Leonora, extremely surprized, would my father refuse me to one of so distinguished a rank as yours? Alas! replied Belflor, it is that very thing that makes me dread his refusal. If you are surprized at it now, you will cease to be so when I have explained the matter to you.[45] Some days ago, Madam, continued he, the king declared his intentions to have me married, without naming the lady he designed me for. He only gave me to understand she was one of the best matches in the kingdom, and that he had this matter much at heart;[46] and as I was then ignorant whether you approved my passion, (for you know your cruelty was such, that I never before this interview, had an opportunity of avowing it) upon that account I expressed no reluctance to submit to his pleasure. After I have told you this, Madam, you may be a judge yourself, whether Don Lewis would run the risk of incurring the king's displeasure in accepting me for his son-in-law.

To be sure, he would not, answered Leonora. I know very well, that however advantageous he might think your alliance, he would renounce it sooner than expose himself to the resentment of the king. But if my father should give his consent, we should be nothing the better for that; for how is it possible you should marry me, when the king has engaged you to another? Madam, I will frankly own to you, replied the count, that I am not a little embarrassed myself upon that head.[47] However, I am not without hopes, that by preserving a proper conduct with regard to the king, I shall be able, considering his friendship for me, to avert this impending blow that threatens me; and, my lovely Leonora, you may easily assist me in this, if you think me worthy of your regard. How is that possible? says Leonora, how can I any ways contribute to break off the match the king has designed for you? Ah! Madam, says the count, with a tender and passionate air, if you would receive my plighted faith, I could yet preserve myself for you, without the king's taking it amiss.

Suffer me, my charming Leonora, said he, (throwing himself at her feet) suffer me to take you as my bride, in the presence of your governess; she will be a witness to answer for the sacred force of our mutual engagements. By these means I shall be able to extricate myself from those fetters they are forging for me; for if after that the king should press me to the match he designs for me, I can throw myself at his feet, and inform him of the violence of my passion for you,[48] and that I have privately married you; and whatever inclination he may have to dispose of me otherways, I am sure he is too good to ravish me from the arms of one I adore, and too just to offer such an affront to your family.

What think you, discreet Marcella, turning to the governante, what think you of this expedient, which love has just now inspired me with? I am charmed with it, answered she; it must be owned that love is very ingenious. And you, my adorable Leonora, what are your sentiments? I hope, tho' still mistrustful and diffident, you will not disapprove of this expedient. No, says the young lady, I have no objections, if my father approves of it; and I don't doubt but he will, when once you inform him of the particulars. You must take care not to intrust him with such a secret, cried the wicked Marcella; it seems you are but little acquainted with Don Lewis: he is too delicate in sentiments of honour to consent to any thing that looks like an intrigue: the name of a clandestine marriage would shock him; besides, his prudence would immediately suggest to him the danger of any step that seemed to thwart the designs of the king: and by this imprudent conduct you would awaken his suspicions; he would be prying into every thing we did,[49] and would, in consequence, make it impossible for you to see one another.

That I should never be able to bear, cries the count. But, Madam Marcella, continued he, (affecting an air of chagrin) do you really imagine Don Lewis would be averse to the affair of a clandestine marriage? He certainly would, replied the other. For my own share, I heartily wish he would come into it; but I know him to be so nice and scrupulous, that he never would agree to dispense with the ceremonies of the church; and if you should be married in that manner, it would immediately become publick.

Ah! my dear Leonora, added the count, (tenderly squeezing her hand) must we, to keep up the ceremony of an idle form, must we, upon that account, run the dreadful risque of, perhaps being separated for ever? It is entirely in your own power to become mine for ever. The consent of your father might perhaps, indeed save you some uneasiness, but as Marcella has shewn the impossibility of obtaining his approbation, receive my hand and my heart; give yourself up to the purity of my passion, and when once it is time to inform him of our engagements, we will let him know the reasons why we concealed it. Well, says Leonora, I consent that we delay, for some time, speaking to Don Lewis. Sound the king first upon this head, before I receive your hand in secret; tell him, if you think proper that you have privately married me; and endeavour under this to see——No, Madam, replied Belflor, I must beg your pardon for that; my sentiments of honour won't permit me to do any thing that approaches near the borders of deceit and falshood; no consideration would make me do that:[50] besides, if the king should but imagine I had imposed upon him, I know him well, and am sure he would never forgive me.

In a word, Signior Cleofas, continued Asmodeus, I should never have done, if I was to repeat, word for word, every thing that was said to shake the virtue of this young creature. I will only add, that the count said every passionate thing that I commonly upon these occasions suggest to you mortals; but all to no purpose.[51] In vain did he swear that he would fulfil, in the eyes of all the world, the private engagements betwixt them. In vain did he adjure heaven by the most solemn oaths. He could not triumph over the virtue of Leonora: and the day, which now began to appear, obliged him, tho' unwilling, to retire.

The next day, Madam Marcella, looking upon it that her honour, or indeed her interest, was concerned in fulfilling her engagements to the count, addressed herself in this manner to her young mistress: Leonora, says she, I am really at a loss how to talk to you. I find you treat Count Belflor's passion for you as if it were a matter of common gallantry; doubtless you have found something in the person of the count that disgusts you. Far from that, says Leonora; he never appeared so amiable in my eyes; and this interview has given him in my affections, the lustre of new charms. If that is really the case, replied the other, I am actually at a loss to comprehend the meaning of your conduct.[52] You say you have conceived a violent passion for him, and yet refuse agreeing to what he has shewn the absolute necessity of.

My good Marcella, says the daughter of Don Lewis, without doubt you have more experience, and are better versed in those things than I; but have you thought of the consequence that must attend a marriage without the consent of my father? Yes, my dear, I have, said the governante, I have reflected upon every thing that can possibly happen; and I am vexed to the soul you should so obstinately stand in the way of making your own fortune. But take care your lover be not disgusted, and that he don't cool upon your hands. Take care lest his passion subside, and he open his eyes to his own interest; and as he offers you his hand, I would advise you to receive it without hesitation. His word binds him; nothing is more sacred to a man of honour. Besides, am not I a witness that he has taken you for his wife? and is not an evidence such as mine sufficient, in a court of justice, to condemn any man who dares to falsify his oath?

By these and other such like conversations, did the perfidious Marcella undermine the virtue of this innocent young lady;[53] who, giving way to the fears she was under of losing for ever the count, some days after yielded, without reserve, to his wicked intentions. The duenna every night introduced him, by the balcony, into her apartment, and let him out the same way.

It happened one night, that staying longer than usual, and the morning beginning to appear, he was in so great a hurry to get down, that he missed his step, and fell into the street; and Don Lewis de Cespides, who lay in the apartment above his daughter's, having risen that morning earlier than usual to dispatch some pressing business, and hearing the noise the count made in his fall, opened his window to see what was the matter, and perceived a man with some difficulty recovering himself,[54] and Madam Marcella on the balcony, disentangling the silken ladder, which the count had made a better use of in getting up than in coming down. He rubbed his eyes, and at first took what he saw for an illusion; but upon reflection he was convinced of the truth of it, and the light of the morning, tho' feeble, sufficiently shewed him the dishonour of his family.

Shocked at this discovery, fatal to his repose,[55] and in the transports of a just indignation, he went down immediately to his daughter's apartment, with a light in one hand, and his sword drawn in the other, looking for his daughter and her guardian, to sacrifice them both to his fury. He knocked at the chamber-door, ordering them immediately to open it, and as they knew his voice they instantly obeyed, trembling. He entered Leonora's apartment with an air full of fury, and presenting to them his naked sword, I come, says he, to wash off the stain that is brought upon my house in the blood of an abandoned child, who has dishonoured her family, and to take vengeance of a perfidious governante, who has abused my confidence.

They both fell down at his feet; and Marcella speaking first, Signior, said she, before you wreak your vengeance upon us, vouchsafe to hear me one moment. Wretch, said Don Lewis, for a moment I do consent to suspend my fury. Speak; let me know all the circumstances of my dishonour. But why do I say all? I know every one but the name of him who has dared thus to dishonour my house. Signior, says Marcella, Count Belflor is the man. Count Belflor! cries Don Lewis, where has he had an opportunity of seeing my daughter?[56] by what means has he been able to seduce her? Conceal nothing from me. Sir, answered the governante, I'll tell you the whole matter with the utmost sincerity. Upon that she gave him a particular account, with infinite art, of every thing she had formerly persuaded Leonora to believe the count had said to her. She set him forth in the most advantageous light, as a tender, delicate, and sincere lover. However, as she could not avoid coming to the conclusion, and was obliged to discover to what lengths the correspondence had been carried, she glossed it over, by enlarging upon the reasons that induced her to consent to a marriage without his privity,[57] and put so good a face upon the matter, that the old gentleman began to abate of his fury. This was immediately perceived by the artful governante, who, to soften him effectually, Sir, continued she, this is what you wanted to be informed of; now wreak your vengeance upon us both, plunge your sword into the bosom of Leonora. But what do I say? Leonora is innocent; she is guilty of nothing but in having followed the advice of one to whom you intrusted her conduct: 'tis I only that ought to suffer. 'Twas I that introduced the count into your daughter's apartment; 'twas I who tied the knot that now joins them. I was wilfully blind to the irregularity of entering into engagements to which you were not privy, in order to secure to your family a son-in-law, who, as you know, is the canal through which all the favours of the court flow. I only consulted the happiness of Leonora, and the advantages your family must reap from such an alliance. The excess of my zeal has made me exceed the bounds of my duty.

While the artful Marcella was talking in this manner, the young lady was in a flood of tears, and in such agitations of grief and sorrow, that her good old father could hold it no longer. He dropped his sword upon the ground, and laying aside the sternness of an inraged parent, Ah! my dear child, said he, (the tears standing in his eyes) what a fatal passion is love! Alas! thou knowest but little the true cause thou hast to wail and lament.[58] Now the presence of an injured and incensed parent, who has surprized you unawares, occasions your grief. You little reflect upon the future scenes of woe that very probably your lover will yet make you feel. And you, indiscreet Marcella, what is this you have done? Into what an excess of misery has your ill-timed zeal for our family thrown us? I own, indeed, that the alliance of such a man as Count Belflor might dazzle you; and that is what pleads your excuse in my breast: but, unthinking woman, should not you have distrusted a man of his character? the greater his rank and power, the more you ought to have been upon your guard against him. If he should break his vows to Leonora, where must I have recourse? shall I find relief in the laws? no, his power and interest will protect him from the severity of justice. I would willingly flatter myself that he will be just to his engagements, and keep his word with Leonora; tho' if it is true, as you have told me, that the king intends to marry him to another lady, 'tis much to be feared that he will interpose his authority in order to compel him. Oh, as to compelling him, says Leonora, there is no fear of that; the count has assured us, that the king will not offer such a violence to his inclinations. I am certain of it, says Marcella. He not only loves his favourite too well to exercise such a tyranny over him, but is too just and generous to give such a mortal wound to the heart of the noble and valiant Don Lewis de Cespides, who has spent all his best days in the service of his country.

Well, says the old man, (sighing) God grant my fears be vain! however, I'll go to the count and bring him to an explanation. The eyes of a father are jealous and discerning. I shall soon dive into the bottom of his intentions. If I find him disposed to do what I would wish, I'll forgive what is past; but says he, (with a severe air) if I find in him a heart that is faithless, both of you shall go directly into a convent, there to mourn your folly all the rest of your days. So saying, he took up his sword, and leaving them to recover from their fright, went up into his chamber to dress.

Asmodeus was here interrupted by our student: The story you are now telling me is extremely interesting, but an affair that I now perceive, keeps me from listening to you so attentively as I otherwise should. I perceive a woman that seems to be handsome, sitting between a young man and an old fellow; they are all three drinking, and I do not doubt but their wine is very good; and while the old gentleman caresses this lady, the baggage stretches out her hand to the young one to kiss: I suppose he is her gallant. Quite the contrary, replies the demon; the old fellow is the gallant, and the young one her husband. The first is a man of figure, a commander of the military order of Calatrava,[59] and ruins himself for the sake of this woman, whose husband has a small place at court. She caresses the old fribbling fumbler out of interest, and grants favours to her husband out of inclination. This is pleasant enough, says Zambullo: pray is not the husband a Frenchman? No, replies Asmodeus, he is even a Spaniard. I can assure you, Sir, the good city of Madrid produces, like other places, complaisant husbands; but they don't spring up so fast any where else as in Paris, which, without doubt, may boast of the glory of its citizens in this respect, above all the rest of the world. I ask your pardon, Signior Asmodeus, says Cleofas, for thus interrupting the thread of your discourse. Please to proceed, Sir, I am infinitely delighted with the story; I find there some refined strokes of art I am extremely edified by. The demon then resumed his narration.

CHAPTER V.

Continuation and conclusion of the amours of Count Belflor.

Don Lewis went out betimes in the morning to meet Count Belflor, who, not imagining his intrigue had been discovered, was surprized at such a visit. He came out of his chamber to meet the old gentleman, and after a number of bows and salutations, How rejoiced I am, said he, to see Don Lewis de Cespides! I hope, Sir, you come to give me some opportunity of serving you. My lord, answered Don Lewis, I desire you will order us to be left alone.

Count Belflor immediately ordered every body out of the room, and they sat down together: upon which the old gentleman began; Count, says he, the quiet and happiness of my life depend upon a proper explanation of an affair I am come to talk to you of. This morning I saw you come out of my daughter's apartments; she has owned the whole affair, and has told me.——She told you that I passionately loved her, interrupted the count, (being willing to avoid a conversation on a subject he had no mind to enter into) but I am sure she would but very lamely describe the sentiments of regard I have for her. I am quite ravished with her; she is the finest creature in the world; has wit, beauty, virtue, and every thing that can make a perfectly accomplished lady.[1] I am told likewise, Sir, you have a son who is following his studies at Alcala: pray has he any resemblance of his sister? I am sure if he has but her beauty, and any share of your good qualities, he must be the most accomplished cavalier in all Spain. I long prodigiously to see him; and if I can be of any service, you may command, Sir, the utmost of my credit and interest in his behalf.[2]

My lord, says Don Lewis, (with great gravity) I am extremely obliged to you; but this is not the affair at present,[3] let us talk upon what—— We must get him into the army immediately, says the count. I'll take care of his advancement; he shall not linger among the croud of subaltern officers, that I give you my word for. Come, my lord, says the other, don't interrupt me in this manner; I demand a direct answer;[4] do you, or do you not, design to keep the engagements you have—— Doubtless I do, says the count, (interrupting him a third time). I will keep my word in what I have said, and will support your son with all my interest; you may be assured of it. This is too much, says Don Cespides (rising). After having basely seduced my daughter, you dare to insult me to my face. But know, my lord, I am a gentleman, and the dishonour you have brought upon my house shall not go unpunished. As he spoke these words, he left the count, his heart ready to break with anger and indignation, and meditating a thousand schemes how to be revenged. As soon as he came home, he spoke to Leonora and Marcella in great agitation of mind. It was not without reason, said he, that I suspected the count. He is false, and I will be revenged upon him. As for you, to-morrow you both go into a convent: prepare yourselves therefore accordingly, and give thanks to heaven that my resentment is satisfied with so slight a punishment. Upon this he retired into his closet, to deliberate with himself what course he should take in an affair of so much delicacy.[5]

As to the young lady, you may easily conceive the condition she was in, when she understood that Belflor was false. For some time she continued motionless. The paleness of death overspread her beautiful face, her spirits failed, and she fell, without signs of life, into the arms of her governess, who thought she had actually given up the ghost. The duenna tried all the means possible to bring her out of this fit, and at last succeeded. Leonora recovered the use of her senses, she opened her eyes, and seeing what pains Marcella was at to relieve her, Ah! how cruel you are, said she, not to let me remain in the state I was in! I was not then sensible of the horror of my fatal destiny. Why did you not let me sleep the sleep of death? You, who know what inexpressible tortures must ever attend my wretched life, why would you endeavour to prolong it?

Marcella tried every method she could think of to comfort her;[6] but all her arguments served only to increase her agony. Every thing you can urge, cried she, is to no purpose.

I will hear no more: 'tis in vain you attempt to mitigate my despair; you ought rather to heighten it; you, who are the occasion of my being plunged into this frightful abyss of misery. Yes, it was you who took upon you to answer for Count Belflor's honour. But for you I should never have abandoned myself to my passion; by degrees I might have overcome it; or, at least, never allowed him to reap any advantage from my weakness. But I will not, continued she, impute my misfortunes to you, I accuse none but myself. I was guilty in following your advice, in receiving the hand of any man without the knowledge of my father. However flattering to my passion, or glorious to my fortune the addresses of the count might be, I ought to have rejected any thing that must be purchased at the expence of my honour. I ought to have distrusted you, distrusted him, and distrusted myself. After having been so weak as to suffer my honour to be betrayed by his false protestations; after the stain I have brought upon my family, and the anguish of heart I have brought upon my aged father, I loath, I detest myself; and far from repining at what they imagine a punishment, my being obliged to retire from the world, would to God I could but hide my shame, was it in the most frightful recesses of a desert.[7]

As she spoke in this manner, she shed floods of tears, tore her garments and her beautiful hair, as if she revenged herself upon them for the perfidy of her lover. The duenna, to conform to the grief of her mistress, appeared to take on mightily; and dropping some tears, which she had always at command, vented herself in terrible execrations against the whole sex, and Count Belflor in particular. Is it possible, cried she, that the count, a man who appeared to me so ingenuous and sincere, should be such a profligate as to deceive us both? I am not able to recover the shock it has given me, nor can I yet believe it to be true.

Why after all, says Leonora, when I consider him at my feet, what woman would not have been deceived by that air of tenderness, those solemn oaths he invoked heaven to witness, those repeated transports of love? his eyes seemed still to express more passion than his words; and, in short, he seemed quite charmed at the sight of me. No, he is not the man they would make me believe him to be. My father has spoke to him with too little respect: they have both been too warm, and that might be the occasion why he rather assumed the state of a grandee, than the behaviour of a lover. But in this supposition, perhaps, I deceive myself. I will, however, get out of this state of uncertainty, and write to Count Belflor, and let him know that I expect him here this evening; and he shall either relieve me from this anxiety, or I will be assured, from his own mouth,[8] of his treachery.

Marcella greatly approved of this expedient; she even conceived some hopes that the count might conquer his ambition, and, melted by Leonora's tears, when they met together,[9] determine to marry her.

In the mean time, Count de Belflor having got rid of Don Lewis, began seriously to reflect upon the consequences that might attend his interview with the old gentleman. He made no doubt but the whole house of the Cespides would make a common quarrel of it;[10] but that reflection gave him small uneasiness. The interruption of his correspondence with Leonora was what touched him to the heart. He thought she would either be sent to a convent, or, at least, so strictly watched, that he should never have an opportunity of seeing her more. This reflection troubled him much, and he was thinking within himself of some means to prevent this misfortune, when his valet de chambre brought him a letter, which Marcella delivered to him from Leonora, the contents of which were these:

"To-morrow I quit the world, and am to be buried in a convent. I have survived my honour: I am become a reproach to myself, and hateful to my family; and all this for having listened to you. Once more I expect you this evening; for such is my despair, that I seek for fresh tortures. Come then, and confess your heart had no share in the vows you so solemnly made, or come and prove the sincerity of them by such a conduct as alone can soften the rigour of my destiny. But as this assignation may be attended with danger, after what has passed between you and my father, I would have you bring a friend along with you; for altho' you have made my life wretched, I cannot help interesting myself in the safety of yours."

The count perused this letter two or three times, and imagining to himself the daughter of Don Lewis in the condition she described herself, he was much moved. Reason, virtue, honour, all which he had violated in the frenzy of his passion, now re-assumed their empire in his breast.[11] The mist that clouded his understanding was now quite dispersed: and, as a man who recovers from a delirium blushes to think of the foolish and ridiculous things he has committed, he was ashamed of the low and base artifices he had made use of to gratify his desires.

Wretch that I am! said he, (to himself) what have I done? some demon surely has possessed me! I promised to marry Leonora; I have taken heaven to witness my protestations. I have pretended that the king had proposed a match for me. Lies, perfidy, perjury! every thing have I made use of to abuse unguarded innocence. Had I not better done all I could to overcome my passion, than satisfy my desires by such dishonest means? And what is the end of all this? I have undone a young lady of family; and now abandon her to the fury of a father, whose dishonour is involved in hers. She has made me happy, and the return I make her is to render her for ever miserable. What a scandal is this to my honour and my name![12] Ought I not immediately to make the reparation that is in my power for the injury I have done her? Yes, I ought, and I will. By marrying her I shall perform the promise I have made, and keep my faith, which I pledged to her so solemnly. And who can with reason blame me for acting thus as a man of honour? Should her favours to me make me suspect her virtue? No; I cannot but be sensible with what difficulty she yielded: and when she did, it was not to the transports of my passion; 'twas to the vows I solemnly made her. But, on the other hand, by marrying in this family I do myself a considerable wrong. Shall I, who may with reason expect one of the first ladies of the kingdom; shall I marry the daughter of a private gentleman, and who can give her but a very small fortune? what will the court say of me? they will surely say I have made a very foolish bargain.

Belflor, thus distracted between love and ambition, knew not what to determine: but tho' he was yet unresolved whether he should marry Leonora, he was resolved, at all events, to go to her according to her appointment, and ordered his valet to give that answer to Marcella.

Don Lewis, on his part, passed the day in reflections how he should best vindicate his honour, and it seemed to him a point of much difficulty. To have recourse to law, would make his dishonour publick: besides, he had all imaginable reason to believe, that tho' justice might be on one side, the judges would be on the other. Nor did he think it adviseable to cast himself at the feet of the king. As that monarch designed Count Belflor for another lady, he did not chuse to make an application that must be fruitless.

There remained nothing but to do himself justice by his sword, and that he concluded upon. In the first transports of his passion, he determined to have sent him a challenge; but reflecting he was too old and feeble to trust his own arm, he thought it would be better to leave the affair to his son, whom he looked upon as fitter for that purpose.[13] He dispatched therefore one of his domesticks to Alcala with a letter, in which he ordered his son to come immediately to Madrid, to revenge an insult offered to the family of the Cespides.

This son of his, whose name is Don Pedro, is a young gentleman of eighteen, extremely handsome, and so brave that he is the very hero of the university.[14] But you know him, says Asmodeus, and therefore I need not enlarge upon his character. True, says Don Cleofas, he is a gentleman of great merit, and remarkable courage.

This young man, continued Asmodeus, was not then at Alcala, as his father imagined. He had come to Madrid to see a lady with whom he had an intrigue.[15] This conquest he had made at the Prado, last time he came to see his father. He was as yet ignorant of her name. It was insisted upon that he should use no means to be informed of who she was; and he was obliged, tho' much against his will, to submit to this cruel condition. A lady of quality had conceived an esteem for him, and imagining that she ought not to trust the discretion and constancy of a student, thought proper to try him, before she would make herself known to him.

He was at that time more taken up in thinking of his incognita, than with the philosophy of Aristotle; and as Alcala is but a little distance from hence, he very often, as well as you, made an elopement up to town;[16] only with this difference, that the object his heart was fixed upon, deserved his regard a little better than Donna Thomasa did yours. In order to conceal these excursions from his father Don Lewis, he used to lodge at an inn in the skirts of the town, where he went by a borrowed name. He never stirred abroad but in the morning, at a certain hour, when he went to a certain house, where this lady, who was such a hindrance to the progress of his studies, had the goodness to come, accompanied by a waiting-woman. For all the rest of the day he remained shut up in his inn; but to make amends for that, as soon as it was night, he used to make a tour thro' all the streets of Madrid.

It happened one night, as he passed through a by-alley, that he heard the sound of some musical instruments, which he liked, and stopped to listen to them. It was a serenade. The man who gave it was naturally a brutal fellow, and at that time drunk, who no sooner perceived our student, but making up to him in a great hurry,[17] without further compliment, said, in a very rude manner, Friend, get about your business; such curious people as you will meet with a very indifferent reception here. Don Pedro, who was nettled at this usage,[18] answered him, That he would have gone, if he had been asked with better manners; but now, says he, I will stay, to teach you how you ought to behave yourself. We shall see presently, says the master of the concert, (drawing his sword) which of us is to give place to the other. Don Pedro, on his part, drew likewise, and they exchanged some passes; and tho' the other acquitted himself as a very good swordsman, he could not, however, parry a mortal thrust Don Pedro gave him, and immediately dropped. All the people concerned in the serenade, who had already quitted their instruments, and drawn their swords in order to assist him, ran up to revenge his death. They fell upon Pedro all together, who, upon that occasion, made appear what he could do;[19] for he not only shewed a surprizing agility in parrying all the thrusts that were made at him, but returned several upon his assailants, and kept them employed all at once.

However, they were so desperate, and withal so numerous, that notwithstanding his skill in fencing, he must have been demolished, if the Count de Belflor, who accidentally passed that way, had not engaged in his defence. The count is a man of honour and courage, and could not bear to see so many people against one gentleman, without taking his part. He immediately drew his sword, and placing himself by Don Pedro's side, they pushed the musicians so briskly, that they took all of them to their heels, some wounded, others for fear of being so.

After they were gone, our student began to thank the count for the generous assistance he had given him; but the other interrupting him, Come, says he, let us leave that subject at present. Are you wounded? No, says Pedro. Well then, said the count, we must make the best of our way from this place; for I see there is a man lies dead by you, and you cannot tarry here any longer, without being in danger of falling into the hands of the officers of justice. Upon which they both marched off as fast as they could, and when they were got at a sufficient distance they stopped.[20]

Don Pedro, who was touched with the most lively sense of gratitude, begged the count not to conceal from him the name of a gentleman, to whom he lay under such a particular obligation. Count de Belflor made no difficulty in telling him, and, at the same time, asked him who he was: but Pedro, who had reasons to be concealed, answered his name was Don Juan de Matos; and assured the count, that, to the last moment of his life, he should retain a grateful sense of what he had done for him.

To-night, answered the count, I will give you an opportunity of acquitting yourself of the obligation. I have an appointment that will be attended with danger, and I was just a-going in search of a friend to accompany me. As I know your bravery, may I take the liberty to ask you to go along with me? Your supposing I would make the least hesitation, is doing me injustice, replied the other. What better use can I make of the life you have preserved, than exposing it for your sake? Come, let us go on, I am ready to follow you. Upon which Belflor conducted him to the house of his father Don Lewis, and they both entered by the balcony into Leonora's apartment.

Here Don Cleofas interrupted the demon. Signior Asmodeus, says he, how is it possible that Don Pedro should not remember the house of his own father? He could not remember it because it was a house he had never seen before; that was the reason, replied the demon. Don Lewis had moved from his former dwelling, and had been in this house about eight days, which his son knew nothing of. I was just a-going to tell you so when you interrupted me, but you are too quick. You have an ugly habit of interrupting people's discourse. You must learn to break yourself of this.

Don Pedro then, continued Asmodeus, did not know he was in his father's house, nor did he perceive it was Marcella that let them in, because she introduced them into an anti-chamber without lights, and Belflor begged his friend to wait there, while he went into his mistress's apartment. The student was content, and sat himself down upon a chair, with his sword in his hand drawn, in case of surprize. He began to ruminate upon the joys with which love crowned the passion of Count Belflor, and earnestly wished himself as happy as he; for altho' he had no reason to complain of his incognita, she had not yet been so complaisant to him as Leonora was to the count.

While he was thus employed in reflections natural to a passionate lover, he heard a door opening softly, which was not the one by which the count entered, and saw a light through the key-hole. He rose up immediately, and getting to the door, which was by that time half open,[21] presented the point of his sword to his father, (for it was he that came into Leonora's apartment, to see whether the count was there). The old gentleman did not imagine at first, that after what had passed, his daughter and Marcella would have dared to receive Belflor again into the house, and that was the reason he had not changed their apartments; but it came into his head, that as they were both to go into a convent the next day, they would be glad to have one more interview with the count, before they finally retired from the world.

Whoever you are, cried Pedro, stop, and come not in here as you value your life. At these words, Don Lewis looked at his son, and his son looked at him with great attention; they recollected each other. Ah! my son, cried the old man, with what eagerness have I waited your arrival! why did not you let me know you was come, was you afraid of disturbing my rest? Alas! sleep is a stranger to my eyes since this fatal accident. My father! cries Don Pedro, (quite astonished) is it you I see? Are not my eyes deceived with a false illusion? Whence arises this amazement? cries Don Lewis. Are you not in your father's house? and did not I acquaint you in my letter that I had moved eight days since? Good God! cries Pedro, what is this I hear? I am then in the apartment of my own sister.

While they were thus talking, Count Belflor, hearing a noise, and imagining his friend was in danger, rushed out of Leonora's apartment with his sword in his hand. As soon as the old man saw him, he became quite furious, and pointing to him, said to his son, Here, cries he, this is the villain who has robbed me of my quiet, and brought an indelible stain upon the honour of our family. Let us revenge ourselves, and punish such a miscreant as he deserves. And immediately drawing out his sword, which he had under his night-gown, he was going to fall upon Count Belflor, but his son Don Pedro prevented him. Hold, Sir, said he, moderate your transports, I beg of you. What do you mean my son? said old Don Lewis. Do you stop my arm? You imagine, perhaps, it is too feeble for this encounter. Well then, do yourself justice for the injury that is done us: it was for that reason I sent for you to Madrid. If you fall, I will come into your place. He must either perish by the hand of one of us, or take away both our lives, after he has robbed us of our honour.

Father, answered Don Pedro, I cannot comply with what you demand of me. Far from

Comte de Belflor Disarms Don Lewis. (Sterling Library, Yale University.)

attempting the life of Count Belflor, I am here for no other purpose but to defend it. My word, my honour is engaged. Come, count, said he to Belflor, let us be gone. Ah coward! said Don Lewis, (looking at his son with fury and indignation)[22] do you yourself oppose a vengeance which ought to engross your whole thoughts? My son, the son of my own blood, is an accomplice with the villain that has seduced my daughter. But think not either of you to escape from my resentment; I will call up my servants, and make them punish his perfidy, and your baseness.

Sir, replied Don Pedro, do your son more justice: I am no coward, nor deserve that odious epithet. This night Count Belflor saved my life; he proposed to me this assignation, without my knowing what or where it was. I offered to accompany him in all the dangers that might attend it; but did not know my gratitude had engaged me against the honour of my own family. So long therefore, as he remains here, I am obliged to protect his life, and by that I acquit myself of the obligation I lie under.[23] But I assure you, the dishonour he has brought upon us, affects me not less sensibly than it does you; and to-morrow you shall see me as eager to shed his blood, as I am now to defend his life.

The count, who had hitherto remained silent, in amazement at this strange adventure, upon that addressed himself to Don Pedro. Mr. Student, said he, you may perhaps find yourself mistaken in the reparation you expect from your sword. I'll propose to you a surer expedient to vindicate your honour. I'll tell you frankly, I had no intention to espouse Leonora till this very day: but this morning I received a letter from her, which made a most sensible impression upon my heart, and since I came here, her tears have removed every remaining obstacle;[24] and the height of my ambition at present is to become Leonora's husband. If the king designs you for another, says Don Lewis, how is it possible you should—The king designs me for no other, replied Belflor (blushing). I ask your pardon for having made such a pretence, and hope you will impute it to my reason being distracted thro' love. It was a crime the violence of my passion made me commit; and I hope you will accept my owning it, as a sufficient atonement.[25]

My lord, says the old gentleman, after such an ingenuous confession, which so well becomes a noble mind, I no longer doubt your sincerity: I am now fully convinced you design effectually to make reparation for the dishonour we have suffered; my anger is cooled by these assurances; and permit me to stifle my resentments in your arms. As he said this, he came forward to the count, who had already advanced towards him, and they embraced one another several times; after which Belflor turning to Don Pedro, And you, said he, the pretended Don Juan de Matos, who are already rivetted in my esteem by your incomparable valour and sentiments of generosity; come, and receive the affectionate embraces of a brother. So saying, he took Don Pedro in his arms, who receiving the compliments of the count with a respectful and submissive air, answered him: My lord, in offering me a friendship so valuable, you thoroughly acquire mine; look upon me as a man you may depend upon to the last drop of my blood.

While the gentlemen were thus engaged, Leonora was standing at her chamber-door, and lost not a word of what passed. At the beginning she was going to rush into the chamber they were in, and throw herself between their swords, without knowing what she did, but Marcella prevented her; however, as soon as this artful duenna perceived that affairs had taken a favourable turn, she was of opinion that her own and her mistress's presence would do no harm; and therefore they came in both together, with their handkerchiefs in their hands, and threw themselves at the feet of Don Lewis. They had good reason to believe, that having surprised them the night before, he would not be quite satisfied with their conduct[26] in repeating the assignation; but the old man took his daughter up in his arms. My child, said he, I reproach you no more. As your lover keeps his word to you, I forget what is past.

Yes, Signior Don Lewis, (says the count) I will marry Leonora; and to expiate my offence, in making a more ample reparation for what I have done, and as a pledge of my friendship to the gallant Don Pedro, I here offer him my sister Eugenia. Ah, Signior, cries old Don Lewis, quite transported, how sensible I am of the honour you do my son. Was ever father so happy! you now give me as much joy, as you formerly caused me pain.

Though the father was charmed at this offer, it was otherways with the son. Being desperately in love with his fair incognita, he was confounded and so thunder-struck,[27] that he could not speak one word; and Count Belflor, without observing his confusion, went away, after telling them, that he would give orders for the necessary preparations to celebrate this double match between the families; and that he thought every moment an age till he was connected with them in such lasting ties of union.

After he was gone, Don Lewis left Leonora in her apartment, and went up into his own with Don Pedro; who speaking to his father with the bluntness of a collegean, begged he would dispense with him from marrying the count's sister. 'Tis enough (says he) that he marries Leonora; that circumstance is sufficient for re-establishing the honour of our family. How, my son! (says the old man) can you have any reluctance to marry the sister of Count de Belflor? Yes indeed I have (says Pedro) that match would be a most cruel affair upon me; and I will tell you the reason. It is about six months that I have loved, or to speak more truly, adored a most charming lady, who has conceived an affection for me.

What an unhappy thing it is to be a father! (cries Don Lewis); we never find our children disposed to do what we desire. But who is this lady, that has made so strong an impression upon you? That I do not know as yet, said Pedro; but she has promised to let me know, as soon as she is satisfied of my prudence and fidelity; though I don't doubt but she is of one of the most illustrious houses in all Spain.

And you imagine, do you, says the old gentleman, changing his tone of voice, that I shall come into this romantic story; and allow you to refuse such an advantageous match as fortune throws in your way; meerly that you may preserve your fidelity to a woman, of whom you know not even the very name? No, no, don't imagine any such thing: get the better of your passion for one who very probably does not deserve it; and think of nothing but to endeavour to shew yourself worthy of the honour Count Belflor does you. All you can say, father, replies the student, is to no purpose. I feel within myself, that I cannot banish the idea of my fair incognita, and nothing can alter my passion for her; was you to propose one of the infantas——Hold, cries Don Lewis hastily, this is too insolent to boast of a constancy that provokes my anger. Be gone, and see me no more, till you are disposed to comply with what I command you.

Pedro durst make no answer to these words of the old gentleman, for fear he should have heard worse. He returned to his chamber, and was there taken up in reflections that in one sense were melancholy, but in another very agreeable. He reflected with uneasiness that he was on the point of coming to a rupture[28] with the whole family, for refusing the count's sister; but on the other hand, it was no small comfort to him to think, that when he discovered this circumstance to his unknown mistress, she could not fail of esteeming him the more for making her such a sacrifice. He likewise flattered himself, that after having given her such a convincing proof of his fidelity, she would let him know her rank and condition, which he had taken in his head was at least equal to that of Eugenia.

In these hopes, he went out as soon as it was day, and walked in the Prado, waiting the hour he should go to Donna Juana's; that was the name of the woman at whose house he used every morning to meet his mistress. He waited very impatiently for the hour of assignation; and as soon as it was come, he went with great speed to the place.

He met there his fair unknown, who had come earlier than usual; but he found her in a flood of tears, and pierced with the most lively grief. What a melancholy sight for a lover! he approached her in great confusion, and falling upon his knees, Madam, says he, what can I think of the situation I find you in? what terrible misfortunes do these tears forbode, which afflict me to the soul? Alas, said she, you little think of the fatal blow I am now to give you. ———We must part for ever, we must never see one another any more.

She accompanied these words with so many sighs, that it was hard to say whether Don Pedro was more concerned at what she told him, or at the grief he saw her in, while she thus spoke to him. All-righteous heaven, cried he, in the transports of a passion he could not contain; can you suffer an union to be destroyed, to the innocence of which you are a witness. But, madam, continued he, perhaps you have taken a false alarm. Are you certain that they intend to tear you from the arms of the most faithful of all lovers? Am I really then the most unhappy of all men? Our misfortune is but too certain, replied the lady. My brother, who has the power of disposing of me, intends this day to marry me to another: he has just now told me so himself. Who is the happy man, answers Pedro hastily; let me know his name, madam: in my despair I'll——I don't know his name, said the lady; my brother would not tell it me; all he said was, that before I gave my hand, he intended I should see him.[29]

But, madam, says our student, do you intend to submit to the will of your brother! will you come to be thus offered up at the altar, without complaining, at least of the violence done you? will you do nothing for my sake? I can tell you, madam, that I have made no scruple to expose myself to the resentment of a father, to preserve myself for you. His threats have not been able to shake my fidelity; and however far he may carry the matter, I assure you I will never marry the lady they design for me, though she is a very great match. And who is she they intend you for? replied the unknown lady. Why, 'tis no other than the sister of Count de Belflor, answered the student. What, cries the lady in astonishment, certainly you are mistaken? are you sure of what you say? is it really Eugenia the sister of Count de Belflor they intend for you?

Yes, madam, the count himself offered her to me, replied Pedro. What, cried Eugenia, are you the gentleman for whom my brother designed me? Heavens, cries Pedro, what do I hear? are you, my fair unknown, the sister of Count Belflor? Yes, Don Pedro,

I am, says Eugenia: though in the transports of joy I feel from what you have now told me, I can scarcely believe I am.

At these words Pedro fell at her feet, and taking her hand, kissed it with all the transports of a passionate lover, who passes at once from a state of despair to the most sublime happiness. While he gave himself up to the transports of his love, Eugenia bestowed upon him a thousand caresses, which she accompanied with words equally kind and tender. What anxiety my brother would have relieved me from, said she, had he only told me the name of my intended husband: what an aversion I have conceived against this husband! Ah! my dear Pedro, you cannot think how much I hated you. My dear Eugenia, says Pedro, what charms do I feel in that hatred! I shall merit it no otherways, than being your slave all the rest of my life.

After these two lovers had shewn one another all the marks of reciprocal affection, Eugenia was curious to know how her lover Pedro had acquired the friendship of her brother Count de Belflor; and he made no difficulty of telling her the whole history of the affair between him and his sister; and gave her a particular account[30] of what had passed the night before. This was an high addition of joy to Eugenia, that her brother was to marry Pedro's sister. Donna Juana loved her friend Eugenia too well, not to partake in her joy upon this happy event. She testified her satisfaction both to her and Don Pedro, who at last parted from Eugenia, after they had agreed not to seem to know each other, when they appeared before her brother the count.

Don Pedro returned to his father, who finding him disposed to obey his pleasure, was not a little rejoiced; and the more so, that he attributed his submission to the resolute and authoritative manner in which he had spoke to him the night before. They waited to hear from Count Belflor; and received a note, acquainting them he had obtained the king's consent for his own and his sister's marriage, with a considerable employment for Don Pedro; that the marriage-ceremonies of both might be performed next day, because the orders he had given for the preparations were dispatched with so much diligence, that they were almost finished. After dinner he came himself, to confirm what he had said, and to present Eugenia to them.

Old Don Lewis shewed all imaginable fondness to this young lady, nor was Leonora wanting in her part. As for Don Pedro, however transported he was with love and joy, he had command enough over himself not to give the count the least suspicion of their former correspondence.

Count Belflor took particular notice of the behaviour of his sister, and fancied, notwithstanding the restraint she put upon herself, that she had no aversion to Don Pedro. To be more certain of it, he took her aside, and made her acknowledge she had no dislike to the gentleman he had destined her for: afterwards he informed her of Don Pedro's birth and family, which he would not do before, lest the difference might have created a prejudice in her breast against him; and which she pretended to hear, as if she had been quite a stranger to what her brother said to her.[31]

To conclude, after a great many compliments on both sides, it was agreed that the marriages should be celebrated in the house of Don Lewis. The ceremonies were performed this evening, and the rejoicings are not yet over. This is the cause of all this mirth and revelry, every one being more overjoyed than another. Dame Marcella is the only person who does not partake in these pleasures, and is this moment crying, while the rest are laughing. For Count Belflor, after the marriage-ceremonies, confessed the whole affair to Don Lewis; and the old gentleman has already provided a place for this virtuous governante in the monastery of the *Arrependitas*,[32] where the thousand pistoles she received as the price of Leonora's virtue, will serve to help her thro' a course of penitence during the remainder of her life.

CHAPTER VI.

What other things Don Cleofas saw, and in what manner
he was revenged of Donna Thomasa.

Let us now cast our eyes another way, continued Asmodeus, and examine new objects. Look into that hotel which is directly under us, and you will observe what is pretty singular.[1] A man deeply in debt, and who notwithstanding sleeps soundly. He must then be a man of quality, says Leandro. It is even as you say, replies the demon; he is a marquis worth an hundred thousand ducats a year, and yet his expence exceeds his income. His table and the ladies he has in keeping oblige him to run in debt; but that is so far from giving him any uneasiness, that when he has a mind to run in debt to any man,[2] he imagines that man greatly obliged to him, as he told a mercer the other day, It is from you, Sir, I will have credit for the future, I honour you with this mark of distinction.

While the marquis thus tastes the sweets of slumber which his creditors do not enjoy, observe that man there, who——Hold Signior Asmodeus, says Don Cleofas, interrupting him, I see a chariot in the street, I cannot help asking you who is in it. Hush! replied Asmodeus, (speaking low, as if he had been afraid of being overheard) you must know that chariot conceals one of the gravest personages in all the Spanish monarchy. He is a president, and is going, after the cares of the day, to make merry with an old Asturian lady, devoted to his pleasures: and that he may not be known, has taken the same precaution Caligula formerly did,[3] who, on a like occasion, put on a peruke to be the better disguised.

Let us now return to the scene I was to have presented to your view, when you interrupted me. You see in the highest part of the marquis's house, a man busy at work in a study, full of books and manuscripts. Perhaps, says the other, that may be my lord's steward, thinking of ways and means how to discharge his master's debts. That's pleasant enough, replies the demon, as if the stewards of such houses trouble themselves about that circumstance. They employ their thoughts more how to make an advantage of the distress of their masters, than to put their affairs in order. The man you see is no steward, he is an author. The marquiss keeps him in his house, affecting to appear a patron of men of letters. This author, replied Don Cleofas, is undoubtedly a writer of great note. You shall judge of that yourself, answered the demon: after ransacking[4] a thousand volumes, he is to make one, in which there will be nothing of his own. He plunders those books and manuscripts; and tho' he has nothing else to do than putting in order what he has so pilfered from others, yet he has more vanity than an original author.

You'll hardly guess, continued Asmodeus, who lives three doors below this hotel; it is no other than La Chicona, that lady of whom I have made such honourable mention in the history of Count de Belflor. Ah! cries Leandro, how I rejoice to see that excellent person so serviceable to youth; she is one of those two old women, I suppose, whom I see in that parlour:[5] one of them leans upon a table, looking attentively at the other, who is telling of money. Which of the two is La Chicona? She who does not tell the money, answered Asmodeus, the other's name is Pebrada, and who follows the same honourable trade; they are partners; and are this moment dividing the fruits of their labour from an adventure, which they have had the good fortune to bring to a happy conclusion.[6]

La Pebrada has the best custom.[7] She is employed by a great many rich widows, to whom she brings regularly every morning her list for them to read. What do you mean by a list? replies the student. That contains, says Asmodeus, the names of all the handsome strangers who come to Madrid, but particularly Frenchmen. As soon as this able brokeress hears of the arrival of any new men, she goes to the inns to inform herself of their country, their birth, their make, their mein, and their age. Then makes a report to the widows her customers, who attentively peruse it, and if they fancy any of the list, La Pebrada procures an interview.

This is vastly convenient, and indeed, in some measure reasonable, replied Zambullo smiling; for to be sure were it not for these good ladies, and they who do business for them, young gentlemen who are strangers here, would lose an infinite deal of time, before they could establish a proper acquaintance. But tell me, are there widows and procuresses of this sort in other countries? A pretty question truly,[8] answered the demon; do you make any doubt of that? I should but ill discharge the duties of my mission here on earth, if I neglected to furnish any great city with a sufficient number of these convenient ladies.[9]

Observe this neighbour of La Chicona, that printer whom you see all alone working at his press; it is now three hours since he has sent away his servants, and will spend the whole night in secretly printing off a book. What may this work then be? says Leandro. It treats of the nature of offences, replied the demon; it proves that religion is more to be regarded than punctilios of honour; and that it is better to forgive than to revenge a wrong. What a rascal of a printer is this! cries the student, he is in the right to print in secret such an infamous treatise; and I would advise the author to keep himself concealed, or I should be one of the first to cudgel him. What! does religion forbid a man to preserve his honour?

We shall not enter into a discussion of that point at present, answered Asmodeus with a satyrical smile: it seems you have made a very good use of the lessons of morality taught you at the university of Alcala; and I give you joy of your proficiency. You may say what you please, replied Cleofas; let the author of this ridiculous work support his theory with ever so plausible arguments,[10] I laugh at them; I am a Spaniard, and hold nothing so sweet as revenge. And as you promised me to punish the perfidy of my mistress, I challenge you to make good that promise.

I yield with pleasure to the transports of your resentment, replies the demon: how I love these growing geniuses, that without hesitation give way to the rising dictates of their passions! I'll do what you desire of me immediately, as the proper time for having your revenge is already come; but I would first entertain you with a most joyous scene. Cast your eyes a little beyond the printing-office, and observe particularly what passes in that apartment hung with crimson. I observe there, answered Leandro, five or six women, who with great eagerness are giving vials to a man who seems to be a valet; and they appear to me in a violent agitation.

These are, replied the demon, devout women, who have reason to be under great concern, as there is in that apartment a member of the holy inquisition who lies sick.[11] This venerable father, who is near thirty five years of age, is in a chamber adjoining to that where you see the women. Two of his dearest penitents are continually with him, one feeds him with slops;[12] and the other, who sits at his pillow, takes care to keep his head warm, and to cover his breast with near fifty blankets. What may his disease be? says Zambullo. He has got a cold in his head, replied the demon, and there is some reason to fear it may fall upon his lungs.

Those other devotees, whom you see in the anti-chamber, upon hearing of his sickness, have come to his apartment in a great hurry, every one bringing different remedies for his disorder: one brings for his cough, syrups of maiden hair, marshmallows, coral and colts foot; another, to preserve his reverence's lungs, syrup of spit-wort, wall flower, and elixir proprietatis: a third, to comfort his brain and stomach, has got balm, cinnamon, and treacle-water, with the essence of musk and ambergrease: a fourth presents him with cordial and bezoardic confections, and another is provided with tinctures of jelly-flowers, coral, corn-poppy, and emeralds.—All these zealous devotees extol their specificks to the inquisitor's servant, whom each takes aside in her turn; and touching him with a ducat, whispers him in the ear: Laurence, my dear Laurence, let my vial have the preference.

My God! what happy mortals these fathers of the inquisition are, cries Don Cleofas. That they are, I give you my word, replied Asmodeus; I myself can hardly forbear envying them; and as Alexander said formerly, that if he were not Alexander, he would be glad to be Diogenes; so I declare to you if I were not a devil, I would chuse to be a father of the holy inquisition.

Come, Mr. Student, continued he, let us go immediately and punish this base woman who has made such ungrateful returns to your tenderness. Upon this Zambullo laid hold of the skirts of Asmodeus's mantle, who a second time winged him thro' the air, and pitched him on the house of Donna Thomasa.

This lady was sitting at table with the four assassins who had pursued Leandro over the tops of the houses;[13] his blood boiled with rage,[14] when he saw them feasting on two partridges and a rabbit, which, with some bottles of excellent wine, he had bought and carried with him to her house: and as a further incitement to his rage,[15] he easily perceived that mirth and joy accompanied this repast; and was convinced by the behaviour

The Sick Inquisitor and His Zealous Devotees. (Sterling Library, Yale University.)

of Thomasa, that the company of these wretches was more agreeable to her than his. O! scoundrels, cried he, with a furious voice, see how they regale themselves at my expence? what a mortifying sight is this to me!

I agree with you, answered the demon, that this is not the most agreeable scene you could behold; but a man that frequents these ladies of pleasure, must expect now and then to meet with such adventures: they happen in France a thousand times to Abbés, to gentlemen of the robe,[16] and commissioners of the revenue. Had I my sword, replied Cleofas, I would immediately fall upon these rascals, and disturb their jollity. It would be no equal match, replied the demon, should you attack them single; let me alone to revenge your cause; I'll do it more effectually than you can. I'll immediately sow the seeds of division,[17] and send among them the spirit of lust, so that they shall quarrel and fall upon each other; you will see excellent sport[18] presently.

At these words, he breathed from his mouth a bluish vapour, which descended winding, like a fire-work, and spread itself over the table of Donna Thomasa; immediately one of the guests, who first felt the power of this infernal blast, drew near to the lady, and caressed her with transport; and the others, who by this time likewise were seized with the same rage, endeavoured to pull her away from him. Every one demanding the preference, and disputing for the prize in his own favour, the fury of jealousy seized them, they came at last to extremities, and drawing their swords, began to fight desperately with one another. In the mean time Donna Thomasa set up horrible shrieks, which alarmed the neighbourhood, who called for the constables of the night. The constables came, and breaking open the door, found upon their coming in, two of these bullies stretched dead upon the floor: they seized the other two, and carried them off to prison along with Thomasa. It was to no purpose that this unhappy wretch shed tears, tore her hair, and shewed all the marks of despair; the people who conveyed her off were as little moved as Zambullo, who along with Asmodeus, burst out into great fits of laughter.

Well, says the demon to our student, are you satisfied? I am not, replied Cleofas; to render my satisfaction complete, you must carry me to the prisons, that I may have the satisfaction to see there, that abandoned woman, who has made such ungrateful returns to my love; for at this moment I feel in myself more detestation against her, than I formerly felt of sentiments of tenderness. I'll do it with all my heart, replied the demon, you shall always find me ready to comply with your inclinations, should they even be contrary to my own, or opposite to my interest, provided they tend to your advantage.

They both flew towards the prison, where the two ruffians arrived very soon, and were put into a dark dungeon. As for Thomasa, they laid her upon some straw, with three or four other women of bad life, whom they had taken up that same day, and who were to-morrow to be carried away to the place appointed for that sort of creatures.

Now, says Zambullo, I am quite satisfied; I riot in the sweets of full revenge.[19] My little dear Thomasa will not pass the night so agreeably as she expected; and we'll go now and continue our observations in what place you think proper. No place can be more proper than where we are, replied the spirit: there are in the prison a great number both of the guilty and of the innocent; it is a place which is the beginning of punishment for the one, and serves to purify the virtue of the other. I must shew you some prisoners of both sorts, and tell you the reasons why they are kept here in irons.

CHAPTER VII.

Of the prisoners.

Before I enter into particulars, you must observe a little the turnkeys, who stand at the entry of these dreadful mansions. The poets of antiquity have placed only one Cerberus at the gates of their hell. You see here a great many. These turnkeys are dead to every sentiment of humanity. The most abandoned of all my brethren would, with difficulty, be able to supply the place of any of them. But I perceive, continued he, that you look with horror on these dismal cells, where a mat is all the furniture; these frightful dungeons appear to you as so many sepulchres. It is not without reason you are shocked at the horrible misery you observe, and that you deplore the condition of these unhappy wretches, whom the hand of justice confines in this dreadful place.[1] However, they are not all alike objects of pity, as we shall see presently, when we come to examine them.

First of all, there is in that great room upon your right hand, four men who lie on two very paultry beds. One is a vintner, who stands accused of having poisoned a stranger, who t'other day drank in his house till he burst; and they pretend that it was the badness of the wine that occasioned the death of the deceased. The master of the tavern, on the other hand, affirms that it was the quantity; and the court will take his word for it, as the stranger was a German. And who is in the right, says Don Cleofas, the vintner or his accusers? Why faith the affair is problematic, replied the demon, and is a moot point.[2] True it is, the wine was adulterated, but it is equally true that the German guest drank such an unmeasurable quantity,[3] that the judges may with a safe conscience set mine host at liberty.

The second prisoner is an assassin by trade, one of those abandoned ruffians whom they call Bravos;[4] and who for four or five pistoles lend their assistance to all who are willing to be at that expence, and want to have any one taken off secretly. The third is a dancing-master, who dresses like a petit-maitre, and has taught one of his female scholars a new way of dancing a minuet;[5] and the fourth is a gentleman of gallantry, who was surprized last week by the watch, as he was getting up by a balcony, into the apartment of a lady of his acquaintance, whose husband was out of the way. He has nothing to do but own his amorous correspondence, to draw himself out of this scrape;[6] but he chuses rather to pass for a robber, and run the risque of his life, than expose the honour of the lady.

Upon my word, says Don Cleofas, this gentleman is a very discreet lover. It must be owned indeed, that our nation exceeds all others in point of gallantry. I'll lay any wager, for example, that a Frenchman would not, like a Spaniard, let himself be hanged, out of such punctilio of delicacy. No, that he would not, I assure you, replied the demon, he would more likely get into a balcony, on set purpose to publish the dishonour of any woman who granted him favours.

In that small place next to the four men, continued he, is a famous sorceress, who has the reputation of being able to do things impossible, by the power of her art. Old rich widows, as they say, find young men who love them without any view of interest; husbands become faithful to their wives, and coquettes love in earnest the rich cavaliers that court them; but nothing of this is true: she possesses no other secret but that of persuading people she does, and from their credulity has been able to pick up a pretty comfortable livelihood.[7] The holy office reclaims this prisoner, and she will probably be burnt the first act of faith that is solemnized.

Below this small room is a dark dungeon, which serves as a place of rest to a young man who kept a tavern. What the devil, cries Leandro, more tavern-keepers? they don't intend surely to poison the whole universe. The case of this man is not the same with the other; they laid hold of this poor wretch the day before yesterday, and the inquisition reclaims him likewise. I'll give you a short history of the affair of his commitment.

An old soldier, who by his courage, or rather indeed by his perseverance in the service, had risen to the dignity of a halbert,[8] came to recruit in Madrid. He enquired at an inn for lodging, where he was told there were rooms enough for him to lie in, but that they could not shew him into any, because of an apparition that haunted the house every night, and insulted such strangers as had the hardiness to take up their residence in them. This was no discouragement to the serjeant: shew me any room you will, says he, and give me some wine, with pipes and tobacco;[9] as for the rest, you need be under no uneasiness. Your spirits know how to respect an old soldier grown weary under the weight of his accoutrements.

The people upon that declaration, shewed this recruiting officer[10] into an apartment, as he seemed so resolute, and brought him what he had called for. He began immediately to smoak and drink, and as it was past midnight before this spirit gave any interruption to the profound silence that reigned in the house, it appeared very probable, that he paid some respect to his new guest: but between one and two in the morning, the halberdeer was alarmed with a most hideous noise, as if it were of chains; and immediately saw a most frightful spectre entering his apartment, clad in black and fettered in irons. The serjeant was in no sort moved at this apparition: without laying down his pipe, he advanced with great tranquillity towards the spirit, and with the flat of his sword, saluted him with a damnable rap over the head.[11]

The ghost not used to such a reception, set up a hideous scream; and perceiving the soldier was about to renew his civility, fell down on his knees, and in a very supplicating tone, For the love of God, most noble serjeant, said he, forbear; take pity on a poor unfortunate devil, who throws himself at your feet, to implore your clemency. I conjure you by the spirit of Jago,[12] who was as you, a mighty and right valiant man at the halbert. If you value your life, answers this old trooper, you must tell me what you are, and speak the truth, and nothing but the truth, or in an instant will I cleave thee in two, as the knights of old served the giants whom they encountered. At these words, the spirit, who plainly perceived what sort of hands he was got into, thought it most adviseable to own the whole truth.

I am, says he, drawer of this inn, and my name is William: I am in love with Juanella, my master's only daughter, and she does not dislike me; but as her parents have in view for her a match above my rank, in order to reconcile them to me for a son-in-law, the young woman and I agreed that I should act the part every night you see me do now; I

Serjeant Hannibal Exposes William the Drawer. (Sterling Library, Yale University.)

wrap myself up in a long black cloak, and hang the chain of the jack[13] about my neck, with which I run up and down the whole house from the cellar to the garret, making the noise you have heard. When I come to my master and mistress's door, I stop and call out, think not that I will give you any rest, till you have married Juanella to your drawer.

After having uttered these words in a hoarse and growling voice, I continue my rounds, and at last go through a window into a little closet, where Juanella lies alone, to whom I give a full account of my proceedings. My noble serjeant, continues William, you may perceive by this, that I have told you the truth; and after such a confession, I am very sensible you may ruin me by letting my master into the secret; but if, instead of doing me this ill office, you will have the goodness to assist me, you may depend upon it, my gratitude——How, in the name of the devil, young man, can I assist you? replies the serjeant. I'll tell you; you have nothing to do, but say to-morrow, that you have seen the spirit, and that he put you in such a fright——How, fright! sblood, sirrah, would you have serjeant Annibal Antonio Quebrantador, say he was frightened? I would rather that fifty millions of devils[14]——No, lord, sir, I did not mean that in the least. Nothing like it, only that you might speak as you thought proper, so that you assisted me in my scheme. Sir, if I have the happiness to marry Juanella, I give you my word and honour, that you and all your friends shall at all times be welcome to my house, without its costing you a farthing. Master William, replies this old battered warrior, you have a taking way with you; you propose to me that I should countenance a cheat; 'tis a very serious matter, but the force of your rhetorick is such as makes me not mind the consequences.[15] Go, begin your noise and rattling again, and tell Juanella what has happened, I'll take upon me to answer for the rest.

Hannibal was as good as his word.[16] The next morning he went to the landlord and landlady of the inn; told them he had seen the apparition, and that he found him a very reasonable ghost. I am, said he to me, the great grandfather of the master of this inn. I had a daughter, whom I promised in marriage to the father of the grandfather of the young man who is his drawer; notwithstanding which, I violated my plighted faith, married her to another, and a short time after died. Ever since that time I remain in torments, and suffer the punishment of my breach of faith. Nor can my departed spirit find any rest, till some one of my generation be married to one of the generation of master William: and for this reason it is that I every night haunt this house; nevertheless, I find it is to no purpose, that I warn them that they marry Juanella with master William. The son of my grandson, as well as his wife, lend a deaf ear to my remonstrances; but tell them, if you please, Mr. Serjeant, that if they do not comply immediately I will proceed to extremities and broil and carbonade them in such a manner as they little think of.[17]

The man of the inn, who is a weak simple fellow, was strangely staggered at this discourse: and his wife, who is yet weaker than he, imagining that she saw the devil at her heels, consented to the marriage, which was solemnized the next day. Master William, a short time after, set up his business in another part of the town, where serjeant Annibal Antonio Quebrantador did not fail very frequently to pay his respects to him; and the young vintner, out of gratitude, gave him as much wine as he could drink; which pleased the halberdeer so much, that he not only brought all his friends, but even his recruits, and made them all drunk at free cost.

But master William began at last to grow weary of furnishing liquor to so many people, and declared his thoughts upon that head to the soldier; who, without reflecting that he had gone beyond the terms of agreement, was so unreasonable as to treat master William as a little ungrateful scoundrel. William answered, the serjeant replied; and the conversation ended in some half dozen blows, which Hannibal bestowed upon the young vintner. Several people who passed by, took the part of master William; the serjeant wounded three or four of them, and would not have stopped there, if a troop of archers had not seized him, as a disturber of the publick peace: they carried him to prison, where he has confessed every thing that I have now told you; and upon his confession they have seized master William; the father-in-law demands that the marriage be annulled, and the holy office,[18] upon information that William is worth some money, wants to look into the affair.

Thanks be to God, cried Don Cleofas, how watchful the fathers of the holy inquisition are! the moment they smell out any affair, from which the smallest advantage[19]—— Hush! replied Asmodeus, take particular care what liberties you give yourself, in regard to that tremendous tribunal: they have spies every where, who inform them even of things that never have been spoke; I myself dare hardly mention their name, but with fear and trembling.

In the place above this unhappy vintner, in the first room upon your left hand, are two men worthy of commiseration. One of them is a young valet de chambre, whom his lady received in private as a lover. The husband happened to surprize them; upon which, she cried out for help, as if the valet had made an attempt upon her virtue. They immediately seized this poor wretch, who, in all probability, will fall a sacrifice to the reputation of his mistress.

The companion of the valet, who is yet less culpable than he, likewise runs the risque of losing his life. He is groom of the chamber to a dutchess, who has been robbed of a fine diamond, and they accuse him of being the thief. To-morrow he will be put upon the rack, and tortured till he confess the robbery; tho' in the mean while the person who stole it is a favourite chambermaid, whom they dare not suspect.

Ah! Signior Asmodeus, says Leandro, for the love of God do some service to this unhappy wretch; his innocence makes me interest myself in his behalf; use your power to free him from those cruel punishments with which he is threatned: he deserves——You don't consider what you say, Mr. Student, replied the demon, interrupting him. Can you think of asking me to oppose an iniquitous action, or that I should hinder an innocent man from perishing? you might as well ask an attorney not to ruin the widow and the orphan.

I must therefore tell you once for all, that you are not to expect any thing from me so directly contrary to my interests, unless at least you can shew that it will considerably tend to your own particular advantage. Besides, were I inclined to do so, do you imagine I could release a prisoner? How, says Zambullo, have you not the power of setting a man free from prison? No, indeed, replied the other, if you had ever read Enchiridion,[20] or Albertus Magnus,[21] you would have known that this is beyond the power of me, or any of my brethren: had I the misfortune myself to be laid hold of by the claws of justice, I could find no other means of escape, but that of touching very feelingly.

In the next chamber on the same side is a surgeon, who is convicted of having taken in a fit of jealousy, the same quantity of blood from his wife, as was taken from Seneca.[22] This day he was put to the torture; and after confessing the crime of which he stood charged, he has owned further, that for ten years past he has taken a pretty extraordinary method to get himself business: In the night time he used to wound people as they passed along, and made his escape through a back door of his own house; and while the persons so wounded cried for help, and the neighbours gathered round about them, the surgeon came there amongst the rest, and finding a man weltering in blood, made him be carried to his shop, where the same hand that wounded, applied the balsam.

But though the surgeon has made this confession, and deserves to die a thousand times, yet he is not without hopes of obtaining a pardon, which may very probably be the case, as he is related to the prince's nurse; besides, I must acquaint you that he has a wonderful kind of wash,[23] which he alone knows how to make; it whitens the skin, and gives the bloom of youth to decrepit old age, and is now made use of for that purpose by three ladies of the court, who have joined their interests to save him. He depends so much upon them, or rather if you will, upon his wash, that he now sleeps soundly, in the agreeable hopes, that when he wakes he shall be discharged out of prison.

I perceive in the same chamber, says the student, another man who lies upon a mat; and who, I think, likewise enjoys the quiet of repose, I fancy his situation is not desperate. It is a very odd affair, replied the demon. This gentleman is a Biscayan, and has made his fortune by a random shot;[24] I'll tell you in what manner. About a fortnight ago, he was hunting with his elder brother, who was possessed of a considerable estate, and by a most unhappy accident killed him, instead of a brace of partridge. That was no bad *quid pro quo* for a younger brother, said Don Cleofas laughing; no more it was, replied Asmodeus; but the other relations of the family, who would fain be heirs to the estate of the defunct, prosecute him as the murderer, and accuse him of having done this, that he might be the only heir of the family. He has surrendered himself of his own accord, and appears so afflicted at the death of his brother, that one cannot imagine he could have any hand in taking away his life. And has he not really, said Leandro, any thing to reproach himself with, but his mistake when he was shooting? No, replied the demon, to be sure he had no bad intentions; tho', for my own share, I would advise all gentlemen of estates, not to go a hunting with their younger brothers.

Observe these two young men, who are lodged in a little hole near the Biscayan, and are as merry as if they were at their liberty. They are two accomplished sharpers;[25] one of them in particular, who will perhaps one day entertain the publick with a detail of his pranks; and is a second edition of Gusman de Alfarache.[26] That is he in the brown velvet, and a feather in his hat.

It is not three months since he lived in this town page to Count d'Oniate, and would have been to this day in the service of that nobleman, had it not been for a trick he played, which is the cause of his being in prison; and which I will give you an account of.

This young fellow, whose name is Domingo, happened to receive when he was in the service of the count, an hundred lashes for something he had been guilty of, by order of the groom of the chambers, and master of the pages. This piece of discipline had for a long time stuck in his stomach,[27] and he was resolved to be revenged. He had often observed that Signior Don Cosmo, for that is the name of this esquire, washed his hands with orange flower-water, and rubbed his body with pink and jessamine; that he took more pains with himself than an old coquet; and that, in a word, he was one of those fops who imagine a woman can't see them without being in love with them. This observation suggested to him a project of revenge, which he imparted to a young hussey in the neighbourhood, of whose assistance he stood in need, and with whom he was so well acquainted, that he could not possibly be more so.

This Abigail,[28] whose name was Floretta, that she might enjoy the pleasure of his conversation with more ease, made him pass for her cousin in the house of Donna Luziana her mistress, whose father was at that time in the country.[29] The arch rogue Domingo, after having instructed his pretended cousin in the part she was to act, came in one morning into the chamber of Don Cosmo, where he found the squire, who was trying on a new suit of cloaths, and was standing before the glass, admiring his own figure. The page, as if he had been in raptures at the sight of this Narcissus, said to him, Signior Don Cosmo, you have the air of a prince. I see all the great lords at court most gorgeously clad; but notwithstanding the richness of their dress, I do not find one of them that carries your noble mien. I cannot say, added he, whether my being so much devoted to you, as I am, may not render me prejudiced in your favour, but in my own opinion, you eclipse all the brilliancy of a birth-day.[30]

Don Cosmo simpering[31] at this discourse, which so aptly suited his vanity, answered with an air of self-complacency, you flatter me my friend, or rather you love me, and your friendship sees more graces in me than what nature has bestowed. I can't allow that, replied this rogue, for every body speaks of you as well as I do. I wish only you had heard what a cousin of mine said t'other day, who is a lady of quality's woman.

The other pricked up his ears at this hint, and asked with great eagerness, what he had heard his cousin say?[32] Say! replied Domingo; she enlarged upon the gracefulness of your stature, that noble and agreeable air, which diffuses itself over your whole person; and what is still more, she told me in confidence, that Donna Luziana her mistress took a singular pleasure in looking at you through her lattice every time you pass by her house.

Who is that lady, said Don Cosmo, and where does she live? What! replies the other, don't you know that she is the only daughter of General Don Fernando our neighbour? Ah! cries Don Cosmo, I now recollect, I remember to have heard a great deal said of the fortune and beauty of Luziana. She is a lady of great distinction, but is it possible she can have any regard for me? Make no doubt of it, says Domingo, my cousin has told me so; and though she is but a waiting maid, I can assure you the girl is not given to lying. I can answer for her as for myself. As that is the case, said Don Cosmo, I should be glad to have a private conversation with your cousin, to engage her in my interest by some small presents, as is usual on such occasions; and if she gives me encouragement to make my addresses to her mistress I'll even try my fortune. I allow there is a great difference between Don Fernando and me; but what then? I am made a gentleman, and am worth five hundred ducats a year. There happens every day more extraordinary marriages than this.

The page encouraged his master in his resolution, and procured an interview between him and his cousin, who finding him ready to swallow every thing,[33] assured him without further preamble,[34] that her mistress was deeply in love with him. She has often spoke to me upon that head, said she to him, and the answers I have given her, have been, I assure you, no ways to your disadvantage.[35] In a word, Signior Don Cosmo, you may safely depend upon it, that Luziana has a secret passion for you. I would advise you without further ceremony, to make her honourable proposals; and demonstrate to her, that as you are the handsomest, you are at the same time, the most polite and gallant cavalier in Madrid: give her serenades, she loves them above all things, and I will take care on my part, to make her put a proper value on these instances of your gallantry, and doubt not but my good offices may be of service to you. Don Cosmo was transported to find Floretta enter so warmly into his interest; and embracing her, put upon her finger a ring of small value, which he had brought on purpose to make her a present. My dear Floretta, said he, I make you a present of this diamond only to begin our acquaintance; I will be grateful, and make you a more solid recompence for the services you shall do me.

No man could be more satisfied than our squire was with this interview. He not only thanked Domingo for having procured it for him, but made him a present of a pair of silk stockings, and some shirts with laced ruffles; promising him besides, that he would let slip no opportunity of doing him service. After which he consulted him on what measures were proper to be taken: my friend, says he to him, what is your opinion, would you have me break my mind[36] to Luziana in a letter, conceived in passionate and sublime expressions? That is, my opinion altogether, said Domingo; declare your love to her in the highest stile, I am certain she will receive it favourably. I believe so too, replied Don Cosmo, and am determined at all events, to begin that way: upon this he immediately set about to write, and after having fouled and tore above twenty sheets of paper, he at last conceived a billet-doux which he fixed upon; this he read to Domingo, who having listened to it with marks of admiration, took upon him to carry it to his cousin. The letter was writ in this lofty and sublime manner.

> Long, long is the time, O charming Luziana, that influenced by the voice of fame's trumpet,[37] which proclaims aloud your perfections through the universe, my heart has been fired with an ardent passion for you; yet notwithstanding these consuming flames that broil my vitals,[38] I have not yet attempted any act of gallantry; but as I understand that you vouchsafe to look upon me with a favourable eye, when I pass by your lattice; that lattice, which from the eyes of mortals invelops your cœlestial beauty; and that even by the fate of destiny[39] (fate thrice happy for me) you entertain on my behalf sentiments of regard, I take the liberty to beg you will permit me to consecrate myself eternally to your service. If I am so happy as to attain this, I renounce all other women past, present, and to come.
>
> Don Cosmo de la Higuera.

The page and the waiting woman did not fail to make themselves merry at the expence of Don Cosmo and his letter; but they did not stop there, they joined their heads together, and composed a tender billet-doux, which Mrs. Abigail wrote with her own hand, and which Domingo gave the next day to the squire, as an answer from Donna Luziana. It was conceived in these words.

I can't imagine who has so well informed you of my secret sentiments. I find I am betrayed by somebody; but whoever it be I forgive them, as it is the occasion of my knowing that you love me. Of all the men I see pass through the street, you are he I take the most pleasure to look at, and am extremely glad you are become my lover; though perhaps it is what I ought not to be glad of, and much less to tell you so: but if I have committed a fault, your transcendent merit is my excuse.

Donna Luziana.

Though this letter was rather too much to be supposed to come from the daughter of a general officer[40] (for the writers of it had not been so nice in their reflections), Don Cosmo had no kind of distrust of it; he had so good an opinion of himself, as to believe that any lady upon his account might transgress the rules of decency and delicacy. Ah! Domingo, cried he, after reading aloud the supposed letter, you see plainly how much the lady is smitten; I shall be in a short time the son-in-law of Don Ferdinand, or my name is not Don Cosmo de la Higuera.

No doubt of it, answered Domingo, you have made a violent impression upon the heart of the young lady. But a propos, continued he, I remember now that my cousin expressly charged me to tell you, that to-morrow at furthest, it would be absolutely necessary you should entertain her mistress with a serenade, to make her still more desperately in love with you.[41] I'll do it with all my heart, replied the other, and you may assure your cousin I will follow her advice; and that to-morrow without fail, she shall hear in her street at midnight one of the most gallant concerts that ever yet was heard in Madrid. Accordingly he went and found an able musician, to whom he communicated his project, and charged him with having it put in execution.

While he was thus busy in making preparations for the serenade, Floretta, whom Domingo had spoke to, finding her mistress in a good humour, had said to her, Madam, I am going to give you a most diverting entertainment. Luziana asked what was the matter. O! replied the other, laughing as if she had been mad, no small matter I assure you. Don Cosmo, who is an original character, and master of the pages to Count d'Onnate, has made choice of you as the sovereign lady of his affections; and that you may not remain ignorant of it, intends to-morrow evening to entertain you with a concert of vocal and instrumental musick. Donna Luziana, who is naturally of a chearful temper, and who besides was in no fear that the gallantries of this master of the pages would any ways hurt her reputation, was so far from being serious on the matter, that she anticipated the pleasure she should have from the serenade; so that this lady without her knowledge, confirmed Don Cosmo in his mistake, for which she would have been very angry with herself if she had been apprized of it.

Next evening there appeared before the balcony of Luziana two coaches, out of which this gallant squire and his trusty confident alighted, accompanied by six other men, singers and players upon instruments, who begun their concert, which lasted a long time. They played a great number of new airs, and sung a great number of new songs, the subjects of which chiefly turned upon the power of love, to unite lovers of different rank and condition; and Luziana was infinitely delighted with every stanza that seemed to have any reference to herself.[42]

When the serenade was over, Don Cosmo sent the musicians home in the same coaches they came, and waited with Domingo in the street, till such time as the curious people, who had come there upon hearing the musick, were retired; after which he came forward towards the balcony, from whence Floretta, by leave of her mistress, spoke to him through a chink of the lattice. Is it you, Signior Don Cosmo? Who asks me that question? replied he in a whining voice. Donna Luziana, answered Floretta, who wants to know if this concert be the effect of your gallantry. To this Don Cosmo answered, that what he had done to-night was only a type of that homage his love would pay to that wonder of the age, if she would deign to receive it from one who was ready to immolate himself a victim[43] upon the altar of her beauty.

Luziana could hardly forbear laughing at this high-strained compliment: however, she got the better of herself, and coming to the lattice, spoke to her gallant in the most serious manner she could: Signior Don Cosmo, I see you are no novice in affairs of gallantry. All gentlemen that are in love ought to make you their pattern in what manner to behave to their mistresses.[44] I am extremely well pleased with your serenade, and shall consider you upon that account accordingly; but you must now retire, people may overhear us; another time we will have a longer conversation with each other. At these words, she shut the lattice, leaving the squire in the street, extremely well satisfied with his reception, and Domingo extremely surprized at her acting such a part in this comedy.

This affair, including the expence of the coach, and the immense quantity of wine drank by the musicians, cost Don Cosmo one hundred ducats; and about two days after, Domingo dipped him into a farther expence, in the following manner. Having been informed by Floretta, that she and some others of her companions were to go a merry-making upon the eve of St. John, a night so celebrated in this city,[45] he undertook to treat them with a magnificent repast at the expence of his master.

Signior Don Cosmo, said the page to him the evening before, you know what a high festival is to be kept to-morrow; and I am to acquaint you that Donna Luziana proposes to be by break of day on the banks of the Mansanarez, to see the dancing upon that occasion. I apprehend this is a hint sufficient to you who are the most gallant of all cavaliers; you are not the man to let slip so fine an opportunity; and I dare answer for it, that your mistress and all her company will be nobly treated to-morrow morning. That you may safely do, replied the governor of the pages, and I thank you for your advice; you shall see whether I know or not how to make use of such an opportunity.[46] And in fact, to-morrow morning by break of day, four of the domestick servants, accompanied by Domingo, and loaded with cold provisions of all sorts, with a vast quantity of sweet-meats and the richest wines, arrived on the banks of the Mansanarez, where Floretta and her companions, habited like nymphs, were dancing to the rising of Aurora.

They felt no small joy when the page interrupted their mirth, by inviting them to partake of a repast in the name of Signior Don Cosmo de la Higuera. They sat down upon the grass, and began immediately to do honour to the entertainment, laughing immoderately at the fool who gave it; for this baggage Floretta had let them all into the secret.

As they were thus employed in mirth and jollity, they saw the squire himself appear, mounted on a pad[47] belonging to the count, and in a very rich habit. He came forward to join Domingo and salute the company, who all got up to receive him with more respect, and returned him thanks for their entertainment. He cast his eyes around amongst all the women to find out Luziana, and pay her a fine compliment, which he had composed as he was pacing along on the road; but Floretta taking him aside, told him her mistress was so ill she could not attend the festival. Don Cosmo appeared mightily afflicted at this information, and asked what was the matter with his dear Luziana. She has got a great cold, replied the other, occasioned by her being almost the whole night upon the balcony without her veil, talking to me of you while you was giving the serenade. The squire, who was greatly consoled for the illness of his mistress from the occasion of it,[48] begged Mrs. Floretta to continue to him her good offices with her lady, and then went home more and more delighted with his good fortune.

It happened when these things were thus in agitation,[49] that Don Cosmo received a bill of exchange from Andalusia for a thousand gold crowns, which came to him by the death of an uncle who died at Seville. This money was paid to him; and after having counted it, he put it into a strong box in the presence of Domingo, who was prodigiously attentive to this action of his master; and was so vastly smit with the beauty of these broad pieces, that he determined to have them in his own possession, and to carry them off to Portugal. He imparted this scheme to Floretta, and proposed to her to take the same journey along with him. Though this proposal deserved to have been well weighed, yet the Abigail, who was as bad as the page, accepted of it without hesitation. In a word, one night, when Don Cosmo was in his study, and busy in composing an emphatic letter to his mistress, Domingo found means to break open the box where the broad pieces were deposited, and having taken them off, got immediately into the street, and coming under the balcony of Luziana, began to mew like a cat. This was the signal agreed on between him and Floretta, who did not make him wait long; and being determined to follow his fortunes any where, they immediately went out of Madrid, imagining they should have time enough to get into Portugal before they could be overtaken, should they be pursued; but unhappily for them, Don Cosmo finding out that very night the robbery, and the flight of his confident, immediately had recourse to justice; and the officers were sent out to all parts to apprehend the thief; they catched him near Zebreros with his nymph, and brought them both back. Mrs. Abigail now enjoys the comforts of a house of correction, and Domingo is in this prison.

Well, says Don Cleofas, doubtless Signior Don Cosmo has not lost his thousand gold crowns. I take it for granted they have been restored to him. O! not at all, replied the demon, you don't consider that these are, in the hands of justice, proofs of the crime; and they never part with such evidence. This governor of the pages, whose story is now publick about the town, remains both robbed of his thousand broad pieces, and is the jest of every basket-woman[50] into the bargain.

Domingo and that other prisoner who now is at play with him, continued the demon, have for their neighbour a young Castilian, who was taken up for having in the presence of creditable witnesses, struck his father. Heavens! cries Leandro, what do you tell me? Can a son arrive to that pitch of wickedness, as to lift his hand against his own father? O! yes, replied the demon, that is nothing extraordinary; I'll give you an instance of the same kind. Under the reign of Pedro the first, surnamed the just and the cruel,[51] the eighth king of Portugal, a young man of twenty years of age was taken up for the same crime. The king, who was, as you are, surprized at the novelty of the case, was determined to interrogate the mother of the criminal, which he did so dexterously, that he drew her into a confession, that the young man had been begot upon her body by a pious son of the church. And if the judges of this Castilian could manage the mother of their prisoner with as much address, they might come to the same explanation.

Cast your eyes upon that large dungeon below the three prisoners whom I have been just now shewing you, and observe what passes. You see three wretches there. They are highwaymen, and are just going to make their escape. They procured a file concealed in a loaf of bread, and have already sawed through a thick iron bar of one of the windows, through which they will get into a court which leads into the street. It is now above ten months since they were committed to prison, and above eight since they ought to have received the public recompence of their crimes; but thanks to the slowness of justice, they are now setting out to commit more murders.

Follow me into this low place, where you see about twenty or thirty men lying upon straw; they are pickpocket fellows that commit all sorts of crimes. Do you observe five or six of them who are pulling about a bricklayer's labourer, who this day has been sent to prison, for having wounded an archer with a brickbat? Why do the other prisoners so worry this poor labourer? says Zambullo. It is, replied Asmodeus, because he has not yet paid his garnish. But, continued he, let us leave these miserable wretches, and get away from this frightful place; we'll go and entertain ourselves with something more diverting.

CHAPTER VIII.

Asmodeus shews Don Cleofas several people, and informs him
what they have been doing throughout the day.

They left the prisoners, and flying away to another quarter of the town, stopt at a great hotel, where Asmodeus said to the student, I have a great mind to inform you of what all these persons about this hotel have been doing to-day: a detail that will probably divert you. I make no doubt of it, replied Leandro, and beg you will begin with that captain whom I see putting on his boots. I suppose he has some affairs of consequence which call him hence. He is, replied the demon, a captain just ready to set out from Madrid; his horse is waiting for him in the street, and he is bound for Catalonia, where his regiment is quartered.

As this gentleman had no money, he applied to an usurer. Signior Sanguisuela, said he, could you not lend one a thousand ducats? Upon my word, Sir, said the usurer, with a pleasant and smiling countenance, I really have not so much myself, but to oblige you, I will try to find a man that may accommodate you with the sum you want; that is, who will give you four hundred ducats down for your note of a thousand, and out of that four hundred, you shall give me, if you please, sixty for my trouble. Money is now adays so vastly scarce——What an unconscionable extortion[1] is this, cried the officer, to demand six hundred and sixty ducats for the loan of three hundred and forty? what piece of villainous knavery? such devouring vultures ought every one of them to be hanged.

My noble captain, replied the usurer with great coolness, don't put yourself in a passion; go and try somewhere else; you have no reason to complain of any ill usage from me; I do not force you to take the three hundred and forty ducats; you may have them or let them alone as you please. The officer, who had nothing to reply to this argument, went away: but after having considered that he was under a necessity of setting out for his regiment; that the time was pressing, and that in short he could do nothing without money, he came back to the usurer this morning, whom he met at his door in a black cloak, a band, with short hair, and a vast large set of beads. Signior Sanguisuela, says he to him, I will take your three hundred and forty ducats; the necessity I am under for money obliges me to comply with your proposal. I am going to mass, replied the usurer very gravely; at my return, if you'll come, I'll give you the money. No, no, replies the captain, that won't do, you must go in again and give it me now. My affairs are so pressing as to admit of no delay. I must be dispatched immediately.[2] That is what I cannot possibly comply with, replies Sanguisuela, I constantly hear mass every day before I enter upon any kind of business; this is a rule I have laid down to myself, and I am determined religiously to observe it during the whole course of my life.

However great the captain's eagerness was to finger the money, he was obliged to give way to the piety of Sanguisuela, and arm himself with patience; and, as if he had been afraid the ducats should have made their escape from him, he followed the usurer to church, heard mass with him, and after that, was preparing to go; but Sanguisuela whispered him in the ear, one of the ablest divines in all Madrid, said he, is going to preach, and I will upon no account lose his sermon.

The officer, to whom the time of mass appeared tedious, was at this new delay almost quite mad; however he staid in the church. The preacher appeared, and the subject of his discourse was against usury; the captain's heart rejoiced at this, and observing the countenance of Sanguisuela, he said within himself, if the heart of this Jew[3] would but so far melt as let me have six hundred ducats, I should depart well satisfied with him. When the sermon was ended and they were gone out, the captain came up to the other and said, well, what think you of this divine, does not his discourse carry with it much energy and conviction? For my part, I am quite moved with it. I am entirely of the same opinion with you, replied Sanguisuela, he has treated his subject perfectly well; I told you he was a man of great abilities, and has done his business accordingly; now let us go and dispatch ours.

What two women are these that lie together in the same bed, and laugh so heartily? cries Don Cleofas; they seem to be jolly girls. They are, replied the demon, two sisters, and have this morning buried their father, who was a man of a peevish temper, and who had so great an aversion to marriage, or rather a reluctancy to part with any thing to his daughters, that he never would give his consent to the most advantageous offers that were made them. The old man was just now the subject of their conversation; he is dead, said the eldest; that unnatural father, who took such a barbarous pleasure in seeing us continue maids, will now no more oppose our inclinations. As for me, said the other sister, I am for what is substantial, and will have a rich man, were he the greatest beast in nature; and the fat Don Blancho shall be my choice. Softly, sister, replies the eldest, we must have those husbands that fate allots us, for marriages are registered in heaven; so much the worse, replied the youngest, for if that is the case, I am afraid my father will tear out the leaf. The eldest could not help bursting into a fit of laughter at this conceit, and they are both laughing at it now.

In the house next that of the two sisters, a female adventurer of Arragon has hired furnished lodgings. I see her admiring herself before the glass instead of going to bed; she congratulates herself upon her charms, which have gained her to-day an important conquest. She studies new airs, and has found out one which to-morrow will be practised with great success upon her lover; and indeed she cannot be too careful of him, for he is well worth looking after, as she herself declared but just now to one of her creditors who came to dun her for money: have a little patience, said she, my friend, and come back again in a few days; I am in terms with one of the most considerable persons belonging to the revenue.

I need not ask you, says Leandro, how that man has been employed that I now see. He must have been busied all the day in writing letters. What a number of them lies upon the table! And what is most remarkable, replied the demon, the subject of all these letters is the same. This gentleman has written to all his friends, imparting to them an affair that has happened to him this afternoon. He was in love with a widow of thirty, who is a fine lady and a prude: she received his addresses favourably, and at last consented to his proposal of marriage. But while they were making necessary preparations for the nuptials, she allowed her gallant the liberty of visiting her at her own house. He was there this afternoon: and as by chance there happened to be nobody in the way to give notice of his coming, he entered the apartment of his mistress, whom he found in a gallant dishabille; or to speak more truly, lying almost naked upon a couch. As she was fast asleep he approached her softly, to make use of the opportunity, and snatched a kiss; upon which the lady waked, and sighing, tenderly said, *What again! my dear Ambrosio, Ah! leave me to my rest.* The cavalier, who is a man naturally well-bred, went away immediately, gave up all his pretensions to the lady; and as he was going out of her apartment met the footman: Ambrosio, said he to him, you must not go in, your mistress desires you would leave her to her rest.

Two doors beyond that of the cavalier, I see in a small apartment a man, who may pass for an original of a husband; for he sleeps soundly, and is lulled to slumber by the continual scolding of his wife, who loads him with reproaches for having been from home all day; and would be still more enraged, if she knew how he had spent his time. I fancy he has been engaged too in some love adventure, says Leandro: you are right, replied Asmodeus, and I'll give you an account of the particulars.

The man you see is a tradesman, his name is Patricio, he is one of those libertine husbands, who live without any regard to wife or children, though he married a young woman of beauty and virtue, by whom he has one son and two daughters, all of them infants. This morning he went out of his house, without enquiring whether he had left a loaf of bread for his family, which very often are without one. He went through the great square, where the preparations for the bull-fighting, which was to-day, occasioned him to stop. The scaffolds were already fitted up all round the square, and the people were beginning to take their places.

As he was considering every thing about him, he spied a lady handsome and well dressed, who in stepping from the scaffold, shewed a fine turned leg, with pink-coloured silk stockings and embroidered garters; a circumstance which was more than enough to put this silly creature of a tradesman beside himself. He immediately went up to the lady, who was in company with another, and who likewise shewed by her behaviour, that they were both women of the town. Ladies, said he, if I can be of any use to you, you need but speak; you will find me devoted to your service. Signior Cavalier, answered the nymph with the pink-coloured stockings, your offer is too good to be refused; we have indeed taken our places, but are quitting them to go to breakfast, for we have been so foolish as to come out this morning without taking so much as a dish of chocolate; and as you are so polite to offer us your service, we will wait upon you any where you please, where we can have something for breakfast, provided it be in a private and retired place; for you know that young ladies cannot take too much care of their reputation.

Patricio, whose sentiments of generosity and politeness, banished all thought of his poverty,[4] carried his princesses to a tavern in the suburbs, where he immediately called for breakfast. What will you please to have? replied the landlord. I have the remains of a sumptuous feast which was given at my house yesterday; crammed fowls, Leon partridges, pidgeons of Old Castile, and above one half of a Bayonne ham.[5] There is more than we have occasion for, says the conductor of these vestals. Ladies, call for what you like, what do you choose? They answered, that whatever was agreeable to him would be so to them. Upon which he ordered two partridges, and two cold chickens; and desired them to show a private room, as he was in company with ladies of honour, who stood upon punctilios of delicacy.

They shewed them accordingly into a private apartment, and in a moment brought what he had ordered, with bread and wine: these ladies of honour, who were sharp set, began immediately to devour the victuals, while the cully[6] who was to pay the reckoning, employed his time in gazing at Luisita, for that was the name of the lady he was enamoured with. He was ravished with the whiteness of her hand, on which sparkled a fine ring she had got in the course of her business. He bestowed upon her all the fine names he could think of, such as angel and goddess;[7] and could not eat a bit, so much was he delighted with being in company with this fine lady. He asked his goddess whether she was married, who answered him she was not, but was under the direction of a brother; if she had told him it was a brother by the family of Adam, she would have told him the truth, but she did not think proper to let him into that secret.[8]

In the mean time these two harpies not only devoured each her chicken, but drank in proportion; so that the wine was out. This gallant went himself to fetch a reinforcement, that he might have it more quickly; and was no sooner gone out of the room, but Jacintha, the companion of Luisita, laid her claws upon the two partridges that remained, and crammed them into a great pouch which she had under her petticoat. Our Adonis returned with his wine, and observing that all the victuals were gone, he asked his Venus if she did not chuse something else. Let them bring us, says she, some of those pigeons the landlord spoke of, if they are extremely nice; if not, a slice of the ham will suffice. She had scarce spoke these words, when Patricio went out to look after the provisions, and ordered three pigeons, with a large plate of ham. These birds of prey began to devour afresh; and while this simpleton of a tradesman was gone a third time to call for more bread, they sent two of the pigeons down to the great pouch to keep company with the partridges.

After this repast, which ended with such fruits as were then in season, the amorous Patricio pressed Luisita to shew him those marks of gratitude he expected from her. The lady refused to comply with his desires, but did not leave him without hopes, telling him there was a time for every thing; and that a tavern was not a proper place for her to shew her gratitude for his politeness. Hearing the clock strike one, she put on an air of uneasiness, and said, my dear Jacintha, how unlucky we are, we shan't, I am afraid, find places to see the bull-fighting. O! I beg your pardon for that, replied Jacintha, the gentleman has nothing to do but to bring us back to the place where he so politely accosted us, and you need be in no pain for the rest.

But before they went out of the tavern, there was a necessity of settling accounts with the landlord, who made the bill amount to fifty reals. Patricio took out his purse, but finding there only thirty, was obliged to leave his rosary in pawn for the rest. Afterwards he reconducted these Lucretias to the place where he had found them, and got them convenient places upon the scaffold, for which the proprietor, who was his acquaintance, gave him credit.

No sooner were they set down, but they began to ask for refreshments. Jesus, cries one of them, I am ready to choak with thirst; this ham has quite parched me up; and I myself, said the other, should be very glad of some lemonade. Patricio, who understood quite well what all this meant, left them to go and get something for them to drink; but stopped in the way, and spoke thus to himself: fool that I am, where am I going? would not any man imagine I had at least a hundred pistoles in my purse or at home, and in the mean time I am not worth a farthing in the world? But what shall I do? if I return to the ladies without bringing them what they asked for, I shall look mean and pitiful;[9] and on the other hand, to give up an affair which wears so promising an aspect, is what I cannot bear the thoughts of.

While he was in this perplexity, he spied amongst the crowd one of his friends, who had often made him tenders of service, which his pride had hitherto prevented him from accepting: but upon this occasion he lost all sense of delicacy, and coming up to his friend with great eagerness, borrowed a double pistole; upon which resuming fresh courage, he immediately ran to a place where these things were sold, and bought such a quantity of liquors in ice, so many biscuits and dried sweet-meats, that the doubloon was hardly enough to pay for them.

The bull-feast ended with the day, and Patricio went to conduct his lady home, in hopes of having his wishes crowned with success.[10] But as soon as he came to the door where she told him she lived, there came out a kind of servant-maid, who running up to Luisita, spoke to her with great seeming confusion; what a time is this for you to come home! Your brother Don Jasper Heridor has been waiting for you above these two hours, and swearing like a devil. Upon which the lady pretending to be greatly frightened, turned round to her gallant, and squeezing his hand, whispered him softly, my brother is most terribly passionate, but his anger is soon over; do you wait in the street, we'll go and pacify him; and as he sups every night in the city, as soon as he goes out, Jacintha shall come and tell you, and conduct you into the house.

Patricio, who was greatly comforted by this assurance, kissed with transport the hand of Luisita, who bestowing some marks of kindness upon him by way of bonne bouche,[11] entered into the house along with Jacintha and the servant-maid, whilst he took his stand in the street, fortifying himself with patience.[12] He sat down upon a bench about two doors off, and staid a considerable time, without suspecting they had any design to put a trick upon him. The only thing that disturbed him was, that he did not see that cursed fellow Don Jasper Heridor her brother come out of the house; and was in a mortal fright, lest perhaps he might not sup in the city that evening.

Whilst he was thus employed in these reflections,[13] he heard the clock strike ten, eleven, twelve: at last, he began to have some doubts and suspicions of his lady's integrity. Upon this he went to the door, and after having entered, groped his way through a dark entry, in the middle of which he found a stair-case. He did not venture to go up, but listened attentively, where his ears were saluted with a concert, composed of the barking of a dog, the mewing of a cat, and the squalling of an infant. He was at last of opinion that he was duped; and what confirms him in it is, that having endeavoured to find the bottom of this dark passage, he found it to be a thorough-fare, and himself in another street than that in which he had so long done duty as a centinel.[14]

He then began to regret the loss of his money, and returned to his lodgings, wishing all pink-coloured stockings at the devil. He knocked at his door; and his wife with her beads in her hand and tears in her eyes, came to open it; and with a tender and pious voice, said, ah! Patricio, how can you thus leave your house, and take so little care of your helpless wife and infants? what have you been doing since six o'clock this morning that you went abroad? The husband not knowing what answer to make to this address, and at the same time vexed within himself for having been the dupe of these two harlots, pulled off his cloaths and went to bed, without saying one word: and his wife, who is at present in the humour of moralizing, has read a lecture which has lulled him to sleep this instant.

Cast your eyes, continued Asmodeus, upon the great house just by that of the cavalier, who has been writing to his friends his adventure with master Ambrosio's mistress. Don't you observe there a young lady lying in a bed of crimson-sattin embroidered with gold? I see, replied Don Cleofas, a person who is asleep; and perceive at the same time a book upon the pillow. Just so, replied the demon; this lady is a young countess of great wit, and a most sprightly humour, who being troubled with want of sleep for about six days past, has just now sent for one of the gravest physicians of all the faculty. When he was come, and she had asked his advice, he ordered her a medicine, which he told her was recommended by Hippocrates. The lady began to be merry upon this prescription; but the physician, whose genius was no ways turned to pleasantry,[15] did not relish her mirth; and told her with a solemn and doctoral gravity, Madam, Hippocrates is not a man to be turned into ridicule. O! Signior Doctor, replied the countess with a serious air, I have no intention to ridicule so learned and so celebrated an author; on the contrary, I have so great an opinion of him, that I am persuaded if I should look into his works, I should be cured of my present complaint. I have in my library a new translation of him by the learned Azero,[16] which they say is the best. You'll hardly believe, continued Asmodeus, what an effect reading sometimes has.[17] The lady had hardly got to the third page, when she fell into a profound sleep.

There is in the stables of the same hotel a poor lame soldier, whom the grooms out of charity, allow to lie upon the straw. In the day-time he begs, and has lately had a pleasant enough conversation with another beggar, who takes his post near to Buen-Retiro,[18] in the high road that leads to the palace, and manages his affairs extremely well; for he lives at his ease, and has a daughter marriageable, who passes amongst the beggars for a rich heiress. The soldier accosting this farthing monger one day, said to him, Signior Mendigo, I have lost my right arm; and, as I can serve the king no longer, find myself reduced like you, to pay my respects to strangers, in order to get a subsistence. I know that it is of all trades that which a man is surest to get his bread by,[19] and all other necessaries, only it is not quite so honourable. Were it honourable, replied the other, it would be a trade not worth following; for every one would take it up.

You are in the right, said the soldier; and now I think on it, as I am of the same calling with you, I should be glad to be allied to you. Give me your daughter, I'll marry her. You don't think of what you say, replied the other; my daughter must have a better match. You are not yet sufficiently docked[20] to be my son-in-law. I must have a husband for her, that will create pity even in the breast of an usurer. What the devil, replied the soldier, am not I in a situation deplorable enough? For shame, replied the other angrily, you, who have only lost an arm, pretend to my daughter! I would have you to know, that I have refused her to a man who has hardly any remainder left of his backside.[21]

I should be in the wrong, continued the demon, to pass by this house, which joins that of the countess; and where there lives an old drunken painter and a satyric poet. The painter went out this morning at seven o'clock to fetch a confessor to his wife, who lay at the point of death; but meeting with one of his friends, who took him into a tavern, he did not return till ten o'clock at night. The poet, who, as fame reports, has often met with a sorrowful recompence for his satyric verses, speaking t'other day in a coffeehouse of a man who was not there, said, with a fierce look, that fellow is a scoundrel, and if I could meet with him, I would give him an hundred kicks on the breech. That you may very well afford to do, replied a wag, for you won't then be out of his debt.

I must not neglect telling you the story of a banker, in this street, who is newly set up in town. It is not above three months since he came home from Peru with great riches. His father is an honest cobler of Vieso de Mediana, a considerable village near the mountains of Sierra d'Avila, where he lived in great contentment with his wife, a woman of the same age with himself, that is, about sixty years old.

It was now a long time since their son was gone from them to the Indies, to seek a better fortune than they were able to give him. They had not seen him for above twenty years, but they often spoke of him, and every day sent up their prayers to heaven for his preservation; nor did they fail to have him remembered to God duly every Sunday by the curate, who was their intimate friend. The banker, on his part, did not forget the old people; as soon as he came home, and had settled his affairs, he resolved to inform him-

self in person of what situation they were in. For this purpose, after having told his servants not to be in any pain for him, he set out about a fortnight ago on horseback without any one to attend him, and came to the place of his nativity.

It was about ten o'clock at night when he arrived, and the honest cobler[22] was fast
asleep with his wife, when he was obliged to get up in a hurry at the noise which the
banker made rapping at the door of their small cottage: they asked who was there?
Open, open, replied the other, it is your son Francillo. Your tricks upon strangers, cried
the cobler, march on, you'll find nothing here worth your while to break into the house
for. Francillo is now either in the Indies or dead. Your son is not in the Indies, replied
the banker, he is returned from Peru, and now speaks to you; do not refuse to let him
into your house. Let us get up, Jacobo, said the wife, it is Francillo; I think I know his
voice.

They both got up in a great hurry; the father lighted a rush candle,[23] and the mother
putting on her cloaths with all expedition, went and opened the door. She looked upon
Francillo, and recollecting him, cast her arms round his neck, and locked him in her embrace. The good old cobler, who felt no less the emotions of tenderness than his wife,
embraced Francillo in his turn; and these three people, so overjoyed to find themselves
together again after so long an absence, expressed their mutual satisfaction every way
they possibly could.

After these agreeable transports of tenderness were over, the banker unbridled his
horse, and put him into a stable, where there was a cow that was a nursing-mother to
the whole house. Then he gave an account to his parents of the success of his voyage,
and of the riches he brought from Peru. The relation was indeed very circumstantial,
and would have tired the patience of any other auditors; but when a son launches forth
into a particular recital of his adventures, he is in no danger of tiring a father and a
mother. The most minute circumstance has to them something interesting;[24] and these
old people heard with the greatest eagerness of attention every particular circumstance,
and felt the alternate impressions of joy or sorrow, according to the different changes of
his fortune.

As soon as he made an end of his own story, he told them he had come to share his
fortune with them; and therefore begged his father would not work any more. Hold,
child, said master Jacobo, I love my trade, and will not leave it off. What, says the banker,
is it not time you should now find rest in your old age? I do not propose you should
come and live at Madrid with me; I know very well the town would not be agreeable to
you, and therefore would not disturb the quiet and tranquillity of your life: what I want
is, that you should give over a painful and laborious occupation; and as it is now in your
power, live here at ease.

The wife joined in the remonstrances of her son, and master Jacobo was at last prevailed upon. Well, Francillo, said the old man, to please you, I will work no more for the
people of the town in general; but you must take this along with you, that I will always
mend my own shoes and the curate's, who is our intimate friend. After affairs were so
compromised, the banker ate a couple of eggs his mother had boiled for him, and lay
down to sleep by his father, with a pleasure none can have an idea of, but such as have
felt the tender workings of filial piety and affection.

The Honest Cobbler and His Wife Greet Their Son. (Sterling Library, Yale University.)

Next morning Francillo returned to Madrid, after having left them a purse of three hundred pistoles; but was not a little surprised this morning to see the old man appear before him. What occasions your coming here? said he to him. Son, answered master Jacobo, I have brought you the purse of gold you left with us, take back your money; I am determined to stick by my trade,[25] for I have not known what to do with myself since I left off working. Well, says Francillo, since it must be so, go back to your own village, and continue your trade, but let it be only to amuse you; take your own purse with you, and do not spare mine. But what would you have me do with so much money? said master Jacobo. Do with it! replied his son; relieve your distressed neighbours, and put it to such uses as your good friend the curate shall advise you. The honest cobler was satisfied with this expedient, and is now returned to Mediana.

Don Cleofas listened to this account with infinite pleasure; and would have bestowed all the praises that were due to the honest good hearted banker, if he had not been interrupted by the noise of some piercing shrieks he heard just by. Signior Asmodeus, says he, what horrible noise is this I hear? It proceeds, replied the demon, from a place that is appointed for the reception of people that are mad, and who are now stretching their throats and lungs in singing and bawling;[26] we are hard by the house. Let us go and see them immediately, said Zambullo. With all my heart, answers the demon; I'll give you this entertainment, and tell you the different reasons that deprived them of their senses. As soon as he had spoke these words, he carried Don Cleofas to the Casa de los Locos.

CHAPTER IX.

Of the bedlamites.[1]

Zambullo cast his eyes over all the different apartments; and after he had observed all the mad people, men and women which they contained, Asmodeus said, you see them here of all sorts, one sex as well as the other; merry and sad, young and old. I must now acquaint you with what occasioned their going mad. We will go over the apartments separately, and begin with the men.

The first man whom you see is of New Castille, born in the very heart of Madrid, a flaming patriot,[2] more jealous of the honour of his country than an old Roman. He turned mad from indignation, at reading in the news papers that five and twenty Spaniards had been beaten by five hundred Portuguese.

He has for his neighbour a young clergyman, who pants so eagerly after a living, that he has been cringing at court[3] for these ten years; and seeing himself always forgot,[4] the disappointment has affected his brain. But this disaster has procured him what his most sanguine hopes could never expect, the archbishoprick of Toledo; for though indeed he is not archbishop, yet he thinks himself so, and in my opinion is much more happy than if he was; for this pleasing dream will last him as long as he lives, and he will not in the other world be obliged to give an account of the use he has made of his income.

The next is a young heir, whose guardian has given him out to be lunatick, that he may for ever have the management of his estate; and the young man has really lost the use of his senses by being thus confined. Next to the minor behold that venerable personage, with a turret of woollen night-caps;[5] he is an ancient schoolmaster, who has cracked his brain in researches[6] after the *paulo post futurum*[7] of a Greek verb: and the other is a merchant, who has not been able to stand the shock of losing a ship in a late storm, though in the former part of his life he had resolution enough patiently to submit to two statutes of bankruptcy.

He whom you see lying in the next apartment, is old captain Zanubio, a Neapolitan gentleman, who came to live at Madrid; a fit of jealousy has reduced him to the state you now see him in. He was married to a young lady, named Aurora, whom he kept from the sight of every human creature. His house was inaccessible to the male sex. Aurora never went out but to church, and then was always attended with her old Tithonus, who carried her sometimes to a country-house he had near Alcantara. A young gentleman called Don Garcia Pacheco had by chance seen her at church, and fell desperately in love with her. He was a young man of an enterprising genius, and extremely well calculated to attract the regard of a young lady unequally coupled.[8]

The difficulty that attended the access to Zanubio's house did not discourage him. As he had not yet a beard, and was very smooth-faced, he disguised himself in women's cloaths, took a purse of an hundred pistoles, and went immediately to the captain's country-house, where he knew he was to come along with his spouse; there addressing himself to the gardener's wife, as if he had been a lady pursued by a giant, My good mother, said he, I fly to you for protection. For the love of God take pity on me, I am a young lady of Toledo of birth and fortune, whom my parents would marry to a man I hate; this night I have made my escape from their tyranny, in order to find an asylum; and I think I cannot be safer any where than here: allow me to stay with you, till such time as my parents come to other resolutions concerning me. There is my purse, continued he, take that, which is all I can at present offer you, but hope the day will come, when I shall have it in my power to shew my gratitude more amply for the services you do me.

The gardener's wife, who was a good-natured woman,[9] was mightily moved with the conclusion of this discourse: Child, said she, I will do you all the service I can. Well do I know the deplorable situation of young ladies who are married to old husbands; alas, poor creatures, how they gnaw the sheets, my heart bleeds for them;[10] and upon such an occasion you could never apply to a fitter person than me. I'll put you into a private room, where no one shall know any thing about you.

Don Garcia was here some days extremely impatient for the arrival of Aurora.[11] She at last came, attended by her old Argus;[12] who, according to his usual custom, rummaged all the rooms, closets, cellars, and garrets, to see that no secret enemy lurked any where about his house. The gardener's wife, who knew him well, prevented the consequence of any discovery, by telling him in what manner a young lady had fled to her house for refuge.

Notwithstanding Zanubio's natural jealousy, he had no suspicion of any deceit here. He was only curious to see the unknown lady, who begged him not to insist upon knowing her name, as that was a decency she ought to preserve in regard to her family, which in some measure she had dishonoured by her escape. Then he told him a long story, with a great deal of art, with which the captain was charmed: he found an inclination grow upon him for this amiable person, to whom he offered his best services; and imagining that his civility to her would be requited one way or other,[13] brought her to his wife.

As soon as Aurora saw Don Garcia she blushed, and was in confusion without knowing why. He perceived this, and imagined she had observed him in the church where he had first seen her: to be satisfied on this head, as soon as he had an opportunity of speaking to her in private, he said to her, Madam, I have a brother who has often spoke to me of you; he once had an opportunity of seeing you at church for a moment; and since that moment which he calls to mind every day,[14] he remains in a situation that deserves your pity.

At this discourse Aurora looking upon Don Garcia more attentively than she had done before, answered him, Sir, you resemble that brother too much for me to be the dupe of such an artifice; and I plainly see you are a man in disguise.

I remember very well one day that I was hearing mass, my veil dropped and you had a sight of me. I looked at you out of curiosity, and observed you kept your eyes upon me; and when I went out of church, I believe you did not fail to follow me, in order to learn who I was, and in what street I lived. I say I believe, because I durst not look back to observe you; for my husband, who was with me, would have taken notice of such a thing, and looked upon it as criminal. The next day, and some days after, I went to the same church, and observed your face so well, that I now recollect your features, notwithstanding your disguise.

Well, madam, then I must pull off the mask, replied Don Garcia; yes, I am a man, and one who is captivated by your beauty: I am Don Garcia Pacheco, whom love has brought here under this disguise. And you imagine, no doubt, replied she, that I will approve of your extravagant passion, and by conniving at this stratagem, join with you in deceiving my husband. But in this supposition you are mistaken, for I'll go immediately and discover the whole affair to him; my honour and my peace depend upon it. Besides, I am glad of such an excellent opportunity to convince him that he has less security in his own vigilance than in my virtue; and that notwithstanding he is so jealous and so suspicious, I am less capable of being deceived than he.

Scarce had she pronounced these words when the captain came into the room and joined the conversation; well ladies, said he, what is the subject of your discourse? Why sir, replied Aurora, we were talking of gentlemen making attempts upon the virtue of young wives that were married to old husbands; and I was a saying, that if any of these sparks should have the boldness to come about your house,[15] I should know how to deal with him as he deserved.[16]

And you, madam, answered Zanubio, turning to Don Garcia, what do you think of this matter, how would you deal with a young gentleman in such a case? Don Garcia was so confounded and so much out of countenance, that he could make no answer; and the old captain must certainly have perceived his confusion, if a servant had not that instant come in to let him know that one from Madrid wanted to speak with him, upon which he went out to know what was the business.

The moment he was gone, Don Garcia threw himself at the feet of Aurora: ah! madam, said he, what pleasure can you take in thus tormenting me? sure you will not be so barbarous as to deliver me up to the fury of an inraged husband? No, Pacheco, replied she smiling, young wives, who have old jealous husbands, are not usually so hard hearted. Take courage, I had only a mind to divert myself a little, by putting you into a breathing sweat;[17] but I'll make you amends for it; you must not think that too dear a price to pay for the favour I allow you of staying here. At these words of consolation, Don Garcia's fears vanished; he even conceived great hopes of success, and the kind Aurora did not baulk his expectations.

It happened one day while they were giving one another reciprocal marks of affection and esteem[18] in Zanubio's apartment, the captain surprised them. Though he had been a man not naturally jealous, he saw enough to convince him that the fair unknown belyed her sex. At the sight of this he became mad with rage, and ran to his closet to fetch his pistols; but in the mean while the lovers made their escape. They double locked the doors of the apartment behind them, carried off the keys, and got with all speed to a neighbouring village, where Don Garcia's servant waited with a couple of good horses; there putting off his woman's dress, he took Aurora behind him, and carried her to a convent, of which an aunt of hers was lady abbess. After which precaution, he returned to Madrid, and there waited the issue of this adventure.

In the mean time, Zanubio finding himself locked in, bawled out and called up his servants. One of them upon hearing his voice, ran up stairs; but as the doors were locked, could not get in. The captain endeavoured to break them open; but not being able to effect that so soon as he wished, in the fury of his impatience, threw himself out of the window with his pistols in his hand: he pitched upon his head,[19] and was so terribly hurt, that he lay stretched upon the ground quite stunned. The servants came, and taking him up, carried him into the hall and laid him upon a couch; when by throwing water into his face, and using other methods, they recovered him from his swoon; but he no sooner came to himself, than his rage returned with as much violence as ever. He asked where was his wife? They told him she was gone with the strange lady through the little garden-gate; upon which he ordered them to bring him his pistols, and they were obliged to obey. He caused his horse to be got ready, and without reflecting that he was wounded, immediately rode off by a different road from what the others had taken. He passed a whole day to no purpose in looking after them; and at last being obliged to stop at an inn to rest himself, the fatigue and his wound brought upon him a fever with a delirium, which had well nigh carried him off.

To make short of the story, he continued in that condition at the inn for a fortnight, and after that returned to his country-seat, where his imagination being continually racked with reflections upon his misfortune, he at last by degrees lost the use of his reason. The relations of Aurora had no sooner got intelligence of this, than they had him brought to Madrid, and shut up in the place appointed for mad people. As for the lady she is as yet in the convent; and they intend she shall remain there some years as a punishment for her indiscretion, or rather misconduct, for which they may thank themselves.[20]

After Zanubio, continues the demon, comes Signior Don Blas Desdichado, a cavalier of distinguished merit. The death of his wife has brought him to that deplorable situation in which you now behold him. God bless me! cries Don Cleofas, what! a husband run mad at the death of his wife! one seldom finds such an exalted instance of conjugal affection. Don't be in such a hurry, replied Asmodeus, interrupting him, the man did not lose his senses out of grief for the loss of his wife; what disturbed his skull[21] was, that as she died without children, he was obliged by a clause in the marriage-contract, to refund fifty thousand ducats to her relations.

Oh, that explanation clears the matter up, cries Leandro, I am not at all surprised at his being in this condition. But tell me, pray, who is this young man that skips like a kid in the next room, and every moment stops, holding his sides and ready to burst with laughter? He seems to me to be quite a joyous fellow; why, says Asmodeus, his madness was occasioned by an excess of joy. This fellow was porter to a man of quality, and one day receiving the news of the death of a rich scrivener to whom he was sole heir, he could not stand it; his head whirled round, and he has not recovered the use of his reason ever since.[22]

We are now come to that great tall boy[23] who plays upon the guittar, and accompanies it with his voice. He is melancholy mad, and is a lover, who the cruelty of his mistress has reduced to such a state of despair, that they have been obliged to confine him. Ah! cries the student, how I pity him, I cannot help bewailing the misfortune of his condition: alas, it may be the case of any gentleman. Were I myself in fetters to an unrelenting beauty, I make no doubt but I might undergo the same fate. This shews you a true Castilian, replied the demon; a man must be born in the very heart of Castile to be able to love to such a pitch, as that the frowns of his mistress could endanger the use of his reason. Frenchmen are not affected so tenderly; and to shew you the difference betwixt them and a Spaniard in this point, it will be sufficient to let you hear the song, which this Castilian has been now composing.

A Spanish love-song.

I weep, I sigh, my smart to cure,
Which I from love's sharp dart endure:
But yet no sighs my fires asswage,
Which burn, thus blown, with double rage.

Thus it is a Castilian cavalier complains under the displeasure of his mistress; and the following verses will shew you how a Frenchman behaves himself under the like misfortune.

A French love-song.

The object, which inflames my tender heart,
Despises Cupid, and a lover's smart;
In vain my paleness, languor, gentle sighs,
Would draw soft pity from her cruel eyes:
But since nor pray'rs, nor tears the fair can move,
I'll end my life, to end the pains of love.
Friendship will decently attend the dead,
Let me be buried at the Bedford-head*.[24]

---

* In the original *Paien*, a noted traiteur[25] of Paris.

This Bedford-head is, I suppose, a tavern, said Don Cleofas. Indeed it is, replied the demon, and a very good one. Let us proceed to examine the rest. We'll now take a view of the women, replied Leandro, I am impatient to see them. That we shall do immediately, replies the demon, but there are two or three unhappy people I want to shew you first, as you may perhaps reap some advantage from the knowledge of their misfortunes.

Observe in the cell adjoining to that of the player on the guittar, the meager, sepulchre-countenance of that man who grinds his teeth, and seems as if he could eat the very iron bars of his window. He's an honest man, but born under such unfortunate stars, that although he had all the merit in the world, and was at all imaginable pains, he was never able to assure himself of daily bread; he went mad upon seeing a low worthless fellow, whom he knew, mount in one day to the highest pinnacle of fortune.

The next to him is an old secretary, whose brain was cracked[26] because he could not support the ingratitude of a courtier, in whose service he had been for sixty years. One can hardly enough commend the zeal and fidelity of this servant, who never demanded any thing, and contented himself with barely mentioning his services and assiduity; but his master, who was not a man like Archelaus king of Macedon, who refused when he was asked, and gave when he was not, has died without considering him in the least: he has only left him what was due to him for wages, and this poor man must remain shut up in this place, and pass the remainder of his life in misery.

I shall shew you but one more, and that is he whom you see leaning on his elbows at the window, and appears to be in a profound reverie. This is no other than Signior Hidalgo de Tafalla; he came to live at Madrid, where he made a rare use of his fortune; he was seized with a frantick itch[27] of being acquainted with all the wits of the town, and treating them. There was nothing at his house but entertainments and feasting every day. And though these ungrateful and ungenerous animals, the race of authors, laughed in his face at the time they were spunging upon him; yet he could not be satisfied till he had got them to eat up the last remains of his small fortune. Then no doubt, said Zambullo, he has gone mad from vexation, at his having so foolishly ruined himself. Quite the contrary, says Asmodeus, he went mad because he had not left wherewithal to go on in the same manner.

Now we come, continued he, to the women. How is this? cried the student, I see but seven or eight of them, there are fewer mad women than I supposed. They are not all here, replied the demon smiling. If you have a mind I'll bring you immediately to a part of the town, where you shall see a house quite full of them. There is no occasion for that, replied Don Cleofas, I'll satisfy myself with these that are here. You are in the right, said the demon, for they are almost all of them ladies of quality; you may judge by the richness of their linnen that they are not persons of common rank, and I will give you an account of the reasons why they are here.[28]

In this first apartment is the wife of a corregidor,[29] whom a lady belonging to the court called a cit,[30] which had so great an effect upon her mind, that she was not herself ever after. In the second apartment is the lady of the treasurer-general of the council of the Indies;[31] her madness was occasioned by the vexation she felt at being obliged in a narrow street to make her coach go back to give way to the dutchess of Medina Celi's. In the third resides a young widow, who was the daughter of a citizen, and whose brain is turned from being disappointed in an expected match with a young nobleman. And in the fourth apartment dwells a young lady of quality called Donna Beatrix, whose story I must acquaint you with.

This lady had a she friend whose name was Donna Mencia: they visited one another every day. A chevalier of the order of St. Jago, a personable and polite gentleman having got acquainted with them, they very soon became rivals of each other, and warmly disputed the possession of the chevalier's heart, which decided in favour of Donna Mencia, whom he soon after married.

Donna Beatrix, jealous of the power of her charms, was touched to the quick with this, which she conceived as an affront put upon her beauty, and like a true Spaniard, was projecting schemes of revenge when she received a letter from Don Jacintho de Romarate, who was in love with Donna Mencia; in which letter he acquainted her, that he, being likewise affronted at the marriage of his mistress, had determined to fight the gentleman who had taken her from him.

This letter was extremely agreeable to Beatrix, who desiring nothing more than the death of the offender, wished only that Don Jacintho might kill his rival. While she was in pious expectations of this event, it happened that her own brother having some difference with Don Jacintho, fought him and received two wounds of which he died. Though it was the duty of Donna Beatrix to prosecute the murderer of her brother, she delayed the prosecution, to give Don Jacintho time to fight the chevalier of St. Jago. This is a convincing proof that nothing interests a woman so much as the reputation of her beauty. This was the case with Pallas * in the affair of Ajax and Cassandra. The goddess did not immediately punish the sacrilegious Greek who had profaned her temple, but waited till he should first revenge her cause for the judgment of Paris. But, alas! poor Donna Beatrix was not so lucky in this case as Minerva, for she has not tasted the sweets of revenge. Romarate was killed in the duel with the chevalier; and the vexation which this lady felt at not having her project of revenge accomplished, has turned her brain.

The two next ladies are, one of them the grandmother of a counsellor, who by her misconduct spent too much of his estate, and he has found ways and means to get her in here, in order to be rid of her. And the other is an old marchioness, who having always idolized her own beauty, instead of growing old with a good grace, bewailed without ceasing the decay of her charms, till at last one day viewing herself attentively in a faithful mirrour, her head gave way all at once.

So much the better, cried Leandro, for my lady marchioness; perhaps in this disorder of her mind, she is not so sensible of the change that time has made in her beauty. As-

---

* When Troy was sacked by the Greeks, Ajax the son of Oileus, ravished Cassandra, Priam's daughter, and virgin priestess of Minerva, in the very temple of the goddess, *Ecce trahebatur,* &c. Virg. Æn. lib. 2. And, for this offence, was on his return home, destroyed with his fleet and companions, as we are told likewise by Virgil in his first book, Ipsa, *Jovis rapidum,* &c. But this instance of the female prudence and finesse of Minerva, in suspending her resentment till she had made use of him to revenge an affront received from another, has, I believe, escaped the observation of the commentators, and therefore the honour of it is justly due to the quick and ingenious conceptions of our author.

suredly not, replied the demon: so far is she from observing the approaches of age upon her face, that she thinks her complexion a mixture of lillies and roses; she fancies she sees the loves and the graces sporting around her; and in a word, believes herself to be actually the goddess Venus. Well, replied the scholar, and is she not more happy in thus fancying herself to be what she is not, than in seeing herself such as she really is? No doubt of it, replied Asmodeus. But there is one lady more whom you must observe. She that is in the furthermost apartment, who is now gone to rest, after having been three days and three nights without one wink of sleep.[32] Her name is Donna Emerenciana, observe her attentively. What do you think of her? I think her extremely pretty, replied Zambullo. What a pity it is such a charming creature should be deprived of her reason. Listen to me with attention, answered the demon, and I'll inform you of the particulars relating to her misfortune.

Donna Emerenciana, the only child of Guillem Stephani, lived happily at Siguenca in the house of her father, till Don Kimen de Lizana interrupted her quiet with his addresses of gallantry, by which he endeavoured to gain her affections. She not only received these marks of gallantry favourably, but even connived at those stratagems he made use of to procure means to speak to her,[33] and in a short time after, they mutually exchanged vows of fidelity to each other.

These two lovers were of equal rank in regard to their families, but the lady was one of the best fortunes in Spain, and Don Kimen only a younger brother. But there was yet a greater obstacle to their union, for Don Guillem mortally hated the family of Lizana; which he evidently made appear in all his discourse, whenever that family happened to be mentioned;[34] and he seemed to have a particular aversion to Don Kimen above any of his race. Emerenciana was greatly afflicted at this disposition of her father, and conceived from it no favourable presage to her love. However she gave herself up without restriction to the violence of her inclinations, and continued her secret interviews with Lizana, who came into her apartment from time to time in the dead of the night by means of a waiting-woman.

It happened one of these nights that Don Guillem, who by chance had not gone to sleep when the gallant came into his house, imagined he heard some noise in his daughter's apartment, which was not far from his own. This was more than enough to create suspicion in a man so distrustful as he. Notwithstanding his suspicious temper, Emerenciana had behaved with so much prudence and address, that he had no notion of any correspondence between her and Don Kimen. But being a man who was not naturally apt to take things upon trust,[35] he slipt softly out of bed, and opened a window which looked into the street, where he had the patience to wait till he saw a man come down from the balcony upon a silk ladder, whom by the light of the moon, he knew to be Don Kimen de Lizana.

You will better be able to judge how Stephani was affected at this sight, when I tell you[36] he was the most revengeful, the most brutal monster that ever Sicily, the country of his nativity, had produced. He did not give way to the transports of his passion, but took care not to do any thing by which the principal object of his revenge might escape the fury of his resentment. He check'd his rage, and waiting till his daughter was up in the morning, entered her apartment; where being all alone with her, and looking upon her with eyes sparkling with fury and indignation, Wretch, said he, who in defiance of the nobleness of your blood and family, are not ashamed to commit the most infamous actions; prepare to receive the just punishment of your crimes. This poignard, added he, drawing a poignard from his bosom, this poignard shall be the immediate instrument of your death,[37] if you do not without reserve make a confession of every circumstance. Who is he that has this night dishonoured my house?

Emerenciana remained quite speechless, so frightned was she at the threats of her father that she could not utter one word. Ah! infamous wretch, continued he, your silence and confusion but too plainly inform me of your crime. What dost thou imagine I am ignorant of what has happened this night? I saw that villain Don Kimen come down from your balcony; was it not enough that you received a man into your apartment in the night-time, but must that man too be the person who is my avowed and declared enemy![38] let me know, however, to what lengths this insult upon my honour has been carried. Speak without reserve, for by that alone you can expect to avoid instant death.

The young lady at these last words, conceiving some hopes of escaping the dreadful fate that threatened her, recovered somewhat from her fright, and answered Don Guillem: Signior, said she, I could not help being sensible to the addresses of Lizana, but I take heaven to witness of the purity of his intentions. As he knows that you are at enmity with his family, he has not yet dared to ask your consent; and it was only to confer together upon the proper methods how to obtain it, that I allowed him some times to come here. Who was it, replied Stephani, you employed to manage this correspondence, and be the carrier of your letters? One of your pages, replied his daughter, does us that piece of service. That's all I wanted to know, replied her father, and I will presently put in execution the scheme I have formed: upon which with the dagger still in his hand, he made her take pen, ink, and paper, and write the following billet to her lover, which he himself dictated:

> My dear husband, the only joy of my life, I send this to acquaint you that my father is immediately going to his country-house, from which he will not return till to-morrow, that you may make use of the opportunity, I flatter myself you will expect night as impatiently as I do.

After Emerenciana had writ and sealed this treacherous letter, Don Guillem said to her, call the page who acquits himself so dexterously in his employment, and order him to go instantly with this note to Don Kimen: but hark ye, don't think to deceive me; I'll go and conceal myself in a place where I can see you[39] when you deliver him this commission, and if I do but observe that you speak a single word, or make but the least signal that may create any suspicion, I'll that instant dip this poignard in your heart's blood. Emerenciana, who knew her father too well to venture upon disobeying him, delivered the letter into the hands of the page in the same manner she had used to do.

After this, Stephani put up his dagger, but did not allow his daughter to be out of his sight the whole day, nor suffered her to speak to any one in private, and took his measures so well, that Lizana could not be apprised of the snare that was laid for him. This young man therefore did not fail to be punctual to the assignation. Scarce had he got into the house of his mistress, when he found himself seized upon by three stout men, who disarmed him before he could defend himself, crammed a handkerchief into his mouth[40] to hinder him from crying out, muffled up his eyes and tied his hands behind his back. At the same instant they put him, in this condition, into a coach, which was ready for that purpose, and into which they all three went, that they might be more sure of the cavalier, whom they conducted to Stephani's country house which was situated near the village of Miedes, about four small leagues from Siguenca.

Don Guillem went immediately after them in another coach, with his daughter, two maids, and a duenna of remarkable crabbed temper,[41] whom he had sent for that afternoon, and hired into his service. He likewise carried along with him all the rest of his family, excepting one old servant who knew nothing of Lizana's being carried off. They came all of them before break of day to the village of Miedes, when the first thing that Signior Stephani took care of, was to have Don Kimen shut up in a dungeon, which received all its light from a vent so narrow, that a man could not pass through it. He then gave orders to his servant Julio, in whom he chiefly trusted, to allow the prisoner for his subsistence only bread and water, with a bundle of straw to lie upon; and to say to him every time he carried him his allowance, here, base deceiver, this is the way Don Guillem treats those who dare to do him wrong.

This cruel Sicilian behaved in a manner no less brutal towards his daughter. He shut her up in a room which had no prospect, would not allow her any servant to attend her, and set the duenna whom he had pitched upon over her, as her gaoler; a duenna, who had no equal for cruelty and barbarity of temper.

In this manner did he dispose of the two lovers, but did not intend to stop here. He determined to have Don Kimen murdered, but was greatly puzzled how he should effect that with impunity. As he had employed his servants in carrying off the cavalier, he could not suppose an action to which so many people were privy, would long remain a secret; he therefore revolved within his mind what expedient he should fall upon to escape the hand of justice, and at last pitched upon one which could only have entered into the mind of the most accomplished villain.[42] He brought all his accomplices together into a place detached from the body of the house, where he declared to them how much he was satisfied with the services they had done him; and that as a mark of his gratitude, he intended to distribute a sum of money among them, after giving them an entertainment: upon which he made them all sit down at table, and in the midst of their feasting, Julio, by his order, poisoned every one of them; after which the master and the man set fire to the place, and before any of the inhabitants of the village could come to give their assistance, they murdered the two waiting women that belonged to Emerenciana, with the young page I made mention of, and then cast their bodies amongst the others. The place was soon in flames, and reduced to ashes, notwithstanding all that the peasants in the neighbourhood could do to extinguish the fire. It would have been worth while to have seen the affected grimaces of the Sicilian upon that occasion; he appeared quite inconsolable at the fate of his domestics.

Having in this manner made himself sure of the fidelity of such as might have had it in their power to betray him, he said to his confident, My dear Julio now am I at ease, and can dispatch Don Kimen when I will; but before I offer him up a sacrifice to my revenge, I would have the pleasure of making him suffer a little. The misery and horrors of a dungeon may be made more cruel to him than death.— And, indeed, true it was, that Lizana deplored, without ceasing, his misery; and despairing ever to be freed from the prison he was in, wished for nothing more than that they would dispatch him.

But in vain did Stephani hope for quiet, even after what he had done. In less than three days he began to be tortured with a fresh uneasiness, and to be under strong suspicions lest Julio,[43] as he brought Don Kimen his allowance, should be tempted by his promises; and the dread of this made him take a resolution of hastening the death of the one, and then to dispatch the other with a pistol: Julio on his part was not without some mistrust, that after his master had got rid of Lizana, he might probably fall a sacrifice next; upon which he had determined to make his escape the first opportunity, and carry off with him what moveables he most conveniently could.

While these two worthy men were conceiving such designs in regard to one another, it happened one day, that they were surrounded about a hundred paces from the castle, by about fifteen or twenty archers of the holy brotherhood of Hermandad,[44] crying out in the name of the king and of justice.

At first Don Guillem was confounded and turned pale. However, putting a good face upon the matter, asked the commandant, who it was he wanted? You yourself, replied the officer, who are accused of having carried away Don Kimen de Lizana; and I have orders to make a strict search in your house for that gentleman, and at the same time to take you into custody.

Stephani, at this answer of the officer's, not doubting but he was ruined, became desperate. He drew a case of pistols, and swore he would not allow one of them to enter his house, and that he would instantly blow the commandant's brains out, if he did not immediately retire with his men. The other,[45] despising his threat, advanced upon the Sicilian, who discharged a pistol at him and wounded him in the face; but this wound cost him his life who had given it; for two or three of the archers let fly at him at once, and laid him quite dead upon the ground, to revenge their commander. As to Julio, he let himself be seized without resistance; and there was no occasion to ask him any questions whether Lizana was in the castle, for he made a full confession of every thing; only as he saw his master lying stone dead, he did not fail to lay the blame of every thing upon him.

At last he brought the commandant and his men to the dungeon, where they found Don Kimen lying upon straw, bound and fettered.

This unhappy gentleman, who was in continual expectation of death, and supposed that so many armed men came into the dungeon only with an intent to murder him, was agreeably surprised to find, that those people he took for his executioners were his deliverers. After they had untied him and set him free, he thanked them for his deliverance, and asked them how they came to know he was confined in that castle? That is what I am going to tell you as briefly as possible, replies the commandant.

The night you was taken away, one of the people concerned in that affair, who had a sweetheart that lived a little way off from Don Guillem's, having gone to take leave of his mistress before he went into the country, was so imprudent as to give her an account of the whole matter. This woman kept the secret for two or three days; but as the fire that happened at Miedes came to be talked of in the town of Siguenca, and it appeared strange to every body, that all the servants of Stephani should have perished in the flames, it came into the woman's head, that he himself must have been the author of it;

Don Kimen Rescued by the Hermandad. (Sterling Library, Yale University.)

upon which, in revenge for the death of her lover, she went immediately to your father, Don Felix, and made a discovery to him of every thing she knew.

Your father, terrified at the thoughts of your being in the power of a man, who, he knew would stick at nothing, brought her before the corregidor, who, upon hearing her story, was convinced that the Sicilian intended to make you suffer tedious and cruel torments, and made no doubt but that he himself had set fire to his house on purpose; and being willing to know the bottom of this affair,[46] he sent orders to me at my house at Retortilo, the place where I live, to get immediately on horseback, and go directly to this house to look for you, and apprehend Don Guillem dead or alive. I happily executed my commission as to what regards you, and am extremely sorry I have it not in my power, to bring the author of your misfortunes alive to Siguenca; for by his resisting, he put us under a necessity of killing him dead on the spot.[47]

The officer having spoke thus to Don Kimen, said, I must draw up a verbal process[48] in relation to every thing that has been done here; after which we will set out and relieve your family from the anxiety they labour under upon your account.

Wait a little, Signior commandant, cried Julio, I must give you some fresh materials for your verbal process; there is another prisoner here, whom you must likewise set at liberty. Donna Emerenciana is locked up in a dark room, with an unrelenting duenna, who eternally teizes and upbraids her, without allowing her one moment's quiet.

O heavens! said Lizana, then this barbarous man has not been contented with exercising his cruelty only upon me: come, let us make haste to deliver this poor lady from the barbarity of her jaylor. Upon this Julio carried Don Kimen and the commandant, attended by five or six archers, to the room in which she was imprisoned.

It is easy to conceive the joy which he felt in finding again his mistress, after he had despaired of seeing her; his hopes were renewed afresh, nor did he make any doubt but his wishes would be now fully accomplished, as the only person who opposed his happiness was dead. The moment he saw her he ran and cast himself at her feet. But how great was his surprize and disappointment, when, instead of finding his mistress ready to receive his transports, he perceived poor Emerenciana out of her senses! She had been so plagued and tormented by her cursed duenna, that she had turned quite mad.

At first she remained in a kind of reverie; then fancying herself to be the beautiful Angelica,[49] beset by the Tartars, in the forest of Albragua, she imagined all the people she saw in the room to be so many Palatines come to her relief; she took the chief of the holy brotherhood for Rolando, Lizana for Brandimart, Julio for Hubert of Lion, and the archers for Antifort, Clarion, Adrian, and the two sons of the marquis of Olivier. She received them with great courtesy, and said to them, Gallant cavaliers, I now dread no more the resentment of the emperor Agrican, nor of the queen Marphisa; your prowess is sufficient to protect me against all the warriors of the universe.

At this strange discourse the commandant and his myrmidons[50] burst out into a fit of laughing, but Don Kimen laughed not: to see his dear mistress in such a situation was torture equal to ten thousand daggers to his heart; and he had like to have gone mad himself;[51] but he imagined she would recover the use of her reason, and in that hope came up to her, and taking her in his arms with great fondness, Emerenciana, said he, my dear, recollect yourself, it is I, your own Lizana; be comforted; our misery is now at an end: heaven has taken pity on us, and would not suffer that hearts like ours, so tenderly united in love, should be separated: your inhuman father, who has used us in this manner, has now no longer power over either of us.

The answer she made to this was still as if she had been the daughter of the king of Gallafron, and addressed herself again to the valiant defenders of Albraca, who were not now disposed to laugh any more: even the commandant himself, though naturally rugged as a flint,[52] could not help being moved with pity, and spoke compassionately to Don Kimen, whom he saw sinking with excess of grief. Signior cavalier, said he, do not despair; the lady may yet recover; you have able physicians at Siguenca, who may probably effect her cure; but we must be gone, we stay here too long. You, Signior Hubert of Lion, continued he, who know all the studs of this great castle, go, and take along with you Antifort, and the two sons of the marquis of Olivier, order them to get ready the fleetest coursers, and put them immediately to the chariot of the princess. In the mean time, I will go and draw up my verbal process.

Upon saying which he took out of his pocket an ink-bottle and some paper; and, after having writ what he intended, gave his hand to Angelica, to help her down stairs into the court-yard, where the Palatines had got a coach and four mules ready to set off, into which he went, along with the lady and Don Kimen, and made the duenna likewise come in, whom he was certain the corregidor would take proper care of. But that was not all, he ordered Julio to be chained, and put in another coach, along with the corps of Don Guillem; after which the archers mounted their horses, and they set out all together on the road for Siguenca.

While they were on their way, the daughter of Stephani said a thousand extravagant things, which were so many stabs to the heart of Lizana; he could not with patience bear the sight of the duenna: barbarous woman, said he, it is you and you alone who have brought Emerenciana to this cruel extremity. The governante justified herself with all the grimaces of hypocrisy, and laid the blame of the whole upon the deceased. Her misfortune, said she, is intirely owing to Don Guillem. This cruel unrelenting father came every day and frighted his daughter, and his threats at last turned her brain.

When they came to Siguenca, the commandant went and gave an account of the success of his commission to the corregidor, who immediately examined Julio and the duenna, and committed them both to prison in this town, where they now remain. The judge likewise received the deposition of Lizana, who immediately after set out for his father's, where his arrival changed the grief of his family into joy and gladness. As to Donna Emerenciana, he took care to have her conducted to Madrid, where she has an uncle by the mother's side.

This affectionate relation, who wanted extremely to have the management of his niece's fortune, was appointed her guardian; and as he could not, with any decency, but appear willing to have her cured, he found himself under a kind of necessity to send for the most famous physicians of Madrid: as it happened, he had no occasion to repent of it, for, after many learned consultations,[53] they at last thought proper to declare her incurable; and the guardian, upon this opinion of the doctors had her immediately shut up in this place, where, in all probability, she will remain for the rest of her life.

Unhappy pair, cried Don Cleofas, my heart bleeds for them;[54] poor Emerenciana deserved a better destiny; and pray, added he, what is become of Don Kimen? what course has he taken? A very wise one, says Asmodeus; when he saw the thing was past remedy, he set out for New Spain; and hopes, that by absence and travelling, he may at last efface from his mind the remembrance of a lady whom his interest and his repose require he should forget. But come (continued the demon) after having shewed you those mad people who are shut up here, I will shew you others, who, though not confined, deserve to be so.

CHAPTER X.

Of which the subject is inexhaustible.

Let us now go to the other part of the town; and when I observe any that deserve to have places here, I will give you their character. I see one already whom I must take notice of; he is newly married: about eight days ago hearing that a lady of pleasure, whom he was in love with, had taken some liberties he did not approve of, he went to her full of fury, broke some part of her furniture, threw the rest out of the window, and the next day married her.

Why really, says Zambullo, I think that gentleman deserves the next vacant place in this college. There is a neighbour of his, replied the demon, that I do not think a bit wiser than he; he is a batchelor of five and forty, with a sufficient competence to live on,[1] and yet is going to enter into the service of a great lord. O there comes a lawyer's widow: this good lady has seen the last year of her twelfth lustrum;[2] and, as her husband is just dead, she is going to retire into a convent. I will do it, says she, to secure the reputation of my virtue from the slander of malicious tongues.

I perceive here two virgins of the age of fifty;[3] they send up their prayers to God Almighty, that he would be graciously pleased to take to himself their father, who keeps them locked up as if they were girls of fifteen;[4] they are in hopes, that after his death they shall find some handsome cavaliers that may fall in love with them. And why not? said the student; there are men in the world of such a strange taste. I allow it, replied Asmodeus; it is not impossible but they may find husbands, but it is not at all probable; their folly therefore consists in expecting any such thing: though indeed there is not any country in the world where women are willing to do themselves strict justice, in regard to their age.

About a month ago, at Paris, a maid of eight and forty, and a married woman of threescore and nine, went before a justice, to attest the character of a widow of their acquaintance, whose reputation had been slandered: the justice first asked the married woman, what her age was? and though the number of her years was written in expressive wrinkles on her forehead, as plain as in the parish-register, she made no scruple to answer, that she was forty. After which, addressing himself to the maiden lady, and you, Mademoiselle, said he, pray what may your age be? I desire your worship would talk of other affairs, said she; these are questions not to be asked people. You don't take the matter right, replied he; you don't consider that the law requires—Pish; there is no law for that, replied the lady briskly; what business has the law to do with enquiring about my age? that is no branch of its business. But I cannot, replied the magistrate, otherwise receive your deposition; your age must be mentioned in it; it is a circumstance absolutely necessary. If it be absolutely necessary, replied the lady, consider me attentively, and set me down according to the dictates of your own conscience. The justice, who was a polite man, looked at her, and set her down twenty-eight. He then asked her, how long she had known this widow? I knew her before she was married, replied the maiden lady. Why then, answered the judge, I must have made some small mistake in your age, mademoiselle; I have set you down but twenty-eight; and it is nine and twenty years since this woman was married. Well, cried the other, then set me down thirty; I may reasonably enough be supposed to have known her when I was a year old. Ay, but that will never do in law; the least we can add is a dozen more. No, indeed but you sha'n't, cried she, all that I will submit to, to satisfy the point of law, is to give you one year more; but I would not add one month more, if my own reputation were at stake.

When these two ladies had given their depositions before the justice, the married woman said to the maiden, what do you think of that old fool, who took us for such simpletons as to give a true account of our age? for my share I think it too much that it should be wrote in the parish-registers; there is no occasion to make a public record of it in their books, for all the world to look at. Should not we make a pretty appearance, think you, to stand in open court, and the clerk reading aloud, Madam Richard, of the age of threescore, and Miss Parenelle, of the age of forty-five, maketh oath, and each for herself saith, &c. As for my share I laugh at such a thing; I have clipt them off a good even score,[5] and I think you are much to be commended for having done the same. The same, replied miss very smartly;[6] what do you mean by the same? I am your humble servant for that; I am but thirty-five at the most. What do you say, my dear, replied the other, with a malicious smile; I saw you born, child; and, God knows I speak of an old story, I have seen your father, my dear, who was no young man when he died, and it is now above forty years since his decease. To this the other replied, with great agitation of spirit, my father, my father, what do you talk of my father; when my father married my mother, it is well known he was too old to be able to get children.

I observe, in the next house, two men, who are not over and above stocked with reason; one is a young heir, who neither knows how to keep his money nor how to spend it, but has fallen upon an expedient to keep himself always in cash; when he is flush of money he buys books, and when his purse begins to grow empty he disposes of them again for half of what they cost him. The other is a foreign painter, who draws portraits of ladies; he is a man of genius, and designs correctly, his colours are warm,[7] and he hits the likeness; but he don't flatter, and yet expects he shall have a run. *Inter stultos referatur.*[8] What a plague, cried Leandro, do you speak Latin too? Are you surprised at that? replied the demon. I speak all languages; I understand Greek and Hebrew, Arabic and Chinese, and yet am not a bit the more proud, or more of a pedant for all that. In this I have the advantage over the literati.

Observe in that great hotel upon the left hand, a sick lady, surrounded with so many women who wait upon her; she is the widow of a famous rich master-builder, but her head is quite turned with notions of quality. She has just now made her will, and has left all her wealth, which is immensely great, amongst persons of rank, merely on account of their great quality, tho' she never beheld them with her eyes. She was asked, whether she would not bequeath a legacy to a certain man to whom she lay under great obligations? Alas! no, replied she with a sorrowful air, and I am heartily grieved I cannot; I am not so ungrateful as not to acknowledge he has done me considerable services, but he is a plebeian, and his name would disgrace my testament.

Signior Asmodeus, interrupted Leandro, pray let me know whether this man whom I see reading in his closet may not perhaps deserve an apartment in the college?[9] He deserves one extremely well, I assure you, replied the demon; he is an old venerable vicar, who is looking over the proofs of a book he has now in the press. Some work of morality or divinity, no doubt, said Don Cleofas. No, not that, replied the demon; it is a collection of bawdy poems which he composed in his youth; instead of committing them to the flames, or letting them perish with him, he has caused them to be printed off during his life-time, for fear lest, after his death, his heirs should be tempted to publish them, and gut them of their spirit and energy.[10] I should be in the wrong, by the bye, to neglect taking notice of a little hump-backed woman who lives with the vicar; she is so much persuaded that she pleases the men, that if any one does but speak to her, she immediately marks him down in the list of her lovers.

But let us now come to a rich prebendary,[11] whom I see just by. This man's case is extremely singular; he lives abstemiously, but not from a principle of mortification or sobriety; nor is it from a principle of avarice that he does not allow himself a coach. What can be the reason that he does not live up to his income? Only, replied the demon, that he may have money. Well then, what use does he make of it? I suppose he disposes of it to charitable uses.[12] No, not that either; he lays it out in pictures, trinkets, and costly pieces of furniture: nor does he even propose to have any pleasure or enjoyment from them during his life-time; his only design is, that they should appear in the inventory of his goods and chattels after his death. What you say cannot be, says Zambullo, it is impossible there should be a man in the world of such a turn. I tell you it is fact, says the demon; this Mania possesses him; his greatest pleasure is in thinking how people will admire the catalogue of his valuable and rich houshold furniture, when they come to be exposed to sale by auction.[13] If he buys, for instance, a rich cabinet, he has it carefully packed up, and laid in his wardrobe, that it may appear intirely new to the toyman[14] who shall come and bid for it.

Let us proceed to one of his neighbours, whom you will find no less a fool than he, an old batchelor lately come to Madrid, with a great estate, which his father, who was auditor of Manilla,[15] had left him. The behaviour of this man is pretty extraordinary; he never misses a day attending the levee of the king and the first minister, though he is a man of no ambition, nor sues for any employment; he wants none, nor asks for any thing. What then, replies Don Cleofas; does he attend only to pay his court, without any other view? Not even that, replied the demon; he never spoke to the minister in his life, and is not so much as known by him, nor does he desire he ever should. What then can his motive be? Why it is this, he would make people believe he is a man of great consequence. What an original coxcomb this is![16] cried the student, bursting into a fit of laughter; what a deal of pains he takes about nothing: you are in the right to rank him amongst the bedlamites. O! replied the demon, I can shew you a great many others, who are as void of common sense as he; look into that great house where you see so many burning tapers, and three men and two women sitting round the table, they have already supped, and are now playing at cards, to pass away the rest of the night; after which they will separate. This is the life these people live, who meet regularly every night, and then go to sleep till the return of the evening; they have bid adieu to the sight of the sun, and the beauties of nature. To see them surrounded in this manner with flambeaus looks like the funeral obsequies of the dead. There is no occasion, says Cleofas, to shut up these fools, for they are so already.

I see a man fast asleep, continued the demon, whom I love vastly, and who has no less regard for me; he is the work of my own hands: I have moulded and fashioned him. He is an old batchelor, who idolizes the fair sex: if you speak to him of a fair lady, you cannot help observing with what pleasure he listens to you; tell him of her pretty little mouth, her vermilion lips, ivory teeth, and alabaster complection; in a word, mention as many particulars as you please, at every one of them he sighs, his eyes sparkle, and his whole frame is in ecstasy of rapture.[17] About two days ago, as he passed by the shop of a shoemaker who works for ladies, he stopt short all of a sudden, to look at a slipper which he perceived, and after having considered it with the greatest attention, said with a soft and tender air to a gentleman who was with him, Ah! my friend, what an idea does this slipper present to my imagination? How pretty must that foot be for whom it is made? But I take too much pleasure in looking at it; we must go from this, it is not safe tarrying here any longer. This old batchelor ought to have a black mark set upon him, says Leandro Perez. Why you are not much in the wrong, replied the demon. And there is a neighbour of his who is not much better, who, because he keeps an equipage of his own, is out of countenance if he is at any time seen in a hackney coach. But we may very well compare this exchequerman with a relation of his, a rector, who enjoys very beneficial livings in the church, and who every day makes use of a hackney-coach, to save two fine horses and four fine mules, which he keeps in his stable.

I observe in the neighbourhood of these two gentlemen, a person who cannot, without great injustice, be refused a place in these apartments: he is a cavalier of threescore, and makes his addresses to a young lady, whom he visits every day, and entertains her with an account of his gallantries in his youth, and what a man he was in days of yore. He is such a fool as to imagine the young lady will like him for what he has been. We may rank along with him another old fellow who lives hard by, a French marquis, who is come to see the court of Madrid. This noble lord is now threescore and ten, and in his former days made a brilliant figure at Versailles; the whole court admired his graceful stature, his gallant air, and were particularly charmed with his fine taste in dress; he has carefully preserved all the suits of cloaths he then wore, and now dresses in what he had appeared in fifty years ago, though in his own country the fashions change every day; but what is more pleasant than any thing, he looks upon himself to be as handsome and graceful as in the prime days of his youth.

Come, says Don Cleofas, we need make no hesitation in regard to him; we may very safely set down this French lord among those who deserve a place in the Casa de los Locos. But I must reserve one apartment, replied the demon, for a lady who lives in a garret near the hotel of the count: this is an old widow, who, out of an excess of tenderness to her children, has given them every thing she had, reserving to herself only a small pension, which the aforesaid children are obliged to pay her; but they are so piously grateful, that it is with great difficulty she can get one farthing.

There is an old batchelor whom I would likewise willingly provide for, said the demon. This man no sooner gets a ducat than he spends it; and as he can't live without expence, makes any shift to get money. About a fortnight ago, his laundress, to whom he owed no less than thirty pistoles, came and dunned him for the money,[18] saying, she had an absolute occasion for it, as she was just going to be married to a valet de chambre, who courted her. Why then, says he, you must have got money besides this; for who the devil would marry you for thirty pistoles? I beg your pardon for that, said she, I have two hundred ducats more. Two hundred ducats! replied he; give them me, and I'll marry you, and so we shall be quit. She took him at his word, and he is now married to his washerwoman.

We must likewise preserve three places more for these three gentlemen who now return from supping in the city, and are going into the hotel upon your right hand, where they live. The one is a count, and values himself upon his taste in the belles lettres; the other is the count's brother, a dignified clergyman; and the third is a wit, who is their follower. They are hardly ever asunder, and for the most part make visits all three together: the count praises none but himself; his brother praises him and himself; but the poor wit has a tripple charge, to praise the other two and himself into the bargain.

There are two vacancies more that may very properly be filled up; one of them I would bestow upon a citizen here, who has taken it into his head truly to be a florist; and though the man is so poor that he hardly can support himself and family, he keeps a gardener and his wife to look after about a dozen auriculas[19] which he has in a little garden. And I would assign another apartment to the use of a player, who, complaining of the vexations that attended the business of the stage,[20] told his companions t'other day, Why faith, gentlemen, I am quite weary of this way of life; I would even rather be a country squire, with only a thousand ducats a year.

Which ever way I turn me, I perceive hardly any thing else but people who are troubled with diseases in the brain. There is one for example, a chevalier of Calatrava, who is so vain and so proud at his having a secret intrigue with the daughter of a grandee, that he imagines himself upon a level with the greatest nobleman about court. He greatly resembles * Villius, who imagined himself son-in-law to the dictator, because he had an affair with Sylla's daughter; and this parallel still is more just, as the chevalier, like the Roman, has a Longarenus, that is to say, a low fellow of a rival, who in a short time

* Villius, a noble Roman, maintained an intrigue with Fausta, only because she was daughter to the dictator; but happening unluckily to call one time when she was engaged with Longarenus, was by him severely drubbed and kicked out of doors. The story, with a dialogue proper for the occasion, is told by Horace in his second satire of the first book. Aulus Gellius mentions, that that grave historian Sallust did likewise undergo the same fate, and received the like chastisement from the hands of her husband Milo.

will supplant him. In short one would imagine that a succession of fools sprout like the heads of the hydra, and that one generation follows close at the heels of another. There is a man who is secretary to a minister, who exactly resembles * Bolanus, who kept no kind of measures with any man, and without any ceremony told every one at first sight if he did not like them. There is an old president, the same as † Fusidius, who lent his money at cent. per cent. And ‡ Marseus (he who gave his house to the actress Origo) lives again in the person of that young heir, who now guttles down with an actress[21] the last mortgage of an estate he has near the Escurial.[22]

Asmodeus was going to proceed, but was interrupted by hearing all of a sudden a concert of music; upon which he said to Don Cleofas, At the end of this street there are musicians, who are going to give a serenade:[23] if you have any inclination to be present at it, I'll take you there immediately. I love those sort of things mightily, replied Zambullo; let us go there; perhaps there may be some singers amongst them. He had no sooner said this than he found himself transported to the top of a house just over the serenade. The musicians immediately struck up some Italian airs; after which two songsters sung alternately the following stanzas.

A Castilian Love-Song.

I.

> If you, my fair, desire of me,
> A picture of your charms to see,
> Attend, and in my verse I'll show,
> With what divine, celestial charms you glow.

* Our author has here again taken the sentiments and authority of his friend Mr. Dacier upon trust, who, in his notes upon the passage of Horace, where he mentions Bolanus, (Sat. 9. lib. I) describes his character just as Monsieur Le Sage does here.[24] But the real state of the case is this—when Horace found himself fallen an unhappy victim, and under the talons of this messenger of satan sent to buffet him, he sends up a pathetic ejaculation, how much he envied that felicity of brain, that happy construction of skull, which Bolanus enjoyed, to whom sense or nonsense, the *tacenda* or *loquenda*, were equally indifferent; and I believe many a man finds himself now and then under the necessity of envying such a character,

> ——*O te, Bolane, Cerebri*
> *Felicem, aiebem tacitus*——

† This Fusidius was so mortally afraid lest people should laugh at him as a spendthrift or a bubble,[25] that, in order to avoid the imputation of either of these characters, he employed his money in lending it out at extravagant usury.

> *Fusidius vappæ famam timet ac nebulonis:*
> *Quinas hic capiti mercedes exsecat.*
> Hor. sat. 2. lib. I.

‡ This is likewise one of Horace's people, whom he takes notice of in the satire abovementioned, as having spent every farthing he had in the world upon Origo, the actress, merely from a pious principle and scruple of conscience, that he would not meddle with other men's wives.

II.

Your forehead, made of iv'ry white,
Calls up a blush in the day's light:
You captivate the gods above,
And vanquish Cupid in his turn with love.

III.

Your scorching eyes victorious shine
With such strong light they put out mine!
You stretch your conquest over all,
'Tis you, not Cupid, who commands the ball.

IV.

Madrid, enchanted with your grace,
Turns pagan to your heavenly face:
In love's soft net all hearts you take,
And Jews turn Christians for your beauty's sake.

V.

Thou'rt Venus, heav'n, the polar star,
Which to love's vessel shines afar:
No lustre can compare to thine
Not gems, or treasure of an Indian mine.

The stanzas, cried Cleofas, are full of gallantry and delicacy. Why yes, replied the demon; you, who are a Castilian, may perhaps think so; but were they translated into French, I assure you they would lose all their bloom. A Frenchman would not at all relish these figurative expressions, and such extravagant sallies would only excite his laughter.[26] But come, said Asmodeus, we'll talk of the stanzas another time; you will be entertained presently with another kind of musick.

Observe these four men, who now appear in the street; you see they are attacking the serenaders, who defend themselves with their fiddles as with shields, but not finding them sufficient defence, they are running away; and you may perceive two cavaliers who come to the assistance of the musicians, one of whom is he who gives the serenade: with what fury do they fall upon the aggressors? but they, who are superior in number and equal in point of skill and courage, receive them with great resolution. How their swords strike fire! see there is one falls, who is the master of the concert, and is mortally wounded; upon seeing of which the other gentleman his companion retires, the aggressors save themselves by flight, and the musicians get off as fast as they can,[27] and there remains none upon the spot but the unfortunate gentleman whose life pays the price of the serenade; but mark, at the same time, the lady[28] who sits at her lattice, and observes every thing that passes. She is so proud and so vain of her beauty, though by the bye, she is but very ordinary, that instead of grieving at this fatal catastrophe, she inwardly rejoices and congratulates herself on the power of her charms.[29] But this is not all, continued Asmodeus; there is still another you must observe, who has come up to the deceased, to give him, if possible, some assistance; but while he is busy in thus discharging the duties of friendship, he is seized by the watch, who carry him to prison, where he will remain a long time, and undergo the same fate as if he had been the murderer of his friend.

How fruitful of misfortunes has this night been? says Zambullo. And this will not be the last, answered the demon; if you were now at the sun-gate[30] you would be frightned with a scene that is going on there. By the negligence of a servant a great hotel is now on fire, which has already consumed a vast deal of furniture. But Don Pedro de Esculano, the master of this hotel, does not, at present, think of the loss of his moveables, however valuable they may be; he thinks only how he may be able to save Seraphina, his dear and only child, who, at this instant, is in danger of perishing in the flames.

Don Cleofas expressing a great desire to see this fire, the demon carried him off in an instant to the sun-gate, where they pitched on the top of a house opposite to the hotel where the fire was.

CHAPTER XI.

An account of the fire, and what Asmodeus did on that occasion.

They immediately heard the confused voices of different people, some crying out, fire, others crying out, water. A moment after, they saw the great stair-case which led to the principal apartments all on fire, and, after that, clouds of smoke and flame bursting thro' the windows. The fire now rages excessively, continued the demon, and has got to the top of the house, from whence you may see it rising in a vast quantity of smoke and sparks, and is so very violent, that all the people who came to assist in quenching it can do nothing but look at it. Do you observe there, in the crowd, an old man in a night-gown; don't you hear his cries and lamentations; that is Don Pedro Esculano; he calls out to the people who are about him, and conjures them to attempt to deliver his daughter, offering any one who will undertake it a great reward; but in vain; there is not one will run the risk of trying to save that young lady, who is but sixteen years of age, and surprisingly beautiful. Finding his intreaties and offers all in vain, he tears his hair and his beard, beats his breast and commits all sorts of extravagant actions, in the excess of grief and despair; while Seraphina, abandoned by her women, is fallen into a swoon by the fright in her own apartment, where the smoke and flame will soon stifle her. It is out of the power of mortal man to save her.

The noble and generous heart of Don Cleofas could not bear the thoughts of this without being in the utmost agitation.[1] Asmodeus, said he, I conjure you to save this young lady from the instant fate that threatens her; I insist upon it as the recompence of the service you are indebted to me for; if you refuse me I have done with you, and shall never be easy all the rest of my life. The devil upon crutches laughed at hearing the student speak in this manner. Master Zambullo, said he, I find you are possessed of all the qualities of a knight-errant; you are courageous, you feel for the misfortunes of your fellow-creatures; and are extremely devoted to the service of the ladies. I suppose now you would not mind rushing into the midst of the flames,[2] like another Amadis, so you could but deliver this lady safe and sound into the arms of her father. Would to God, replied Don Cleofas, the thing was practicable on these conditions: I would run the risk of my life without hesitation. And your life would pay the price of such a notable exploit, replied the demon. I have already told you, that it is not in the power of man to save her; and therefore to satisfy you I must take the affair personally upon myself. Wait here, and observe in what manner I will act upon this occasion.

He had no sooner spoke these words, than, to the infinite amazement of Don Cleofas, he assumed his make and figure, mixed among the people, pressed through the crowd, and darted into the flames, his own element, in full view of all the spectators, who were terrified at the rashness of the action, and who, by their shouts and murmurs, seemed to blame such a hazardous attempt. What a desperate fool this must be, says one. How can any views of interest prompt a man to run himself into so much danger? No, said another; this bold adventurer must be a lover of Esculano's daughter, who in the frenzy of his grief is resolved to save his mistress, or to perish with her. In short, they all looked upon it that he would undergo the fate of Empedocles*; but in less than a minute they beheld him come through the flames with Seraphina in his arms. The air resounded with acclamations, and every one bestowed aloud a thousand praises on the brave cavalier, who had performed so glorious an atchievement. Rash actions, when attended with success, meet with applause; and this prodigious feat was looked upon by the mob as a natural effect of the heroism of the Spanish nation.

As the lady was still in a swoon, her father durst not give himself up to the transports of joy which he felt, being afraid lest his daughter, after having been so miraculously delivered from the flames, should expire before his eyes, from the dreadful apprehension the danger she had been in might have upon her brain; but he was soon comforted: She recovered from her swoon by the care that was taken of her, and looking upon the old gentleman, said to him in an affectionate manner, Signior, I should be more grieved than rejoiced at being saved from these devouring flames, if I did not find you in safety likewise. Ah! my child, replied he embracing her, as I have not lost you, I am easy about the rest; but let us return our thanks, said he, to this young and gallant cavalier, presenting Don Cleofas to her; this is your generous deliverer; it is to him you owe the preservation of your life: we can never sufficiently shew our gratitude, and the reward which I promised shall never discharge our obligations to him.

Upon this the demon replied in a gallant and polite manner, Signior Don Pedro, said he, the reward you promised was, I assure you, no inducement to me to attempt that piece of service I have had the happiness to do you. I am a gentleman born, and a Castil-

---

* This Empedocles was a great humourist, and extremely whimsical. The last whim he took into his head, was to jump down into the cauldron of mount Ætna, when it was raging in a fit of burning: and Horace is of opinion, that if any friend had ventured in after him, in order to pull him out, that the other, instead of being thankful, would have cursed him for his pains.[3]

ian. The pleasure of having prevented your affliction, and of having saved this beautiful lady, is all the reward I ask or looked for.[4]

The generosity and disinterestedness of the cavalier made Don Esculano conceive an infinite esteem for him: he begged he would come and see him, and be united with him in the bonds of mutual friendship. After a great many compliments on both sides, Don Pedro retired with his daughter to a house which was at the bottom of the garden, and Asmodeus rejoined Don Cleofas, who seeing him return in his original figure, Signior Diable, says he, don't my eyes deceive me? Was not you this moment in my shape? You'll excuse the liberty I took, said the other, when I tell you the reason of my transfiguration: I am plotting for you,[5] and have in my view to make you the husband of Seraphina. By appearing in your shape, I have been able to inspire the lady with very favourable sentiments in regard to your worship, and her father Esculano has likewise a high opinion of you; for I told him that the danger I ran, in saving the life of his daughter was only from a motive of serving them both, without any view of other reward, as the honour of having been the instrument of saving the life of such a fine lady was recompence enough to a gentleman of Castile. Don Pedro Esculano has a noble soul, and will be outdone by no man in point of generosity. I can assure you, he is this moment deliberating with himself, whether he shall not make you an offer of his daughter, in requital of the service he imagines you have done him.

But let us leave him to come to some resolution, and in the mean time repair to another place, more proper for us to take our observations.[6]

END of the First Volume.

The Devil upon Crutches

VOLUME TWO

THE
DEVIL upon CRUTCHES:
FROM THE
DIABLE BOITEUX
OF
Mr. LE SAGE,
A
NEW TRANSLATION.

To which are now firſt added,

ASMODEUS's CRUTCHES,
A CRITICAL LETTER upon the WORK;

And DIALOGUES between Two CHIMNEYS
of MADRID.

Adorned with CUTS.

Michael from Adam's Eyes the Film remov'd
---Then purg'd with Euphraſy and Rue
The viſual Nerve, for he had much to ſee.   MILT.

The SECOND EDITION, corre_cted_,

IN TWO VOLUMES.
VOL. II.

LONDON:
Printed for T. OSBORNE, A. MILLAR, R. BALDWIN,
S. CROWDER, J. RIVINGTON and J. FLETCHER,
and I. POTTINGER.

MDCCLIX.

THE
CONTENTS
OF THE
SECOND VOLUME.

THE
DEVIL
UPON
CRUTCHES.

CHAPTER I.

Containing the history of the dead; some tombs, and a parcel of ghosts.

We will for a while, said Asmodeus, suspend our examination of the living, and for some moments interrupt the repose of the dead; let us take a cursory view of the sepulchral monuments in this cathedral, of the persons they contain, and examine into the reasons why they were erected.

The first that you see on the right hand contains the sorrowful remains of a general officer, who, like Agamemnon*, on his return from the wars, found an Ægisthus in his house. In the second there lies a young gentleman of a noble family, who being minded at a bull-feast to give his mistress a sample of his valour and dexterity, fell a sacrifice to the rage of these fierce animals. And in the third there rests an old prelate, who departed this life somewhat before his time;[1] for when he made his will he was in good health. But having read it to his domestics, to each of whom, like a kind master, he had bequeathed something, his cook became impatient, and would wait no longer for his legacy.

This fourth tomb receives the ashes of a man, who never concerned himself with any thing but being constant in his devoirs at court. For sixty years together he made his appearance there morning and evening;[2] and the king, to reward his faithful attendance, loaded him with favours. And this courtier, replied Don Cleofas, was he a man apt to serve his friends? He served no one, replied the demon. No man could be more liberal of promises, but he never kept one of them. What a wretch! said Cleofas: if human society was to be lop'd of all its useless excrescencies, courtiers of such a stamp deserve first to be discarded from it. This other monument, continued Asmodeus, is the repository of the mortal part of a noble lord, zealous for the interest of his country, and the

---

* Agamemnon, king of Mycenæ and son of Atreus, chosen generalissimo of the combined forces of the Greeks in the war of Troy, upon his return home was slain by his own cousin Ægisthus the son of Thyestes, brother of Atreus, at a banquet, by the instigation of Clytemnestra, with whom he had lived in adultery during the absence of Agamemnon. She and Ægisthus were afterwards slain by her own son Orestes. This has lately been the subject of an English tragedy.[3]

glory of his king. He spent his whole life in embassies at Rome, in France, in England, and in Portugal; and in the course of his ministry so effectually ruined his fortune, that when he died he did not leave sufficient to bury him; but the king, in gratitude for his past services, defrayed the expences of his funeral.

Let us now go and take a view of the tombs on the other side. The first is that of a great merchant, who left immense wealth to his children; but, lest they should forget from whence they came, caused his name and quality to be engraved on his monument; for which his posterity at this day are no ways thankful to his memory.

The superb mausoleum next to this, which surpasses all the rest in the magnificence of its structure, is a master-piece of art, which strangers look at with admiration. I do the same, says Zambullo, and am particularly taken with these two figures upon their knees. They are highly finished, and the sculptor must have been an exquisite artist; but pray inform me of the persons whom they represent. You see, says Asmodeus, a duke and his dutchess. The first was a great officer of state, and filled his post with honour; and his lady lived in the highest devotion. I must tell you a story of this good lady; you may perhaps think it a little odd for one of her piety, and it is this.

She had for a long time as her director, a friar of the order of Merci,[4] named Jerom d'Aguilares, a good man, and a famous preacher, with whom she was quite satisfy'd; when there happened to start up a dominican, who preached in such a manner, that all the people of Madrid were in raptures with him. This new orator was called brother Placidus, and cardinal Ximenes[5] was not followed as a preacher more than he. In short, his reputation was such, that he preached to the court, by whom he was even more applauded than he had been by the people. At first the dutchess piqued herself upon not being influenced by the fame of this new orator, and not indulging her curiosity so far as to go and hear him. But she had a further motive, she wanted to convince her director that he had a penitent of so much delicacy, as could feel for the chagrin and uneasiness this new comer might occasion him. But she could not be so much mistress of herself for ever. The dominican made so much noise, that at last her curiosity got the better of her.[6] She saw him, heard him preach, relished his doctrine,[7] followed him, and the inconstant creature even formed a project for getting herself under his direction.

The first step she was obliged to take was to get rid of the friar, which was no easy matter, for a spiritual guide is not shaken off so soon as a gallant. A devotee does not chuse to be thought a jilt in spiritual matters, and to lose the esteem of the director she quits. Well, how did my lady duchess manage the matter, think you?[8] Next time she saw father Jerom, she spoke to him in a manner that testified real affliction. Father Jerom, said she, I am on the brink of despair. This moment I labour under unutterable affliction, anguish, and astonishment. Bless me, said Aguilares, what is the matter with your grace? Oh Sir! would you think it? answered she. My lord, who has hitherto never suspected my virtue, and who, without uneasiness, has let me be so long under your direction, is all of a sudden seized with a fit of jealousy, and insists you shall have me no longer for your penitent. Did you ever hear of such a capricious whim? I expostulated the matter with him to no purpose: I told him what an outrage he committed against common decency, to entertain a jealousy of a man of the most exalted piety, and who was quite dead to all lusts of the flesh. In short, my defending you served only to confirm his suspicions.

Asmodeus Teaches Don Cleofas the Truth about the Dead.
(Sterling Library, Yale University.)

Father Jerom, cunning as he was, became the dupe of this feigned story. Certain it is, she affirmed the truth of all the circumstances in such a manner as might have deceived an angel;[9] and though the pious priest had many substantial reasons for not losing such a penitent as my lady dutchess, he could not get off desiring her to comply with the will of her husband. But his reverence judged, some time after, otherwise of the matter, when he found his most noble penitent was under the spiritual guidance of brother Placidus.

Next to this grandee and his ingenious lady, a less superb monument contains the odly coupled remains of a director of the Indies and his young wife. This man of many plums,[10] in the three-score and third year of his age, married a girl of nineteen. He had by a former venter two children, whom he was just going to disinherit, when he was prevented by an apoplectic fit; and his wife followed him within the four and twenty hours, in a fit of madness that he had not slept with his fathers a few days later.[11]

We are now come to the most honoured, the most respected monument of this abbey. The Romans had not the tomb of Romulus in greater veneration than the Spaniards have this. What great man must this be? said Leandro Perez. A man, said Asmodeus, who in his life-time was absolute minister of the Spanish monarchy,[12] which perhaps never saw his equal. The king his master, with perfect confidence, reposed upon him the whole charge of government, and neither he nor his people had cause to repent it. His administration increased the happiness of the people and the glory of the empire, nor was he more distinguished for his high abilities in the art of government, than for the private virtues of humanity and piety. But notwithstanding that even in his dying moments his heart had nothing to reproach him with, yet the very nature of the employment he had filled, made him that he could not meet death without trembling.

Beyond the monument of this great man, so deservedly regretted, observe, in that corner yonder, a piece of black marble fixed to a pillar. Shall I open the sepulchre below, and shew you the remains of a city-beauty, who died in the flower of her age, and whose charms dazzled the eyes of every one? Lo now she is reduced to dust.

When alive she was so inchantingly beautiful, that her father lived in continual apprehensions, lest some one or other should run away with her, which very probably would have been the case, had she lived much longer. Three gentlemen, who adored her, were, at her death, drove to despair, and, as a proof of it, they all killed themselves. Their tragical story is engraved in letters of gold upon that piece of marble, and these three small figures, represent the despairing lovers in the act of making away with themselves.[13] One swallows poison, another falls upon his sword, and the third is fitting a rope about his neck to hang himself.

The demon observing that Don Cleofas laughed at this prodigiously, and seemed hugely diverted at seeing three such figures placed over the tomb of a citizen's daughter, said to him, Signior Cleofas, since I find this entertains your fancy so much, I have a great mind this instant to carry you to the banks of the Tagus, and shew you a sepulchral monument, which a dramatic author caused to be erected for himself in the church of a village near Almarus,[14] whither he hath retired, after having led at Madrid a long and jovial life. This author had furnished the theatre with a great many pieces stuff'd with all manner of lewd ribaldry; for which he repented before his death. On his tomb he caused to be represented a kind of funeral pile, consisting of his own works, with the figure of modesty holding a torch ready to set it on fire.

Besides the remains of the dead shut up in these tombs I have been now shewing you, there are vast numbers of others buried without any sepulchral monuments. I see their ghosts wandering up and down; passing and repassing one another without intermission, but without interrupting the solemn repose of this sacred abode. They speak not indeed to one another, but in their silence I can read their thoughts. How vex'd am I, says Leandro Perez, that I cannot enjoy, with you, the pleasure of beholding them. That satisfaction I can give you, said Asmodeus; nothing is easier to me. At that instant the demon touch'd his eyes, and by an illusionary vision, made him behold an infinite number of fleeting spirits, cloath'd in white.

At the sight of these phantoms Don Cleofas shuddered. What, says Asmodeus, do you tremble at the sight of these spectres? Do they terrify you? Let not their dress discompose you; on the contrary, from henceforward accustom your mind to the idea of it; for it is the uniform of the manes,[15] and what in time you yourself must put on. Take courage then, and fear nothing. I am surprised your resolution should fail you on this occasion, who have had the boldness to stand the sight of me; for I assure you these you see are far more harmless than I.

At these words the student summoning all his courage, beheld these passing shades, without so much emotion.[16] Consider them all attentively, said Asmodeus to him. The man who lies under the superb mausoleum here mixes with him that rests under the humble turf. The different degrees of grandeur, that made the distinction between them while in the world, here subsists no more. The great officer of state, and the first minister are here reduced to a level with the lowest of mankind. Like as the hero of the tragedy becomes himself again when the curtain drops,[17] so these great men, with the course of their lives, finish their course of grandeur.

One thing I observe here, said Leandro; I see a spirit wandering all alone, and seemingly to avoid the company of the others. If you said the others avoided it, answered the demon, you would say truly. Would you know who this shade is? It is the ghost of an old scrivener, who had the vanity to order himself to be buried in a lead coffin; which has given such offence to all the other ghosts of his own rank, who have been interred more modestly, that, to mortify him for his arrogance, they are determined none of them shall keep him company.

I have something else to observe to you, replied Cleofas. Two ghosts here, in passing by, stopped for a moment to look at one another, and then continued their course. These are the shades of two intimate friends, replied Asmodeus, one a painter, and the other a musician. They were indeed every now and then guilty of the sin of drunkenness, but in other respects very honest fellows, and both died in the same year. As often as the manes of these two friends meet, struck with the remembrance of pleasures past, they say to one another in pathetic silence, Ah! my friend, so merry as we two have been![18]

Mercy on me, cries Cleofas, what a couple of ghosts are these I see walking together at the end of the church. How strangely different they are both in their mien, and in the size of their bodies. One of them is of an immense stature, and stalks with a most stately gravity; the other is a meer pigmy, and skips along as if he were in the step of a minuet. The large one, replied the demon, is a German who died a martyr to the emperor's health, which he drank in three vast bumpers[19] of wine mixed with tobacco; and the other little fluttering thing[20] is the spirit of a departed Frenchman, who according to the gallantry of his own nation, thought proper one time, as he was going into a church, to shew his politeness, by offering holy water to a young lady as she was coming out; and that very same day received the reward of his good breeding from the mouth of a pistol.

I distinguish in the croud, cries Asmodeus, three pretty remarkable ghosts, and I must let you know in what manner their souls came to be disunited from their bodies. They formerly animated three actresses, who made as much noise at Madrid, as ever Origo, Citheris, and Arbuscula[21] did at Rome, and, like them, were fully instructed in the art of pleasing men in public, and ruining them in private. Now, such was the end of these famous Spanish actresses. One died suddenly of envy at the applause the audience gave a new actress. The other shortened her days in the excess of a debauch; and the third, happening to over-heat herself on the stage as she acted the part of a vestal, died of a miscarriage behind the scenes.

But now, continued Asmodeus, let us leave to rest in peace the manes of the dead; we have examined them sufficiently already. I am now to present to your sight an object, which ought to make even a stronger impression on your mind than the sight of these departed spirits. By the same power that I have shewed you the spirits of the dead, I will make death himself appear before your eyes. You shall see this formidable foe of mankind, who incessantly lies in wait without being seen; who, in the twinkling of an eye,[22] traverses the globe, and, in an instant, sheds his baleful influence over all its inhabitants.

Look towards the east, and perceive him coming.[23] What flocks of obscene, ill-omened birds attend this king of terrors, and, with dismal screeches announce his approach. His never-wearied arm sustains the fatal scythe, which mows down succeeding generations. On one of his wings are painted war, pestilence, and famine, conflagrations, and shipwrecks, with all the other fatal events incident to men, which every moment make them become his prey; and, on his other wing, you see represented young graduates in physic, receiving their degrees in the presence of death, who gives them the doctoral cap, after they have taken the oath, never to prescribe otherwise than according to the present practice.

Though Don Cleofas was fully convinced that what he saw was purely imaginary, and that Asmodeus only shewed him death in this form, to divert himself at his expence, yet he could not look upon the phantom without horror. However, he took courage, and said to the demon, This griesly spectre will not, I am persuaded, pass through Madrid, without leaving behind him some tokens of his being there. That you may be assured of, replied the demon; he comes not here for parade only. You may, if you please, be witness to what he is about to execute. With all my heart, replied the other, let us go and observe his progress, and what unhappy families are to fall his victims. What tears will he cause to be shed! No doubt he will, answered Asmodeus; but a great many of them will be crocadile's tears;[24] for death, all-terrible as he is, occasions, upon the whole as much joy as sorrow.

Our two observers immediately set out, to accompany death in his progress; who directly entered into the house of a tradesman, that was extremely ill in his bed. He touched him with the mortal scythe, and the man immediately expired, in the midst of his family, who set up most howling lamentations. There is no grimace here, said Asmodeus. This man was tenderly beloved by his wife and children, and, besides, now that he is gone, they know not how to subsist; so that their grief is undoubtedly sincere.

But it is not the same in regard to what passes in this other house, where you see death stretching his withering hand over that old man who has been bed-ridden for some time.[25] He is a counsellor, who has always lived single, and has not allowed himself the necessaries of life, in order to heap up wealth, which he leaves to his three nephews, who gathered about him as soon as they heard he drew near to his end. They affected the deepest affliction, and acted their parts to admiration; but now they take off the mask, and begin to play the part of heirs in good earnest, after having whimpered in the character of tender relations. They begin to rummage every where, and will find vast store of gold and silver. One of the heirs has been just now saying to the other, What a blessing it is for poor nephews to have miserly uncles, who forego all the enjoyments of life, only to procure it for their representatives. A pretty funeral oration this, says Cleofas. Oh! replies the demon, I can tell you, that most fathers who are rich, and live long, may expect the same elogium from their own children.

While these young gentlemen, in the height of joy, are searching the coffers of the deceased, their late much honoured uncle, death has winged his way to that grand hotel, where lives a young nobleman, who is ill of the small pox. This lord, the most amiable person about court, is just going to be cut off in the flower of his youth, in spite of the famous physician who attends him, or perhaps it may be, because that very physician does attend him.

Observe how rapid the operations of death go on. Already has he cut the thread of that young lord's destiny, and is now preparing for another exploit. You see he takes his stand on the top of a convent, descends into one of the cells, and encountering a pious ecclesiastic, puts an end to a life of forty years penance and mortification. But though death, in all his terrors, does not frighten this blameless priest, it is far otherwise in regard to that great house there, which he will fill with dread and horror; for he is now just on the point of grappling with a rich licentiate, lately promoted to the see of Albarazin. This prelate thinks of nothing but of preparations to enter upon his diocese, with all the pomp and magnificence, now a days usual with the bishops of the church. Death is the farthest from his thoughts, though this moment he will set out for the other world, and with as few attendants as the holy recluse, nor am I sure that he will be received as favourably.

Merciful God, cries Zambullo, he goes into the palace of the king: how I tremble lest a touch of that tremendous scythe, should throw all Spain into unspeakable consternation. You have reason to be afraid, said Asmodeus, for death knows no distinction between sceptered monarchs and the lowest of their subjects. But, for this time, you may be easy; he does not yet visit the king, but one of his courtiers, one of those great lords, whose only business it is to attend the levee, and pay their court; and you know these are not the men of the nation the most difficult to be replaced.

But as far as I can perceive, said Cleofas, he is not satisfied with having taken off this courtier, for he makes a stop yet, at the palace, over the apartments of the queen. So he does, answered Asmodeus, and for a very good purpose; he is calling to him a good for nothing woman, whose delight was to sow the seeds of division in the court of the queen, and is fallen ill merely out of chagrin to see two ladies, between whom she had occasioned a difference, again heartily reconciled to each other.

Don't you hear terrible shrieks? continued the demon. This merciless destroyer has just been in that great house upon the left hand, which is now the scene of as mournful a catastrophe, as any we see upon this great theatre of the world. Fix your eyes there on that deplorable spectacle. I do perceive, says Cleofas, a lady, who tears her hair, and is struggling in the arms of her women: why is she so miserably afflicted? Look into the apartment over against her, replied Asmodeus, and there you will find the cause. You observe a young gentleman, stretched dead upon that magnificent bed; he was her husband, and she is in despair for the loss of him. The story is moving, and deserves to be recorded. I have a great mind to tell it you.

You will do me an infinite pleasure, said Leandro Perez; for though I laugh at the ridiculous, I feel for the distressed. The story is somewhat long, said Asmodeus, but too interesting, to tire you. Besides, I own to you that, devil as I am, I am quite wearied in accompanying death in all his ravages: let us leave him to himself to look out for his prey. I am entirely of your mind, replied Zambullo, and would rather hear the recital of the story you mention to me, than see the whole race of Adam perish one after the other.[26]

CHAPTER II.

The Power of Friendship.

A NOVEL.

A young gentleman of Toledo, attended only by his valet de chambre, was making his way, in all haste, from the place of his nativity, to avoid the consequences of a tragical adventure; when being about two leagues from the town of Valencia, at the entrance of a wood, he met with a lady, who was alighting from her coach in great seeming confusion. She had no veil over her most beautiful face, and this charming creature appeared so much in distress, that the gentleman, imagining she might stand in need of assistance, offered her the protection of his sword.

Generous stranger, replied the lady, I will not refuse the offer you tender me of your assistance. Perhaps heaven has sent you here to avert the misfortune that threatens me. Two cavaliers have made an appointment to meet one another in this wood, and I expect to see them come every minute. They are to fight a duel, and therefore I beg you come and assist me to part them. As she said this, she advanced farther into the wood; and the Toledan, leaving his horse with his servant, followed her.

Scarce had they gone a hundred yards, but they heard the clashing of swords, and perceived among the trees, two men furiously engaging one another. The Toledan ran up immediately, to part them; which having accomplished by entreaties, and other means, he asked them the ground of their quarrel.

Gallant stranger, said one of them, my name is Don Fadrique de Mendoza, and the name of my adversary is Don Alvaro Ponza; we are both in love with Donna Theodora, the lady whom you see. She has paid no regard to our sighs, and, whatever proofs we have given of our passion, the cruel fair one has never given us any encouragement. As for me, I am determined still to continue her slave, notwithstanding her indifference; but my rival, instead of doing the same, has thought fit to send me a challenge.

It is true, interrupted Don Alvaro, I have taken this method, as I believed that, if I had no rival, Donna Theodora might favour my pretensions; and upon this account I seek the life of Don Fadrique, to get rid of a man who is the bar to my happiness.

Signior cavalier, said the Toledan, I do not approve your having recourse to arms, as it must injure Donna Theodora; it will be immediately known over all the kingdom of Valencia, that you fought a duel upon her account; and the honour of your mistress ought to be dearer to you, than your own quiet or even your lives. Besides, what advantage can the vanquisher hope to reap from his victory? Does either of you imagine, that after having exposed the reputation of the lady, she will afterwards look with a more favourable eye upon you, on that account? What an infatuation is this![1] Take my advice, and let each of you get a victory over himself, which will be more worthy the honour of the names you bear. Get the better of the fury that transports you,[2] and engage yourselves by an oath to acquiesce in that method of accommodation which I shall propose. Your quarrel may be easily made up without shedding of blood.

How! cries Don Alvaro, after what manner can that be effected? This lady, replied the Toledan, must declare her choice of Don Fadrique or of you; and the discarded lover, instead of arming against his rival, must decamp, and leave the coast clear.[3] I agree, said Don Alvaro, and swear by every thing that is sacred, I will faithfully perform the conditions. Let Donna Theodora determine our pretensions; let her, if she so pleases, prefer my rival to me; that preference will be less terrible than the racking uncertainty I now labour under.[4] And I, said Don Fadrique, likewise take heaven to witness. If the divine object, whom I adore, declares against me, I will that instant withdraw from the sight of her charms, and, if I cannot remove her from my thoughts, I will at least never see her more.

Then the Toledan, turning towards Theodora, said, Now, Madam, it is your turn to speak. You can, with one word, disarm these two rivals, and have nothing to do but name him whose constancy you incline to recompence. Signior cavalier, said the lady, I beg you would find out some other expedient to make up their difference. Why should I be made the sacrifice? Doubtless I esteem both Don Fadrique and Don Alvaro, but have no passion for either of them; and it would be an injustice in me to prevent a stain upon my reputation at the expence of giving any of them hopes of what my heart tells me neither of them can expect.

Come, Madam, said the Toledan, this affectation is unseasonable; it is necessary you should declare in favour of one of them. Though these two gentlemen are equally handsome in their persons, yet I am fully convinced you have a tendre for one rather than the other, and I build this confidence on the mortal fright you was in when I met you.

You judge of that wrong, replied Theodora. The death of either of these gentlemen would, no doubt, greatly affect me, and I should never cease reproaching myself, though I was the innocent cause. But when you saw me so much alarmed, the fright I was in proceeded from the danger that threatned my own reputation.

Don Alvaro, who was naturally impetuous,[5] upon this lost all patience. This is too much, said he, fiercely; since the lady will not terminate the quarrel amicably, our swords must. So saying, he put himself again in a posture to attack Don Fadrique, who likewise prepared for his defence.

Upon this Theodora, more frightened at seeing them prepare to fight, than determined by any particular affection, called out with great emotion, Hold, gentlemen, I will satisfy you: since there is no other way of deciding a difference that so much concerns my honour I declare that I give the preference to Don Fadrique de Mendoza.

As soon as she had pronounced these words, Don Alvaro, without uttering one syllable, ran to untie his horse, and casting looks full of fury upon his rival and his mistress, immediately disappeared. The happy Mendoza, on the contrary, was overwhelmed with joy; sometimes he was on his knees before Theodora, and sometimes embracing the Toledan; nor could he find words sufficient to express his gratitude to both.[6]

Mean while the lady, who, since the departure of Alvaro, was recovered from her fright, began to reflect, with great uneasiness, that she had engaged herself to suffer the addresses of a lover, whose merit though she greatly esteemed, yet her heart was no ways prepossessed in his favour.

Signior Don Fadrique, said she to him, I hope you will not abuse the preference I have given to you; you owe it to the necessity I was under of deciding between you and Don Alvaro; not but that I have always had a greater regard for you than for him, and am very sensible he don't possess your good qualities. I must do you the justice to own, that you are the most accomplished cavalier in all Valencia; and will farther own, that the addresses of such a man may flatter the vanity of any woman; yet how much so ever it may redound to my honour being courted by you, I must tell you plainly, it is at present so indifferent to me, that you may with reason complain of your fate in loving me so tenderly as you seem to do. I would not, however, have you despair of one time gaining my heart. My indifference, perhaps, is owing to the grief I yet feel for the loss I sustained, about a year ago of my husband, Don Andreas de Cisuentes. Though we lived but a short while together, and he was old when my parents, dazzled with his great riches, obliged me to give him my hand, I was nevertheless greatly afflicted at his death, and to this day regret him every hour.

And indeed, continued the lady, I have all the reason in the world to respect his memory. He was far from being one of these peevish and jealous old dotards, who not imagining it possible that a young wife can put up with their infirmities, are perpetually watching and brooding over them; or have every step of their conduct pryed into by old duennas, the ministers of their tyranny. On the contrary, he had such a confidence in my virtue, as is hardly to be met with in a young husband, who knows himself to be beloved; and his complaisance was without bounds. I dare say, the only study of his life was to anticipate me in all my wishes.[7] Such was my late husband, Don Andreas de Cisuentes.

Don Fadrique on His Knees before Donna Theodora. (Sterling Library, Yale University.)

You may therefore judge yourself, Mendoza, whether one can easily forget so amiable a character. Indeed he is ever present to my thoughts; and, no doubt, that circumstance greatly contributes to render me insensible to whatever pains may be taken to win my affections.

Don Fadrique could not help, here, interrupting Theodora. Ah, Madam! cried he, what joy have I in hearing from your own mouth, that it is not an aversion to my person has hitherto made you insensible to my sighs; and I do not despair but you may one day yield yourself to the constancy of my love. It will not be my fault, replied she, if that does not happen, as I allow you to visit me, and sometimes talk to me on the subject of love. Endeavour to inspire me with favourable sentiments for you: do what you can to instil a passion in my breast,[8] and whenever you succeed in gaining my heart, I will not conceal it from you. But if, notwithstanding all you can do, you should not succeed, remember, Mendoza, you will have no just reason to reproach me.

To this Mendoza would have answered, but was prevented; for Donna Theodora taking the Toledan by the hand, turned about towards her coach. He went and disengaged his horse from a tree, to which he had been tied, and, leading him by the bridle, followed the lady, who got into her coach in as much agitation of mind as she had alighted from it, though from a very different cause. Don Fadrique and the Toledan escorted her on horseback to the gates of Valencia, where they parted: the lady went to her own house, and Mendoza carried the Toledan along with him.

Don Fadrique made him repose himself, and entertained him with a handsome collation; after which he asked him particularly what brought him to Valencia, and if he intended making any long stay. I shall be here as short a time as possible, replied the other. I wait only for an opportunity to get to sea, and intend to embark in the first vessel that sails from the coasts of Spain; for I am in no manner solicitous what corner of the world it be, provided I finish the course of a wretched life, far from these fatal shores.

What is it you say? answered Don Fadrique with astonishment. What can make you disgusted with your native country, and hate that which all men so naturally love? After what has happened to me, replied the Toledan, my country is become hateful to me, and the height of my wishes is to leave it for ever. Ah! Signior cavalier, said Mendoza full of tenderness, how impatient am I to know your misfortunes: if I cannot heal your grief, I can, at least, share it with you. Your appearance has already prepossessed me in your favour; your deportment charms me, and I feel somehow or other, that I am deeply interested in your destiny.

Signior Don Fadrique, replied the Toledan, this is the greatest balm I could receive to my wounds;[9] and, to shew myself in some measure sensible of your goodness, I can tell you in my turn, that during the little time I saw you with Alvaro Ponza, I found myself biassed in your favour. That instantaneous moment of affection, which I never before felt for any one, had such an effect that I was in pain lest Theodora should have given the preference to your rival, and felt a sudden flow of joy[10] when I found she determined in your favour. You have since so heightened that first impulse of friendship, that, instead of having any reserve, I long to unbosom myself to you, and have a sensible pleasure in imparting to you the secrets of my soul. Listen then to the history of my misfortunes.

Toledo is the place of my birth, and my name Don Juan de Zarates. In my infancy I lost my parents; so that I was early in possession of an estate of four thousand ducats a year, which they left me. As I was my own master, and looked upon my fortune as sufficient not to oblige me to regard fortune in the choice of a wife,[11] I married a girl exquisitely beautiful, without minding the little she brought me, or the inequality of our conditions. On the contrary, I rejoiced in my own good fortune, and, the better to relish the enjoyment of one I loved so much, a few days after my marriage, I carried her down to a country house I have a few miles from Toledo.

Here we lived in perfect happiness and union, when the Duke of Naxera, whose castle is in my neighbourhood, one day as he was hunting, came to refresh himself at my house, and seeing my wife fell in love with her; at least I believed so; and what confirmed me in my suspicion, he courted my friendship with great eagerness, though before he had treated me with neglect. I was always of the party with him when he hunted, he sent me several presents, and he made me frequent offers of his service and friendship.

At this discovery I was greatly alarmed, and once resolved to carry my wife back to Toledo, which thought heaven certainly inspired me with; for had I deprived the duke of all opportunity of seeing her, I should have avoided the misfortunes that have since befallen me; but the confidence I had in her virtue banished all apprehensions. I looked upon it as impossible, that a woman I had married without any fortune, and whom I had raised from obscurity, could be so ungrateful as to forget my generosity; but to my sorrow I was mistaken. Vanity and ambition, the ruling passions of the sex, shone remarkably in her.[12]

As soon as the duke found means to impart to her his passion, she plumed herself in so important a conquest. The addresses of a man who was called *Your Grace* enflamed her pride, and filled her head with strange fancies. From that time she thought more of herself and less of me. What I had done for her, instead of waking her gratitude, made me fall into contempt with her. She looked upon me as one unworthy to possess a woman of her beauty, and made no doubt but if the noble duke had seen her before she was married, he would have made her his dutchess. Full of these fantastical notions, and seduced by the presents that soothed her vanity, she abandoned herself to his desires.

They exchanged many billet-doux with one another, without my having the least suspicion of their correspondence; but at last I was unhappy enough to have my eyes opened. One day I returned from hunting sooner than usual, and entered into the apartment of my wife, who did not expect me. She had just received a billet from the duke, and was preparing to give an answer. She could not conceal her confusion at my appearance. I was shocked at this, and seeing pen, ink, and paper upon the table, suspected she had betrayed me. I urged her to shew me what she had been writing, but she excused it; so that I was obliged to use force to satisfy my jealous curiosity. In spite of her resistance, I pulled from her bosom a letter, which contained as follows:

Must I languish for ever in expectation of a second interview? How cruel you are, after giving me the most flattering hopes, so long to retard their completion! Don Juan is every day engaged in hunting, or goes to Toledo, and ought we to let slip such precious opportunities? Think on the violent flame that consumes me, and take pity on me, Madam. Consider, that if it is the highest pleasure to obtain the hopes of what one desires, it is the cruellest torture to wait long for the enjoyment.

I could not read this letter without being transported into fury. I laid my hand upon my sword; and in the beginning of my rage intended to have deprived the perfidious wretch[13] of life, who had robbed me of my honour. But reflecting that this was revenging myself by halves, and that my resentment required another victim, I suppressed my fury, and even used dissimulation. I spoke to my wife with all the calmness I possibly could. Madam, said I, you was in the wrong to listen to the duke; the splendor of his quality should not have dazzled you, but I know young people are apt to be seduced by such things; and I am willing to believe that is all your crime, and that you have not quite betrayed my honour. On that account, therefore, I pardon your indiscretion, provided that you return to your duty, and for the future shew, by your behaviour, you are sensible of my tenderness, and do every thing in your power to deserve it. After having spoke to her in this manner, I went out of her appartment, both to give her an opportunity to recover from the confusion she was in, and to retire myself, in order to quiet my thoughts after the passion this discovery had put me in.[14] Though I could not recover the peace of my mind, I affected, at least, to do so for two days; and on the third, pretending I had some important business at Toledo, I told my wife I was obliged to be gone for some time, and begged her in the mean time to be careful of her honour during my absence.

I set out; but instead of continuing my journey to Toledo, came back privately in the twilight, and hid myself in the apartment of a faithful servant, from which I could see every one that came into the house. I made no doubt but the duke was informed of my absence, and that he would not fail to make use of so favourable an opportunity; so that I thought of catching them together, and glutting my vengeance on both.[15]

However, I was disappointed in my expectations. It was so far from appearing as if they had a mind to admit a gallant, that I observed they were extremely careful to lock the doors, and secure the house: and after being there three days and no duke appearing, nor any of his people, I was persuaded my wife had repented of her folly, and had in earnest broke off all correspondence with her gallant.

Fully persuaded of this, I lost all desire of revenge, and giving way to the transports of affection which my anger had stifled, I ran to my wife's apartment. I embraced her tenderly. My dear, said I, I here make you a tender back again of my esteem and affection. I was not at Toledo, I only pretended it to try your sincerity; and you ought to pardon this in a husband, whose jealousy, you know, was not altogether without foundation. I was afraid that your mind, carried away by illusionary dreams of grandeur, could not have been recovered; but thanks to heaven you are sensible of your error, and I hope, for the future, nothing will be able to disturb or interrupt our mutual union.

My wife appeared sensibly touched at these words, and dropped some tears. Wretch that I am, cried she, for having given you reason to suspect my fidelity. In vain do I detest myself for having so justly provoked your indignation. In vain have my eyes, for these two days, shed floods of tears. My grief, my repentance, my remorse are useless, never shall I regain your confidence. Madam I do here restore it to you, said I, quite moved at the grief she seemed to be in; as you so thoroughly repent, I promise you I will never think of what is past.

And indeed I was sincere.[16] From that moment I had the same regard for her I had ever had, and again tasted those pleasures which had been so cruelly interrupted. The relish of them was even heightened; for my wife, as if she had intended to efface from my memory all remembrance of her past misconduct, was more assiduous in her endeavours to please me than she had ever been. I found her endearments more lively and passionate, and was almost glad that that had happened which had occasioned me so much disquiet.

I chanced to fall sick; and tho' my distemper was not dangerous, it is hardly to be conceived how much my wife appeared alarmed. All day she was at my bed-side, and at night, for I lay in a separate apartment, she never missed coming two or three times to inform herself how I did. In a word, she seemed intent on nothing else but to be beforehand in getting every thing she thought I might stand in need of.[17] One would have believed her life had been locked up in mine. As for me I was so touched with all the marks of affection she shewed me, that I thought I could never sufficiently express my sense of them. Notwithstanding, Signior Mendoza, they were not so sincere as I imagined.

One night, when I was somewhat recovered, my valet de chambre waked me: Signior, said he to me in great agitation, I beg your pardon for disturbing your rest, but my duty will not allow me to conceal from you what is now doing in the house. The duke of Naxera is at this moment with my lady.

I was so thunderstruck at this piece of intelligence, that for some time I looked at my servant, without being able to answer him. The more I reflected on what he told me, the more I thought it impossible. No, Fabio, cried I, it cannot be; my wife cannot be guilty of such treachery. You are not sure of what you say. Sir, said he, would to God I could doubt of it, but I am not deceived by false appearances. Since you have been ill, I have had a suspicion that every night they let in the duke into my lady's apartments; and I hid myself to be convinced of the truth, and am but too well persuaded my suspicions are just.

Upon this I got up, quite furious with rage: I put on my night-gown, and with my sword in my hand went directly to her apartment, attended by Fabio, who carried a light. At the noise we made in entering the apartment, the duke, who was sitting upon the bed, got up, and taking a pistol he had on his belt, came up and discharged it at me; but he was in so much agitation and confusion that he missed me, and I immediately advanced upon him and plunged my sword into his heart. Then I came up to my wife, who was more dead than alive: And you, said I, infamous wretch, receive the reward of your baseness: so saying, I stabbed her to the heart with my sword yet smoking with the blood of her lover.

Signior Don Fadrique, continued Zarates, I blame the transport of my fury: I own I might have punished a faithless woman without taking away her life; but after all, what man is able to govern himself on such occasions? Think of this base woman's attending me so carefully in my sickness; think of all the demonstrations of affection, the circumstances and aggravations of her perfidy, and then judge whether a husband ought not to be pardoned for her death, when so justly provoked to the transports of rage and fury.

To make an end of this tragical story; after having satiated my revenge, I put on my cloaths in great haste, judging I had no time to lose, as the relations of the duke would search for me all over Spain; and as the interests of my family could not be put in competition with theirs, so I could have no security but in a foreign country. For which reason, taking two of the best horses, and all the money and jewels I had, I went from my house before break of day, attended by my servant, who had given me such proofs of his fidelity. I took the road to Valencia, designing to go on board the first ship that sailed for Italy. As I passed by the wood to-day where you was, I met Donna Theodora, who begged me to follow her, and assist to part you and Don Alvaro.

After the Toledan had done speaking, Don Fadrique addressed himself to him: Signior Don Juan, said he, you have taken a just vengeance on the duke of Naxera; and give yourself no pain about what searches his relations may make after you. If you please to accept of my house, it is at your service, 'till you find an opportunity of passing into Italy. The governor of Valencia is my uncle. You will be safer here than any where else, and will be with a man who from henceforth will be proud to join himself with you in the strictest ties of friendship. Zarates answered Mendoza in terms full of gratitude, and accepted the asylum he offered him.

Admire the power of sympathy, Signior Cleofas, continued the demon. These two young gentlemen conceived an affection for one another, that in a few days grew into a friendship equal to that of Pylades and Orestes *. Their merit was in all respects equal, and such a sympathy was in their tempers, that what was agreeable to Don Fadrique was surely so to Don Juan. They made, as it were but one individual, and were modelled by nature to have a friendship for each other. Don Fadrique in particular was charmed with the behaviour of his friend, and was, on every occasion, speaking extravagantly in his praise to his mistress Donna Theodora.

They very often together visited that lady, who still continued to hear with indifference the addresses of Mendoza. This greatly mortified him, and he often complained to his friend, who, to comfort him, would say, even the most insensible of the sex are some time or other got the better of.[18] Lovers must have patience, and wait for the critical minute. Don't be discouraged, said he, for sooner or later your mistress, depend upon it, will reward your constancy. Such discourses of his friend, though founded on experience, did not satisfy the mind of the anxious Mendoza, who despaired of ever making himself agreeable in the eyes of the widow of Cisuentes. The apprehension of this threw him into a languishing state of health, which drew pity from his friend Don Juan; but Don Juan in a little time was more to be pitied himself.

However much reason our Toledan might have to be thoroughly disgusted with all

---

* Their friendship is celebrated by all antiquity; insomuch that Cicero, as a signal mark of honour to these two friends, distinguishes the height of friendship by the name of *Pyladean friendship*.[19] Orestes, as has been said, slew his mother Clytemnestra, and her adulterer Ægisthus, for the murder of his father. He is a principal character in those noble tragedies of *Sophocles* and *Euripides*, whose plans and subjects are founded on the fates of the house of Agamemnon, and were represented in all the splendor and magnificence of the Athenian theatre. He makes his appearance likewise, in his turn, upon our stage.[20]

woman-kind, after the monstrous perfidy of his wife, he could not, notwithstanding, help falling in love with Theodora. However, far from indulging a passion so highly injurious[21] to his friend, he, on the contrary, thought of nothing but how to stifle it; and being convinced he could effect that no how but by flying from the object that gave it birth, he resolved to see Theodora no more. So that when Mendoza desired him to go along with him, he always found some pretence to excuse himself.

On the other hand, Don Fadrique never went once to see his mistress, that she did not ask him why Don Juan did not come along with him. One time she put this question to him, he answered with a smile, my friend has his reasons. Reasons! replied Theodora, what reason can he have to avoid me? Madam, answered Mendoza, this very day, when I desired him to come along with me, and shewed some surprize at his refusing my request, he imparted to me a secret, which I must communicate to you for his excuse: he told me his heart was engaged with a lady, and as his stay here was to be very short, he had no time to lose.[22]

At this Theodora reddened, and said, she was not at all satisfied with that excuse. How deeply soever, said she, a man may be in love, he ought not to forsake his friends. Though Don Fadrique observed her to change colour, yet he imputed it only to her vanity, and that she was piqued to find herself neglected; but he was mistaken. A passion much stronger than vanity was the occasion of her sudden emotion; though being apprehensive he should guess at the true cause, she immediately changed the subject of their conversation, and put on such an air of chearfulness, as would have deceived Don Fadrique, had he even at first guessed the true reason.

As soon as she was alone, her reflections became serious, and crouded upon her.[23] She then felt all the power of that passion she had conceived for Don Juan de Zarates, and believing her love had met with another sort of return than it really had, she sighed bitterly.[24] Cruel and unjust deity, cried she, why dost thou thus sport with unhappy mortals? Don Fadrique loves me even to adoration, but I feel no sentiments of affection towards him:[25] I, on the other hand, love Don Juan to distraction, while his heart is the captive of another. Ah! Don Fadrique, reproach me not for my coldness to you, your friend has sufficiently revenged your quarrel.

As she spoke these words, seized with grief and jealousy, she could not help shedding tears; but hope, ever at hand to assist anxious lovers, relieved her by more pleasant prospects. That representing to her imagination her rival not so dangerous as she had at first thought her; that Don Juan was, perhaps, less the captive of her charms, than inveigled by her arts and coquetry; and that in time she should be able to break such slender engagements. But, in order to judge herself how matters were, she was determined to have a private conversation with Zarates. She sent him word she wanted to speak with him; upon which he immediately waited upon her, and as they were alone she began in this manner.

I never could have imagined, said she, that love could have made a polite gentleman forget the respect that is due to ladies; yet I find Don Juan, since he has been in love, comes no more to see me; for which I think I have reason to complain, though I am willing to believe it is not from your own inclinations; I suppose your mistress has laid her commands upon you that you see me no more. Come, Don Juan, own the truth, and I forgive you. I well know, that a man in love is not his own master, and that he must be obedient to the will of his mistress.

Madam, replied Zarates, I own my conduct is such as may justly surprise you; but for God's sake, Madam, don't oblige me to come to an explanation. Whatever the reason be, replied Theodora with the utmost emotion, I insist upon it you tell me. Well, Madam, replied Don Juan, since you insist upon it, there is no avoiding it; but then I expect you will not be offended, if I discover to you more, perhaps, than you desire to know.

Don Fadrique, continued he, has already acquainted you with the affair that obliged me to leave Castile. When I went from Toledo, my heart was so full of resentment against all women, that I thought myself secure from ever again falling into their snares.[26] In this temper of mind I was, when, approaching towards Valencia, I met you, and, perhaps what had never before happened to any one, I stood the first sight of you with indifference. I even saw you again without losing my liberty; but, alas! Madam, how dearly have I since paid for these days of peace! You are at last become the conqueror. Your beauty, your wit, your charms have had a full triumph. In one word, I feel for you all that passion which even you are capable of inspiring.

This, Madam, is what has banished me from your presence. The lady you was told I was in love with is an imaginary one: it was a feigned story I told Don Fadrique, to prevent any suspicion he might have on account of my constantly declining to come and see you.

This eclaircissement[27] which Donna Theodora no ways expected, caused in her such a sudden emotion of joy, that she could not conceal it; though indeed she was at no pains to conceal it, and instead of looks of anger and disdain, she cast her eyes upon the Toledan, full of tenderness and affection: Don Juan, said she, you have made me the confidante of your secrets; listen to me, and I will in the same manner open my heart to you.

No ways touched[28] with the passion of Alvaro Ponza, and not much more with the addresses of Mendoza, I led a quiet and happy life, till fortune made you pass by that wood where we first met. Though I was then in the greatest agitation of mind, I could not help taking particular notice of the politeness of your behaviour when you offered me your assistance; and the means you used to disengage two furious rivals from killing one another, gave me a high opinion, both of your prudence and valour. Indeed the expedient you proposed was no ways agreeable to myself, for it was a great violence to my inclinations, to be obliged to make choice either of one or the other; though, to speak freely, I believe even at that time, you was a good deal the occasion of my then reluctance; for though my words declared (when I was obliged to make such declaration) for Don Fadrique, my heart declared for the unknown stranger. Since that time, which I now ought to account the happiest period of my life, after the declaration you have made me, your merit has daily increased my love and esteem.

You see I make no mystery of my inclination to you; I tell it you with the same frankness that I told your friend I did not love him. A woman who has the misfortune to love a man, who has not, or must not have the same affection for her, ought to keep her sentiments secret, and be revenged upon herself for her weakness, by an eternal silence; but

I apprehend one may, consistent with the strictest rules of honour, own an innocent passion for a man, whose views are no otherwise than honourable. Yes, Don Juan, that you love me is the highest joy I can have; for which I make no scruple to return thanks to heaven, who, doubtless, has destined us for one another.

After the lady had expressed herself in this manner,[29] she stopped to give Zarates an opportunity of speaking, and to testify those marks of joy and gratitude, with which she made no doubt she had inspired him: but, instead of shewing transports of joy at what he had just heard, he remained sorrowful and pensive.

What is the meaning of this, Don Juan? said she. What! after having made a discovery to you, which another might have received with transport, even disregarding the delicacy and punctilios which my sex ought to preserve; after disclosing to you the secret passion of my soul: instead of receiving such a declaration with transport, do you appear cold? I even perceive that grief and anguish stand fixed in your eyes. Ah! Don Juan, how ill my favours are requited![30]

And what other effect, Madam, said Zarates sorrowfully, what other effect do you think they can have upon a heart like mine? The more love you shew to me, alas! the more miserable I am. You know, Madam, what Mendoza has done for me. You know the strict union of friendship that binds us. Can I, Madam, resolve to procure my own happiness at the expence of what is most dear to him? Your sentiments of friendship are too delicate, replied Theodora.[31] I can give you my hand without his being able to reproach me, and you may receive it without breach of friendship. I own, indeed, that the thoughts of a friend in affliction must give you disquiet: but, Don Juan, is that to be put in the balance with the smiling destiny that attends you?

Yes, Madam, said he with a resolute air. Such a friend as Don Fadrique has more power over me than you imagine. If you knew or could conceive all the tenderness, all the warmth of our friendship, you would pity me from your soul. Mendoza has concealed nothing from me, and has interested himself in every thing that concerns me. The least trifle that respects me does not escape the assiduous attention of his friendship. In a word, I share his soul with you.

Ah, Madam, continued he, had I known these favourable sentiments you honour me with, before I had entered into the ties of so strict a friendship, I then might have availed myself of them. Regarding nothing else but my own good fortune in being so happy as to please you, I should have then treated Mendoza as a rival. My heart then would have been upon its guard against those marks of affection he has shewn me. I would not have made him the same returns of mutual friendship, nor allowed myself to have lain under these obligations to him I do now. But now, Madam, it is too late. I have accepted of all the instances of friendship it was in his power to shew me: I have conceived an affection and friendship for him: Both gratitude and inclination engage me to him, and reduce me to the cruel necessity of renouncing that happiness you now offer me.

At this Donna Theodora, whose eyes flowed with tears, took out her handkerchief to wipe them. This incident shook the constancy of Zarates; he found himself begin to waver, and resolved therefore to break off. Adieu, Madam, said he, while his sighs interrupted his words, adieu! my honour is in danger whilst I stay with you. I cannot stand your tears, they are too many for me. I go from you for ever, to bewail the loss of those charms, which the honour of my friendship demands as a sacrifice. At these words he went away, though all the resolution he could summon up was hardly able to bear him through the conflict.

After he was gone, the lady found herself agitated by a thousand different reflections. She was ashamed at having owned her passion to a man she could not captivate by the power of her charms.[32] But as she had no manner of doubt that he had the same passion for her as she had for him, and that it was only out of regard to his friend that he declined the offer she had made him, her good sense made her, instead of being offended with him, admire the uncommon effects of so generous a friendship. However, as it is impossible for any lady not to be chagrined, when disappointed of what she earnestly wishes for, she determined to go next day into the country, in order to assuage her grief, or more truly to increase it; for love rather grows than declines in the retirement of solitude.

Don Juan, on his part, not finding Mendoza at home, shut himself up in his apartment to give a freer loose to his grief.[33] After having done the part of a man of honour to his friend, he thought he might warrantably be allowed to indulge himself in sighs. Don Fadrique returned very soon, and interrupted him in his solitary musings; and imagining by his looks that something extraordinary was the matter with him, testified so much anxiety on that account, that Zarates, to make him easy, was obliged to tell him he wanted only a little rest. The other retired immediately to leave him to his repose; but as he went out, shewed so much concern, that it awaked afresh the tenderness of his friend. Just heavens! said he to himself, why must the delicate sentiments of the most tender friendship embitter my whole life?

Next day Don Fadrique was not got out of bed, when one of his servants brought him word, that Donna Theodora was set out with all her equipage for her seat at Villareal; and that it was likely she would not soon return. This news did not give him so much uneasiness on account of being deprived of the sight of one he so passionately loved, as that her departure was made a secret of to him. Without knowing the meaning of such a conduct, he gathered from it but very bad omens.

He got up to wait upon his friend, both to talk with him upon this affair, and to learn the state of his health; but as he was just dressed, Don Juan came into his apartment, and said to him, I will make you so far easy as to acquaint you, that to-day I am quite well. This makes me some amends, said Mendoza, for the disagreeable news I have now received. The Toledan immediately asked what that was; and Don Fadrique, after making his servants quit the room, told him, that Donna Theodora had that morning gone into the country, where it was believed she would continue a considerable time. I am astonished at this. Why was it made a secret of from me? What think you of it, Don Juan? don't you think I have reason to be uneasy?

Zarates took great care not to give his friend the least hint of what he himself conjectured upon this occasion;[34] he endeavoured to persuade him, that Theodora might very well go into the country without his having any reason to be alarmed. But Don Fadrique, no ways satisfied with the reasons his friend offered in order to make him easy, interrupted him: All you can alledge, said he, cannot remove the suspicion I harbour in my breast.[35] Doubtless I have done something imprudently to disoblige Theodora; and to punish me she has withdrawn into the country, without so much as vouchsafing to let me know my fault.

But however the case may be, continued he, I will remain no longer in this state of uncertainty. Come, Don Juan, let us go find her. If you take my advice, replied the Toledan, you will take no one with you: such an explanation ought to be without witnesses. Don Juan, replied Fadrique, is to be looked upon as nobody: Theodora knows you are privy to my most secret thoughts; besides, she esteems you so greatly, that far from injuring me on such an occasion, you will be the fittest person to solicit her in my favour.

No, Don Fadrique, replied the other, my presence can be of no use to you: Go alone, I conjure you. My dear Don Juan, replied Mendoza, I will not: I expect this of your friendship. What tyranny is this, replied the Toledan with a very dissatisfied air,[36] why require of my friendship what it ought not to grant?

These words, the meaning of which Fadrique did not comprehend, and the hasty manner they were spoke in, strangely surprised him. He looked upon his friend with eager attention; Don Juan, said he, what means that which I have just now heard? What horrible suspicions are now engendering within my breast? It is too much to put a constraint both upon yourself, and torture me: Speak; say, what occasions this reluctance to see Theodora?

I would willingly have concealed it from you, answered the Toledan; but since you yourself force me to an explanation, I must not dissemble with you. Let us not for the future, my dear Don Fadrique, congratulate one another upon the conformity of our inclinations, alas! they are but too much alike. The arrow that has pierced your heart, has not missed your friend. Donna Theodora——

What! interrupted Mendoza, turning pale, are you then my rival? Ever since I first perceived the growing of my passion, answered Don Juan, I have resisted it: I have constantly avoided the lady. This you know to be true, and have often chid me on that account. If I could not eradicate it from my breast, I have at least been able to triumph over it.

But yesterday the lady sent me word, that she wanted to speak with me, and accordingly I went. She asked me the reason why I seemed as if I industriously shunned the sight of her. I invented excuses, which did not satisfy her; and at last was obliged to tell her the real cause; believing, that after such a declaration, she would approve of the resolution I had taken, to see her no more. But, as my unhappy stars would have it, shall I speak it, Mendoza? Yes, I will tell you; she had conceived a passion for me.

Though Don Juan's friend was a man of the sweetest disposition, and had the greatest command of temper,[37] he fell into a fit of fury at this, and could not help interrupting him. Hold, Don Juan, cried he, sheath rather your sword in my bosom, than kill me by this fatal narration. What! is it not enough to tell me you are my rival, but you must likewise tell me, that you are the beloved object? Just heavens! what a horrible secret you impart to me! You put our friendship to too severe a trial. But why do I say our friendship? That you have given to the winds, after maintaining such a treacherous correspondence as you have now mentioned.

How much have I been mistaken! I took you to my heart,[38] believing you a man of generosity and honour; but find you have proved false, as you have been capable of entertaining a passion so highly injurious to me. This is an unexpected stroke, and quite disconcerts me: I feel it too the more sensibly as it comes from one—Sir, interrupted the Toledan in his turn, you must do me more justice: have but a moment's patience, and you will find I am not to be taxed with breach of friendship. Hear what I have to say, and you will soon repent of having laid to my charge such an infamous imputation.

He then gave him a succinct account[39] of the particulars of what had passed between him and Theodora; the passionate declaration she made him, and the arguments she made use of to engage him to comply with the dictates of his love. He likewise told him in what manner he had answered her importunities; and when he came to touch upon the firmness and resolution he had shewn, in being determined to resist all her enticements, Don Fadrique found his anger quite appeased. In a word, continued Don Juan, friendship got the better of love: I refused myself to Theodora, who shed tears at the disappointment. But, good God, what a struggle did these tears excite in my breast? I cannot now think of it, without trembling at the danger I was in. I began to accuse myself of barbarity, and for some moments, Mendoza, my heart was unfaithful to you. I did not, however, yield to my weakness, but saved myself by a speedy flight from those so dangerous tears. But it is not enough I have escaped this time, I ought to dread what may happen hereafter, and to hasten my departure, that I be no more exposed to the dangerous sight of Theodora. After this, will Don Fadrique yet accuse me of perfidy and ingratitude?

No, answered Mendoza, embracing him; my eyes are opened, and I pronounce you innocent. Forgive the first transports of passion in a lover, who sees himself fallen from all his hopes. Alas! how could I imagine it to be otherwise?[40] or think that Donna Theodora could see you long, and not love you; or be able to resist the charms of your behaviour, the effect of which I myself have experienced? You are a real friend, and I impute my misfortune to my own unhappy destiny; and far from cooling in my friendship,[41] I find the sentiments of affection even stronger in my breast. What! renounce the possession of Donna Theodora on my account? Make so great a sacrifice to our friendship, and I not be duly sensible of it? You had resolution enough to conquer your passion, and shall not I make at least an effort to conquer mine? It is my duty to make a suitable return to such generosity. Yes, Don Juan, obey the dictates of love; give your hand to the widow of Cisuentes; and though my heart should break, yet Mendoza presses you to it.

You press in vain, replied Zarates; though I must confess my inclinations are violently attached to Theodora, I nevertheless prefer your repose to my own happiness. But can her repose be a thing indifferent to you? said Don Fadrique. Let us not deceive ourselves: her inclination to you has decided my fate. Should you even absent yourself from her, and, on my account, lead a wretched life, far distant from the sight of her charms, that would be of no service to my love. As I have never yet made an impression on her heart, I never shall: heaven has reserved that conquest for you. She was in love with you from the first moment she saw you; and her affection for you is a natural passion, nor is it possible she can be happy without you. Receive then her hand, and accomplish her and your happiness. Leave me to the rigour of my cruel destiny; and involve not three persons in misery, when one can be a sacrifice for all.[42]

Asmodeus was here obliged to stop, to hear our student, who said to him, Is it really a fact, that there does exist men of such a finished character? As for me, I see men quarrelling with one another, not for such mistresses as Theodora, but for downright arrant jilts. Do you think a lover can renounce the adorable object of his passion, and reciprocally beloved too, only not to render his friend miserable? I believe there exists no where such characters, excepting in romances, where human nature is represented what it ought to be, rather than what it really is. I agree with you, replied the demon, it is not very common; but at the same time is to be met with, not only in romantic characters, but every where, as often as you find human nature polished to perfection.[43] This is so true, that, since the flood of Noah, besides this instance, I have known some few examples of it. But let us return to our history.

The two friends continued to make each other a mutual sacrifice of their passion; and as the one would not yield in point of generosity to the other, their amorous thoughts were for a few days suspended. They never discoursed of Theodora; they durst not even mention her name. But if friendship triumphed over love within the walls of Valencia, love, on the other hand, as it were to be revenged, tyrannized, with a cruel hand, in another quarter, and made his will be obeyed without resistance.

Donna Theodora was at her seat at Villareal, situated near the sea; where she abandoned herself to the violence of her passion. Night and day she thought of Don Juan, and could not help entertaining some hopes, that, one day or other, he might become her husband; though she had small ground for such hope, after the sentiments of friendship he had declared for Don Fadrique.

One evening, after sun-set, as she was attended by one of her women, taking a walk along the sea-shore, she saw a boat rowing towards land. She imagined, at first, she perceived seven or eight men in it of a very bad aspect; but after having seen them nearer, and considered them more attentively, she was of opinion she had mistaken their countenances, and that they were masks; as indeed they really were people masked, and armed with swords and bayonets.

She was frightened at the sight of them; and drawing no good presage from their preparing to land, she immediately turned about, and went towards the castle. She looked behind her from time to time, and observing they had gained the shore, and were pursuing her, she run with all her might: but as she could not run so well as Atalanta*, and the people in masks were swift and stout fellows, they came up with her, and seized her at the gate of the castle.[44]

Theodora and her woman shrieked most terribly, which, in an instant, brought some of the domestics out of the castle; and they giving the alarm to the rest, all Theodora's servants came running out, armed with clubs and pitchforks. In the mean time, two of

---

* This lady was remarkable for her swiftness, and if she did not like any of her suitors, proposed a match of running, on condition that if they won the race, they should have her, but if they were beat, they must suffer death; by which means she put an end to the passion of a great many of her lovers. However, one Hippomanes undertook her after all, at the instigation of Venus, who gave him three golden apples, which he threw away at a distance, as he found himself worsted in the race; and Atalanta, not being able to resist the temptation of going out of her way, and stopping to gather them, by that means lost the wager.

the strongest among the masks, taking Theodora and her woman in their arms, carried them towards the vessel, in spite of what resistance they could make; while the rest kept the people of the castle in play,[45] who attacked them very fiercely. The fight lasted some time; but the people in masks at last executed their enterprize, and got to the boat, fighting as they retreated. And it was high time for them to retire; for they had not all got on board, when, on the side of Valencia, they perceived four or five people on horseback riding full speed, who seemed as if they intended to rescue the lady. On this the ravishers made such haste to put off to sea, that the intended assistance of the cavaliers came too late.

These gentlemen were Don Fadrique and Don Juan; the first of whom had that day received a letter from a friend, who acquainted him, that he had received certain intelligence, that Alvaro Ponza was in the island of Majorca; that he had fitted out a sloop;[46] and that, with the assistance of twenty desparate fellows, ready to engage in any attempt, he proposed carrying off the widow of Cisuentes, the first time she should be at the castle. Upon receiving this advice, the Toledan and he, with their valets de chambre, had set out immediately from Valencia, to communicate their intelligence to Theodora. They had discovered, at a distance from the shore, a considerable number of people, who seemed as if they were fighting; and, suspecting it might be what they so much dreaded, they put on with all their might,[47] to prevent the attempt of Alvaro. But notwithstanding all their haste, they came only time enough to be witnesses of the rape they wanted to prevent.

In the mean while Alvaro Ponza, glorying in the success of his attempt, carried away his prize, and the boat went off to join a small armed vessel that waited for them out at sea. One can hardly conceive more lively grief and affliction than at that time possessed Don Juan and his friend Mendoza. They uttered a thousand imprecations against Alvaro, and filled the air with piteous but vain complaints. All the servants of Theodora, after their example, likewise poured forth their lamentations. The shore resounded with their cries. Fury, despair, and desolation, were spread around these melancholy mansions.[48] The rape of Helen caused not greater grief and consternation at the court of Sparta.

CHAPTER III.

A fray that happened between a comic and tragic poet.

Here the demon was interrupted. Signior Asmodeus, says our gentleman, though I have the greatest pleasure imaginable in listening to what you say, I cannot get the better of my curiosity, and must beg you will explain to me the meaning of something I have now before my eyes. I see two strange figures of men in their shirts, holding one another by the hair and the ears, and kicking desperately,[1] with a number of people in night-gowns, endeavouring to part them. I beg you will be so good as to let me know the meaning of this. That I will with pleasure, says Asmodeus, as, my only business at present is to satisfy your curiosity.[2]

These two figures you see battling with each other are two poets, one a writer of tragedies, and the other of comedies. They are Frenchmen. The rest of the company, who endeavour to part them, consist of one Fleming, one Italian, and two Germans. They live all in the same place, which is a house of furnished lodgings only for foreigners. The tragic poet having undergone some mortification in his native country, is come to Spain; and the comedian, not being quite satisfied with his success at Paris, has undertaken the same journey, in hopes to better his fortune at Madrid.

The tragedian, though an assuming, insignificant fellow, had procured to himself no small degree of reputation in his own country, in spite of the judicious part of the public. To keep his muse in breath, he exercises her every day, and is eternally composing.[3] This very night, not being able to sleep, he began a new piece, the subject of which is from the Iliad, and in a twinkling finished a scene.[4] As he has, like the rest of the fraternity (though we may reckon it one of his least faults) an insatiable itch of tormenting innocent and well-meaning people with a recital of his works, he immediately got out of bed, and, taking his candle, began to rap with great vehemence at the door of his brother Bard, who, employing his hours much better, at that time indulged himself in profound snoring, and bid defiance to the Muses. However, waking at the noise, he started up and opened the door, when immediately the tragedian, with the air and gestures of a bedlamite, Down, said he, down upon your knees, and worship a genius, whom Melpomene inspires. I am just now brought to bed of twins; of most beautiful couplets.[5] But why do I say I? 'Tis not I, 'tis Apollo himself; they are his legitimate offspring. Were I at Paris, I this moment would go about and rehearse them from house to house; and I only wait the approach of morn, to pay my compliments to our ambassador here. Oh! how he and all the French in Madrid will be charmed with them! However, Sir, before any one should see them, I thought proper to give you the preference.

Sir, says the comedian, with a horrible yawn, I am infinitely honoured with this mark of distinction. The only grievous circumstance is, that you have chose a very improper time. I happened to go to bed very late, and am so overpowered with slumber, that I cannot answer for myself, but that I may fall asleep in the very time you are repeating. Oh! as to that, replies this writer of tragedies, I will take upon me to answer for your vigilance. Fall asleep while I repeat! No, no; were you shrouded in the sepulchre, the scene that I have composed would make your dry bones live.[6] My versification is no farrago of trite sentiments and common-place phrases, supported only by rhime; 'tis the true, the genuine spirit of poetry, which searches the heart and tries the reins. I am none of those little poetasters, whose flimsy productions go off the scene, like spectres, and may be sent to the cape of Good-Hope to divert the Hottentots. My productions, worthy to be consecrated with my statue in the Palatine library,[7] bring crouded audiences even after the thirtieth night. But come, continues this mirror of modesty, let us come to the lines themselves, of which, brother, I here offer you the first-fruits.

This is my tragedy. The death of Patroclus. Scene the first. Enter Briseis, and other captives of Achilles. They tear their hair, and beat their breasts, and are not even able to support themselves. This, you are to observe, is the effect of their grief for the death of Patroclus. Overcome by despair, they all at once, as if their heels were tripped up,[8] fall down upon the stage. This you'll perhaps say, is somewhat bold, but that is the very thing I aim at. Let your little geniuses, a Gad's name, confine themselves within the narrow bounds of rule and imitation.[9] With all my heart; it may be, perhaps, well judged in them to be so chaste and reserved; but for me, I say that I love to strike out something new, and hold it a maxim, that to melt and ravish the passions of an audience, images ought to be represented such as no man ever dreamt of, or could any ways expect. Well, then, the captives are on the ground: Phœnix, the governor of Achilles is with them, who raises them up, not at once, but one after the other, and then begins:

> Priam, with Hector and his town must fall;
> His comrade dear Achilles will revenge;
> Atrides fierce, Camelus the divine,
> The godlike Nestor, with Eumelus brave,
> Leontes dextrous at the sword and spear,
> Ulysses sly, and Diomedes strong.
> For combat fierce, Achilles does prepare,
> And towards Troy his steeds immortal drives,
> With speed more rapid than his fiery rage,
> Speed scarce distinguished by the following eye.
> Advance, quoth he, my Xanthus dear, and thou,
> Beloved Balius; when with carnage tired,
> And when the Trojans to their walls retire,
> Regain our camp, and bring me back secure.
> Then Xanthus, bowing low, to him reply'd;
> Our duty, great Achilles, we will do;
> And your impatience shall be satisfy'd;
> But soon the moment of your death will come,
> Thus beef-ey'd Juno taught the horse to speak.
> And then the hero's chariot seem'd to fly.
> The Greeks beheld him and with cries of joy
> At once the lofty walls of Ilion rung.
> The prince, with his Vulcanian arms adorned,
> Appear'd more glittering than the morning star,
> Or like the sun beginning his career
> When he gets up to light the nether world;
> Or shining like the fire which peasants make
> In a dark night upon the mountain's top.

But I stop to give you time to breathe; should I repeat the whole scene, the beauties of the versification, the sublimity of sentiment, and the brilliancy of expression would be too much for you. You might be in danger of being choaked. Observe but the propriety of that simile, *Or shining like the fire which peasants make*, &c. Every one, indeed, cannot see the beauty of it; but you, who have true taste and delicacy, I am sure cannot miss being charmed with it. Oh! to be sure, Sir, replies the other, screwing up his face into a satyrical grin,[10] nothing was ever wrote so fine; and I persuade myself that in the course of the work, you will not fail to mention the circumstance of Thetis flapping away the Trojan flies from the body of Patroclus. Pray, good Sir, don't you be witty upon that circumstance, replies the tragedian; and to let you into a secret, that incident is, perhaps, the most proper of any in the whole piece, to give one, like me, an opportunity of making pompous verses. I shall not neglect to put the finishing hand to it,[11] I assure you, Sir. Take my word for it, added he, all my works are true sterling; being obliged to stop at the end of every line, when I repeat, to receive the applause of the auditors. I remember I read a tragedy in a house at Paris, where every day all the most famous wits meet at dinner, and where I assure you, without vanity, I do not pass for a dunce. The celebrated countess of Vieille-Brune happened to be there. Her taste is inexpressibly pure and delicate, and I am her favourite poet. Her cheeks were bedewed with tears, from the very first scene. In the second act she called for another handkerchief: during the third act she did nothing but sob and sigh; and in the fourth was taken with a fit of the cholic; but at the catastrophe I was afraid she actually would have expired with the hero of my tragedy.

The comedian had hitherto kept the muscles of his countenance in a proper decorum,[12] but could hold no longer, and bursting into a fit of laughter, Ah! well do I know that lady, says he; that is her very character; she cannot bear comedy: so great is her aversion to it, that before the entertainment[13] begins, she generally quits the house, to carry off all her grief. Tragedy is her favourite passion; be the piece good or bad, if you but introduce unhappy lovers, you are sure to melt the heart of her ladyship.[14] To be plain with you, if I composed serious pieces, I should make choice of better judges.

Oh! I have others too, replied the tragedian: a thousand people of quality, male and female, are my admirers. And I should be as diffident of them, cries the comedian. I would as little trust to their judgment; and do you know the reason why? The greatest part of the time you are rehearsing, these kind of people are thinking of something else, and only catch at the beauty of a single verse, or the delicacy of some one particular sentiment; and that is sufficient for them to praise a whole piece, let all the rest of it be ever such stuff.[15] And, for the same reason, if they happen to attend to any verses, which may be either low or stiff, they very often, upon that account, damn the whole of a good play.

Come then, says the tragedian, if you will not admit people of that sort as proper judges, I refer myself to the applauses of the pit. Pish! replies the other, don't tell me of the pit; the pit often shews the caprice of its decisions. The audience there are so shamefully misled in their judgment, that sometimes they are ridiculously besotted[16] to a most wretched performance, two whole months together. Indeed when the piece comes to be printed, they are undeceived; and the author falls into disgrace, after a run of the most happy success.

Well, that may be as it will, but is what I have nothing to apprehend from, answers the tragic writer. My works undergo as many editions as representations. I own, indeed, it is not the same in respect to comedies; there the publication is sure to discover the failings, as they are but insignificant performances, and the productions of a low genius. Softly good Mr. writer of tragedies, replies the comedian; I say again softly. You don't seem to be apprized that you begin to be warm. I desire you will speak of comedy, at least before me, with a little more reverence. Do you imagine, Sir, that a comedy is not as difficult to compose as a tragedy? Undeceive yourself, and give me leave to tell you, Sir, that it is as difficult to make people of taste laugh, as to make them cry. Know, from henceforward, that the design of a comedy, which comprehends the manners of common life, if it is properly conducted, requires as much address and skill in the execution, as the plan of any subject founded upon the most heroic actions.

O lord! replies the tragic poet, with a sneer, I am glad at my heart to hear you talk after this manner. Come, Monsieur Calidas, we'll end all disputes. There's my hand: and to convince you of my sincerity, I give you my honour, that for the future I will esteem your works as much as I have hitherto despised them.

I value your contempt much, Monsieur Giblet, says the other, with quivering lips;[17] and to give a proper answer to these insolent airs of yours, I will tell you candidly my opinion of those verses you have been just now plaguing me with. The images on the whole are ridiculous, and though taken from Homer, are ne'er a bit the less so for that. Achilles speaks to his horses, and his horses answer him. This idea is low; and the simile of the swains making a fire upon the top of a mountain is every whit as bad. It is doing no honour to the ancients to pilfer from them in this manner. Doubtless they abound in noble and refined strokes of genius; but I hope, Sir, you will not take it amiss if I am of opinion, it is otherguise folks than you that are able to distinguish them.[18]

To this Giblet replied: As you have not taste enough to relish the beauties of my poetry, and to punish you for having dared to criticize on my scene, you shall not hear the end of it. End of it! replied the other, God help me, I am punished enough already, in having been obliged to hear the beginning. You pretend to despise my comedies: Lookee, Sir, I tell you, that the worst comedy I can make, will be still beyond the best of your tragedies. And let me tell you further, 'tis much easier done, to veil nonsense in fustian and bombast, than to hit off the elegance and pleasantry of wit.

I thank God, replied the tragedian, with an air of contempt, if I am not so happy as to have your esteem, I think I may comfort myself under that affliction. However, the court happens to judge more favourably of me: and the pension the king has been pleased—Poh! don't think to bambouzle me[19] with your pension, says Calidas; I know better things: I know too well how they are obtained, to have the better opinion of your writings for that. Once more I repeat it, you must not imagine yourself superior to comic writers; and to shew you how much I think tragedy inferior to comedy, the moment I return into France, if I have not success in comedy, I will humble myself to the writing of tragedy. Why really, replies Giblet, for a farce-maker methinks you shew a little too much vanity. And for a mere versifier, cried the other, who has no other merit than a little sublimated fustian,[20] methinks you take rather too much upon you. You are an insolent fellow, my dear little Monsieur Calidas, and were I not in your chamber, the *Peripetie*[21] of this adventure should teach you to pay more respect to the buskin. O my great and mighty Monsieur Giblet, I beg that consideration may be no manner of obstacle: if you have a mind to enter into that method of argument, I like my own chamber for the scene of action as well as any other place.

At that instant they grappled. The comedian with his left hand seized this writer of tragedies by the right ear, the tragedian did the same by him: and in that attitude, they made alternate applications to each other's jaws, while their feet kept a kind of concert

Quarrel between the Tragic and Comic Poets. (Sterling Library, Yale University.)

by various and repeated kicks.[22] An Italian who lodged in the next room, overhearing this conversation, and judging what it would end in, got out of bed, and called up the people of the house, in compassion to these two miserable Frenchmen, though he was not of their country. A Fleming, and two Germans, whom you now see in night-gowns, came up, and after some difficulty disengaged them from each other.

This fray of the poets, says Don Cleofas, diverts me much; and by what I can learn from it, it would seem that in France the composers of tragedy value themselves above the writers of comedy. Doubtless, says Asmodeus, the one thinks himself as much above the other, as the heroes in tragedy are superior to the valets de chambre in comedy. But whence arises this vaunted superiority? says Don Cleofas. Is it that composing a tragedy is really so much more difficult than to write a comedy? The question you propose to me, replies the demon, has been the subject of a thousand disputes, and is still undecided. As to me, my judgment is this; (no offence, I hope, to those who may be of a different opinion) I say it is as difficult to write a comedy as a tragedy; for if the last was a sign of more universal genius than the other, it would conclude, that a tragedian was more capable of writing a comedy than the best comic author. Now daily experience convinces us, that this is not true. So that these two different species of poetry require a genius equally able, though of a different character, properly to execute them. But it is now time, added the demon, to resume the thread of our story, which this digression has interrupted.

CHAPTER IV.

Continuation and conclusion of the Power of Friendship.

Tho' Theodora's servants had not been able to rescue their lady from the ruffians that carried her off, they had, however shewn a deal of courage, and their valour proved fatal to some of Alvaro's people. Among others, there was one so dangerously wounded, that he could not follow his companions, and was found stretched almost lifeless upon the sand.

They remembered this unhappy wretch to have been a valet belonging to Alvaro; and as they found he still breathed, had him brought into the castle, and did every thing they could to bring him to his senses, which, at last, they effected, though the vast quantity of blood he lost had reduced him to the last extremity. To engage him to make a discovery of what he knew, they promised to take care of his life, and not deliver him into the hands of justice, provided he told them whither his master intended to carry Theodora.

This promise encouraged him, though he was in such a situation, that he could have little hopes of reaping any great advantage from it. He exerted the small strength he had left, and with a feeble voice confirmed the intelligence Don Fadrique had received; and added, that the design of Alvaro was to carry her to Saffari, in the island of Sardinia, where he had a relation, under whose protection and authority he promised himself a sure asylum.

This discovery eased the minds of Mendoza and the Toledan. They left the wounded man in the castle, where he expired a few hours after, and returned to Valencia, consulting what course was proper for them to take on this occasion. They determined to go and find out their common enemy in his retreat; and accordingly they both embarked, without any attendants, at Denia, for Portmahon, from whence they supposed they should easily find a passage over into the island of Sardinia; and they were hardly arrived there, when they heard that there lay in the harbour a ship freighted for Cagliari, that was just ready to sail; which opportunity they made use of accordingly.

The ship set sail with as fair a wind as they could wish; but about five or six hours after they were becalmed, and at night the wind coming contrary, they were obliged to lye-by, in hopes it would change. In this manner they continued for three days, and on the fourth, about two in the afternoon, they espied a ship under full sail, bearing directly down upon them. At first they took her for a merchant-man; but finding she came within cannon-shot of them, without hoisting any colours,[1] they made no doubt but she was a corsair.

And they were right in their guess. She was a pirate of Tunis, who believed that the Christians would have struck without fighting; but when they perceived that they trimmed their sails, and were getting ready their guns, they imagined they should have hotter work than they looked for; so that they stopped, trimmed their sails likewise, and prepared for the engagement.

They began firing their guns on both sides, and the Christians, at first, seemed to have the advantage; but an Algerine of greater burthen and more men than any of the other two, happening to come up in the midst of the action, sided with the corsair of Tunis; and coming down full sail upon the Spaniard, laid her between two fires.[2]

The Christians upon this were dismayed; and not being willing to continue any longer such an unequal fight, ceased firing. There appeared then on the stern of the Algerine vessel a slave, who called out to the people in the Spanish ship, that if they expected quarter, they must strike to the Algerine.[3] After this summons, a Turk, who held in his hand a flag of green silk, embroidered with half-moons of gold and silver intermingled together, displayed it in the air. The Christians seeing that all resistance was in vain, gave over thoughts of further defence, seized with all the horror of grief and despair, which the idea of slavery presents to men born free; and the master of the vessel being afraid lest a longer delay should exasperate these barbarians, struck the flag from the poop, threw himself into the boat with some of the sailors, and went on board the Algerine.

The pirate ordered a party of his men to search the Spanish ship, that is, to plunder it of every thing they could find. The corsair of Tunis gave the same order to his men; so that all these unhappy wretches, who were passengers, were, in an instant, disarmed and stripped of every thing; after which they were brought on board the Algerine, where the two pirates divided them by lot.

It would have been some consolation to Mendoza and his friend, had they fallen to the share of the same master. Their chains would have sat lighter upon them, had they bore them in company with one another; but fortune, who had a mind to make them undergo the most rigorous destiny, gave Don Fadrique to the pirate of Tunis, and Don Juan to the Algerine. You may imagine the grief and despair of these two friends, on finding themselves separated; they threw themselves at the feet of the masters of the corsairs, conjuring them in the name of heaven not to separate them. But these rovers, whose minds were proof against the most piercing scenes of misery, were no ways moved: so far from it, that judging them to be people of quality, and that each of them was able to purchase their liberty at a great sum, they determined to separate them, in order to enhance the price of the ransom.

Mendoza and Zarates, finding they had to do with men unsusceptible of humanity, looked at one another, and, by their looks, testified the excess of their affliction. But when the pirates had made an end of sharing their booty, and the Tunis corsair wanted to depart for his own port, with the slaves that had fallen to his share, these two friends had like to have died away of grief. Mendoza approached the Toledan; and holding him fast in his arms, Must we then, said he, be parted? What a fatal necessity! Is it not enough that an impious ravisher remains unpunished, but must we be deprived of the happiness of mingling our tears and complaints? Ah! Don Juan, what crime have we committed against heaven, that it should so wreak its vengeance upon us? You need impute our misfortunes to no other cause but me, replied Don Juan. The death of two people whom I sacrificed to my fury, though excusable in the eye of man, has undoubtedly drawn upon me the wrath of heaven, who likewise punishes you, for having received into your friendship a wretch whom justice pursues.

As they spoke to one another in this manner, they shed such floods of tears, and sighed so bitterly, that the rest of the slaves were no less touched at their misfortunes than at their own. But the Tunis soldiers, yet more barbarous than their commanders, thinking that Mendoza was too tedious in getting out of the vessel, brutally tore him from the embraces of his friend, and, beating him unmercifully,[4] dragged him along with them. Adieu! my dear friend, cried he, whom I am never to see more: Theodora is not yet revenged. The cruel usage I am to receive from these barbarians, will be the lightest affliction of my bondage.

Don Juan could answer nothing to this. The manner in which he saw his friend treated threw him into an agony that deprived him of speech. As the thread of our story requires that we should follow the Toledan, we will leave Don Fadrique aboard the Tunis corsair.

The Algerine returned to his port, where being arrived, he first brought all his slaves before the bashaw, and afterwards to the public mart, where they use to sell them. An officer belonging to the dey Mezomorto bought Don Juan for his master, and they employed this new slave to work in the gardens of the Haram *. Such employment, though hard upon a gentleman, was nevertheless agreeable to Don Juan, as it afforded him the retirement of solitude. In the situation of mind he was in, nothing could be more agree-

* What we call Seraglios are called by the Turks Haram, all except that of the Grand Signior. 'Tis his alone that is known by the name of the *Serail*.[5]

able to him than reflecting upon his misfortunes. He reflected on them every moment; and so far was he from endeavouring to remove those melancholy ideas from his imagination, that he seemed to take a pleasure in recalling them to his memory.

It happened one day as he was at work, he was singing to himself a sorrowful ditty, without perceiving the dey, who walked in the gardens. Mezomorto stopped to listen to him; and liking his voice, out of curiosity came up to him, and asked his name. He answered it was Alvaro: for when he was sold to the dey, he thought proper to change his name, as all slaves for the most part do, and had taken that of Alvaro; because as he was continually ruminating on the rape of Theodora by Alvaro Ponza, it came more readily into his head than any other. Mezomorto, who understood Spanish tolerably well, asked him several questions relating to the customs of his country, and particularly what methods the men used to make themselves agreeable to the ladies. All which questions Don Juan answered to the dey's satisfaction.

Alvaro, said the dey to him, you seem to me to be an ingenious man, and, I suppose, above the common rank: however, let that be as it will, you have the good fortune to please me, and I intend to honour you with my confidence. At these words Don Juan threw himself at the feet of the dey, and rose up, after he had put the hem of his garment to his mouth, his eyes, and afterwards upon his head.

And as a proof of my confidence in you, said Mezomorto, I will acquaint you that I have in my Serail some of the finest women in Europe; one in particular who has no equal: I don't believe the Grand Signior himself is possessed of so perfect a beauty, though his ships are ever bringing him women from all parts of the world. Her countenance is like the reflected sun; her stature like the shooting trees that are planted in the gardens of Eram.[6] I am quite enchanted with her.

But this surprizing creature of such exquisite beauty, still continues in a most melancholy sorrow, which neither time nor the ardour of my love is able to conquer. Though fortune has put her in my power, I have never gratified my inclinations; I have hitherto always suppressed them; and, contrary to what is practised by people of my rank, who desire nothing but to indulge the pleasures of sense, I have tried to win her heart by a complaisance and respect which the meanest mussulman would be ashamed to shew to a christian captive.

Notwithstanding which, all my endeavours to please her only increase her melancholy, even to an obstinacy which begins now to tire my patience. The ideas of slavery dwell not so strong upon the mind of any of the rest; my caresses have soon removed all such impressions. This uninterrupted grief of hers becomes extremely uneasy to me.[7] However, before I yield to the transports of my passion, I will make one effort more to conquer her obstinacy, and intend to make use of you as the means of bringing her to reason. As she is a Christian, and of your nation, she will very probably put a confidence in you, and may, perhaps, be persuaded by you sooner than another. You may impress her with high ideas of my riches and grandeur. Tell her, I will distinguish her from all my other slaves. You may even, if it is necessary, give her hopes that it is possible she may one day become the wife of Mezomorto; and tell her, moreover, that I shall regard her more than I would a sultana offered me by the Grand Signior.

Don Juan prostrated himself a second time before the dey; and though he did not much like the service he was going upon, promised he would do every thing in his power to succeed with the lady. That's enough, said the dey; leave your work and follow me. I am going, contrary to the customs of my country, to introduce you to a private conversation with this fair captive; but dread to abuse this confidence, for if you do, torments unknown even to Turks shall be your portion. Endeavour to sooth her melancholy, and remember that your own liberty depends upon your success in this commission.[8] Don Juan then left his work, and followed the dey, who went before, to take the necessary steps to prepare the lady to receive him.

She was sitting with two old slaves, who retired as soon as Mezomorto entered. The fair captive made her obeisance to him with great respect, but could not help trembling, which she constantly did as often as she saw him. The dey perceived this, and to comfort her said, Lovely captive, I come only to acquaint you, that there is among my slaves a Spaniard, with whom, perhaps, you would be glad to converse. If you choose to see him, I will allow him to wait upon you, and that without any one else being present.

The lady answered, she should be extremely glad of such an opportunity. I will go then and send him to you, said Mezomorto; and heaven grant his conversation may be able to assuage your sorrows. So saying he went out, and meeting with Don Juan, whispered him softly,[9] you may go in, and after you have discoursed with her, come into my apartment, and let me know what has passed.

Zarates, pushing open the door, immediately entered the apartment of the fair slave, and paid his respects without looking at her, which she in like manner received without looking stedfastly at him; but when all of a sudden they viewed one another with attention, they both skreamed out with joy and surprize. Oh heavens! cried the Toledan approaching her, am I not deceived by an imaginary phantom? Is it possible! Can you be Donna Theodora? Ah! Don Juan, replied she, is it you who speak to me? Yes, Madam, said he, tenderly kissing one of her hands, it is Don Juan himself. Know me, Madam, by these tears, which my eyes cannot help pouring forth at the sight of you. Know me by these transports your presence alone is capable of inspiring. I repine no longer at my destiny, since it restores you to my vows. But alas! whither does the excess of my joy hurry me? I forget that you are a captive in chains. By what new caprice of destiny, Madam, have you come into this situation? How have you been able to escape the brutal attempts of Alvaro? Ah! what cruel anxieties have I laboured under, and how I yet dread that heaven has not effectually protected your virtue.

Heaven, answered Theodora, has avenged me of Alvaro Ponza. Had I time to relate to you——You have time enough, interrupted Don Juan; the dey allows me to be here with you, and, what is more surprising, all alone. Let us avail ourselves of these happy moments. Recount to me the particulars of what has befallen you, since you was carried away by Alvaro. How came you to know that Alvaro was the person who forced me away? I know it but too well, answered Don Juan; and thereupon gave her a particular account of the intelligence that had been received, and how he and Mendoza having set out in search of the ravisher, were taken by the Barbary pirates. After he had finished his story, Theodora thus began the recital of her adventures.

It is needless for me to mention the astonishment I was in at finding myself seized by a set of people in masks. I swooned away in the arms of him that carried me; and when

I recovered from the fit, found myself alone with Ines, at sea, in the cabin of a ship, sailing full before the wind.[10] That wretch Ines began to exhort me to patience; and from her manner of talking left me no room to doubt that she was in concert with my ravisher, who had the assurance to come before me, and throw himself at my feet: Madam, said he, forgive Alvaro, for using such means to accomplish his wishes. You know what pains I have taken, and with what warmth and zeal I disputed the empire of your heart with Don Fadrique, ever 'till that day in which you gave him the preference to me. Had my passion for you been less violent than it is, I should have been able to get the better of it,[11] and in time have wore out the impression of my misfortune; but my fate is ever to adore your charms: slighted as I was, I could not withdraw myself from the tyranny of your beauty; though you have nothing to fear from the violence of my passion. I have made no attempt upon your liberty, with a design to offer the least insult to your virtue. No, Madam, I mean no more than, in the retreat I design to conduct you to, by sacred and solemn bonds perpetually to unite our destinies.

He spoke to me a great deal more, which I cannot remember; but to hear him talk, one would have imagined he had used no violence to me; and that I ought rather to have considered him in the light of a passionate lover, than an audacious ravisher. Whilst he was speaking, I did nothing but weep, and shew signs of despair; for which reason he left me, without spending any more time in persuading me; but as he went out, he made a sign to Ines, which I found was for her to support, with all her skill, the reasons he had offered to vindicate his conduct.[12]

She did not fail to execute her office. She represented to me, that after the noise my being taken away must make in the world, I could not dispense with marrying Alvaro, whatever aversion I might have to him; that my reputation required my heart should make that sacrifice. This was not the way to dry my tears, to point out the necessity of such an odious match; so I remained inconsolable. Ines was at a loss what to say more, when all of a sudden we heard a great noise upon the deck, which drew our attention that way.

The noise we heard was made by Alvaro's people, on seeing a large vessel bearing down upon us full sail;[13] and as our ship was not so good a sailor as the other, there was no getting away. They came close up to us, and we immediately heard a cry of *strike, strike;*[14] but Alvaro Ponza and his people chusing rather to die than surrender, resolved to stand an engagement. The action was very desperate, of which I will not trouble you with the particulars. I shall only tell you, that Alvaro and every one belonging to him were killed, after having fought like men in despair. As for us, they made us go aboard the corsair, which belonged to Mezomorto, and was commanded by Aby Aly Osman, one of his officers.

Aby Aly looked at me a long time with some surprize, and knowing by my dress that I was Spanish, he spoke to me in the Castilian tongue. Moderate your grief, said he, and take comfort, notwithstanding your falling into slavery; that misfortune you could not possibly avoid: but why do I say misfortune? It is a happiness for which you will have reason ever to be thankful. You are too beautiful to be confined to reign over the hearts of Christians. Heaven did not form such as you for that miserable race of mortals: You deserve the homage of the greatest of mankind; none but mussulmen are worthy to possess you. I will go immediately back to Algiers, continued he: though I have taken no other prize, I am certain the dey, my master, will be satisfied with the success of my cruize. I am not afraid of his condemning my impatience to deliver into his hands a beauty, that will be the pleasure of his life, and the ornament of his seraglio.

At this discourse, which let me know what I was to expect, I redoubled my lamentations. Aby Aly, who saw in another light than I the cause of my fears, did nothing but laugh, and made towards Algiers, whilst I was overwhelmed with despair. Sometimes I sent up my cries to heaven, imploring its protection. Sometimes I wished some Christian vessels would come and attack us, or that the billows might swallow us up; and after that wished my grief and my tears might render me so frightful an object, as that the dey might look upon me with horror: empty wishes, which my alarmed virtue made me suggest. We arrived in the port, where they conducted me to the palace, and brought me before Mezomorto.

I know not what Aby Aly said when he presented me to his master, nor what answer his master made him, because they spoke Turkish; but thought I perceived by the looks and gestures of the dey, that I was so unhappy as to please him; and what he said to me immediately after, confirmed me in my despair, as it confirmed me in that opinion.

In vain did I throw myself at his feet, and promise whatever he could ask for my ransom. It was in vain I tempted his avarice by the offer of all I was worth: he told me, that he esteemed me before all the riches in the universe. He ordered this apartment to be got ready for me, which is the most magnificent in all the palace; and since that time has spared no pains to remove the grief and melancholy with which he sees me overwhelmed. He brings to me all the slaves of either sex, who can sing or play upon any instrument. He has removed Ines from me, thinking she indulged my melancholy reflections, and I am at present served by two old women, who are perpetually entertaining me with discourses of their master's love, and of the manifold pleasures reserved in store for me.

But every thing they do to divert me has a quite contrary effect; I am not to be comforted. Shut up a captive in this detestable palace, which ecchos every day with cries of oppressed innocence, I suffer even less in the loss of my liberty, than in the horrors which I feel at the addresses of the dey; and though hitherto he has behaved as a complaisant and respectful lover, I am notwithstanding under perpetual terrors, and every moment dread, lest, growing weary of a conduct which, no doubt, is irksome to him, he should make a brutal use of the power he has over me. The apprehension of this haunts me night and day like a spectre, and every moment of my life is a fresh repetition of my torment.

Donna Theodora could not utter these last words without tears, which pierced Don Juan to the heart. It is no wonder, Madam, said he, that your fears of what may happen should be so horribly frightful; I tremble at the thoughts of it as much as you; and the respect of the dey towards you will wear off sooner than you imagine; the complaisant lover will soon assume another character:[15] I know it but too well, and am too sensible of the danger you are in.

But, continued he, changing his tone of voice, if such a thing should happen, I will not be a tame spectator; slave as I am, in my despair, I am still to be dreaded. Before

Mezomorto commits any violence on you, this dagger shall—Ah! Don Juan, interrupted the widow of Cisuentes, what a scheme is this you propose? Take care not to entertain any such resolution. What would be the consequence, think you, of your killing the dey? Would not the Turks revenge his death with tortures hitherto unthought of——I tremble when I think of it. Besides, would it not be exposing yourself to certain destruction, without answering any end?[16] Suppose you killed him, should I by that be restored to my liberty? On the contrary, I should very probably be sold to some ruffian, that would not treat me with near so much humanity as Mezomorto. Just heaven! to you it belongs to shew your justice. You know the secret designs of the dey: you forbid me the relief of poison or dagger; to you therefore it belongs to prevent my committing a crime with which you are offended.

Yes, Madam, said Zarates, and heaven will prevent it. Something within my breast tells me it will. What I have this moment thought of, is doubtless an inspiration from above. The reason the dey has allowed me to see you is, to bring you over to a compliance with his love, and I am to go to him to give an account of our conversation, and must deceive him. I will tell him, you are not now so inconsolable as you was; that the delicacy of his behaviour towards you,[17] has begun to have some effect; and that by a continuance of the same conduct, he need not despair of at length gaining your heart. And you, on your part, must second me in this. When he sees you again, you must appear less sorrowful than usual, and even seem as if you took some pleasure in his company.

What a violence this is committing upon one's self,[18] said Theodora, for a liberal and ingenuous mind to stoop to such dissimulation? And after all what will be the effect of such a painful complaisance? Mezomorto, answered he, will be satisfied with himself for treating you with so much delicacy and respect, and will continue the same means of gaining your affection. During which time, I will be contriving some method of setting you at liberty. The attempt, I own, is difficult; but I know a slave who is extremely expert and ingenious, whose talents and industry I doubt not to make a proper use of.

I must leave you, continued he, for our business admits of no delay; we shall see one another again soon. I must go find the dey, and amuse him with some feigned tale or other; and as for you, Madam, you must prepare yourself to receive him properly. You must dissemble, and put a restraint upon yourself; however obnoxious the sight of him may be to you, you must not appear with looks of hatred or aversion; and tho' you open not your mouth at any time but to deplore your misfortunes, you must now use such a language as will flatter his inclinations. Be not afraid of giving him too much hope; you must promise every thing, that you may have it in your own power to grant nothing. Very well, replied Theodora, I will do every thing you desire, as the impending danger that threatens reduces me to this cruel necessity. Go, Don Juan, do what you can to rescue me from bondage. The reflection of its being owing to you, will give additional joys to the sweets of liberty.

The Toledan, according to the orders of the dey, went and waited upon him. Well, Alvaro, says he with great eagerness, what news from the fair captive? Have you brought her into better temper? If you bring me word that I must not hope to conquer her obstinate reluctancy, I swear by the head of the Grand Signior, my lord and master, that this day I will accomplish by violence, what I cannot obtain by entreaty. Sir, answered Don Juan, you have no occasion to make this tremendous oath; you will be under no necessity of having recourse to violence, in order to satisfy your passion. Your slave is a young lady, whose heart as yet is a stranger to love. So insensible has she been to the power of this passion, that she has rejected the addresses of the greatest grandees of Spain. In our own country she lived as a sovereign princess, and here she is a captive; and a mind such as hers, must be for a considerable time deeply affected with such a change of fortune; but, nevertheless, this haughty Spaniard will, like others, be soon reconciled to this state of captivity. I can even venture to assure you, that her chains begin already to sit lighter upon her. The generosity of your behaviour, that respectful deference you have always shewn her, and which she did not expect, begin to win upon her, and, by degrees, get the better of her grief; and you ought, Sir, to make the most of this turn and disposition of mind, which is so much in your favour. If you continue to her the same conduct and behaviour, you may depend upon it she will very soon, without reluctance, lose in your arms all regret for the loss of liberty.

I am rejoiced with what you tell me, replied the dey; the hopes you give me throw me into an extasy of joy.[19] Yes, I promise you, I will restrain the ardour of my desires, to give her the more complete satisfaction. But don't you deceive me, or are you not deceived yourself? I will go this moment and wait upon her, to see if I can observe, in her looks, such a favourable change of mind as you would make me hope. After that he went away to see Theodora; and the Toledan returned towards the garden, to meet the gardener, who was that expert slave whose assistance he intended to make use of to deliver the fair captive.

The gardener, whose name was Francisco, was of Navarre; he knew Algiers perfectly well, for he had been in the service of many masters, before he came into that of the dey. My friend Francisco, said Don Juan, I am at present in great affliction; there is in the palace a young lady, of one of the most considerable families in all Valencia; she has begged Mezomorto to name her ransom, but he will accept no price of redemption, because he is in love with her. And why are you so concerned at that? replied Francisco. Because I am of the same town, answered Don Juan, and our families lived most intimate with one another. There is nothing in my power I would not do to contribute to setting her at liberty.

This is no easy matter, replied Francisco, yet I assure you I could bring it about, if the lady's relations be such as would pay one accordingly for such a piece of service. You may be assured of it they are, answered the other; I take upon me to answer for the gratitude of all her friends, and for her own in particular. Her name is Theodora, and she is the widow of a man who has left her a vast fortune, and is as generous as she is rich. In a word, I am a Spaniard and a gentleman, that is sufficient.

Well, with all my heart, replies the gardener; on the faith of your promise I'll go and see to find a renegade[20] Catalan, whom I know, and propose to him——How! says the Toledan, quite surprised, would you trust such an affair as this to a miserable wretch, who has impiously renounced his religion? Renegade as he is, interrupted Francisco, he is for all that an honest man. He deserves rather to be pitied than detested, and I could willingly excuse him, if his crime would admit of one. His story is briefly this:

He is a native of Barcelona, and was a surgeon by profession; but finding he had little business there, determined to go and set up at Carthagena, hoping that by changing his place of residence, he should better his business.[21] He sailed therefore for Carthagena, along with his mother; but in their voyage they met with an Algerine pirate, who carried them in here. They were both sold for slaves, his mother to a Moor, and himself to a Turk,[22] who used him so cruelly, that he turned Mahometan, to put an end to his own slavery, and likewise procure his mother's liberty, whom he saw very ill used by the Moor her master. Afterwards he insinuated himself into the service of the dey, went several times a cruizing, and got a considerable sum of money;[23] part of which he gave for the ransom of his mother, and, to make the most he could of the rest, determined to turn pirate.

He made himself a captain,[24] bought a galley, and, with some Turks who were willing to share his fortune, went and cruized between Alicant and Carthagena; from which cruize he returned loaded with spoils. He set sail again, and was so fortunate, that in a short time he was able to man a large ship, with which he took several valuable prizes; but his good fortune at last forsook him.[25] One time he attacked a French frigate, who handled him so roughly, that it was with great difficulty he could get back to the port of Algiers. As in this country they judge of the merit of corsairs by the success of their expeditions, the Catalan, by this misfortune, fell into contempt with the Turks, which vexed and sowered him to such a degree, that he sold his ship, and retired to a house a little way from town, where he has lived ever since upon what he had got, with his mother and some slaves.

I very often go to see him, for we once served together the same master, and we are very intimate; he imparts to me his most secret thoughts, and it is not three days ago since he told me, with tears in his eyes, that he had never enjoyed a moment's peace since he had abjured his faith; that to quiet the stings of his conscience, which knawed him without intermission, he had been often tempted to trample the turban under his feet; and at the hazard of being burnt alive, make reparation, by a public act of repentance, for the scandal he had brought upon Christianity.

This is the true character of that renegado, to whom I intend to apply on this occasion; and I think such a man may be safely trusted. I will go out, under pretence of repairing to the place where all the slaves of the dey usually meet,[26] and will take care to find out my friend. I intend to tell him, that instead of pining and tormenting himself with the remorse of having left the bosom of the church, he ought rather to think of some means, whereby he may be again received into the communion of the catholic faith; and that, to accomplish this, he has nothing more to do than equip a vessel, as if, being tired with the life he now leads, he designed to return to his old trade of cruizing, and that by means of this ship we may reach the coasts of Valencia; after which, Donna Theodora will give him wherewithal to pass the rest of his days comfortably at Barcelona.

Yes, my dear Francisco, cried Don Juan, transported with the hopes this gardener had given him, you may make what promises you please to the renegado: you and he both may rest assured of being made easy all the rest of your lives. But do you think that our project will go on successfully, in the manner you propose to execute it? There may happen some difficulties which I do not at present foresee, replied Francisco; but the Catalan and I will take care to get over them. Alvaro, added he, parting from him, I conceive good hopes of our success, and doubt not but when I see you again, I shall bring you agreeable tidings.

Don Juan waited the return of Francisco with great impatience. In about four hours he came back and told him that he had seen the renegado, and had imparted to him their design; and that, after mature deliberation, they had come to a resolution, that he should buy a small vessel ready equipped; and as it is allowable to take slaves for mariners, that he should take all his own along with him; that for fear of suspicion, he should engage twelve Turkish soldiers to go with him, as if he was really going on a cruize; but that two days before that on which he should appoint them to be on board, he should embark himself with his slaves, weigh anchor without any noise, and take us up in his pinnace at a little gate of this garden, which is just by the sea. You may let the captive lady know of this, and you may assure her, that in a fortnight, at farthest, she shall be delivered from her captivity.

What joy was this to Zarates to have it in his power to bring such intelligence to Theodora? That he might have an opportunity of seeing her, he went next day to wait on Mezomorto, and having seen him, Pardon me, Sir, said he, if I have the boldness to ask you in what temper you found the fair captive. Are you now better satisfied? I am charmed with her behaviour, replied the dey. Yesterday her eyes did not as usual avoid my tender and passionate looks. Her conversation, which formerly used to turn on nothing but constant reflections on the misery of her situation, was free from all complaints of her own; she even seemed to listen with a kind of compassion to mine.

It is to you, Alvaro, I owe this great change, I perceive you well know the genius of the women of your own country; and I would have you converse with her once more, to finish what you have so happily begun. Make use of all your ingenuity and address to hasten the hour of my happiness, and I will soon set you at liberty. I swear by the soul of our great prophet, I will send you back into your own country, loaded with such presents, that the Christians, when they see you, will not believe you return from slavery.

The Toledan did not fail to take advantage of the error of Mezomorto. He seemed greatly moved by his promises, and under the pretence of hastening what he so much wanted, he left him to go and see the lady, whom he found alone in her apartment, the old women her attendants being busied somewhere else.[27] He informed her what Francisco and the renegado had agreed on together, on the faith of the promises he had made them.

This was matter of infinite consolation for Theodora, to understand such well concerted measures were taken for her deliverance. Is it possible, cried she, in an extasy of joy, that I should ever hope to see again Valencia, the dear place of my nativity? What rapturous pleasure will it be, after so many toils, so many perils, to live there in peace and tranquillity with you. Ah! Don Juan, how flattering is this prospect to my imagination! Do you share in it with me? Are you thinking just now, that while you rescue me from the power of Mezomorto, you are taking from him your own wife?

Ah! Madam, replied Zarates, what pleasing music these enchanting words would be to my ears, if the sorrowful remembrance of an unhappy friend did not embitter all the comfort, all the pleasure they can give me? Forgive me, Madam, this delicacy, and own yourself, that Mendoza deserves your compassion. It was for your sake he left Valencia; for you he has lost his liberty; and I make no doubt but even now at Tunis, the weight of his chains affects him less than the affliction he suffers at the thought of your not being revenged.

Doubtless he deserves a better fate, replied Theodora. I call heaven to witness, that I am truly sensible of all he has suffered upon my account; and I tenderly compassionate the disquiet I have caused him;[28] but by a cruel and fatal destiny it is impossible my heart can ever be the recompence of his services.

Their conversation was interrupted by the coming in of the two old women who attended Theodora. Don Juan immediately changed the discourse, and talking as the confidant of Mezomorto, Yes, fair captive, said he, you have enthralled him who now holds you in chains. Mezomorto, the most gallant and most amiable of all the mussulmen, your lord and mine, has conceived an esteem for you. Persevere to receive him with affection, and you will quickly find an end of all your miseries. He went away after speaking these last words, the true meaning of which was understood only by Theodora.

Things remained in this situation in the dey's palace for about eight days. In the mean while the Catalan had purchased a small ship almost quite equipped, and was getting ready for his departure; but about six days before he could put to sea, Don Juan met with fresh alarms.

Mezomorto sent for him, and taking him into his closet, Alvaro, said he, you are free; when you please, you may go for Spain; the presents I promised you are ready for you; I have seen my fair captive this day, and she is quite another thing from what she was before,[29] when her melancholy gave me so much uneasiness. I perceive that every day more and more effaces from her mind the ideas of captivity. In a word, I have found her so sweetly charming, that I am come to a determined resolution to marry her. In two days she shall be the wife of Mezomorto.

At this Don Juan changed colour, and notwithstanding every thing he could do to conceal his trouble and surprize, the dey perceived it, and asked him the reason.

Sir, said Don Juan, in the midst of his confusion, I cannot help testifying my surprize, that one of the most considerable princes of the Ottoman empire should humble himself so far as to take to wife one that is his slave. I am very sensible that there are not wanting instances of it among your nation; but then, the illustrious Mezomorto, who may demand the daughter of any of the greatest officers of the port[30]——I agree with you, interrupted the dey; I might aspire to the daughter of the grand vizir, and even reasonably expect to succeed my father-in-law in his post; but I have vast riches with little ambition. I prefer the ease and pleasure I enjoy here, to the splendor of the vizirate; that dangerous precipice of honour,[31] to which we hardly sooner mount, than the jealousy of the sultan, or the envy of those who are about his person, throw us headlong down. Besides, I am in love with my slave, and her beauty renders her worthy of that high rank to which I am going to advance her.

But, added he, there is a necessity that this very day she change her religion, to merit the honour I confer upon her. Do you think that any ridiculous prejudices will make her hesitate at that? No, Signior, replied Don Juan, I am persuaded she will sacrifice every thing to so glorious a prospect. But allow me, Sir, to say, that in my opinion you ought not to marry her so hastily, and hurry on the match so fast; for it is not to be imagined but that the thoughts of renouncing what she has sucked in with her mother's milk, will at first shock her; and therefore I think she should have some time to make proper reflections. When once she considers, that instead of offering her any dishonour, or letting her grow old among the rest of your slaves, you join her to yourself by a marriage so glorious for her, there can be no doubt, but gratitude and ambition will soon get the better of her scruples. Defer, therefore, for at least eight days the execution of your purpose.

Mezomorto remained some time in suspence. The delay his confidant proposed did not at all suit with the eagerness of his desires; however, he thought the advice was very judicious. Alvaro, said he, I am convinced by your reasons; and however great my impatience is to enjoy my amiable captive, I will wait eight days more. Do you go and see her immediately, and bring her to a compliance against that time; and I intend, that the same Alvaro, who has done me such good offices with her, shall have the honour of giving me her hand.

Don Juan went in all haste to the apartment of Theodora, and informed her of what had passed between him and the dey, that she might take her measures accordingly. At the same time he acquainted her, that the renegado would have his vessel ready in six days; and as she seemed to be extremely uneasy in regard to what way she could get out of her apartment, supposing the doors of the chambers between hers and the stair-case should be locked, he told her, she need be in no pain about that, as she was to come out at the window of her own room, which looked into the garden, by a ladder, which he would take care to provide for that purpose.

The six days being at last expired,[32] Francisco told the Toledan, that his friend the Catalan would be ready to sail the next night, and you may imagine that night was expected with great impatience. It came at last, and, to add to their good fortune, it was very dark. As soon as the time was come to execute their enterprize, Don Juan placed the ladder under the window of her apartment, which she perceiving, came down in great hurry and agitation; after which she leaned upon Don Juan, who brought her to the gate of the garden that opened towards the sea.

They went forwards together at a great pace, and anticipated the pleasures of being rescued from slavery; but fortune, with whom these two lovers were not yet quite good friends,[33] prepared for them a blow more cruel than what they had yet ever felt, and what, of all others, they least expected.

They were now got out of the garden,[34] and were upon the sea-shore ready to get into the boat that waited for them, when a man, whom they took to be one of those that attended them in their escape, and of whom they had not the least suspicion, advanced towards Don Juan with his naked sword, and plunging it into his breast, Perfidious Alvaro Ponza, said he, it is thus Don Fadrique de Mendoza thinks he ought to punish a cowardly ravisher: you deserve not to be treated according to the laws of honour.[35]

The Toledan could not resist the force of the blow, which brought him to the ground; and at the same time Theodora, who supported herself upon him, seized at once with grief, fear, and astonishment, fainted away. Ah! Mendoza, said Don Juan, what have you done? It is I, your friend Don Juan, whom you have killed. All gracious heaven, cried Don Fadrique, have I assassinated—I forgive you my death, interrupted Zarates, our unhappy destiny is alone to blame; or perhaps we ought to be thankful, as by this means an end is put to our misfortunes. Adieu, my dear Mendoza, I die contented, as I deliver unto you Donna Theodora, who will satisfy you that I have never betrayed our friendship.

Too generous friend! (said Don Fadrique, agitated with despair); but you shall not go alone; the same weapon that gave you the blow, shall revenge you on your assassin. If my mistake frees me from the guilt of a crime, it does not satisfy my own mind. At these words, turning his point to his breast, he run himself up to the hilt, and fell upon the body of Don Juan, who fainted away, occasioned more from his surprize at the despair of his friend, than by the loss of blood he had sustained.

Francisco and the renegado, who were about ten paces distant, and who had their own reasons for not assisting Alvaro, were astonished to hear these last words, and behold this last action of Don Fadrique. They then knew that he was mistaken, that the wounded gentlemen were two friends, and not mortal enemies, as they had before believed. Upon that they run to their assistance; but finding them speechless, as well as Theodora, who had fainted away, they knew not what to do. Francisco was of opinion they should carry off Theodora, and leave the gentlemen on the shore, as in all probability they would die soon, if they were not dead already. But the renegado was not of the same mind: he said it was wrong to abandon people in their condition, whose wounds, perhaps might not be mortal: that he himself would dress them on board his ship, where he had all the instruments belonging to his former profession, which he had not yet forgot; and Francisco yielded to his opinion.

As they very well knew how necessary it was to make haste, the renegado and Francisco, with the help of some slaves, brought the unhappy widow of Cisuentes, and her two lovers, yet more unhappy than she, into the boat. In a few minutes they reached the ship; and as soon as they were on board, some unfurled the sails, while the others were on the deck upon their knees, imploring the protection of heaven, with all that fervency which the dread of being overtaken by the ships of Mezomorto could inspire.

As for the renegado, after having given the charge of the ship to a French slave, who was an excellent seaman, his first care was to look after Theodora, whom he restored to the use of her senses; and, by the help of his medicines, Don Juan and Don Fadrique came likewise to theirs. The lady, who had fainted away on seeing Don Juan fall, was astonished to see Mendoza; and though in the situation she saw him, she imagined that he had fallen upon his own sword, out of grief for having wounded his friend, yet she could not look upon him otherwise than as the murderer of the man she loved.

Nothing could be more affecting than to see these three people together, after they had recovered the use of their senses. The situation they had been in just before, though next a-kin to death, was not near so piteous. Theodora eyed Don Juan with looks that signified the strongest passions of grief and despair; and the two dying friends looked at one another, at the same time sighing bitterly.

After having for some time preserved a mournful and tender silence, Don Fadrique began, by addressing himself to Theodora: Madam, said he, before I die, I have the pleasure of seeing you delivered from slavery. Would to heaven your liberty had been owing to me; but providence has ordered it that you should owe that obligation to the man you love; and I love this rival too well to complain at it. I only wish the wound I have been so unhappy as to give him may not prevent his enjoying the effects of your gratitude. The lady answered nothing to this declaration. So far was she then from deploring the hard fate of Mendoza, that she felt for him sentiments of aversion, when she reflected on the condition Don Juan was in.

In the mean time, the surgeon began to examine and probe their wounds. He began with Zarates, whose wound he found not dangerous, as the sword had only glanced under the left breast, without hurting any of the vital parts. This report of the surgeon diminished the affliction of Theodora, and gave great joy to Don Fadrique, who turned towards that lady, Madam, said he, I am now content; I quit the world without murmuring, as my friend is out of danger, and I die not under your displeasure.

He pronounced these words in so passionate and tender a manner, that Theodora could not help being moved. As her fear for Don Juan was over, so was her hatred of Don Fadrique; and beholding him now in the light of one who deserved her pity, Ah! Mendoza, said she, in a generous transport, suffer your wound to be dressed; perhaps it is not more dangerous than that of your friend; allow yourself to be taken care of, and live, Don Fadrique. If I cannot make you happy, I will not make any other. Out of compassion and friendship for you, I will not give my hand to Don Juan, as I intended; and will make you the same sacrifice of him, as he has done of me.

Don Fadrique was going to have replied; but the surgeon, who imagined it would hurt him, obliged him to keep silence, and examined his wound; which appeared to be mortal, the sword having entered the upper part of the lungs, as appeared from an hemorrhage, or loss of blood, which threatened fatal consequences. As soon as the surgeon had finished the dressings, he left the two gentlemen together in the cabin, on two small beds, to take their rest, and carried Theodora to another place, as he imagined her presence would do neither of them any good.[36]

Notwithstanding all their care, Mendoza feavered, and towards the evening the hemorrhage increased. The surgeon then told him he could not live; so that if he had any thing to say to his friend or the lady, he had no time to lose. This threw the Toledan into a terrible agony; but Don Fadrique received it with great calmness. He desired they would call Theodora, who came and sat down by him, in a condition more easy to be conceived than expressed.

She shed floods of tears, and sobbed so violently, that Mendoza could not bear it. Madam, said he, I am not worthy these precious tears: dry them up, I beseech you, and listen to me for a moment: and I make the same request to you, my dear Zarates, added he, perceiving the grief and anguish his friend was in, I know this separation will bear hard upon you; your well-proved friendship will not allow me to doubt of it. But wait both of you till I am laid in the dust, and honour me, in my death, with these marks of tenderness and friendship. 'Till then suspend your sorrows, which pierce my heart more sensibly than the agonies I now endure;[37] and learn by what labyrinths the destiny that pursues me, conducted me to these fatal shores, which I stained with the blood of myself and of my friend.

You are, no doubt, in pain to know how I came to mistake Don Juan for Alvaro, which I will give you an account of, if the short remainder of my life will give me time for this melancholy explanation.

Some hours after the ship, in which I was, had left the Algerine, on board of which was Don Juan, we met a French privateer who attacked us, and having made himself master of the Tunis corsair, set us on shore near Alicant. The first thing I thought of after I had regained my liberty was redeeming my friend: for this purpose I set out immediately for Valencia, where I got all the ready money I could raise; and, upon being informed, that there were fathers of the redemption[38] at Barcelona ready to sail for Algiers, I went thither; but before I went, begged my uncle, Don Francisco de Mendoza, Governor of Valencia, to employ all his interest at the court of Madrid, to obtain Zarates's pardon, whom I told him I designed to bring back with me; and to procure a restitution of his estate,[39] which had been forfeited since the death of the duke of Naxera.

As soon as I arrived at Algiers, I immediately went to the quarter of the slaves: I examined them all, but in vain; I found not him whom I sought for. I happened to meet the Catalan, the master of this ship, whom I remembered to have been in the service of my uncle; to him I communicated the motive of my coming to Algiers, and begged him to make strict inquiry after my friend. I am sorry, replied he, I can't serve you; for this night I am to sail with a lady of Valencia, a slave of the dey's. And pray, said I, what is the name of that lady? He answered, her name was Theodora.

The surprize I discovered at the name of Theodora shewed the Catalan that I had an interest in that lady: he discovered to me the scheme they had laid to procure her liberty; and as in the account he gave me, he made mention of the slave Alvaro, I made no manner of doubt but it was Alvaro Ponza himself. Assist me in my revenge, said I with transport to the renegado, give me an opportunity of destroying my mortal enemy. You shall have that satisfaction presently, said he; but tell me first the ground of your quarrel with Alvaro. Upon which I related to him all the particulars, and when I had done, It is very well, said he, you have nothing to do but come along with us this night, when you will be shewn your rival; and when you have revenged yourself upon him, you may take his place, and accompany us to conduct Theodora to Valencia.

But however great my impatience was, I did not forget Don Juan; I left money for his ransom in the hands of an Italian merchant, called Francisco Capali, who resides at Algiers, and who promised me to redeem him, if he could get any intelligence of him. At last, night came, and I went to the renegado, who conducted me to the sea-shore. We stopped at a small gate, from whence a man came directly towards us, and pointing with his finger to a man and a woman, who were coming after him, These are, said he, Alvaro and Donna Theodora who follow me.

Upon this my rage became furious;[40] I drew my sword, and run to the unhappy Alvaro, and, fully believing it was my hated rival I was going to strike, plunged my sword into the breast of that dear friend I had been in quest of. But, thanks to heaven, added he tenderly, my mistake will neither cost him his life, nor be the occasion of perpetual grief to Theodora.

Ah! Mendoza, said she, you don't do me justice,[41] I shall never cease lamenting the loss of you; should I even marry your friend, it will be but to mingle our sorrows and tears. Your unhappy love, your friendship, your misfortunes will be the constant subject of our conversation. This is too much, Madam, replied Don Fadrique, I am not worthy of being bewailed or remembered. Let me conjure you, Madam, with my latest breath, to marry Zarates, as soon as he has avenged you upon Alvaro Ponza. Alvaro Ponza is no more, replied Theodora: the same day he carried me away, he was killed by the corsair that took us.

Madam, said Mendoza, this news gives me pleasure; my friend will then be so much the sooner made happy. Indulge, without constraint, your passion for each other. I perceive, with joy, the moment approach, which will remove the obstacle your pity and his generosity made to your mutual felicity. May your days peacefully glide along in uninterrupted tranquillity, in a perfect union, which the jealousy of fortune may never be able to disturb! Adieu, Madam; adieu, Don Juan: think both of you on a man who never loved any thing so much as he did you.

Don Juan and Theodora, instead of answering him, redoubled their tears, which Don Fadrique perceiving, and, at the same time, finding himself approaching towards his end, went on in this manner: I find that I indulge my fondness too much; death already surrounds me, and I forget to supplicate the divine goodness to pardon me for having, with my own hand, shortened the period of a life which heaven alone ought to dispose of. Having uttered these words, he lifted up his eyes to heaven, with all the signs of unfeigned repentance, and immediately the hemorrhage caused a suffocation, which carried him off.

Upon this Don Juan, in a fit of despair, laid his hand on his wound, and tore off the dressings, endeavouring to make it incurable; but Francisco and the renegado seized him, and prevented the effects of his fury. Theodora, frightened almost to death, joined her intreaties to the assistance of the Catalan and Francisco, to prevent his intentions: she spoke to him in so tender and affecting a manner, as brought him to himself. He allowed them to put on the dressings again, and by degrees the lover began to prevail over the friend. But though his reason became predominant, he made use of it only to check the rash and hasty transports of despair, not to efface the pious remembrance of friendship.

The renegado, amongst many other things which he carried with him into Spain, had some balm of Arabia and exquisite perfumes; with which he embalmed the body of Mendoza, at the request of Theodora and Don Juan, who expressed their desire of performing his funeral obsequies in the town of Valencia. During the whole voyage they mingled their tears and lamentations; but it was not so with the rest of the people in the ship; for as the wind continued still favourable, they came in view of the coast of Spain.

As soon as they descried land, all the slaves were transported with joy; and when the ship had safely arrived in the port of Denia, they disposed of themselves different ways. But Don Juan and the widow of Cisuentes dispatched a courier to Valencia, with letters to the governor and to Theodora's family. The news of this lady's return gave infinite joy to all her relations; but Don Francisco de Mendoza was deeply afflicted at the account of the death of his nephew, of which he gave very sensible proofs;[42] for he came with Theodora's relations to Denia, to see the corpse of the unhappy Don Fadrique, which the good old man bathed with his tears, and mourned over him with such sorrow

The Death of Don Fadrique. (Sterling Library, Yale University.)

and affection, as melted the hearts of all who were present. He then asked by what mishap his nephew had come to this unhappy end.

I will give you an account of the particulars, Signior, said Don Juan. Far from wanting to efface it from my memory, I indulge a melancholy pleasure in ever presenting it to my imagination, and cherishing my grief. He then gave him an account how this fatal accident came to pass; and as this drew from his eyes fresh tears, so it redoubled those of Don Francisco. As for Theodora, her relations testified their joy at seeing her again, and congratulated her upon the miraculous escape she had made from the tyranny of Mezomorto.

After a proper explanation of the various incidents attending their fortune, they put the corpse of Don Fadrique into a coach, and carried it to Valencia: but he was not buried there, because the time of Don Francisco's vice-royalty being on the point of expiring, this nobleman was preparing to set out for Madrid, where he intended to carry the body of his nephew.

Whilst they were making these preparations for their departure, the widow of Cisuentes shewed her gratitude in the fullest and most generous manner to Francisco and the renegado. Francisco went into Navarre, his native country, and the renegado, with his mother, returned to Barcelona, where he was received again into the bosom of the church, and where he yet lives very happily. During this time Don Francisco received a packet from court, with a pardon for Don Juan, which the king, notwithstanding the regard he had for the house of Naxera, could not refuse to the importunate solicitations of all the Mendozas, who unanimously joined their interests to obtain it. This was so much the more agreeable to the Toledan, as by that he had an opportunity of attending the body of his friend, which otherways he durst not have ventured to have done.[43]

At last the funeral procession set out, accompanied by a vast number of persons of quality; and as soon as they arrived at Madrid, they interred the body of Don Fadrique in a church where Zarates and Donna Theodora, by the permission of the Mendozas, erected a magnificent monument over his tomb. Nor did they stop there; they wore mourning for their friend a whole year, as a perpetual token of their grief, and the memory of their friendship.

After having given such illustrious proofs of their regard to Mendoza, they were married; but by an unprecedented effect of the power of friendship, Don Juan, for a long time, could not shake off a melancholy, which nothing was able to conquer. Don Fadrique, his dear Don Fadrique was ever present to his imagination. Every night his fancy presented him to him in the visions of dreams, and, for the most part, such as he was in his dying agonies.[44] But at last his mind began to be weaned from these melancholy ideas. The charms of Theodora, of whom he every day grew more passionately fond, by degrees began to dispel this sorrowful gloom. In a word, Don Juan was beginning to be restored to the peace and quiet of his mind: but a few days ago, as he was hunting, he fell from his horse, by which accident he received a wound in his head that formed an abscess, and the physicians have not been able to save his life. He is gone; and Theodora, the lady whom you see in the arms of the two women, will immediately follow after.

CHAPTER V.

Of Dreams.

When Asmodeus had finished the recital of this story, Don Cleofas said to him, this is indeed a noble picture of friendship; but if it is so rare a thing now a days to find two men love one another with such disinterested friendship as Don Juan and Don Fadrique, I believe it would be still more difficult to find two rival friends of the other sex, who would so generously make a mutual sacrifice to one another of the beloved object.

You are in the right, answered the demon, that is what never has happened, and what never will; for women have no friendships. Let us suppose, for example, two women perfectly united; let us suppose their friendship to be even carried to such a height, that the one does not speak ill of the other behind her back; and that you see them both, and discover an inclination for one, the consequence is, the other is all in a fury; not that she has any affection for you; but she cannot bear not to be preferred before the other. Such is the character of women. They are too jealous of one another to be capable of cherishing sentiments of friendship.

The story of these two nonpareil friends is a little romantic, and has taken us up rather too long, said Leandro Perez; the night is far gone, and we shall presently see the light of the sun. I expect from you a new scene of amusement; for I perceive a vast number of people asleep, and I want you should tell me[1] the subject of their dreams. With all my heart, answered Asmodeus, I see you love variety of lots, and I will give you the satisfaction you desire.

I doubt not, says Zambullo, but I shall find these dreams extremely ridiculous. Why so? answered the demon; you who are master of Ovid *, don't you know what that poet says, that it is towards break of day dreams are truest, because then the fancy is less clogged with the fumes of indigestion. As for me, answered Cleofas, Ovid may say what he pleases, but I put no faith in dreams. In that you are very wrong, replied Asmodeus; they ought neither to be treated as chimeras, nor all of them believed. They are liars that sometimes speak truth. The emperor Augustus, whose head-piece was perhaps as good as any student's of Alcala, did not set so light by dreams that concerned him; so far from it, that before the battle of Philippi, he left his tent, on the report of the particulars of a dream that respected himself.[2] I could mention a thousand other instances, which would convince you of your error, but I shall let them alone now, and satisfy your curiosity in what you want to be informed of.

---

* Hero, in her letter to Leander, mentions a dream she had in the latter part of the night, towards the dawn of the morning, a time, she says, that the visions which appear to the fancy generally prove true. Tibullus prays the Gods against some dreams, that they might not prove true, though dreamt when the night was far spent; and Horace founds his belief of the reality of an apparition he saw, (when old Quirinus came to him in his sleep, and exhorted him not to plague his brain with composing Greek couplets) upon the time it appeared to him, namely, after midnight.[3]

And let us begin with this fine house upon the right hand. The lord of this hotel, whom you see asleep in this magnificent apartment, is a nobleman of vast fortune and great gallantry. He dreams that he is at the opera, hearing a young actress sing, and that he is inchanted with the song of this syren.

In the apartment next to his lies my lady countess, who is desperately fond of play; and is dreaming that she has no money, and is obliged to pawn her jewels, but dreams in rapture, that the goldsmith lets her have three hundred pistoles upon what she thinks very moderate interest.[4]

In the next hotel to this lives a marquis of the same character with the count, and is in love with a famous coquette. He now dreams that he is borrowing a sum of money to give her in a present; and the steward who lies above him is dreaming that he gets an estate on the ruins of his master's fortune. Now, what do you think of these dreams, are they visionary illusions? No, really, says Don Cleofas. I find my friend Ovid is in the right. But I want much to know who this man is whom I observe: he has his whiskers done up in papillotes,[5] and even whilst he is asleep preserves such an air of importance, that he seems to me to be a man of some distinction. He is a country squire, said Asmodeus, a man of estate in Arragon; but an empty-skulled coxcomb.[6] He is now dreaming that he is in company with a grandee, who yields him the precedency at a public ceremony.

But I see, in the same house two brothers of the faculty, who are mortified with very affecting dreams. One of them trembles in his sleep, thinking that an act has passed, which forbids all physicians receiving any fees 'till the patient is cured. And the other dreams, that an act is passed, ordering all physicians to appear in mourning at the burial of the several patients that die under their care. I should be extremely glad, said Zambullo, that this last act was really in force; and that a physician was obliged to attend the funeral of his patient, as in France the judge is obliged to assist at the execution of the criminal he has condemned.[7] I like the comparison extremely well, answered the demon; and in such a case it might be said with truth, that the one goes to see his sentence executed, and that the other has already performed the execution of his.

Oh Lord! cries the student, who is this that rubs his eyes, getting up in so great a hurry? A man of quality, answered the other, who sollicits the government of New Spain; he has just now dreamt that the minister looked drily upon him. I perceive likewise, a young lady that wakes, and who seems not at all pleased with her dream. She is a lady of fortune; beautiful and witty, and has two sweethearts both greatly smitten with her.[8] One of them she loves tenderly, and the other she hates with thorough aversion. This moment she saw at her feet the lover she detests, who shewed so much passion, and was so very pressing and importunate, that it was well she waked, for she was on the point of granting him favours she had never thought of bestowing on the man she loved. During our sleep, nature is not under the restraints of reason and virtue.

Look into that house, at the corner of the street, it belongs to an attorney. You see him asleep with his wife in a room adorned with old tapestry hangings: the man himself dreams that he is going to see one of his former clients, who is in a hospital, and to make him restitution of some of his money; and his wife dreams that her husband is turning out of doors a great brawny clerk, of whom he is become jealous.

Bless me, says Don Cleofas, what a snorting I hear! I fancy it must be that fellow, whom I see in a small room near the attorney. Yes, says Asmodeus, it is a canon, who dreams that he is saying his *Benedicite.*

He has for his neighbour a mercer, who sells his goods at a great price, but on credit, to persons of quality. He has on his books above an hundred thousand ducats. He dreams, that all the people who owe him money are come to pay him; and his foreign correspondents are dreaming, that he is on the point of becoming a bankrupt. These two dreams, said the student, do not issue from the temple of sleep by the same gate. Assuredly not, replied the demon; but you may depend upon it, the first comes thro' *Porto Cornea**.

* *La porte de corne*, the *horn-gate.* The poets have given two gates to the temple of sleep, one of horn and the other of ivory; through one of which proceed true, and from the other false dreams. Penelope telling Ulysses a dream she had dreamt, makes mention of the gates of sleep; Λοιαι γαρτι πυλαι &c. See Hom. Odyss. lib. 19. towards the end, which Virgil has translated into the Æneid. Lib. 6.

> *Sunt geminæ somni portæ; quorum altera fertur*
> *Cornea, quâ veris facilis datur exitus umbris*
> *Altera, caudenti perfecta nitens elephanto,*
> *Sed falsa ad cælum mittent insomnia manes.*

There are two gates of sleep; one of them called the horn-gate, through which issue such dreams as have their foundation in truth and reality: The other of polished ivory, and exquisite workmanship; but is the gate through which the manes send into the world false dreams and deceitful illusions. Mr. Le Sage, therefore, must certainly have mistaken one gate for the other, unless the printer has done him the favour to put *le premier* for *le dernier, the first* instead of *the last.* For what he means undoubtedly is, that, whether the dream of the mercer's creditors, in regard to his turning bankrupt, be true or not, his own dream of his quality-debtors coming all to discharge their bills is certainly false; so of consequence, in setting out to him, ought to have taken the ivory, not the horn-road.

It is hardly credible what disturbance these lines of Virgil, above quoted, have occasioned. They have created both public dissention and private animosities; insomuch that intended matches between the children of authors have, upon that account, been put a stop to. The difference of opinion in regard to this passage has not only affected the peace and quiet of their minds, but has likewise produced fatal effects upon their bodies. Two of them died lately at Munster, raving mad. The original cause of this critical Mania, which has continued so many centuries, and still rages with the same violence, is what immediately follows,

> *Natum*——————
> *prosequitur dictis, protaque emittit eburna.*

He takes leave of his son, and conducts him thro' the ivory gate; which has given a handle to the adverse party to say, that he diverts himself, at last, with his own sublime philosophical system, and sends it up into the air as boys do a paper kite.

But whoever has a mind to satisfy himself about this passage of Virgil, (which is, in fact, puzzling) will find a new and ingenious attempt to discuss the difficulties attending it, supported with great learning, in Mr. Warburton's Divine Legation of Moses, where the descent of Æneas into hell, in all its particulars, is cleared and accounted for, by a reference to the progressive ceremonies of initiation into the Eleusinian mysteries.[9]

In the house next the merchant's lives a famous bookseller; he some time ago published a work that sold extremely well. He agreed with the author for fifty pistoles, if it came to a second edition; and he now dreams that he is actually printing a second edition without the author's knowledge.

As to that dream, says Zambullo, we may easily guess through what gate of sleep it has proceeded: there is no doubt but it will prove one of the true ones. These honest gentlemen, the booksellers, stand upon little ceremony with authors in such points as these.[10] What you say is undoubtedly true, replied Asmodeus; but at the same time, pray Sir, inform yourself a little better in regard to the character of these honest gentlemen the authors, and you will find their consciences, in that respect, pretty much upon a foot with the others. A trifling affair, that happened not above a hundred years ago at Madrid, will set this affair before you in a true light.

Three booksellers were drinking a glass of wine together at a tavern, and as they drank, complained bitterly of the scarcity of new books, that were good for any thing. Gentlemen, said one of the three, our complaints in the main are certainly too well grounded, but as we are all friends I will tell you a secret; within these few days past, something extraordinary has fallen in my way.——I have purchased a copy from an author, that cost me, most certainly, a pretty round sum; but what then? It is a brilliant of the first water.[11] Upon this, another of the booksellers declared, that it was very same case with him; having, as he said, upon his honour, made a most valuable and inestimable acquisition in the republic of letters, no longer ago than the day before yesterday. Upon this, the third bookseller stood up and spoke, My friends, said he, since you have been so free, I will likewise impart to you, that this very day is come into my possession the choicest manuscript that these modern times have yet produced. When this last had uttered these words, the three booksellers put their hands to their pockets in vast hurry, as it were in defiance of each other. They soon perceived that every one had purchased the copy of a play, but did not know, 'till they compared the originals, that each of them had separately paid so much money for the Wandering Jew.

In the next house, continued Asmodeus, there is a timorous and bashful lover, who makes his addresses to a lady, who is good flesh and blood, and a widow besides. He has this moment awaked, and was dreaming that he was with his mistress in the thicket of a wood, and that he was talking to her in a most soft and tender strain; to which she answered: You are so insinuating and seducing! was I not upon my guard against the snares of you men, even my virtue, in such a place, might be in danger; but I know you too well, you're all deceitful: actions, not words, must convince me. Actions, Madam, what actions do you require of me? replies the lover. Must I undertake the twelve labours of Hercules, to convince you of the violence of my passion? No, Don Nicasio, said she tenderly and leaning back;[12] no, I can be satisfied with less than an Hercules. Upon this the man awaked.

Pray, said the student, tell me why that man, who is in that bed yonder, is in such agitation? he is tossing to and fro, as if he were possessed by the devil. He is, replied the other, a learned clergyman, who is now in a dream that gives him great uneasiness. He thinks he is disputing with and maintaining the immortality of the soul against a little doctor of physic, who is as good a christian as he is a physician.

In the second story over the clergyman, lays a gentleman of Estremadura, whose name is Balthazar Farfaronico. He has rid post[13] to Madrid, to ask a place at court for having killed a Portugueze. You will hardly guess what the subject matter of his dream is. He had already, as he thinks, got the government of Antiquera, but is very dissatisfied, imagining he deserves the government of the Indies.

I perceive in an inn two people of consequence, who are both of them plagued with very uneasy dreams. One, who is governor of a fortified town, dreams that he is besieged, and after a short defence obliged to surrender prisoner of war with his garrison. The other person is the bishop of Murcia: the court has appointed this prelate to preach the funeral sermon for one of the princesses, which he is to perform in two days. He dreams that he is in the pulpit, and that he stops short after the beginning of the discourse. Why, says Zambullo, it is not impossible but that may happen to him. No, really, answered the demon; for it is what did happen to his lordship not long ago, upon a like occasion.

Shall I shew you one that walks in his sleep? You need but look into the stables of that inn, and there you will perceive one. I observe, says Leandro, a man walking in his shirt, holding in his hand what seems to me a curry-comb. He is, replied Asmodeus, the ostler of the inn, and is quite asleep. He gets up every night, and curries the horses, after which he goes to bed again without waking. The people of the inn think it is the devil, and the ostler himself believes it more than any of them.

In the great house over-against the inn lives a knight of the golden-fleece,[14] formerly vice-roy of Mexico: he is fallen sick, and fearing he shall die, begins to have some troublesome reflections; and indeed the manner he behaved in during the period of his government, may, in a good measure, justify his uneasiness; for the chronicles of New Spain do not make very honourable mention of him. He has just now dreamt a dream, the horrors of which still dwell upon his imagination, and will very probably be the cause of his death. This dream must be somewhat extraordinary, said Zambullo. You shall hear what it is, replied Asmodeus; it is indeed a pretty odd one.[15] He has been dreaming that he was in the valley of death, where all the Mexicans that had been the victims of his cruelty and injustice flocked round him, and loaded him with reproaches and curses. They were even going to have tore him in pieces, but he made his escape, and saved himself from their fury. After which he thought he was got into a spacious room, hung quite round with black cloth, where were his father and grandfather sitting at a table with three covers; these two pensive shades made signs for him to come near, and his father, with a ghostly gravity,[16] said, We have expected you a long time; come and take your place by us.

This was no very pleasing dream, said our student, and I am not surprised his excellency's imagination did not relish it. But, to make amends, said the demon, his niece, who lies in the apartment over him, passes the night deliciously; Morpheus visits her in pleasant slumbers. She is a lady between five and twenty and thirty, ugly and crooked. She now dreams that her uncle is no more, to whom she is sole heiress; and in the vision of dreams, beholds around her all the fine noblemen of the court disputing the prize of her heart.

If I am not mistaken, said Don Cleofas, I hear somebody behind us laughing. You are not mistaken, replied the demon; 'tis a woman laughing in her sleep, a little way from this; a widow, who affects to be a prude, and loves slander with all her soul. She now dreams that she is gossiping with an old devotee, whose conversation gives her infinite delight.

And as for me, I laugh in my turn at a citizen, who lies in the apartment under the widow: it is with great difficulty he makes a shift to live honestly with the little he has; but dreams that he is hoarding up gold and silver in heaps, and the more he hoards the more he finds, so that he has already filled several chests. Poor man, says Leandro, how soon this mighty treasure will vanish! When he wakes, answered the demon, he will be like the real rich man who dies; his wealth and him will bid adieu to each other.

If you have any curiosity to know the dreams of two actresses, who are neighbours, I will inform you. One of them dreams that she is luring birds, which, as soon as they are catched, she plucks their feathers, and gives them to a great boar cat,[17] of whom she is desperately fond, and who enjoys all the fruit of her labours: the other dreams that she is driving from her house greyhounds and Danish mastiffs, in which she formerly greatly delighted; and will now only keep a little lap-dog, one of the handsomest that ever was seen, whom she has lately taken into favour.

These are two ridiculous dreams, said our student. I fancy if there were at Madrid, as formerly at Rome, interpreters of dreams,[18] they would be pretty much puzzled to explain them. Not much puzzled, answered the demon; if they knew but ever so little of the manners and character of our modern actresses, they would soon produce a clear and solid interpretation.

For my own share, said Cleofas, I comprehend nothing of the matter, nor do I give myself any trouble about it. I would much rather know who that lady is, whom I see asleep in a rich velvet bed, with gold fringes, and who has by her bedside a book and a candle. That is a right honourable lady, said the demon; one who rides in a splendid equipage, and whose chief ambition is to have young fellows of good mien, and well-made, appear in her livery. She is used every night to read before she goes to bed, other-wise she could not sleep a wink. Last night she was reading in Ovid's Metamorphoses, and that has given rise to a whimsical dream that now occupies her fancy. She dreams that Jupiter is, at that instant, making love to her in the form of a brawny footman.

But now we are upon this subject, I perceive a metamorphosis which is pleasant enough; a player who now, in the dead of sleep, enjoys a most pleasant reverie. This actor is so very old, that scarcely a man in Madrid remembers his first appearance upon the theatre; he has trod the stage so long, that he is now, if one may say so, theatrified. He has merit in his way, but is so vain, and values himself so much upon it, that he considers himself above the race of men. Can you imagine, for example, what this Cothurnian hero[19] dreams of? Why that he is dead, and that there is an extraordinary council of the gods convened, to determine what is to be done with so extraordinary a mortal. He is now listening attentively to the speech of Mercury; who is haranguing to the assembly of the gods, that this famous player, after having so often represented Jupiter, and the other immortal deities upon the stage, ought not to be subject to the common fate of men, but ought to be enrolled among the celestial powers. Momus seconds Mercury's motion; but some others, both gods and goddesses, seem to be against this new species of canonization; and Jupiter, to put an end to their dispute, transforms him into a scenical figure of decoration.

The demon who was going on, when Zambullo interrupted him: Stop, Signior Asmodeus, you seem not to be aware that day now appears. I am mortally afraid we shall be seen upon the top of this house: if the people once get a sight of your worship, we shall have a mob about us, that will not be dispersed so soon.

They will see nothing of us, answered the other. I have the same power as these fabulous divinities we have been talking of; and as Jupiter, the son of Saturn, erst inveloped mount Ida with clouds of smoke, to hide from all the universe his caresses with Juno; in like manner shall we be immediately wrapt up in a thick vapour, which, though impenetrable to the eyes of other mortals, will be no hindrance to you from perceiving all these objects I have a mind to shew you. In an instant they found themselves in the midst of a smoaky cloud, extremely dark, but which did not occasion any dimness to the eyes of Don Cleofas.

Now as to our dreams——But hold, added he, I don't consider that I have kept you up all night, and that the manner I have entertained you with must have greatly fatigued you. I will therefore carry you home, and leave you, some hours, to rest; whilst, in the mean time, I traverse the four quarters of the world, and discharge the duty of my mission here on earth, after which I will return, and entertain you with some new scenes. I have no inclination to sleep, nor am I at all fatigued, answered Zambullo; therefore, instead of leaving me, I beg you would do me the favour to inform me, what those people are about, who are now stirring, and, it seems, preparing to go out; I want to know what is their scheme of the day, and why they get up so early. What you want, answered the demon, is well worth your while to be informed of. By that you will come to the knowledge of the views, intentions, and designs of poor mortals; the pains they take to kill the time,[20] and fill up the short space of duration that is alotted them between their birth and the grave.

CHAPTER VI.

Where may be seen several originals, that are not without copies.

Let us begin first with the troop of beggars whom you see already in the streets. Most of them are born of creditable parents, but through laziness and debauchery, have taken to this course of life; they live in common like monks, and pass the night in all manner of riot, in a house, belonging to the society, which is well stored with wine and all manner of provision. They are now separating, to act their parts at the doors of the churches. At night they will meet, and drink the health of those charitably disposed

Christians who relieve their necessities. It is worth while to observe how these rogues turn and twist themselves to raise pity. A coquette knows not better to practise her airs in the glass, than these fellows do to act their grimaces.[1]

Observe them three there, all together. He who supports himself upon crutches, whose body shakes as if in the fit of an ague, and who walks with so much pain, that one would imagine he was to tumble to the ground every moment, though he looks old and decrepit, and has a long, white beard, is nevertheless a young fellow so nimble and agile, that he could out-run a stag; and that other there, whose scald-head[2] is covered with a clout, has a head of hair fit for one of the pages of the court; and the third, who appears quite lame, is a rascal who begs so lamentably, that at the sound of his doleful voice, there is hardly a good old woman in Madrid, but will come down three pair of stairs to give him a farthing.

Whilst these idle vermin, under the pretence of poverty, are preparing to cheat the public, I can perceive a great many honest, laborious tradesmen, who, though Spaniards, are preparing to earn their bread by the sweat of their brows; and a number of people, of all sorts, going about their different employments. How many projects, concerted over night, will, this day, be executed, or vanish into air? What variety of operations will love, interest, and ambition occasion?

What is this I see in the street? said Cleofas. Who is that woman loaded with medals*, conducted by a footman, and going in so great haste. Doubtless she must be sent for on some pressing occasion. You are in the right, answered Asmodeus; she is a venerable matron, and is going, in all haste, to a house where her assistance is immediately wanted. She is now got into the apartments of an actress, who is in labour; and just by her you see two men in great concern; one of them is the husband, and the other a gentleman of fortune, who is interested in what passes; for the lying-in of these princesses pretty much resembles that of Alcmena; there is, for the most part, a Jupiter and Amphytrion concerned.

To see that gentleman mounted on horseback with his carabine, one would imagine he was equipped for the field to make war upon the hares and partridges about Madrid; but he goes neither to hunt nor to course. He has another design; and is going to a country village, where he will dress himself as a peasant; and in that disguise get into a farmer's house, where he has a mistress, who is under the eye of a strict and watchful mother.

This young clergyman, who goes past us in so great a hurry, pays his respects regularly every morning to an old canon, his uncle, whose prebendship he has in his eye; and if you look over the way, you will see a man taking his cloak, and making ready to go out. He is an honest and rich citizen, who has a very serious affair upon his hands that does not a little perplex him.[3] The case is, he has an only child, a daughter, to dispose of in marriage; and is not a little in doubt, whether he should bestow her upon an attorney, who makes his addresses, or to a proud country squire, who demands her in marriage.

* It is a common thing in Spain for women, in particular, to make shew of their extraordinary piety, by having loads of these medals hanging about them, (made mostly of stamped pewter) representing saints, miracles, and all sorts of traditionary legends.

He is going to take the advice of his friends upon the matter; and between the two the citizen is really much puzzled. For if he makes choice of the squire, he is afraid of a son-in-law that will despise him; and if he gives his daughter to the attorney, he dreads lest he should take into his house a moth, that may, in time, consume his substance.

In the house next to this anxious father, observe in that apartment of rich and magnificent furniture, a man dressed in a morning gown of brocade and flowers of gold. That is a bel esprit, a fellow come from the dunghill, and affects the airs of a man of quality.[4] Not ten years ago he had not sixpence, but is now worth ten thousand ducats a year. He keeps a splendid equipage, but that he saves from the crumbs of his table, for he never has any one to dine with him, but sits down to his bit by himself; except now and then, that out of ostentation he pretends to give entertainments to people of quality. To-day he is to give a dinner to some of them, and upon that account has sent for a cook and confectioner, with whom he haggles for a farthing,[5] and sets down upon the paper particular dishes he bargains for. What a pitiful dog[6] this is! said Zambullo. All beggars, answered Asmodeus, who spring on a sudden to the top of fortune's wheel, become either misers or spendthrifts; that is a standing rule.

Let me know, says Zambullo, who that lady is at her toilet, in conversation with a very handsome gentleman. Upon my word, said the demon, what you observe is worth your attention. She is a German lady, and a widow, who lives at Madrid upon her jointure, and keeps extreme good company; and he that is with her, is a young nobleman called Don Antonio de Monsalvo.

Though his family is one of the greatest in Spain, he has made this widow a promise of marriage, and has moreover, given into her hands a deed of obligation to perform his engagements, under the penalty of three thousand pistoles; but he finds himself strongly opposed in his designs by his friends, who threaten to have him shut up, if he does not break off all correspondence with her, whom they look upon to be no better than she should be.[7] The cavalier, extremely mortified to find them all united to thwart him in his love, last evening went to his mistress, who, observing him to be chagrined, asked him the cause, which he told her, assuring her, at the same time, that all the opposition he might meet with, on the part of his family, should never one moment divert the constancy of his passion. The lady seemed charmed at his fidelity and resolution, and about midnight they parted, quite satisfied with one another.

This morning Monsalvo came back again to see his widow, whom he found at her toilet, and began afresh to talk of his love. While they were conversing together, the lady took her papers from her hair; one of which Monsalvo taking up without thinking, unfolded it, and found it to be his own hand-writing. What then, Madam, said he smiling, is this the use you make of my billets-doux? Yes, Monsalvo, said she, you see what use I make of the engagements of lovers, who would marry me against the consent of their families; I use them for papillottes. When Don Antonio found that it was, in fact, the writing he had signed for the forfeiture of the three thousand pistoles, he could not help admiring the generous disinterestedness of the lady, and swore, anew, eternal fidelity.

Cast your eyes upon that tall, lean man, who is going along the street, just below. He has a large book of paper under his arm, an inkhorn on his belt, and a guittar on his back. This looks to be an odd sort of fellow, says Zambullo, and I durst to say is an original.

Certainly, replied Asmodeus, he is a queer sort of mortal. You have heard of Cynic philosophers; you have them in Spain, and there goes one.[8] This man is walking towards Buen-Retiro, to a place where there is a fine meadow, in the midst of which pours a fountain of clear water, which winds its serpentine rills, amidst the flowers that deck the enamelled fields. There will he stay the whole day long, contemplating the riches of nature, playing upon the guittar, and minuting his reflections down in his place-book;[9] and his pockets supply him with plenty of bread and onions, his daily sustenance. Such is the sober life this man has led for these ten years past; and if Aristippus was to say to him, as he did to Diogenes, if you knew how to make your court to the great, you would not munch onions; this modern philosopher would answer him, I could make myself agreeable to the great as well as you, if I could debase human nature so far as to cringe to another.

In fact, this sage was formerly a follower and attendant of great men, and they even made his fortune; but as he found their friendship was only an honourable servitude, he suddenly broke off all communication with them. He kept his chariot, but laid it down, because he imagined it might in the streets bespatter more worthy men than himself, and gave all he had got to his indigent acquaintance, reserving only to himself as much as would support him in the manner he now lives; for this philosopher thinks it as shameful to beg his bread among the people, as to cringe to the minister.

You ought to pity that gentleman who follows the Cynic, and who is attended only by his dog. He may boast of representing one of the best families in all Castile, and was formerly in possession of a large fortune, which, like Lucian's Timon,[10] he squandered away in constantly regaling his friends, but more particularly in costly entertainments on the marriage or birth-days of princes and princesses; and indeed on every occasion where there were public rejoicings in Spain. The moment these sharks, who had been devouring him, found the tables turned,[11] they knew him no more. His friends, his servants all have forsaken him; one only remains faithful to him, his old dog Argus.

Tell me, Signior Asmodeus, said Don Cleofas, to whom that chariot belongs, which stops before that house. It belongs to a rich banker, answered the other, who visits there every morning, where lives a Galician beauty, whom this old sinner[12] keeps, and of whom he is desperately fond. Yesterday he was informed that she was false to him. In the fury of passion this news put him in, he wrote her a letter full of threatnings and reproaches; and you would hardly guess, I believe, how this little jilt behaved on the occasion. Instead of the common method of impudently denying the fact, she this morning sent him a letter, in which she acknowledges the just reason he has to be incensed against her; that he ought, for the future, to look upon her with contempt and indignation, as she has been capable of falshood to so fine a gentleman; that she was not only sensible of her fault, but abhorred herself for it, and, to inflict some degree of punishment, had already cut off her fine hair, of which he knows she is passionately fond; in a word, that she had taken a resolution to retire, and devote the rest of her days to repentance.

The old fumbler[13] was strangely melted at these pretended remorses of his mistress, and got up betimes to pay her a visit. He found her all in tears; and this excellent actress has played her part so well, that he has not only entirely forgiven what is past, but will do more. To make her amends for the rape of her locks,[14] he has this moment promised to make her the lady of a manor, and to buy her a fine country-house, which is now to be sold near the Escurial.[15]

All the public shops, and other places, are now opened, said the scholar; and I perceive a gentleman so early as this going into a tavern. That gentleman, said Asmodeus, is the heir of a good family; but has got the furor of writing upon him, and cannot be happy unless he passes for an author: and yet, on the main, the man has sense; nay, has genius enough to make tolerable observations upon almost all the plays that appear upon the stage, but not enough to compose a tolerable one himself. He is gone into this tavern to order a handsome dinner, and is to entertain four players, whose protection he wants for a vile play of his own writing, which he is to offer to their company.

Apropos. Now we are talking of authors, continued Asmodeus, there are two of them that meet in the street: how scornfully they grin one at another, as they pull off their hats. They have a sovereign contempt for each other, and indeed not without reason. One writes as easily as Crispinus*, whom Horace compares to the blowing of a pair of bellows, and the other has wore himself down to skin and bones, in composing works of dry and tasteless insipidity.

Who is that little man who is getting out of his coach, at the door of a church? says Cleofas. He is, replied the demon, a person worth remarking. About ten years since he gave up the study of the law, though he had been head-clerk to a notary public, and entered into a Carthusian monastery[16] at Saragossa. In the sixth month of his noviceship, he departed from the convent, and came to Madrid; and they who were acquainted with him, were vastly surprised to find him all of a sudden appear one of the principal members of the council of the Indies. To this day people talk with surprize of such a sudden elevation. Some are of opinion he sold himself to the devil; others, that he was kept by a certain lady of a great jointure; others, that he had found a treasure. Well, but you know the meaning of all this, interrupted Zambullo. O yes, I know it, replied the demon, and will unravel the mystery to you.

While this monk was in his noviceship, it happened that as he was digging very deep in the garden to plant a tree, he found a copper chest, which he opened, and within it a gold casket, containing about thirty fine diamonds; and though he knew nothing of the value of precious stones, yet he made no manner of doubt but what he found was a valuable purchase. And as Gripus†, in one of Plautus's plays, renounces the fishing-nets, after he had found a treasure; so this monk leaving the cassock, and being a fisher of

---

* Crispinus was cotemporary with Horace, at whose success and reputation he was so enraged, that he sent him a challenge; desiring him to name his time and place, and he would meet him, and write with him for what he would; the conditions to be, that he who wrote most in the same time, should be deemed the conqueror, and to prevent any foul play, proposed they should each of them write in the custody of centinels. The other declined accepting this invitation, alledging in his excuse, his natural timidity; but sent his adversary a piece of exhortation, which was, to repair to a smith's forge, and there finish his studies, carefully observing the motion of the bellows, and taking example therefrom. Vid. Hor. lib. 1. Sat. 4.

† This is a fisherman in the play of Plautus, called Rudens, what we would call the tempest. About the beginning of the fourth act, he makes a long soliloquy, what he would do with his treasure; that he would build a town, and call it Gripus, &c.

men, returned to Madrid, where by the assistance of one of his friends, he changed his diamonds for ready money; and his ready money for a post, which enables him now to stand a distinguished publican at the receipt of custom.[17]

CHAPTER VII.

What things more the demon shewed Don Cleofas.

I must make you laugh a little, continued Asmodeus, at that man who is just now entering that coffee-house; he is a Biscayan physician, and is going to have a dish of chocolate, after which he will sit and play all day at chess.

But whilst he is so busy, you need be under no apprehension for his patients, for he has none; and if he had, the time he bestows at play would be no loss to them. Every night he visits a beautiful and rich widow, whom he greatly wants to marry, and with whom he pretends to be deeply in love. During the time he sits with her, a rogue of a valet, who makes up all the number of his domestics, and with whom he is in very good intelligence, brings him a list of the lord knows how many people of quality,[1] who have sent for the doctor. The widow lady believes all this to be literally true, and the doctor is on the point of gaining her consent.

Let us stop at this hotel near us. I must not let pass, without observing the people who dwell in it. Cast your eyes over the apartments, and remark what you discover. I perceive ladies of most exquisite beauty, answered Leandro; some of them are getting up, and others of them are already risen. What beauties they disclose to my sight! Methinks I see the nymphs of Diana, just as the poets describe them.

If these ladies you so much admire rival the nymphs of Diana in the charms of beauty, I assure you they cannot boast of their chastity. These are five or six women of the town, who live in common, and share their booty.[2] As the fine ladies in inchanted castles, did, in days of old, by their charms, allure the knight-errants who passed by their castles, so do they lure young people into their snares; and unhappy they who listen to their syren-songs. Indeed to warn people, who pass by, of their danger, there ought to be marks placed before the house, as there are buoys set up to keep ships from coming upon the shoals.[3]

I need not ask you where these noble lords are driving in their chariots; they are, no doubt, going to the king's levee. They are, answered the demon; and if you have a mind to go too, I'll take you along with me; we may be able to make there some pretty observations. You could not propose any thing more agreeable, said Zambullo. I am so fond of it, that I already anticipate the pleasure I shall receive.

Upon which, Asmodeus, willing to satisfy the curiosity of Don Cleofas, carried him off towards the palace; but before they got there, our student perceiving several workmen busy in raising a very high gate, asked if it was not the portal of some church. No;

answered the other, 'tis for a new market-place, and is very magnificent, as you see. But if they should rear it as high as the tower of Babel, it will never come up to the two Latin verses, that are to serve for an inscription.

What say you? cries Leandro. You give me such an idea of them, that I am impatient to know what they are. I will tell you, answered the demon, and be sure you take heed to them.

> * *Quam bene Mercurius nunc merces vendit opimas.*
> *Momus ubi fatuos vendidit ante sales.*

There is in this distich,[4] a turn of words exquisitely pretty. I don't yet perceive all the beauty in them you mention, said our student; for I don't comprehend these *fatuos sales*.[5] That is, answered Asmodeus, because you don't know that the place this market is built on, for the sale of provisions, was formerly a college of monks, a seminary of learning for young people. The regents of this college made the scholars act most vile dramatic performances, with such ridiculously extravagant *ballets* in the interludes, that preterits and supines danced horn-pipes.[6] Oh! replied Don Cleofas, say no more of it; I well know what sickening stuff the college-pieces are. I like the inscription hugely.

Asmodeus and Zambullo were scarcely got on the stair-case of the palace, when they saw a great number of courtiers going up the steps. As these lords passed one by one, the demon stood nomenclator.[7] There, said he to Leandro, pointing with his finger to them, one after another, that is the count de Villalonsa, chief of the house of Puebla d'Ellerena; that is the marquis of Castro Fueste; this is Don Lopez de los Rios, president of the finances; and that other the count de Villa Hombrosa. But he was not satisfied with mentioning their names, he must needs give their characters: in giving of which, this evil spirit, following the biass of his own diabolical nature, always intermixed some satyrical stroke, not much to the honour of these great personages.[8]

He would say, for example, this lord is of a temper obliging and affable; if you address him, he receives you with an air of sweetness and good nature; do you beg his protection, he generously grants it, and offers to employ all his interest in your favour. What a pity it is, that a mind so turned to humanity and benevolence should be clogged with any natural infirmity. But so it is. He labours under such a defect of memory, that for the blood of him he cannot remember a quarter of an hour any thing of what he has said to you, or what you have said to him.[9]

And this great duke, he would add, speaking of another, is one of the most amiable characters about court. He is not, like most others of his distinguished rank, whimsical and capricious, varying every hour like the weather; no, he has none of that; his temper is even, and consistent with itself at all times. And, moreover, if you shew an attachment to his person, he is far from being insolent or ungrateful; and if you are so fortunate as to do him any particular service, you are sure of being handsomely requited; but then,

---

* This means, "How properly does Mercury now sell wares and commodities, in a place where Momus formerly vended insipid attempts to wit and pleasantry." What pun, or *jeu de mots* is in it, must be on a double signification of the word *sales:* but it is not worth while to say any more about it; for it is at best, a low monkish conundrum.

amidst all this, in bestowing a recompence for services done, he is so monstrously long-winded, that, services apart, you think your very attendance has dearly purchased his favours.

After Asmodeus had entertained Leandro Perez with an account of the good and bad qualities of a great number of the lords about court, he brought him into a large hall, where were men of all ranks and conditions; but in particular such a cluster of chevaliers, that Don Cleofas could not help saying, What a number of knights! My God! Spain must certainly abound with them. That you may take my word for, said the demon; nor is it any ways surprising; for a chevalier of the order of St. Jago or Calatrava,[10] don't require the same qualification as a Roman knight, to be worth twenty five thousand crowns. No, a qualification here comes much cheaper.

Look upon that little, flat-faced man behind you there. Don't speak so loud, said Zambullo; the man will hear you. No he won't, replied the demon; for by the same power that we are rendered invisible, we likewise cannot be overheard. Observe him again, and remark his figure; he is a Catalan, just returned from the Philippine islands, where he had been a privateer in the service of Spain. Tho' to look at him, one would not take him for an Achilles, yet this man has performed prodigies of valour. This morning he is to present a petition to the king, praying for some place, in recompence of his services; but as he has not first addressed himself to the minister, I question much whether he will succeed.

On the right hand of the buccaneer, said Leandro Perez, I see a large, fat fellow, who would appear a man of consequence. To judge of him by the important loftiness of his carriage, one would take him to be some great lord. He is far from it, said Asmodeus; a poor, broken, country squire, who keeps a gaming table under the protection of a nobleman.

But I observe a doctor in divinity here, who is well worth remarking: that is he, I mean, at the first window, in conversation with the gentleman in brown velvet. They are talking of an affair that was yesterday decided by the king, of which I will acquaint you with the particulars.

About two months ago the doctor, who is a member of the academy of Toledo,[11] published a book of morality that gave great offence to all the Castilian authors. They found the language in general, as they thought, too bold, and many words newly coined. Upon this they all, to an author, entered into a confederacy against him, had a meeting upon the affair, and agreed to draw up a petition to the king, praying him to condemn the doctor's book, as contrary to the elegance and purity of the Spanish tongue.

His majesty thought the subject-matter of the petition worthy of his consideration, and appointed three people to examine the book. They reported, that the stile certainly deserved censure, and the more so as it was plausible and florid.[12] Upon which report, the king decided in the following manner; he ordered, under pain of being punished for disobedience, that those academicians of Toledo, whose stile was formed after the taste of the doctor's, should write no more books for the future; and further, to preserve the purity of the Castilian language, that these academicians, after their death, should be succeeded by none but persons of the first quality.

Such decision, indeed, said Zambullo smiling, appears marvellous. The partizans of the common vernacular language, will have now nothing to fear. Pardon me, answered the demon; the authors, who are enemies to that noble simplicity which charms the judicious, are not all of them members of the academy at Toledo.

Don Cleofas expressed a curiosity to know who he was in the velvet, that discoursed with the doctor. He is, answered Asmodeus, a younger brother of a good family in Catalonia, and is an officer in the Spanish guards. A spritely young fellow he is, I assure you; to convince you of it, I will tell you a repartee he made t'other day to a lady, in a great deal of good company; but to make you understand it,[13] you must know that he has a brother, named Don Andreas de Prada, who some years ago had, as his brother has now, a commission in the guards.

It happened one day, that a farmer of the king's revenue, a man worth a vast deal of money, accosted Don Andreas in this manner; Signior de Prada, said he, I am of the same name as you, but our families are different. I know you to be of one of the best families of Catalonia, but at the same time, that you are not rich. Now I am rich enough, but of a mean family. Suppose we should share with one another what each of us separately possesses? Are you in the possession of the heraldry of your family? Don Andreas answered he was. That being the case, said he, give it to me; I will put it into the hands of an able genealogist, who shall fall to work, and make us cousins, in spite of our grandfathers; and if you do that, I will in my turn, give you thirty thousand pistoles. Is it agreed? Don Andreas was dazzled with the greatness of the sum, gave his coat of arms to the other, and with the money he received, bought a fine estate in Catalonia, on which he has lived ever since.

But his younger brother, who got not a shilling by this bargain, happened to dine at a place where they talked of Signior Prada, farmer of the revenues: upon which a lady in the company, addressing herself to the captain, said, Sir, are not you the farmer's relation? No, Madam, answered he, I have not that honour, it is my brother.

Don Cleofas burst into a fit of laughter at this repartee, which he thought extremely smart.[14] Then perceiving a little man who followed a lord up and down, My God! cried he, what does this little creature want, who sticks so closely to this courtier, and makes him so many bows? he certainly solicits him for something. What you observe, said Asmodeus, is worth your knowing, and I will tell you the meaning of all this. The little man is an honest citizen, who has a very fine country house not far from Madrid, at a village where there are famous mineral waters, which he gave the use of, for three months, to this noble lord, (who went there to drink the waters,) without costing him a farthing. The citizen is intreating him, with great earnestness, to serve him in an affair, in which he has immediate occasion for his interest; and the nobleman, with the greatest politeness, refuses to do him the least service.

I must not let this plebeian cavalier escape our observation; he that you see pressing and jostling through the croud, as if he was a man of the first quality. He is grown lately excessively rich, by his knowledge in the science of numbers. In his house there are as many servants as in the hotel of any nobleman; and his table surpasses that of the minister for elegance, and the number of dishes. He keeps an equipage for himself, another for his wife, and a third for his children. Not many days since he bought a set of horses, which even the prince of Spain had refused, because they were too dear. What insolence! cried Leandro. If a Turk was to see this fool of fortune mounted so high upon her wheel, he would not fail to prophecy, that his fall was very near.[15] I know nothing of futurity, said Asmodeus; but I am very much inclined to be of the same opinion with the Turk.

What is this I see? cried the demon with surprize. I can scarcely believe the testimony of my senses. I see at court a poet that I am sure has no business here.[16] How can the man have the assurance to shew his face in this place, after having lampooned almost all the grandees in Spain?[17] I wish he don't depend too much upon the contempt they hold him in.

Consider attentively that venerable personage, who comes in, supported by a gentleman. See with what respect he is received, and how the crowd of courtiers make a lane to let him pass. This is Don Joseph de Reynaste, and Ayala, grand judge of the police,[18] who comes to make a report to the king, of what has passed this night in the city of Madrid. Observe that good old man, with veneration.

Indeed, says Zambullo, he has greatly the air of a good man. Much were it to be wished, replied Asmodeus, that the inferior judges and magistrates under him, would model their conduct after his example. He is not one of those hasty and violent tempers, who are swayed only by passion and caprice. He will not send a man to prison on the bare information of a bailiff, a secretary, or a justice's clerk. He knows too well what sort of fellows, for the most part, they are;[19] that their low and venal souls are capable of most shamefully corrupting the stream of justice. For which reason, therefore, when an accused person is to be committed, he strictly examines into all the circumstances, and must be convinced himself of the truth of what is laid to the charge of the criminal; by which means, he never sends an innocent person to prison. Whoever are committed by him are guilty of the crimes for which they stand accused; nor even those does he abandon to the barbarity practised in the dungeons. He goes himself in person to see these miserable wretches, and interposes the protection of his authority, that the just severities of the law be not made more bitter by the scourges of inhumanity.

What a delightful character! replied Leandro. What an amiable old man is this! I wish, with all my heart, I could hear him speak to the king. I am very sorry, answered the other, that I cannot gratify you in this, without manifestly exposing myself; for I am not allowed to come into the presence of sovereigns; that would be breaking into the province of Leviathan, Belphegor, and Ashtaroth. I have already told you, that these three spirits have the charge of kings and princes; and there is a strict order, that no other devil shall presume to go to court, so that I can hardly think what I was dreaming of, when I took it into my head to carry you here. I must own it was a very rash and imprudent step; for if these three demons should espy me, they would immediately fall foul of me, and, between you and I, I should come but scurvily off.[20]

As the case is so, replied Zambullo, for God's sake let us make what haste we can to get away; for it would break my very heart, to see you tossed about in the air like a tennis-ball by these devils your brethren,[21] and I have not it in my power to assist you; for, I suppose, if I was to take your part, I could be of no great service to you. Service! no; replied Asmodeus, they would not feel your blows, but you would soon fall under the weight of theirs.

But continued he, though I cannot give you the satisfaction of being closetted with your monarch, I can give you an equivalent pleasure in the room of it. As he had spoke this, he took Don Cleofas by the hand, and winged him through the air towards La Merci.

CHAPTER VIII.

Of the Slaves.

They both stopped short on the top of a house near that monastery, at the gate of which there was gathered an infinite concourse of people of both sexes. What a world of folks are here! said Leandro. What public ceremonial makes them flock together in such numbers? A ceremony you have never yet seen, answered the demon, though it is frequently performed at Madrid. Three hundred slaves, all subjects of Spain, are this moment landed from Algiers, where the fathers of the redemption have been to ransom them; all the streets through which they pass will be crowded with spectators.

It is true, answered Zambullo, that I have never hitherto been curious enough to see this spectacle; and if this be what your worship reserved for my amusement, I will tell you plainly, that I do not think you had so much reason to boast of it. I am too well acquainted with you, replied Asmodeus, not to know, that the sight of miserable objects is no entertaining amusement for you: but when you are apprised, that in bringing you to see them, I intend to relate to you the most remarkable particulars in the captivity of some, and the perplexities that attend others upon their return to their own country, I am persuaded you will not think yourself disagreeably entertained. No, to be sure, replied the student, you are in the right; what you say now alters the case; and I shall be much obliged to you, for affording me so much satisfaction.[1]

Whilst they were conversing together in this manner, they were interrupted by the noise of great shouts, which the people set up as the slaves passed by, who marched in the following order: they went on foot two and two, in the dress they wore when in slavery; every one carrying his chains on his shoulders. A considerable number of the friars of La Merci, who had gone to meet them, went at their head, mounted upon mules, that were covered with black, as if they had been in mourning, and one of these good fathers carried the standard of the redemption. The youngest of the slaves went first, and the oldest last; and behind them all, came mounted upon a little horse, a religieux of the same order, who looked like one of the ancient prophets, and was chief of the mission. He attracted the looks of all the spectators, by the great gravity of his mien, and a long, grey beard, which made him still more venerable; and one might read in the countenance of this Spanish Moses, the exquisite pleasure he felt in having been the instrument of restoring so many christians to their liberty, and native country.

These captives, said the demon, are not all equally glad at having recovered their liberty. If some are rejoicing at the thoughts of seeing once more their relations, there are others, who dread lest they should hear of things having happened in their families, during their absence, more afflicting to them, than even the miseries of bondage.

For example, the two that march first are in this last class. One, a native of a little village in Arragon,[2] after having been ten years a slave among the Turks, without having ever heard any tidings of his wife, will now find her married to another man, by whom she has five children; and the other, a woolen-draper's son of Segovia, was taken by a corsair twenty-five years since. He is afraid, that in so long a time, the face of affairs in his family may be changed; and his apprehensions are not ill grounded; for his father and mother are both dead, and his brothers, who shared their effects between them, have squandered away the whole, by their bad management.

I cannot help observing, with attention, one particular slave, said Cleofas; and I judge, from his air, that he huggs himself[3] at the thoughts of his being no more in dread of the bastinado.[4] This captive, whom you observe, answered the demon, has more than ordinary cause to be rejoiced at his deliverance, as he has got intelligence that his aunt, to whom he is sole heir, is just dead; by which he will immediately become master of a splendid fortune. The thoughts of this have an agreeable effect, and give that air of satisfaction which you remark.

It is far otherwise with that unhappy gentleman who walks by his side. A cruel anxiety gnaws him without ceasing, and the cause is this; when he was taken by an Algerine corsair, going from Spain to Italy, he was in love with a lady, and was beloved by her; and he is now racked with uneasiness, lest, during the time of his captivity, there should be a change in the constancy of his mistress. And has his captivity been long? said Leandro. Eighteen months, answered the other. Poh! said Zambullo, he can have no reason to be alarmed, his fears are certainly groundless. He has not put his mistress's constancy to a sufficient trial to make him jealous of her fidelity. That is your mistake, answered the demon; for his Dulcinea[5] no sooner heard of his being a slave in Barbary, than the first step she took, was, to provide herself in another gallant.

Pray, Mr. Student, continued the demon, could you imagine, that this man who follows close after the other two we have been talking of, he whom you see in that frightful figure, with a clotted, red beard;[6] should you, think you, take that man, at first sight, for a very pretty fellow? I believe not; yet, I give you my word, he is one, and under the appearance of that shocking figure, you behold a man, who forms the hero of a very extraordinary story, which I will relate to you.

His name is Fabricio; and he was scarce fifteen years of age, when his father, who was a rich farmer of Cinquello, a considerable town in the kingdom of Leon, died; and he lost his mother a short while after. So that being an only child, he was master of a very pretty fortune and was left under the guardianship of one of his uncles, a man of worth and probity. Fabricio finished his studies, which he had already begun at Salamanca.[7] After which he learned to fence, to ride the great horse, and made himself master of all the accomplishments of a gentleman, in order to render himself worthy the regard of Donna Hypolita, the sister of a poor country squire, whose seat, such as it was, lay at a small distance from Cinquello.[8]

This young lady was, indeed, very handsome, and much about the age of Fabricio; who, having been accustomed to see her from his infancy, had, as one may say, sucked in with his mother's milk, a passion for Hypolita; and she, on her part, looked upon Fabricio as a very handsome, pretty fellow; but as he was the son of a farmer, did not think him worth her notice; for she had an insupportable pride, as well as her brother, Don Thomas de Xaral, who, for pride and poverty, perhaps had not his fellow in all Spain.

This poor and proud squire lived in the country, in a place he called a castle, but, indeed properly speaking, it was the rubbish of an old house; for it hung disjointed, and threatned ruin to every one that passed by.[9] But though he could not afford to mend a broken pane in any window of this chateau; though he frequently could have no idea of a dinner,[10] yet he had a valet to wait upon his honour, and a black woman to attend mademoiselle his sister.

It was quite a joyous sight to behold Don Thomas de Xaral appear in the village on sundays and holidays, with a suit of crimson velvet, that looked as if he had employed a barber to shave it, and a shallow brimmed hat, with a feather of a sickly yellow;[11] which, on weekdays, were laid by with all the care, as if they had been so many holy relicks.

Thus equipped in these splendid patches, which he valued himself upon, as so many authentic proofs of the antiquity of his family, he strutted with the utmost insolence,[12] and thought he did more than repay any salute that was made him, if he condescended to return it with a nod. Nor was his sister less ridiculous than he, in this notion of her family; and besides, so absurdly vain in regard to her beauty, that she expected daily some nobleman of the first rank would come and demand her of her brother in marriage.

Such were Don Thomas and his sister Hypolita. This Fabricio well knew, and to make himself agreeable to people so vain and so haughty, resolved to distinguish himself, in paying them a most extraordinary deal of homage; and carried on this so well, that both the brother and sister vouchsafed to allow him to come frequently to them, and pay the tribute of his respects. But as he was apprised of their miserable poverty, as well as their pride, he greatly wanted an opportunity of offering them the service of his purse; but was always prevented by the fear of shocking their pride. At last, however, his generosity found out an ingenious expedient to relieve their necessity, without putting them to the blush. Signior, said he one day to this poor squire, as they were alone, I have two thousand ducats I want to put into somebody's hands, will you be so good to do me the favour to take and keep them for me?

It is needless to ask if Don Thomas condescended to grant this favour. Besides his being so wretchedly poor, he had a conscience quite clear of all kind of scruples upon such an occasion;[13] so that he received the sum in charge, and no sooner had it in his custody, than, without any sort of ceremony or excuse, he laid out part of it in repairing his castle, and equipping himself with several little affairs he stood in need of. A suit of fine blue velvet was ordered and made at Salamanca. A new plume of green feathers supplied the place of the yellow one, which, for so long time, had possessed the honour of adorning the skull of Don Thomas de Xaral. The beautiful Hypolita likewise came in for her share, and was very decently rigged out.[14] Thus it was this man made use of the money given him in trust, without once reflecting it was none of his own, and that it was a thing impossible for him ever to make any restitution. But these things never disturbed his conscience; nay, he even thought it was but right, that the son of a husbandman, as the other was, should pay for the honour of being acquainted with a squire of his dignity and family.

All this Fabricio very clearly foresaw, but then imagined, that in return for his ducats, Don Thomas would treat him with greater familiarity; that Hypolita, by degrees, might be brought to be reconciled so far, as not to be shocked at his boldness in aspiring to a lady of her quality; and certain it is, his access to them both was much freer than it had been formerly, and they honoured him with marks of friendship they had never shewn till then; for a rich man will always be acceptable to the great, if he lets himself become a milch cow; and Xaral and his sister, who before had never known what money was, but by report, no sooner tasted the sweets of it, but they considered Fabricio as one that ought to be looked after, and behaved to him with such gracious affability and complaisance, that the man was transported. He began to imagine his person was not disagreeable to them, and that undoubtedly they had reflected how several antient families, in order to support their gentility, were often obliged to match with plebeians. Pleased with these hopes, which flattered his love, he resolved to ask Hypolita in marriage.

The first favourable opportunity he had of speaking to Don Thomas, he told him, he passionately coveted the honour of being his brother-in-law, and that if he would give his consent, he would quit him of the two thousand ducats he had in his hands, and make him a present of a thousand pistoles besides. The haughty Don Thomas reddened at this proposal, which he looked upon as offering an ignominy to his family;[15] and in the first emotions of his pride, was going to have shewn to Fabricio, in what contempt he held the son of a country farmer. But notwithstanding the indignation he conceived at this insult, he restrained himself; and, without appearing to be any ways shocked, answered, he could not immediately determine himself in such an affair; that he must speak to Hypolita upon the subject, and also have a meeting of their relations.

He sent away the lover with that answer, and did, in fact, summon a diet of as many of the Hidalgos[16] in the neighbourhood, as were his relations, all of whom laboured under the disease of pride and poverty, as much as himself.[17] Of these he called a council, not to deliberate whether he should give his sister to Fabricio; but to think of some proper means to punish that insolent wretch, who notwithstanding the meanness of his original, had the impudence to think of marrying a lady of Hypolita's quality.[18]

After he had laid before this assembly the audaciousness of the attempt, at the very name of Fabricio, and the son of a farmer, the eyes of all these noble personages sparkled with fury and indignation: they denounced fire and fury against the criminal; and one and all agreed, that he ought to be beat to death, in order to expiate the outrage he committed upon their family by proposing so shameful an alliance. However, after considering the thing more maturely, the diet came to a resolution, to let the wretch escape with life; but that to teach him not to forget himself another time, they would serve him a trick he should remember the longest day he lived.

They proposed divers expedients, and at last concluded upon this; that Hypolita should pretend an inclination for Fabricio, and under that pretence, to comfort the unhappy lover for Don Thomas's refusal of the proposed match, she should make an assignation with him in the castle, to which he should be introduced by Hypolita's waiting-woman, the black, and that people should be placed there on purpose to oblige him by force to marry her.

Hypolita agreed to this scheme, without reluctance. She looked upon it, that her reputation, and the honour of her family required she should resent the affront of having a marriage proposed to her, by a man so much below herself. But these first emotions, suggested by her pride, soon gave place to those of pity, or rather love, which, on a sudden humbled the haughty spirit of this young lady.

From that moment she considered the matter in another light. The meanness of Fabricio's pedigree appeared to her over ballanced by his many good qualities; and she now beheld him as a gentleman altogether deserving her esteem and affection. Admire with me, Signior student, the prodigious change the power of this passion is capable of effecting. This very lady, who imagined that a prince hardly deserved her, in an instant becomes in love with the son of an husbandman, and encourages his addresses, after having rejected them with disdain and indignation.

As she therefore gave way to the violence of her inclinations,[19] so far was she from being instrumental to her brother's designs of revenge, that she kept a secret correspondence with Fabricio, by means of the old Moorish woman, who sometimes, by night, introduced him into the house. Don Thomas began to have a suspicion of what passed, and was not satisfied with his sister's conduct; he watched her, and was convinced by his own eyes, that instead of favouring his designs, she had betrayed them. He communicated this to two of his cousins, who, kindling into rage at this news, called aloud for vengeance;[20] and Xaral, who was of a disposition that needed not much spurring on, to revenge an affront of this nature, told them, with the gravity of a Spaniard, that they should see what use he could make of his sword, when there was occasion for him to draw it in defence of his honour; he begged them therefore to come to his house early in the evening of a certain day which he appointed.

They came very exact to the time; and Don Thomas letting them in himself, hid them in a little room, without being perceived by any one; then left them, saying, he would come back, as soon as the gallant came into the house, if so be he came that night. And this happened accordingly; for, as the ill-fortune of our lovers would have it, they had appointed that very night for a private interview.

Fabricio was now with his dear Hypolita; and they had begun a conversation upon a subject they had entertained themselves with a hundred times before, but though ever so often repeated, has always the charms of novelty to lovers: when they were disagreeably interrupted by three cavaliers, who lay upon the watch to surprise them. Don Thomas, and his two courageous cousins, fell all at once on poor Fabricio, who had but just time to draw, and imagining they had a design to murder him, fought desperately; he wounded them all three, and still presenting them the point of his sword, got to the door, and made his escape.

Upon which Xaral finding his enemy had escaped with impunity, after having dishonoured his house, vented his rage against the unhappy Hypolita, and plunged his

Don Thomas Avenges His Family's Honor. (Sterling Library, Yale University.)

sword in her heart; and his two cousins, greatly vexed at the bad success of their scheme, returned with their wounds to their own homes.

But let us stop here, added the demon; I will finish his story as soon as we have seen the rest of the captives pass by; I will then acquaint you, how, after all he was worth had been confiscated, on account of this fatal adventure, he was afterwards taken prisoner on the seas, and carried off as a slave into Barbary.

Whilst you was recounting to me the particulars of what you have now told me, I observed among the captives, a man who had so melancholy and languishing an air, that I had several times a mind to have interrupted you, and asked the reason. Well, says the demon, you have lost nothing by delay; I will acquaint you with the reason of it. This slave, whose sorrowful looks you take notice of,[21] is a young gentleman of Valladolid, of a good family, and was two years a slave to a master, who had a very handsome woman for his wife, who was most desperately in love with him, nor did he return her passion with neglect. His master having some suspicions of this, sold him in a great hurry, fearing lest, if he staid longer with him, he might have an inclination to become the father of a young Turk. Ever since, this passionate Castilian mourns the loss of his mistress; nor is he to be comforted, even with the joy of recovering his liberty.

Says Leandro Perez, I observe a mighty good looking old man, who attracts my attention. Who is he? He is a barber, answered Asmodeus; a native of Guiposcoa, who is returning into Biscay, after forty years of slavery. When he fell into the hands of the corsair,[22] he had a wife, two sons, and one daughter, who are all dead, except one of his sons, who, more fortunate than his father, having been at Peru, is returned, with immense riches, into his own country, where he has purchased two fine estates.

What an exquisite pleasure is this! replied the scholar. What transports of joy will he feel, to find his aged father returned from slavery; and that he has it in his power to make him pass the rest of his days in peace and pleasure.

You talk, replied Asmodeus, like a dutiful and affectionate child; but the Biscayan is of a disposition a little more callous. The unexpected return of his father will rather vex than rejoice him. Instead of keeping him with him at his house at Guiposcoa, and doing every thing in his power to testify his joy at his redemption from slavery, he will put him into some kind of office[23] upon one of his estates.

As you are taken with the looks of that old man, please to observe that countenance just behind him; he is a physician of Arragon, and as exactly resembles an old ape, as one egg is like another.[24] He has been but a fortnight at Algiers; for when the Turks understood what profession he was of, they would keep him no longer among them, and chose to deliver him without ransom to the fathers of La Merci, who refused to give one farthing for him, and who have, with the utmost regret, brought him back into Spain.

You who feel so compassionately for the distress of another, how would you bewail the fate of that poor wretch, whose bald pate is covered with a cap of brown cloth, if you knew the miseries he has undergone for the space of twelve years, under an English renegado, who was his master. And who is that unhappy man? A Franciscan friar, replied the demon; though for my own share I am not at all sorry for his sufferings, since, by his persuasions, above a hundred Christian slaves have refused to take the turban.

And I with the same frankness, said Don Cleofas, will tell you, that I am heartily sorry this good father has been so long at the mercy of such a barbarian. You have neither reason to be sorry, nor I to be glad, answered Asmodeus; for this holy priest has profited so much by his twelve years suffering, that it is better for him to have passed that time even in the misery he has undergone, than to have been in his cell warring against the lusts of the flesh, which he would not all times have been able to have overcome.

The slave that comes next after the Franciscan, said Zambullo, looks extremely calm and easy for a man just redeemed from bondage; and I have a great curiosity to know who he is. You anticipate my intentions, answered the demon; I was just going to have pointed him out to you. In that man, who is a citizen of Salamanca, you see an unhappy father, a man that has experienced misery to such a degree, that he is at last become insensible to its sting. I have a great mind to recount his melancholy story, and take no more notice of the rest of the captives; as, excepting this man, there are but few of the others, whose adventures are worth mentioning.

Signior Zambullo, who began to be weary of seeing so many dismal figures, testified his approbation. Upon which the demon gave him an account of what is contained in the following chapter.

CHAPTER IX.

Containing the last history with which Asmodeus entertained the student of Alcala. How in finishing it, he was all of a sudden interrupted; and in what disagreeable manner the demon was obliged to leave him.

Pablos de Bahabon, the son of a man who was mayor of a town in Old Castile, after having shared with his brother the effects their father had left them (which, though he was extremely covetous, were very small) set out for Salamanca to compleat his studies in that university. He was extremely handsome, had a great deal of wit, and was then twenty three years of age.

As he had a thousand ducats in his pocket, and was of a most generous disposition, his arrival at Salamanca soon became the subject of conversation. All the young people of the town were each fonder than another of his acquaintance,[1] that is, of partaking of those parties of pleasure, which Don Pablos was making every day, I say Don Pablos, because he had taken the title of Don, that he might live in great familiarity with those students, whose rank might otherways have laid him under a restraint. He loved good company, and good cheer too well for his money to last long; so at the end of fifteen months, his purse was eased of its burthen.[2] However, he was not yet a-ground altogether, for his credit, and a few pistoles he borrowed, kept him above water a little longer; but at last he was left quite destitute of all resource.

His friends, when they perceived he could treat no longer, gave him no more trouble, and in the room of them his creditors began to wait upon him. Though he assured these last, that he every day expected remittances from his friends, some of them pressed extremely hard, and followed him up so close, that he was on the point of being arrested, when, as he happened one time to be taking a walk on the banks of the river Tormes, he met an acquaintance, who accosted him; Signior Don Pablos, said he, take care of your person, for I assure you there is a bailiff and his followers[3] looking after you; and they design to arrest you, as soon as you come back into the town. Bahabon, terrified at this piece of intelligence, which agreed but too well with his circumstances, immediately went off, and took the road to Corita. But he quitted that, and went into a wood, in the thickest part of which he hid himself, resolving to lie there concealed, 'till the shades of night should come on, that he might proceed in his journey with greater safety. It happened to be in the season, when the trees swelled in all their foliage;[4] he got up into the top of one of them, and sat upon a branch which covered him with its leaves.

Imagining himself to be quite snug in his present situation, he began, by degrees, to lose the dread of the bailiff; and as men, after they have committed faults, for the most part moralize, and make prodigious sage reflections upon the vanities and follies of human nature, so Don Pablos represented to himself all his past bad conduct, and made strong resolutions, that if ever he came into luck again, he would make a better use of his talents;[5] but made a vow, above all things, to have never any thing to do with those false friends, who intice a young man into debauchery and expence, and whose friendship passes away with the fumes of the wine.

As he busied himself in these reflections, that crouded into his mind one after another, night came on, when, disengaging himself from the branches and leaves that surrounded him, in order to slide down, he imagined, that, by the glimmering of the moon, he perceived the figure of a man. This brought his former terrors back upon him, for he made no doubt it was a bailiff, who had dogged him into the wood, and was there in search of him; and his apprehension increased, when he saw the very man whom he had spied sit down at the bottom of the tree he was in, after having walked three or four times round it.

The demon here, of his own accord, interrupted the thread of his story. Signior Zambullo, said he, let me divert myself a little with the perplexity you are now in. I know you want impatiently to know, who that man could be, who came there so unseasonably, and what business could bring him into the wood. Well, you shall know presently; I will satisfy your curiosity.

That man having sat down at the foot of the tree, whose leaves were so thick, that they entirely concealed Don Pablos from his view, remained there some little time; and afterwards began to dig with his dagger, and having made a pretty deep hole, put into it a leathern bag; then filled it again with the earth, and covering it with the turf, went away. Bahabon, who had observed very minutely every thing that passed, and whose fears were changed into transports of joy, waited only till the man was at a proper distance, to go down from the tree, and dig up the bag, which he doubted not was full of either gold or silver, and, for this purpose, made use of a knife he had about him; though he had not an instrument, his eagerness for the work was such, that, with his hands alone, he would have dug into the very entrails of the earth. As soon as he was in possession of the bag, he felt it, and having no longer any doubt of its being filled with money, made all

Don Pablos Observes Ambrosio Burying Money. (Sterling Library, Yale University.)

imaginable haste to get out of the wood with his booty, fearing then to meet the bailiff much less than to meet the owner of the bag. So transported was he at what had happened, that he travelled all night with great ease, not keeping any certain road, and no ways wearied, or fatigued with the load he carried; but at break of day he stopped under some trees near the town of Melorido; and then, not so much to rest himself, as to satisfy his curiosity in regard to the contents of the bag. He untied it with all that tumultuous rapture which seizes you, when you are on the point of enjoying some exquisite pleasure; and finding it contained good double pistoles, had the farther satisfaction of counting them to the amount of two hundred and fifty.

After having feasted his eyes with the sight of them, he began next to think in good earnest what he should do; and after he had resolved on the course he was to take, secured the doubloons in his pockets, threw away the bag, and came to Melorido; where, after he had found an inn, he breakfasted, hired a mule, and returned that same day to Salamanca.

He soon perceived, by the surprize they shewed at his return,[6] that the reason of his disappearing was no secret; but he was prepared, and had his tale ready. He pretended, that having occasion for money, and not receiving any from the people who managed his estate, though he had wrote twenty times for them to make remittances, he had determined to go down himself; but that the evening before, as he was at Melorido, he had there met his steward, coming to him with cash; so that he had it now in his power, to undeceive all those who imagined he was not a gentleman of fortune; and added, he would let his creditors know, that they did very wrong to press so hard an honest man, who would long ago have paid them every farthing, if it had not been for the negligence of his stewards, in not punctually remitting him the rents of his estate.

And the next day he actually summoned his creditors together, and paid them to the last farthing. Those very friends who in his distress had abandoned him, no sooner heard that he was again flush of money,[7] than they came to beset him as formerly; they began to cringe, and to flatter him, hoping they should be merry at his expence as heretofore; but he was not so to be served a second time; he kept them at a distance, and, mindful of the promise he had made in the wood, broke off all correspondence with them. Instead of following his former course, he applied himself to the study of the laws, devoting his whole time to the attaining of useful knowledge.

However, you will say, he was all this time without scruple making use of the doubloons which were none of his own. I allow it; he did what more than three-fourths of mankind would do on the like occasion; but was always resolved to make restitution, if by any chance he should come to know whose property they were. Resting, however, on his upright intentions, he made use of them, in the mean time, without scruple, waiting patiently till such discovery should be made, which happened about a year after.

A report run in Salamanca, that a man of that town, one Ambrosio Piquillo, having been in a wood, to search for a bag filled with pieces of gold, which he had concealed, had found nothing but the hole he had dug to put it in; and that this misfortune had reduced the poor honest man to beggary.

To the praise of Bahabon be it said, the reflections his conscience made on that occasion had a proper effect upon him; he immediately informed himself where Ambrosio lived, and went to see him in a little, low room with only a stool and a wretched bed. My friend, said he to him with a hypocritical air, I have heard the report of the unhappy accident that has befallen you, and the duty of charity obliging us to relieve one another's necessities, I am come to give you a small matter, but I want to know from yourself the particulars of this affair.

Signior Cavalier, answered Piquillo, I will tell you my story in a few words. I had a son who, I found, robbed me; and upon my perceiving it, was afraid he would have laid his hands on a bag which I had of two hundred and fifty good doubloons; and thought I could take no surer method of securing them from him, than burying them in a wood, which I was so unhappy as to do. Since that unfortunate day, my son has stripped me of every thing I had, and has suddenly disappeared with a woman whom he had ravished before. Finding myself quite reduced by the evil courses of this undutiful child, or, indeed, rather by my own unwarrantable indulgence of him, I was at last obliged to have recourse to my bag of doubloons; but when I came to look for it, my last and my only resort, alas! I found it had been taken from me likewise.[8]

The poor man could not utter these words without a renewal of his affliction, and shed a flood of tears. At this Don Pablos was greatly moved, and said to him; Ambrosio, we must bear patiently the cross accidents of life. Your tears are to no purpose; they will never find you your doubloons again, which are irrecoverably lost to you, if any rogue has laid his fingers upon them; but who knows but they may have fallen into the hands of an honest man, who may restore them to you, as soon as he understands they are yours? You may, therefore, possibly get them again, at least you ought to live in that hope;[9] and in the mean time, till you receive so just a restitution, added he, (giving him six doubloons, of the very same the poor man had put in his bag) take this, and come and see me in eight days. After which he told him his name, and the place of his abode, and parted from him quite confused at the thanks poor Piquillo returned, and the prayers he put up for his prosperity. Actions of generosity are very often of the same kind; we should not admire a great many of them so much as we do, did we know the motives from whence they proceeded.

At the end of eight days, Piquillo, who did not forget what Don Pablos had said, went and waited upon him. Bahabon received him with great civility, and said to him, My friend, I have heard so good a character of you from every body, that I have determined to contribute as much as in my power, to set you up again in the world once more; and to that end will use (besides what I give you myself) all the credit I have with my friends.[10]

And in order to make a beginning towards re-establishing your affairs, I have done something already. I am acquainted with some great people of a very charitable disposition, and have succeeded so well with them in my representation of your unhappy circumstances, that I have collected for you two hundred crowns, which I will now give you. Upon which he went into his closet, and returned with a silk purse, into which he had put that sum in silver, and not in double pistoles, for fear Piquillo, receiving so much of that species of money, should have suspected the truth; instead of which, by that means, he attained more surely his ends, which were to make restitution, and at the same time preserve his reputation, while he satisfied his conscience.[11]

So the man received the crowns, without ever in the least imagining, that what he got was part of his own returned him, but took them, really believing that a collection had been made for him, and after again returning Don Pablos his thanks, went home, thanking God for having raised him up a friend, who so warmly interested himself in his behalf.

Next morning he met in the streets an acquaintance, whose affairs were not in a much better condition than his own. This man told him, that in two days he was to set out for Cadiz, to embark on board of a ship that was to sail for New Spain. I am not at all contented with my lot here, said he, and my mind bodes that I shall better my affairs in New Spain: I would counsel you to go along with me, if you can but only raise two hundred crowns.

I could do such a thing as that, answered Piquillo, and should have no objections to undertake the voyage, was I sure of being able to get a livelihood in the Indies. Upon this, his friend spoke much to him, what a fine, fertile country New Spain was, and told him how many ways there were of getting rich; so that Ambrosio being persuaded by the other, determined to set out along with him for Cadiz. But before he left Salamanca, he took care to send a letter to Bahabon, in which he wrote him, that having found a favourable opportunity to go over to Mexico, he had determined to embrace it, and try if fortune would not be kinder to him elsewhere, than she had been in his own country; that he took the freedom to acquaint him of this, and, at the same time assure him, he should preserve an everlasting remembrance of his favours.

The departure of Ambrosio gave Don Pablos some uneasiness; as by that he found himself prevented of his design to make him restitution by degrees; but reflecting, that in a few years he would probably return to Salamanca, he at last made himself easy, and applied himself more closely than ever to the study of the civil and canon law; and made so great a proficiency, by his application, and the strength of his genius, that he became the ornament of the university, who chose him their rector. The dignity of which office he not only supported by a most profound knowledge, but took so much pains upon himself, that he adorned his own mind with every civil and social virtue.

During the time of his rectorship, he heard there was in the prisons of Salamanca, a young man accused of a rape, and likely to lose his life; this making him recollect that the son of Piquillo had ravished a woman, he enquired who the prisoner was, and finding it was actually the same, he himself undertook his defence. What is particularly to be admired in the science of the law is, that it furnishes arguments equally strong, pro and con; and as our rector understood it thoroughly, he made a most excellent use of it for the defence of the accused. Though to this he joined his own, and the interest of his friends, which, with the strongest solicitations, perhaps contributed more to save the criminal, than even the learned pleadings of the rector.

The accused person got himself honourably acquitted, and went to thank his deliverer,[12] who told him, it was out of regard to his father he had done him that piece of service. I love him, said he, and to give you a farther proof of it, if you will remain here, and lead a regular life, I'll take care to provide for you. Or if you chuse to follow your father to the Indies, you may depend upon fifty pistoles, whenever you choose to call for them. To which young Piquillo replied, since I have the happiness, Sir, to be taken under your protection, it would be wrong in me to leave a place where I enjoy so singular an advantage. I will not leave Salamanca, and I engage to observe such a conduct as you will be satisfied with. Upon this declaration, the rector put into his hands twenty pistoles, saying, Take this, friend; follow some honest employment, and if you make such a good use of your time as you ought, you may always depend upon my assistance.

About two months after this, it happened, that young Piquillo, who always came from time to time, to pay his respects to Don Pablos, appeared before him all in tears. What's the matter? said Bahabon. Signior, said he, I have received a piece of news, that stabs me to the very heart. My father is taken by a corsair of Algiers, and is actually in chains. An old man of this town, who is returned from Algiers, being lately ransomed by the fathers of La Merci, after a ten years captivity, has just now told me, that he left him there a slave. Alas! added he, tearing his hair, and beating his breast, what a miserable wretch am I! 'Twas I who, by my wicked course of life, obliged my father to hide his money, and quit his native country; and 'tis I who have delivered him over into the hands of the barbarian who now loads him with irons. Ah! Signior Don Pablos, why did you save me from the hands of justice? Since you love my father, you ought to have been his avenger, and to have left me to expiate, with my death, the numberless miseries I have occasioned him.

At this discourse, which looked so much like the repentance of a prodigal son reformed, Don Pablos was greatly moved with the deep affliction he saw young Piquillo in. My child, said he to him, I see with pleasure that you are sensible of your past misconduct; but dry up your tears; it is enough that I know where your father is; you may rest satisfied that you shall see him, as his deliverance only depends upon a ransom, which I take upon me to pay; and whatever misfortunes he may have suffered, I am persuaded, that when he returns, and finds in you a son reformed, and full of filial affection towards him, he will not repine at his past afflictions.

By this assurance, Don Pablos sent away the son of Ambrosio full of joy, and in a few days afterwards, Bahabon set out for Madrid, where, as soon as he arrived, he sent a purse of a hundred pistoles to the fathers of La Merci, with a paper, on which were written these words: *This sum is given to the fathers of the redemption, for the ransom of a poor citizen of Salamanca, called Ambrosio Piquillo, a captive at Algiers.* And the good fathers in the voyage they undertook, did not fail to comply with the directions of the rector. They have ransomed Ambrosio, who is that slave whose tranquil air you so much admire.

I imagine, says Don Cleofas, that Bahabon and Piquillo are now quits.[13] Don Pablos don't think so himself, answered Asmodeus. He will pay him principal and interest; his delicacy in point of conscience carries him so far as even to scruple keeping the possession of what he has made by the income of his rectory; and when he again sees old Piquillo, intends to address him in this manner: My friend Ambrosio, look on me no longer as your benefactor; in me you see the thief who dug up the money that you had hid in the wood. It is not sufficient, therefore, that I make you restitution of the two hundred and fifty double pistoles; for as it was by means of that I came to enjoy what I now do, all I am worth belongs to you; I will retain nothing for myself but what you please, and——Here the *Diable Boiteux* stopped short all at once; he was seized of a sudden with a fit of trembling, and his colour changed.

What is the matter with you? cried the student. What extraordinary emotion shakes you so, and of a sudden stops you in your speaking? Ah! Signior Leandro, answered Asmodeus, with a faultering voice, what a dreadful accident has befallen me! The magician who confined me prisoner in the phial has perceived that I have made my escape; and is going to call me back, by the power of such magical incantations, as are impossible for me to resist. How grieved I am! said Don Cleofas, with great concern. What a loss is this to me! Alas! we separate for ever. I don't believe so, replied the demon; this necromancer may stand in need of my assistance; and if I have the good fortune to do him any remarkable piece of service, he may, perhaps, in gratitude, give me my liberty. If that should happen, according to my expectations, you may lay your account upon seeing me again, on condition you never reveal to any one what has passed this night betwixt us; for if you are so indiscreet as to trust that secret to any one, I tell you now, that you will never see me more.

One thing comforts me a little, that though I am obliged to part with you, it is not before I have made your fortune. You will marry the beautiful Seraphina, whom I have inspired with a passion for you; and Signior Don Pedro Esculano has come to a resolution to bestow her upon you, and be sure you don't let slip such a glorious opportunity of at once making your fortune. But, mercy on me, added he, I already feel the incantations of the magician. Hell itself is dismayed at the words uttered by this tremendous cabalist. I can stay not a moment longer, so good b'ye, dear Zambullo. In saying these words he embraced Don Cleofas, and then vanished, after he had carried him to his own apartments.

CHAPTER X. AND LAST.

What Don Cleofas did after the Devil upon Crutches had left him;
and after what manner the author has thought proper to end this work.

Immediately after Asmodeus was gone, our student finding himself fatigued with having been the night long without once sitting down,[1] and in such extraordinary motion besides, undressed, and went to bed, to enjoy some repose; but the agitation of his spirits was so great, that it was with difficulty he could compose himself for rest. At last, however, paying with usury, that tribute to Morpheus which all mortals do, he fell into such a dead sleep, that he did not wake all that day, nor the following night.

He had been thus twenty-four hours, when Don Luis de Lujan, a young gentleman of his acquaintance, coming into his chamber, called out with all his might, Holla! Signior Don Cleofas, rise; get up! At the noise of this, Zambullo awaked. Do you know, says Don Luis, that you have been asleep since yesterday morning? That's impossible, answered Leandro. But nothing is more certain, replied his friend. You have had a nap of twice twelve hours;[2] every one in the house has assured me of it.

Leandro, quite astonished at his having been asleep so long, began at first to think his adventure with the demon was an illusion: but could not let himself believe it; for he reflected upon so many circumstances, that he could not doubt of the reality of what he had seen. However, to be more certain, he got up and dressed himself immediately; then went out with Don Luis, whom he carried towards the gate of the sun, without letting him know wherefore. When they had got there, and Don Cleofas perceived the hotel of Don Pedro reduced almost to ashes, he feigned a surprize. What is this? said he. What horrible devastation has the fire made here? To whom belongs this unfortunate hotel? Is it a long while since it was burnt?

To these two questions Don Luis replied: This house being burnt, said he, occasions less talk in the town, as to the prodigious damage it has done, than in regard to a certain particular affair, which I will inform you of. Signior Don Pedro Esculano has an only child, a daughter, fair and beautiful as the morning. They say, that she was in a room full of fire and smoke, and must inevitably have perished, had she not been rescued from the flames by a young gentleman, whose name is not yet known. This adventure is the common talk of Madrid. People cry up to the skies the heroic gallantry of the cavalier; and it is generally believed, that, though he be but a private gentleman, his bravery will be rewarded with the daughter of Esculano.

Zambullo heard Don Luis, without appearing any wise interested in what he told him; then parting, on pretence of some business, he went to the prado, where, sitting himself down under the trees, he fell into a deep reverie. I can never, said he to himself, sufficiently regret the loss of my dear Asmodeus. In a short time, by his assistance, I might have made the tour of the whole globe, and travelled free from those inconveniences that generally attend travellers. Certainly I suffer a great loss; but who knows, added he, but that it may not be irreparable. Why should I despair of seeing again that demon? It may possibly happen, as he said himself, that the magician will very soon grant him his liberty. Afterwards turning his thoughts upon Esculano and his daughter, he determined to go and wait upon them, merely to have an opportunity of seeing the beauteous Seraphina.

The moment he appeared in the presence of Don Pedro, that nobleman run to him with open arms. Welcome, gallant cavalier, said he, welcome to my house. I was beginning to complain of you. What, said I to myself, the gallant Don Cleofas, after the pressing instances I made him to come and see me, not yet to have paid me a visit! How ill he repays the impatience I feel, to testify the friendship and esteem I have for him.

Don Cleofas, at this obliging reproof, made a respectful bow, and told Don Pedro, in his own excuse, that he was afraid a visit might have been unseasonable, so soon after the confusion he judged they must certainly be in the day before. I don't admit of that excuse, replied Esculano. A visit can never be unseasonable from a man in a house, which, but for him, must have been a scene of most inexpressible sorrow and anguish. But, added he, follow me; you have other acknowledgments to receive than mine. As he spoke thus, he took him by the hand, and led him to the apartment of Seraphina.

That young lady had been taking her nap. My child, said her father to her, let me introduce this gentleman to you, who so courageously rescued you from the flames. I desire you will now express your gratitude for what he has done for you, as the condition you was in at that time rendered you then incapable. Upon which, Signiora Seraphina opening her rosy lips, made such a speech to Leandro Perez, as would give infinite delectation to the reader, if I could repeat it word for word; but as I have had the misfortune to receive an imperfect account of it, I choose rather to say nothing at all, than to disgrace it by butchering mutilations.[3]

But one thing we can aver with truth, and what our readers may depend upon for fact,[4] that Don Cleofas Leandro Perez Zambullo thought he heard a goddess speak, and that he found himself suddenly seized two ways at once, viz. by the eyes and the ears; and that he instantaneously conceived for her a most outrageous passion. Though far from looking upon Seraphina as one he could not miss of having for his bride, he was in great doubt, notwithstanding all the assurances the demon had given him, whether they would crown the services they imagined he had done them, with such a glorious recompence; and the more he was enamoured of her, the more he doubted whether he should obtain her.

And what confirmed his fears, that he should not be so happy, Don Pedro, in the long conversation he had with him, never touched upon that string; he only loaded him with civilities, but never gave the most distant hint, that could make him suppose he had any inclination of becoming his father-in-law. Seraphina, on her part, equally polite as her father, in her conversation used many expressions signifying her gratitude, but not one that could give Don Cleofas any reason to fancy she entertained an affection for his person. So that at last he took his leave of Signior Esculano, much in love, but with very little to hope.

My friend Asmodeus, said he to himself going home, as if he had still been in conversation with that demon, when you assured me, that Don Pedro had determined to make me his son-in-law, and that Seraphina was possessed with a violent passion for me, which you had inspired into her; I fancy, good Sir, you had a mind to make yourself merry at my expence; else you must acknowledge, that you know the present better than that which is to come.

Our student was now sorry that he had been to see the lady, and looking upon the love he had for her as an unhappy passion, which it was necessary he should overcome, was determined to spare no pains to get the better of it.[5] He went farther, and reproached himself for having gone so far, even supposing her father had been inclinable to the match; and thought it a stain upon his honour, to be beholden for his good fortune to any artifice.

He was full of such reflections, when Don Pedro, sending for him the next day, said, Signior Leandro Perez, it is now time for me to demonstrate to you, by my actions, that in obliging me, you have not had to do with one of those grandees, who, were they in my place, would repay your services with a sprinkle of court holy-water. I design no less than Seraphina herself for the reward of the danger you have run upon her account. I have spoke to her upon that head, and find her willing to obey me without reluctance. Nay, I must go farther, and do her the justice to tell you, that when I proposed to her for a husband her deliverer, she shewed a generous transport of joy, by which I knew her to be my own blood, and her gratitude answered to mine. It is a thing, Sir, determined on; you shall have my daughter.

Signior Esculano having spoke in this manner, and expecting with reason, that he should have received in his turn from Don Cleofas, very lively expressions of gratitude, was not a little surprised to find him remain in confusion, and not speak a word. Why don't you answer me, Zambullo? said he. What am I to think of the disorder I see this proposal puts you into? What objections can you have against my daughter? How is it that a private gentleman hesitates at an alliance which a man of the first rank might embrace as an honour? Has the nobility of my house received any stain of which I am ignorant?

Signior, said Leandro, I am very sensible of the difference heaven has made between us. Why then, answered Pedro, do you hesitate at an offer which does you so much honour? Come, tell the truth, Don Cleofas, you are in love with some lady to whom you have plighted your faith; and it is your regard for her, that now stands in the way of your making your fortune. I assure you, answered Signior Cleofas, had I a mistress to whom I was engaged by promise, no temptation whatsoever should make me violate my engagements; but I have no such reason to prevent me from complying with the offers of your generosity. A punctilio of honour[6] makes me decline accepting the splendid fortune you dazzle me with; but far from taking any advantage of your mistake, I will undeceive you, Signior; I am not the deliverer of Seraphina.

What is this I hear, said old Esculano with astonishment; Did not you deliver her from the flames that were ready to devour her? And was it not you who undertook this hazardous attempt? No, Signior, answered the other; all mortal help would have been in vain, and therefore I am obliged to declare to you, that a demon saved your daughter.

These words increased the astonishment of Don Pedro, who, not supposing he was to take it as meant literally, begged the student to explain himself more clearly. Upon which, Leandro, without any regard to preserving the friendship of Asmodeus, told every thing that had happened between that demon and him. After which, Esculano said to him, This confidence you have now put in me, still confirms my resolution to give you my daughter. You was her first deliverer. If you had not begged of that Devil upon Crutches to rescue my daughter, he would have let the flames consume her; so that it is still you who have preserved the life of Seraphina: in a word, you deserve her; and I make an offer of her to you, with the half of my fortune.

Leandro Perez, at these words, which at once removed all his scruples, threw himself at Don Pedro's feet, to thank him for his goodness. A short while after the marriage was celebrated with a magnificence suitable to the heiress of Signior de Esculano, and the great joy the parents of our student felt upon such an occasion, who found himself nobly recompenced for the few hours liberty which he had procured the Devil upon Crutches.

DIALOGUES,

SERIOUS and COMIC,

Between two Chimneys of MADRID.

DIALOGUE I.

The Chimney A. and the Chimney B.

A. It is all over with me, my dear neighbour, I am quite ruined; the Lares, my protecting Gods, now freeze by my hearth, and the same chilliness seizes myself from head to foot. B. I am startled at what you tell me. How has this terrible distemper seized you? And how comes it you are so suddenly changed from hot to cold? for I have constantly seen you all in a fire. A. Alas, I must of necessity follow the destiny of my friend, the scholar and the poor man.— B. What has happened to him? A. O! the greatest of misfortunes. His income, that is to say, the profits of his pen, are quite put a stop to. B. I can't say, neighbour, that I yet understand you. A. Why then I'll explain myself. I talk of an author. His finances depended on the sale of small pamphlets calculated for amusement, which he composed, and they have forbid all writings of this kind. B. What, did these pamphlets support him? A. Yes; and at his ease too; for he did not take up his time in correcting and publishing a volume; he entertained the public with these flying numbers, at least seven or eight in the year.[1] B. What a pity it is to deprive the world of the industry of so good a hand; and how comes it they forbid writings of amusement, the very best things in the world? The public loves to be entertained, and why are they not at their liberty to buy what diverts them? A. You are certainly in the right; and this prevailing taste makes both for authors and booksellers. But then this is the ground of the clamour against that kind of writings; they say that nothing is wrote now-a-days, but low nonsense and mere bagatelle;[2] and that posterity will distinguish this age for the *Age of romances, and all sort of futility.* They say, moreover, that there is a general depravity of taste; that these broken numbers[3] are a real tax upon the public; that by this means a romance is swelled to an intolerable size; and that an author is now actually proposing a scheme, to divide one of them into three hundred and sixty-five parcels; that he may be able to supply his customers every day in the year. B. Why, after the thousand and one nights, the thousand and one days, the thousand and one quarters of an hour, and so many other thousand and one things, I think they may very well put up with a romance split into no more than three hundred and sixty-five divisions. A. Judge then, if they ought to find fault with my author, who, in no work, has ever divided beyond number eight. B. Indeed, my dear friend, I pity you, as I do the chimneys of all authors and booksellers, who will soon become as cold as yours. A. It is but cold comfort[4] for the afflicted to have others as miserable as themselves. B. You are to be pitied; and I do pity you; what else is in my power to do? Besides, I must tell you freely, that a long time since, I have heard many people say, it was high time to check that prevailing taste for low, trifling amusements, and to put a stop to romance-writing. A. What is this you say? B. Yes, it is true. And men of discernment, who are unprejudiced, say now, that this inhibition is of great service to polite writing. That people ought to have some useful end in view, or not write at all. This is their judgment upon the affair, and all the world come into their sentiments. A. But is not that which pleases, at the same time useful? B. Yes, what gives pleasure is so far useful. But besides the utility arising only from pleasure, readers of taste want something solid and instructive, something that has its foundation laid in the real truth of manners. For example, the Devil upon Crutches is so far a romance, but at the same time more instructive than a treatise of morality. There the fable is both pleasant and useful; that is, useful by joining pleasure with instruction. Let your author write such another, and I'll answer for his having permission to print it, provided, though, he don't publish it in eight numbers; for that, you know, is robbing the public to enrich the bookseller. A. Come, let us put an end to this conversation. One may easily perceive that you are a chimney belonging to a change-broker. You are a tasteless, insipid creature, and ignorant, in the superlative degree of every thing concerning literature; your narrow genius does not reach beyond a sum in addition; and I am ready to hang myself for having been so free with you, as I have been. B. What, do you insult me in return for my shewing such concern for your misfortunes? A. Is that shewing concern for one's misfortunes, to commend those who are the cause of them? Go, once more, I tell you, you are as great a dunce as him you belong to. B. For one that complains of being almost froze to death, methinks you shew a good deal of warmth. But, in the mean time, I desire you will let my brother alone; one dash of his pen is worth all the volumes of Parnassus. Every thing he writes is sensible, agreeable, and universally approved. And so long as his writings are but legible, I fear not the cold; my hearth will be kept as warm as if it had been the eternal fire of the vestals, and your poor chilled author[5] will bless himself to be allowed to sit down by it. As for you, notwithstanding your ill usage of me, all the harm I wish you, is, such another brother as mine,[6] to put you into heat again.

DIALOGUE II.

The Chimney C. and the Chimney D.

C. What a prodigy! what a miracle is this! Do you know, my friend, what has happened to me? D. Is it long since? C. About an hour ago. D. No, my dear neighbour, I know not; for I was obliged to assist at a marriage, which was celebrated in the apartment I belong to. C. A marriage! D. Yes, and a couple the best matched that can be.

Lysander and Celimene have taken me witness to their vows. The Penates, my household gods, are the only guarantees of their mutual engagements, and the faith they have plighted to one another. No mortal was present at this ceremony, excepting Lizetta, the faithful servant of Celimene. They are now enjoying the pleasures of this mysterious union. C. This marriage, to be sure, is very solemnly ratified. D. Why yes, I know as well as you, there are some little formalities wanting, but what then? Love will supply the place of all. They love one another, and I am convinced, let their parents do what they please, will continue so to do; and pray, do you find that common in marriages solemnised according to the rites of the church?[1] C. No, really. Marriages, for the most part, are only so many civil contracts, that bind two persons eternally together, who are so far from loving, that they generally hate one another, during the whole course of their lives. D. Well, I can answer for it, the bonds which unite Lisander and Celimene, are more sacred and solemn, for they are the bonds of love. C. I wish you joy, my dear neighbour; and I like you all the better for interesting yourself so much in the happiness of lovers. It is what we owe them as confidants of their secrets; and I myself would do all in my power to serve them, which you will easily believe, when I tell you what has happened to me, which is pretty much such another affair as yours. You know the apartment I belong to is a real cell. D. Ay, and the cell of the charming little Julia. C. Julia was beloved by a very pretty fellow of an officer, named Trason, and Trason did not bestow his love on one that was ungrateful. D. Now, I did not know that. C. There was nothing wanting to complete their mutual happiness, but a favourable opportunity; and Julia's mother had more eyes than Argus. The cell where this unhappy young creature lay was more inaccessible than the tower of Danae. D. Bless me, how learned you are! You understand the ancient fables. I fancy before you had Julia, some poet had studied by your fire-side. But since you mention the tower of Danae, you remember it could not keep out a shower of gold. C. True, and you remember likewise, that Danae was courted by Jupiter; and you know a God can change water and stones into gold; but Trason's pockets had been pretty well drained by three campaigns, so that it did not at all suit him to have recourse to that expedient. D. What other expedient then did he fall upon? C. The most simple and obvious one that could be. He lives but just by; and without the help of any other magic than pure love, up he gets through his chimney to the ridge of the houses, comes to the head of my chimney, which he easily removed; for I had no mind to hinder him; and then slides down through the funnel into the chamber of Julia, supporting himself by his hands and his knees. D. Did she expect his coming? C. No, she only wished it; and far from running with open arms to receive her lover, was in a most mortal fright at seeing him come down. D. She swooned away, I warrant you. C. If she did not at first, she would have done so very soon. Come, none of your joking: This gallant of a chimney-sweeper cast himself at the feet of Julia, and she soon knew him to be her dear Trason. You never saw any thing more moving than the situation they were both in at that time. This is the advantage we chimnies enjoy; we are witnesses to a thousand sights that man would pay any price for seeing. At present Julia's fears are over; she feels emotions of quite a different kind. D. There now, my good neighbour, in one night two marriages pretty much alike. C. Why, very nearly so, indeed. Though my couple not only exchange the solemn vow; but the consequences will, very probably, oblige the mother of Julia to acknowledge Trason for her son-in-law; and I rejoice before-hand in the thoughts of what perplexity this good woman will be reduced to.[2] D. And I in the pleasures her dear child at this moment enjoys.

DIALOGUE III.

The Chimney E. *and Chimney* F.

E. Pray tell me, if you please, good neighbour F, how you can, without being tired, put up with having no body besides your two old maids? For from morning till night no one comes near your fire-side; you have always the same people, and always the same subject of conversation. Indeed I should imagine that by this time your patience was wore out. F. I must indeed own to you, that I often wish they would change their quarters; though, perhaps, in that case, I should be hard put to it how to breathe, as, in all probability, I should not have so good a fire; for they are extremely devout, so of consequence take no less care of their bodies than of their souls; especially when a certain abbot, whom I could name, comes to visit them; then they spare no cost; their kitchen then may vie with that of a lord, and the smoke I breathe upon, is a perfect perfume. E. As far as I perceive, you love nothing but smoke. Well, every one to their own taste, I love variety.[1] New faces and new adventures are my delight. I am, as I suppose you know, the chimney of a furnished lodging. F. And as such it is very happy for you that you have a turn for variety. E. I have so great a turn that way, that I should be extremely sorry to see the same lodgers six months together; and have reason to be thankful that it is a thing never happened to me since the first moment of my existence. F. Belike, then, you are not the oldest of your neighbourhood. E. No, not by a great deal; but for all that, I believe I have the most experience. F. Impart to me then some of your adventures; I beg you to do it, as you would oblige a neighbour. E. With all my heart, if it don't tire you; and will begin from the time I first commenced chimney. He who first sat down by my fire, was the younger son of a good family, but of a country where the portion of younger sons consists only in their sword, joined to a happy impudence of bullying every one with their being born gentlemen.[2] This talent my gentleman possessed in an eminent degree; but had another at the same time much more profitable; for he played with constant good luck, and his good luck was the effect of the most assiduous study; every day he was busy in calculating the various chances upon the cards, and at night put his theory in practice. F. He must, at that rate, have been always flush of money.[3] E. No, you are mistaken; for he squandered it away as fast as he got it; so that he was always needy. Indeed sometimes he cut a great slash; that is a disease peculiar to his nation, but then it never lasted long.[4] His good fortune exasperated the students, who frequented the same nurseries of education, against him, and they brought him into several scrapes, so that at the end of four months I lost him. He was, however, a mighty good lodger, and I regret the loss of him to this day. F. Who came in his room? E. A man the most singular, perhaps, that ever yet lived. A husband faithful and affectionate even beyond the grave; that could not be comforted for the loss of his dear rib: in short, a phenix of a husband.[5] The moment he came, he ordered his room to be hung with black, shut up his windows against the rays of the sun; and had no light in his chamber, but the dim glimmerings of a lamp. Enclosed in this frightful gloom, his constant employment was to sob and shed tears without ceasing. Very often, as if he had been possessed, he would speak aloud to an urn that stood upon a table covered with black cloth, and which he seemed to adore. He would converse with that precious relick, and speak to it as if it answered his passionate expostulations. F. 'Tis a chance but some spirit was enclosed in that same urn. E. A spirit! What a simpleton you are! No, it was the heart of his wife; that was the object of his vows and adoration. F. This was tenderness of grief to excess. I can scarce believe what you tell me. E. Nor should I, if I had not seen it. I remember, sometime or other, to have heard one of my lodgers reading a book which mentioned a story of the same sort of fidelity, or madness, in an English philosopher,[6] which I do not believe to this day, notwithstanding what I have told you; for an example of this kind ought to stand alone. F. But how long did your lodger continue in this fit? E. Full three months. True it is his eyes, the fountains of his tears, began to dry up, and refused to furnish him with fresh supplies of continued grief; and, by degrees, his devotions to the urn, seemed to relish of form and ceremony. Happily for him, his friends found him out, and, of consequence, relieved him. I believe he yielded to the violence they made use of with only a seeming reluctance. However, away they took him, and I was freed of this mournful guest. F. And, I suppose, did not much lament the loss of him. E. Not in the least, I assure you.[7] The room was afterwards let to a woman, at which I rejoiced mightily, as I had hitherto been acquainted only with men. A kind of quaker's dress, and a certificate of forty years marked upon her forehead, gave her a matron air, which struck me at first sight; and by what I had heard of devotees, I immediately judged her to be one. F. Now perhaps, you might be mistaken. E. I was very soon convinced of my error; for the woman was a woman of sense and conduct; she loved pleasure, yet regarded her reputation, and came from the country, a great way off, to Madrid, that she might be sheltered from the malice of slander; and a very short time after, the gentleman on whose account she had undertaken the journey, followed her. Bless me! how surprised I was at the first visit she received from her lover; she flew with transport into his arms; her demureness was changed into a wanton sprightliness, and the glow upon her cheeks effaced the traits of her age. F. A pretty lady for a devotee, truly. E. As she loved her man with all the violence of passion, she made use of every method to preserve her conquest. She was very well apprised that, at her age, it is allowed for women to embellish the charms of nature by art, and accordingly she used every thing she could for that purpose. F. And what arts pray, must she use for that purpose? E. I will tell you. Besides black and white, which painted her complexion to what height of colour she pleased; she called in every other thing to her assistance, dress, baths, and perfumes. She was at her toilet always till her gallant came, and repaired to it again immediately, when he was gone away. She was perpetually at her glass, practising the different airs, either sprightly or languishing, which she imagined might do execution. As for the artillery of endearments and caresses, that she was perfect mistress of. F. With all that, methinks, it was hardly possible she could miss of making herself beloved. E. But then she had other charms infinitely more powerful over the heart of a young lover. She was liberal and rich, and one must have a heart of flint not to love a generous mistress. But the appointed days of man are numbered: when these two lovers were now at the height of mutual felicity, the gallant fell sick, and died a few days afterward, spite of all the assistance that could be administered by the most able physicians. F. The lady, no doubt, took on mightily. E. Yes, she wept, resumed her former demure air, and went back into her own country, to edify her neighbours by her example. My chamber was not long empty; it was taken by another woman, who was, by profession, a go-between, a match-maker. F. A rare kind of occupation, truly. E. It is an occupation that is very common. Negociators of this sort require a deal of address, and this good lady did not want for that. She carried the proposals, procured interviews, and very often brought the matter to a final conclusion. How many of those contracts have been ratified in my apartment! She would make a younger brother, not worth a shilling, pass for a gentleman of fortune, and set off a demi-rep for a pattern of illustrious virtue.[8] F. What an admirable woman this was! E. All this she could do with the greatest ease, and could take in the most cautious and wary; so that by her dexterity she had got a pretty fortune; but at last she began to have scruples, and her remorses carried her so far, that she retired into a convent, there to repent of her former scandalous life. Thus a fit of devotion deprived me of this experienced brokeress. F. Well, but happily for you the natural indifference of your temper prevented your regretting the loss of her. E. That is true; however, after her I had a great many people of common characters in life, men and women, for example, that were concerned in law-suits, a very troublesome sort of lodgers, or people who came from the country to see what a clock it was at Madrid, and returned home, for the most part, as wise as they were before.[9] But it now begins to grow late, so, neighbour, I wish you a good night; another time when we meet, I will give you an account of some more original characters whom I have had at my fire-side. F. Adieu, good neighbour; I will not fail to put you in mind of your promise.

APPENDIX A:
INDEX TO THE 1759 SECOND EDITION
COPY-TEXT

Both the 1750 first edition and the 1759 second edition contained an index to each of the two volumes of *The Devil upon Crutches*. Although the indexes are not part of Smollett's text, they have been reproduced in this appendix as a convenience for the reader. Smollett, who always had a sharp eye for details, neither compiled the indexes nor read proof for them, as the large number of errors and the inconsistency of the entries indicate. The compiler, paid by Smollett's bookseller John Osborn, is unknown, but he had little familiarity with the novel. A few examples will suffice. In the first edition, the vice-roy of Mexico is given a "daughter" in the index when the text clearly states he had a "niece" (155). Although this particular error was corrected in the index for the second edition, perhaps by an alert compositor, "courtiers" in the first edition is absurdly changed to "countries" in the second edition (163). The activities of "Julio" are entered under "Jago" in both editions (84–88). The entries under the topic "Madness" in the first volume do not follow the order in which they appear in the text, here corrected (80). When the editors felt an error might confuse or mislead the reader, it has been corrected silently. The compiler of the indexes failed to supply headings for several of the entries, and they have been added in square brackets. The subentries enclosed in square brackets appeared in the first edition but were deleted in the second edition. The index to each volume of the 1759 second edition copy-text is reprinted below with the page numbers changed to fit the present text.

INDEX TO THE FIRST VOLUME

ASMODEUS, alias the Devil upon Crutches, brought under the power of a magician, by force of incantations, 14. Gives an account of the other demons, and the functions they discharge here on earth, ib. And of himself, 14–15. Is the same as the god Cupid, 15. His figure, appearance, and dress, 16. His magic robe, with its various emblems, ib. Compared to the shield of Achilles, 17. How he came to be lamed in an engagement with Palliardoc, ib. His fray with Palliardoc, and the occasion of it, ib. Wings Don Cleofas through the air, and pitches him on the top of St. Salvador, 19. Opens to his view the inside of the houses in Madrid, and gives him an account of what passes, 19, &c. Has another quarrel with Palliardoc, 21. The manner of their reconciliation, ib. His reasons for not relieving a prisoner, 59. Speaks Latin, 90. The great advantage he has over the literati, ib. Is entreated by Zambullo to rescue Seraphina, 96–97. Puts on Zambullo's shape, and darts into the flames, 97. Rescues Seraphina, ib. What he says to her father, Esculano, 97–98. His conversation with Zambullo on that subject, 98. Carries Zambullo to another quarter, to continue their observations, ib.

ASHTAROTH, appointed with Leviathan and Belphegor to attend crowned heads, 14.

ATTORNIES, their case debated in the Pandemonium, 23. Determined they shall have a demon allotted for their particular use, ib.

ABBE, a young Abbé attending a lady's toilet with patches and paint, 16.

APOTHECARY, how he and his wife, and apprentice are employed at the same time, 21–22.

AUTHOR, what sort of one kept in the house of a patron, 50–51.

[ADVENTURER] A female adventurer's answer to one of her creditors, 68.

AURORA, a young lady, married to captain Zanubio, 76. Discovers Don Garcia Pacheco to be in disguise, 77. Threatens to acquaint her husband, ib. What she says to Zanubio, ib. Comforts Don Garcia, 77–78. Is surprised with him, and escapes to a convent, 78. Vid. *Zanubio*.

AGE, the great difficulty women of all countries find in doing justice to their age, 89. Remarkable instance that happened at Paris, 89–90.

B.

BELPHEGOR, one of the court-demons, 14.

BAR, under the care and direction of Flagel, 14.

BEELZEBUB, who committed to his charge, 14.

BEAU, one of threescore, how employed, 20. An account of his sister, ib. The great loss she sustained, ib.

BROTHER, an accident that happened to an elder from a younger, 60. Advice of consequence to elder brothers, ib.

BEDLAMITES, an account of them, 75–89.

BAILIFFS, an instance of where one of them was moved with pity, 88.

BELFLOR, (Count de) falls in love with Leonora, daughter of Don Luis de Cespides, 26. His artifices to seduce her, 27, &c. Gains over her governante Marcella, 29, &c. Procures an interview, 33. Debauches her, 36. Is discovered coming out of her apartment by her father Don Luis, 36. His conversation with him upon that subject, 38–39. Receives a letter from Leonora, 41. Questions and reasons with himself, as a man of honour, ib. Adventure between him and Pedro, Leonora's brother, 43, &c. Comes to see her before she goes into a convent, 43. Marries her, 49–50, and gives his sister Eugenia to Don Pedro, ib. Vid. *Leonora* and *Cespides* (Don Luis de).

BEATRIX, (Donna) jealous on account of a gentleman's addresses to her friend, 81. Defers prosecuting the murder of her brother, that he may fight her friend's husband, ib. Is disappointed of her project of revenge, and goes distracted, ib.

BOLANUS, a minister compared to him, 94. Our author follows the opinion of Mr. Dacier, ib. Notes; that passage of Horace explained, ib.

BUFFOON, the distinguished good fortune of one, 23–24. And how caressed by the nobility of Madrid, ib.

C.

CLEOFAS, vid. *Zambullo*.

CITIZEN, œconomy of a rich one, 19–20. An account of one who is a florist, 93.

COQUET, a superannuated one, 20.

CONCERT *of Musick*, ridiculous one, 20–21.

CICERO, what he writes to Volumnius, 23. Notes.

CASTILIAN, courts his mistress after the manner of the ancients, 24, and notes. Castilian newsmonger, reason of his going mad, 75. Castilian love-song, 79.

CESPIDES, (Don Luis de) discovers Count Belflor coming out of his daughter's apartments, 36. Threatens to kill her and her governante Marcella, 36–37. Melts into tenderness, and bewails the misfortune of his daughter, 37. Sees count Belflor, and the subject of their conversation, 38–39 &c. Resolves to send Leonora and Marcella into a convent, 39. Sends for his son Don Pedro to fight the count, 42. Finds count Belflor again in the apartment of Leonora, 44. And is prevented by his son from attacking him, ib. Strange explanation and consequences of this adventure, 46. Forgives his daughter, and is reconciled to count Belflor, 47. His conversation with his son Pedro, and the consequences of it, ib. Has the marriage of his daughter Leonora with count Belflor, and of his son Pedro with Eugenia, the count's sister, celebrated in his own house, 49. Vid. *Belflor* and *Leonora.*

COBLER, has a son who returns immensely rich from the Indies, 72. Is prevailed upon by him and his wife, with great reluctancy, to leave off trade, 73. Insists upon leave to mend his own and the curate's shoes, ib. Repents and goes to his son to return him his money, 75.

CLERGYMAN, the great preferment of one from his going mad, 75. Of one that published a book of bawdy on his death-bed, 91. Of one that saved his money, and from what motive, ib. Method of one to save his set of horses, 92. The behaviour of one to a lord and a wit, 93.

CHICONA, wheedles Marcella, Leonora's governante, 27. Entices her and Leonora into her house, where she had concealed count Belflor, 28. Dissuades the count from making farther attempts on Leonora, 29. Shews an aversion to appear before a justice of the peace, ib. Enters into partnership with Pebrada, 51. Their occupation and business, ib.

COUNSELLOR, stratagem of one to get rid of his grandmother, 81.

CAVALIER, a superannuated one; ridicule of his address to a lady, 92. Another of the same stamp, ib.

CARD-PLAYER, what sort of them deserve to be shut up in Bedlam, 92.

COSMO, Don Cosmo de la Higuiera, description of him, 61. Made to believe, that the daughter of a general officer is in love with him, 61–62. Writes her a letter in the sublime stile, 62. Receives an answer, 63. Gives her a serenade, 63–64. Proposes an entertainment for her on the banks of the Mansanarez, 64–65. Is robbed of a thousand pistoles by his servant Domingo, 65.

COMMISSARY *at Paris,* strangely puzzled in settling the age of two women, 89–90. A dialogue between the two women on that subject, 90.

D.

DEMON. See *Asmodeus.*

DOCTOR *of the University,* his wife assisted by Asmodeus, 15.

[DRAWER] William, drawer of an inn, story of one with his master's daughter, 56–58. Vide *Quebrantador.*

DACIER, (Monsieur) mistake in his commentary on a passage of Horace, 19–20, notes. Different explanation from him of another passage of the same author, 94, notes.

DEBTORS, clause in the twelve tables of the Roman laws, concerning them, 19–20, notes. Man in debt, who sleeps sound, 50. His obliging behaviour to his creditors, ib.

DEDICATION, new method of composing one, 22. Great fall of their price of late years, ib. One wrote by a lady of quality to herself, ib.

DRINKING-MATCH, 25.

DUENNAS, what alone makes them faithful to their trust, 29.

DANCING-MASTER, his new method of teaching young ladies, 55.

DOMINGO, his adventures, 60. The way he took to be revenged of his master, 61, &c. Robs him, 65. Is taken together with Floretta, and sent to prison, ib. Vid. *Cosmo.*

E.

ENGLISH *Gentlemen,* a polite act of gallantry of one of them, 16.

ESTATE, a man of great estate, his motive for attending the levée, 91.

EMERENCIANA, (Donna) her story, 82. Her correspondence with Don Kimen de Lizana, ib. Discovered by her father Stephani, ib. Is obliged to write a letter to Lizana, 83. Forcibly carried

away by her father, 84. Locked up with a merciless duenna, 84. Relieved from her imprisonment
by Lizana, 87. Is found mad, ib. The extravagance of her conversation, 87–88. Is conducted to
Madrid, 88. Confined in Bedlam by her uncle, ib. Vid. *Stephani* and *Lizana.*

ESCULANO, (Don Pedro de) his house on fire, 96. Offers a reward to save his daughter from the
flames, who is in danger of instantly perishing, ib. What he says to Asmodeus, who was in the
shape of Zambullo, 97.

F.

FLAGEL, the spirit of the bar, 14.

FABULA, (Donna) account of her lying-in, 21.

FOOTMAN, the tranquillity of one, notwithstanding the situation of his mistress, 21.

FLORETTA, maid to Luziana, joins with Domingo, in putting a trick upon his master, 61, &c. from
whom she receives presents, 62. Cajoles him to an entertainment on the banks of the Mansanarez, 64. Goes off with Domingo, 65. Taken and sent to the house of correction, ib.

FRANCILLO, a banker and son of a cobler, 72. Returns from Peru with great riches, ib. Goes to see
his father and mother, 73. Their conversation, and the consequences of it, 73, &c.

FAUSTA, the daughter of Sylla, her affairs with Villius, 93, and notes.

FUSIDIUS, an old president compared to him, 94. Who he was, and his character from Horace, ib.,
notes.

G.

GRIFFAEL, angel of the attornies, 23.

GAMESTERS, how differently agitated, 16. Gaming, its fatal effects; tragical story of two gentlemen, 24.

[GROOM] Groom of the chambers falsely imprisoned, 59.

GARCIA, (Don Garcia de Pacheco) in love with Aurora, the wife of Zanubio, 76. His scheme to get
access to her, ib. And the prevailing argument he made use of with the gardiner's wife, ib. Is discovered by Aurora, 77. And put into a mortal fright, ib. Surprised by Zanubio and escapes with
his wife, 78. Vid. *Aurora.*

H.

HORACE, a passage of him misinterpreted by Monsieur Dacier, 19–20, notes. Another passage of
his explained differently, 94, notes. His story of Villius and Sylla's daughter, 93, notes. What he
says of Fusidius, 94, notes. Of Marsaeus and Origo, ib.

HUSBANDS, instance of a complaisant one, though a Spaniard, 38. Of one who went mad on the
death of his wife, and the reason why, 78–79.

HUNTING, the danger of it to an elder brother, in company with a younger, 60.

HEIR, reason of a young heir turning lunatic, 76. Ingenious expedient of a young one to keep himself in cash, 90. One compared to Marsaeus, 94.

I.

INQUISITORS, story of rich one attended by his penitents, 52. Declared by the demon to be the happiest of mortals, ib. Their great alertness in matters of profit, 59. Not to be spoke of but with the
greatest reverence, ib.

[JULIO. See *Jago*.]

JUSTICE, what evidence in matters of justice, are never to be parted with, 65.

JAGO, privy to Stephani's treatment of Don Kimen de Lizana, 84. By Stephani's order poisons all the servants, ib. And murders Emerenciana's two women, ib. Is seized by the officers of justice, 85. Discovers where Lizana is confined, ib. Discovers where Emerenciana is confined, 87. Carried in irons to Madrid, 88. Vid. *Stephani* and *Lizana*.

K.

KIMEN. Vid. *Lizana*.

L.

LEANDRO *Perez*. See *Zambullo*.

LUCIFER, The nature of his charge, 14.

LEVIATHAN, attends the court, 14.

LEVITE, on his death bed, deserted by his relations, 25.

LADIES *of Pleasure*, 25–26. The singular happiness of footmen, 26.

LEONORA DE CESPIDES, daughter of Don Luis, in love with count Belflor, 26. Who endeavours to seduce her, 26–27, &c. Is decoyed into the house of la Chicona, 27. Her resolution and virtue, 28–30. Her innocence practised upon by her governante Marcella, 30–33. Her inexperience and credulity got the better of, 36. Yields to the treacherous arguments of Marcella and the count, ib. Is discovered by her father, ib. Who threatens to kill her, ib. Is to be sent to a convent, 39. Writes to count de Belflor, before she retires from the world, 41. Is visited by the count, 43. Who marries her, 49. Vid. *Belflor* and *Cespides*.

LOVERS, instance of great honour in one, 55. How a Frenchman would behave on the like occasion, 55, 79. Of one that lost the use of his reason, 79. The song he composed on the cruelty of his mistress, ib. And the song of a Frenchman under the like misfortune, ib.

LUZIANA, countenances the trick put upon Don Cosmo de la Higuiera, 61–62, &c. Speaks to him from her lattice, 64. Vid. *Cosmo*.

LADY's *Looking-glass*, the occasion of her madness, 81.

LIZANA, (Don Kimen de) in love with Emerenciana, daughter of Stephani, 82. Gains her affection and corresponds with her, ib. Is seen coming out of her apartment by her father, ib. Receives a letter of assignation from Emerenciana, 83. Seized by Stephani's people, and carried off, 83–84. His cruel treatment in a dungeon, 84. Reduced to the extremity of misery, 84–85. Set at liberty, 85. Finds Emerenciana gone distracted, 87–88. Leaves his country, and sets out for New Spain, 89. Vid. *Stephani* and *Emerenciana*.

LONGARENUS, beats Villius out of Sylla's house, 93, notes.

M.

MOUNTEBANKS, their tutelar demon, 14.

MUSSULMAN lord, 16.

MAGICIAN, his great power, 18. His insolence, ib. The reason of his falling out with Asmodeus, ib.

MARCELLA, governante to Leonora de Cespides, wheedled by la Chicona, 27. Her adventure with the man in the grey beard, ib. Her rage and indignation, 29–30. Is corrupted by the count. And undertakes to seduce her ward, 30. Practises upon the inexperience of Leonora, 30, &c. And at

Z.

INDEX
TO THE
SECOND VOLUME

A.

B.

G.

GRATITUDE, instance of the gratitude of kings, 103.

GERMAN, dies of bumpers, 108.

GATES. See *Sleep*.

GIBLET, a tragic poet, retires from Paris to Madrid, 127. Lodges in the same house with a writer of comedies, ib. Rises in the night, and calls him up, ib. Repeats to him part of a tragedy, ib., &c. His applauses of himself, 127–29. Their conversation and dispute, ib., &c. Giblet offended and in great wrath, 130. Enters into a manual argumentation with his opponent, 130–31. They are parted, 132. Vid. *Calidas*.

GERMAN lady, her adventure with a young Spanish nobleman, 159.

H.

HORACE, his reason for thinking a dream to be true—Subject of one of his dreams, 151, notes. Receives a challenge from Crispinus. His answer and advice, 161, notes.

HYPOLITA, her story, 168, &c.

I.

JEROM, father Jerom, how tricked by a dutchess, his penitent, 104. By what means he found it out, 106.

JUAN, Don Juan de Zarates, 110. Flies from Toledo, ib. Meets with Theodora, at the entrance of a wood, ib. His adventure with Don Fadrique de Mendoza and Don Alvaro Ponza, 111, &c. Prevents their fighting, ib. Goes to the house of Don Fadrique, 114. Acquaints him with his history, 115, &c. Marries a woman of no fortune, ib. Whom he suspects of having an intrigue with the duke of Naxera, ib. Finds a letter to her from the duke, ib. His behaviour on that occasion, 116, &c. Is reconciled to her, 117. [Finds afterwards the duke, with her, ib.] Kills him and his wife, ib., and flies, 118. Contracts an intimate friendship with Don Fadrique de Mendoza, ib. Falls in love with Theodora, Don Fadrique's mistress, 119. And declines visiting her, ib. Laid under a necessity of owning his passion, 120. Finds her prepossessed in his favour, ib. But refuses the offer of marriage she makes him, 121, &c. Comes to an explanation with Don Fadrique upon that subject, 123, &c. Sets out along with Don Juan for Theodora's house, 126. Finds her carried off by Alvaro Ponza, ib. Is informed where Alvaro designed to carry her, 133. Goes with Don Fadrique in quest of them, ib. Attacked by two Barbary corsairs, ib. Taken prisoner, ib. Separated from Mendoza, 134. Bought for the service of the dey of Algiers, ib. And employed in his gardens, ib. His conversation with the dey, 135, &c. Becomes the confidant of his amours, 136. Is introduced by him to a lady in his seraglio, ib. Whom he finds to be Theodora; their conversation, ib., &c. Proposes the means of her escape, 139. What pass'd between him and Mezomorto, 139–40. Concerts methods with Francisco, 140–42. Persuades Mezomorto to defer his marriage with Theodora, 144. Carries her out of his seraglio, ib. Is stabbed by Mendoza, by mistake, for Alvaro Ponza, ib. What he says to his friend, 144, &c. Carried on board a ship, 145. His wound dress'd, and found not to be dangerous, 146. His despair on the death of his friend, 148. Arrives in Spain, ib. His conversation with Don Fadrique's uncle, 148, 150. Receives his pardon for the death of the duke of Naxera, 150. Mourns for his friend Don Fadrique, ib. Marries Theodora, and soon after dies, ib.

L.

LADY's dream on reading Ovid, 156.

LADY's (German) adventure, 159.

LADIES of the town, an account of some of them, 162.

M.

MENDOZA. Vid. Don *Fadrique.*

MERCHANT, disobliges his posterity, 104.

MONUMENT, a magnificent one, its history, 104.

MINISTER, his great abilities and distinguish'd probity, 106. Afraid of dying, ib.

MODESTY, sets fire to an author's funeral pile, 107.

MANES, their uniform, 107. To be worn by all, ib. Harmless though frightful, ib. No distinction of grandeur among the Manes, ib.

MIDWIFE, sent for to an actress, 158.

MONSALVO, (Signior) his adventure with a German lady, 159.

MEZOMORTO, dey of Algiers, buys Don Juan as a slave, to work in his garden, 134. Makes him the confidant of his amours, 135, &c. His sentiments in regard to a beautiful captive, ib. Employs Don Juan to speak to her, ib. Refuses to accept a ransom for Theodora, 138. Falls violently in love with her, ib., &c. Deceived by Don Juan, 139, &c.

N.

NEPHEWS, their lamentations over their deceased uncle, 109.

NAXERA, (duke of) his intrigue with the wife of Don Juan de Zarates, 115. Killed by him, 117.

O.

OFFICER, general officer, undergoes the fate of Agamemnon, 103.

ONIONS, philosophical food, 160.

OVID, his opinion of dreams, 151, notes. Dream of a lady after reading in his Metamorphoses, 156.

ORESTES, his friendship with Pylades, 118. A great character in ancient tragedies, ib., notes.

P.

PRELATE, death of one owing to his own imprudence, 103. Reception of one in the other world, 109.

PLACIDUS, a famous preacher, his great reputation, 104, 106. Wins the heart of a dutchess, ib., &c.

PRIEST, his encounter with death, 109.

PLAYER, dream of one, 156.

PHYSICIANS, to assist at the funeral of their patients, 152. An account of one, how he spends his time, 162.

PIQUILLO, his behaviour to Bahabon after his acquital, 179. Acquaints him with his father's captivity, 180. His repentance, ib.

PABLOS. Vid. *Bahabon.*

Z.

APPENDIX B:
GUIDE TO PHARMACEUTICALS
AND RELATED TERMS

As a pharmacist and a surgeon's mate, Smollett took care with his translations of Le Sage's ingredients for various preparations, ranging from laxatives to aphrodisiacs. Therefore, it has seemed useful to provide definitions of these ingredients and comments on their uses. We have consulted John Quincy, *Pharmacopoeia Officinalis & Extemporanea, or, A Compleat English Dispensatory* (1722), and Nicholas Culpeper, *The English Physician* (1649; reprinted as *The Complete Herbal*, 1983). Antoine Furetière, *Dictionnaire universel* (1690; revised by Jean-Baptiste Brutel de la Rivière, 1727; reprinted, 1972), has proved helpful on occasion as well. In some cases, Smollett substituted an English term for the French term; these are duly noted in the entry. Each entry includes a description of the ingredient and remarks on its properties and uses.

AMBERGREASE. Modern ambergris. A valuable and legendary perfume ingredient, distilled from the secretions of the sperm whale. A stimulating cordial, believed to be an aphrodisiac, ambergris was used both internally and externally.

BALM. "Eaux de Melisse." A fragrant garden herb used in many soothing preparations, both external and internal.

CINNAMON. "Canelle orgee." Cinnamon was considered a universal curative; in this case, it is being used to prevent discharges and to strengthen the stomach and bowels.

COLTS FOOT. "Thussilage." Coltsfoot is described as a perennial herb with leaves the shape of a horse's hoof. Rendered into a syrup, coltsfoot was used in restorative preparations for respiratory problems.

CORN-POPPY. "Mille fleurs." Also known as red poppy, the corn poppy was rendered into a syrup that relieved catarrhs and discharges from the head. This term does not correspond to Le Sage's "mille-fleurs," which is described as "cow's urine, received into a vase in order to take as a remedy" (Furetière).

ELECTUARY. A prepared powder or paste mixed with honey or wine to cure stomach disorders.

ELIXIR PROPRIETAS. An elixir is a sweetened alcoholic medicinal solution. This particular mixture of saffron, myrrh, aloe, and sulphur was considered a good stomach medicine and cathartic.

EMERALD. Powdered emeralds, as well as crushed rubies and sapphires, were long used in medicine. By the eighteenth century such ingredients were already considered dangerous and largely used "more to countenance the extravagant Price of a Composition than to contribute any real efficacy thereunto" (Quincy).

JELLY-FLOWER. "D'oillets." Clove-gillyflower, also known as July-flower, because it blooms in that month. Sweet and pleasant tasting, it was used in syrups and cordials.

MAIDENHAIR. A perennial fern, maidenhair was used in balsamic preparations for coughs, asthma, and pleurisies. Maidenhair does not correspond to Le Sage's "jujuba" (modern jojoba), described by Quincy as an "Italian fruit." However, jojoba could be used to cure the same ailments.

MARSHMALLOW. "D'althea." Described as a perennial herb, marshmallow was used in emollient preparations for easing coughing and pleurisies.

MUSK. The most powerful of all perfume fragrances. Considered a stimulating cordial by its fragrance and volatility, musk, extracted from the sac in the male musk deer, was taken internally and applied externally. Also considered an aphrodisiac.

ORANGE FLOWER WATER. An all-purpose cordial composed of oranges, spices, herbs, and white wine, used both "outwardly and inwardly" (Quincy).

SPIT-WORT. Spit-wort cannot be completely identified. Possibly a corruption or regional version of starwort or spleenwort, both herbs frequently used in medicinal preparation. Does not correspond to Le Sage's "sirops of longuevie."

TINCTURE. An alcoholic preparation of a medicinal substance.

TREACLE-WATER. "De l'Eau Thericale." Composed of treacle mixed with many herbs and spices, treacle-water was hailed as the finest antidote against poison.

WALL-FLOWER. "Veronique." Wallflower is a generic term for a variety of herbaceous perennials of the mustard family. Also known as *Veronicae maris* as well as Paul's betony and male speedwell. Used for nervous disorders, apoplexy, paralysis, and pains, wallflower was also used in diuretics and in preparations to relieve maladies of the skin and to discharge pulmonary secretions.

NOTES TO THE TEXT

Quotations from the French are taken from a contemporary edition of *Le Diable boiteux* (Paris: Chez Prault pere, 1737), with page numbers in parentheses immediately following. For a full discussion of the principles and methods followed in preparing the notes, see the preface (xi–xii).

The Author's Dedication

1. "ILLUSTRIOUS DON LEWIS VELEZ DE GUEVARA": Luis Vélez de Guevara (1579–1694), prolific Spanish playwright, poet, and prose writer, is chiefly known for *El diablo cojuelo* (1641), upon which Le Sage modeled *Le Diable boiteux*.

Asmodeus's Crutches

1. "*paulo post futurum*": "*Paulo-post-futurum*" (250). The tenses of Greek verbs are notoriously difficult; the schoolmaster has gone mad studying an obscure form of the future tense.
2. "cit": "Bourgeoise" (269). Short for citizen, but usually applied contemptuously to townsmen or shopkeepers to distinguish them from gentlemen *(OED)*.

Volume 1

Chapter 1

1. "quadrants": "quadrans" (11). Variation of "quadrate," an instrument formerly used for measuring altitudes and distances, consisting of a square plate with two graduated sides *(OED)*.
2. "musæum": "réduit" (12). A museum in this sense is a building or apartment dedicated to the pursuit of learning; a scholar's study.
3. "into the bargain": An addition by Smollett.
4. "plugged up": "enfermé" (13).
5. "do you sit in the house of peers, or are you only a plebeian?": "Si vous êtes un Démon noble ou roturier" (13). Smollett's translation of this passage echoes Milton's description of his vision of the gathering and organizing of the fallen angels and their building of "*Pandæmonium*, the high Capitol / Of Satan and his Peers" (*Paradise Lost* 1.756–57).
6. "he is the demon of grooms and governantes": "c'est le Patron des Marchands, des Tailleurs, des Bouchers, des Boulangers, & des autres voleurs du tiers-état" [he is the patron of merchants, tailors, butchers, bakers, and other thieves of the third estate] (14).
7. "Who a plague are you then?": "Il faut donc" (14).
8. "He presides over the inns of court": An addition by Smollett.
9. "that are not worth a groat": "Amans qui n'ont point de fortune" (16). A groat was a coin of low value or one that had been debased *(OED)*.
10. "drums, routs, beatups": An addition by Smollett. All words indicate violent criminal activity. "Drums" means to ring or knock on a door to ascertain if a place is unoccupied so that it can

be robbed. "Rout," which has many meanings of general violence, seems here to mean a riot or a disturbance. "Beat-up" means an assault *(OED)*.

11. "Agrippa": Agrippa von Nettesheim, 1486–1535. His *De Occulta Philosophia* (1531) was perhaps the best-known work about demons in the Renaissance. Agrippa ranked Asmodeus as the leader of the fourth order of demons, the "revengers of evil."

12. "talmud of Solomon": Actually *The Testament of Solomon*, once believed to be an apocryphal book of the Bible. Supposedly Solomon's warning to Israel against demon worship, recent scholarship regards it as an essay in popular demonology and magic, written in early Christian times and drawn from Jewish, Roman, and Greek sources. The work relates how Solomon acquired powers over demons and used them to build the Temple. Praying for God to deliver the demon Ornias into his hands, who is disrupting work on the Temple, Solomon then orders Ornias to bring his fellow demons before him. In section 5, Asmodeus appears and names his functions and deeds, which include plotting against newlyweds, marring the beauty of maidens, and spreading madness among women. See H. F. D. Sparks, ed., *The Apocryphal Old Testament* (Oxford: Clarendon Press, 1984), 741–42.

13. "I did not . . . mine to you": "je vous gardois celui-là pour le dernier" (17).

14. "have been pleased . . . the loveliest babe in the world": "ces Messieurs me peignent fort avantageusement" (17).

15. "I am equipt": "j'ai" (17).

16. "you have got rammed into": "qui vous recéle" (17).

17. "I see no way . . . get you out": "je pourrai vous délivrer de prison" (18).

18. "and to be plain with you": "entre nous" (18).

19. "it would be a kind of presumption": "comment" (18).

20. "your tutelar demon . . . the familiar of Socrates": "Démon tutelaire, plus éclaire que le génie de Socrate" (19). Plutarch's "Discourse Concerning Socrates His Daemon" describes Socrates' wisdom as so rational that it "was seen to come from a Daemon . . . which, going before him, shed a light upon hidden and obscure matters, and such could not be discovered by unassisted human understanding" (*Moralia* 588e).

21. "I make a tender of myself to you": "je me donne à vous" (19).

22. "but gentlemen of your cloth": "mais vous autres Messieurs les Diables" (20).

23. "tickled": "charmé" (21).

24. "by degrees": "peu à peu" (21).

25. "a kind of scarf": "de toile jaune" (22).

26. "white parchment": "parchemin vierge" (22). Either virgin parchment or a parchment outstanding for its smooth, white texture. In the second case, the parchment may have been treated by a paste made of lime, quicklime, flour, and egg white. The mixture was applied and rubbed down with a damp cloth, and this treatment created a "surface which, when dry, was extremely smooth, hard, and of an even white appearance" (Ronald Reed, *The Nature and Making of Paper* [Leeds: Elmete Press, 1975], 91).

27. "cabalistick characters": "caractéres talismaniques" (22). In this sense, a secret or special series of signs known only to a small party *(OED)*. Based on the word "cabala," an historical and literary term associated with Jewish mysticism. Beginning in the thirteenth century, cabalistic speculation attempted to peer beyond the senses to penetrate the mysteries of heaven and earth in order to discern the nature of God, the angels, the afterlife, and the magical significance of numbers and the letters of the alphabet.

28. "China ink": "encre de la Chine" (23). India ink *(OED)*.

29. "in horrible confusion": "tout en désordre" (23).

30. "petit-maitre": "Petits-Maîtres François" (23). A fop, an effeminate man *(OED)*.

Chapter 2

1. "to do the quicker execution": "faire aimer brusquement" (26).
2. "so confoundedly ugly": "un peu laid" (26).
3. "nether": "moïenne" (27).
4. "I can make shift": "je ne laisse pas d'aller bon train" (27).
5. "sylphid": "Sylphide" (28). Figuratively, a graceful young girl. Because he is a sorceror, Asmodeus's captor might very well be meeting a true sylph, one of a race of beings or spirits that inhabit the air *(OED)*.
6. "and it would . . . in the same manner": "il pourroit bien vous y mettre aussi" (28).
7. "necromancer": "Enchanteur" (28). Two paragraphs later, Smollett uses the same translation for "Négromancien" (29). A necromancer is a sorceror who raises images of the dead for evil purposes *(OED)*.
8. "book on Restrictions": "Livre de la *Contrainte*" (28). Smollett's close following of the French in the second edition contrasts with the first edition of his translation. For reasons known only to himself, he preferred "*Satan's Invisible World* by the rev. Mr. Baxter" in the first edition. This in itself is a source of confusion, because *Satan's Invisible World Discovered* (1685) was actually written by George Sinclair (d. 1696), a professor of philosophy and mathematics at Glasgow. The Presbyterian divine Richard Baxter (1615–91), however, did address the supernatural in *The Certainty of the World of Spirits* (1691). A collection of letters and accounts describing various people's encounters with the supernatural, the work was intended, as Baxter avowed, to frighten people into the fear of God.
9. "we are ignorant . . . of futurity": "nous ne sçavons pas ce qui doit arriver" (29).
10. "bubbled": "grandes duppes" (29).
11. "I supported the interests of another candidate": "je voulois la faire donner à un autre" (31).
12. "whose interest was too prevalent for the conjurations": "dont le nom l'emporta sur le Talisman" (31).
13. "he thought it preferable to running the risk": "il aima mieux l'accepter, que de demeurer exposé" (31).

Chapter 3

1. "church of St. Salvador": "Tour de *San-Salvador*" (32). Established and named in 1257, Saint Salvador was one of the oldest parish churches in Madrid. Jerónimo de Quintana in his *History of Antiquity* (Madrid, 1629) named it as one of the grandest and most noble churches in Madrid, noting that its lofty steeple was called the "watchtower."
2. "why I have pitch'd you here": "pourquoi je vous améne ici" (33).
3. "you shall see . . . as clearly as if it were noon-day": "le dedans va se découvrir à vos yeux" (33).
4. "Louis Velez de Guevara": See note 1, "The Author's Dedication," above.
5. "forces your attention": "vous regardez avec tant de plaisir" (34).
6. "to explain those parts they are now acting on this stage of your world": "je veux vous expliquer ce que font toutes ces personnes que vous voïez" (34).
7. "most inward and hidden motives": "motifs de leurs actions" (34).
8. "city miser": "bourgeois" (34).
9. "distress of a seizure": "*Alcalde de Corte*" (34). The French term means a bailiff, charged with carrying out the court's order, such as a seizure of property.
10. "M. Dacier": André Dacier (1651–1722), the prolific and highly regarded translator.

11. *"Rogabat . . . Farris libra foret"*: "At the last he [Messius Cicirrus] asked why he [Sarmentus] had ever run away, since a pound of meal was enough for one so lean and puny" (Horace *Satires* 1.5.67–69).

12. "beau of threescore, who is come home quite warm from an intrigue": "Galant sexagenaire qui revient de faire l'amour" (36).

13. "utmost effort and perfection": "épuisé" (37).

14. "disputed their pretensions to her so warmly": "se disputent ses bonnes graces" (37).

15. "I give them joy with all my heart": "Les enragés!" (37).

16. *"qui eum vinctum habebit, libras farris indies dato"*: The Twelve Tablets, from which Smollett quotes, are some of the most ancient Latin in existence and are, as such, very different from the Latin of Horace and Cicero. The passage is a digest that begins with Law IV and extends to Law VII: "(Law IV) Where anyone, having acknowledged a debt, has a judgment rendered against him . . . thirty days shall be given to him. . . . (Law V) After the term of thirty days . . . their creditors shall be permitted to forcibly seize them and bring them into court. . . . (Law VI) When a defendant . . . does not satisfy the judgment; or, in the meantime, another party . . . does not pay it out of his own money, the creditor . . . can take the [debtor] with him and bind him or place him in fetters; provided his chains are not of more than fifteen pounds weight. . . . (Law VII) If . . . [a debtor] desires . . . he shall be permitted to support himself out of his own property. But if he has nothing on which to live, his creditor, who holds him in chains, shall give him a pound of grain every day, or he can give him more than a pound, if he wishes to do so."

17. "groats in our jails": "Groats" was a popular term for the allowance of four pence a day provided for debtors under the "Benevolent Act," 32 George II, c. 28. Under this act, creditors were to supply imprisoned debtors with their sustenance; however, this was rarely carried out; see John Howard, *State of the Prisons* (1777; reprint, New York: E. P. Dutton, Everyman's Library, 1929), 2.

18. "some government": "une Vice-Royauté" (38); a province or colony administered by a royal appointee.

19. "her husband, Don Torribio": "vieux Don Torribio" (39).

20. "pierce him to the heart": "lui perçent l'ame" (39). Smollett does not translate the next clause in Le Sage's text: "Il est pénétré de douleur" [he is pierced by pain] (39).

21. "With what officious earnestness he hurries up and down to fetch things for her": "Avec quel soin & quelle ardeur il s'empresse à la secourir!" (39).

22. "who was a-going to begin the world": "songeoit à s'établir" (41).

23. "monk": "mauvais Moine" (41).

24. "chimerical bubble": "belle chimére" (42).

25. "subterraneous student": "souffleur" (42). Smollett seemed to have confused *souffleur* (to blow) with *souterrain*, which literally means "underground" and perhaps here takes on the figurative sense of "underhanded."

26. "prolifick bolus": "pillule prolifique" (42). Medicine formed into a round shape for ease of swallowing and larger than an ordinary pill. The term was frequently used contemptuously (*OED*).

27. "astringent pills": "drogues Astringeantes" (42). Such preparations "constringed the fibres" to prevent immoderate discharges (*OED*).

28. "fat bishop": "Prélat" (43).

29. "flock-bed": "grabat" (43). A crude or rough bed (*OED*).

30. "joint-stool": "placet" (43). A stool made of parts joined or fitted together (*OED*). Although distinguished from a stool made by cruder methods, a "joint-stool" here suggests a rough chair.

31. "something that resembles a table": "une table" (43).

32. "What strange faces . . . as he walks!": "A le voir s'agiter & se démener comme il fait en se promenant" (43).

33. "this rare performance": An addition by Smollett.

34. "deluge of trash": "pitoïables productions" (45).

35. "compter": "comptoir" (46). A table or bureau in which valuables were stored (A Dictionary of the Older Scottish Tongue).

36. "has bit them": "les a prévenus" (46).

37. "but now wants to get clear of the incumbrance": "qui veut cesser de l'être" (47).

38. "a fat, jolly batchelor": "gros Bâchelier boiteux" (48).

39. "Volumnius": Publius Volumnius, a philosopher who accompanied Brutus on his campaigns against the triumvirs and recorded the portents that preceded Brutus's last battle (Plutarch Brutus 48.2, 51.2, 52.2–3).

40. "batchelor Donoso": "Bachelier" (49). A university graduate.

41. "urbanitatis possessionem, in qua . . . contemno cæteros": "My proprietary rights in wit and humor: . . . in that department I fear no man but you; as for the others, I despise them" (Loeb translation).

42. "he has no such hopes": An addition by Smollett.

43. "the very essence of romantick love": "qui file l'amour parfaite" (50).

44. "Dulcinea": "Infante" (50). Dulcinea, Don Quixote's beloved, when used to describe a young lady, is a Smollettian trademark that occurs throughout his work. "Infante" (prince) is a mistake in the French text for "infanta," literally meaning a Spanish princess, but also a fanciful term for a young lady.

45. "he is big with some mighty project": "qu'il roule dans sa tête quelque grand projet" (51).

46. "money-scrivener": "Contador" (51). An accountant (Spanish).

47. "brace of plums": "quatre millions de bien" (51). "Plum" is slang for £100,000 (OED); a brace is a pair, so the gentleman is worth £200,000.

48. "he shall be able to make a compensation for his former iniquities": "Il se flate qu'après une si bonne œuvre il aura la conscience en repos" (51).

49. "knight of St. Jago": "Chevalier de saint Jacques" (52). An affluent military order founded in 1161. Its seat of power was in Santiago de Compostela; the order originally guarded the borders against Muslim attacks and protected pilgrims traveling to the shrine of Saint James in Compostela. During Ferdinand and Isabella's reign, the order was vested in the crown, and the title became honorific.

50. "Me tuo . . . Lydia dormis": "Sleepest then, Lydia, while I, thy true love die throughout the livelong night" (Horace Odes 1.25.7–8).

51. "these portal hymns, these ἄωρα κλαυσίθυρα": The Greek translates as something like "unseasonable laments" and may allude to a poetic topos, popular in antiquity, of the "occlusus amator," "the lover shut out," who sings a song of lament to the closed door of his beloved, while enduring inclement weather.

52. "Levite": "Chanoine" (54). Levite, from Hebrew, means a descendant of the tribe of Levi, members of which acted as assistants to the priests in temple worship. Here it is used as contemptuous slang for a clergyman (OED).

53. "their deceased uncle": An addition by Smollett.

54. "What a simpleton you are": "Que vous êtes jeune" (58).

55. "they don't value these great men one farthing": "elles n'ont pas la moindre amitié pour ces Seigneurs" (58).

56. "every man that bleeds freely is the husband for the time being": "tout payeur est traité comme un mari" (58).

57. "coming in for the second course at free cost": "de les avoir *gratis*" (59).

Chapter 4

1. "who perceived the count's passion by his looks": "qui s'étoit apperçûë de l'attention que le Comte avoit pour elle" (61).

2. "and the only difference . . . quicken the operation": "c'est qu'elle corrompt peu à peu les cœurs, au lieu que je les séduis brusquement" (61).

3. "who was counting": "qui tenoit à la main" (62).

4. "received extreme unction": "est à l'extrêmité" (63). Extreme unction is the sacrament of anointing a sick person with oil. A penitential rite, it is given when death is approaching and recovery not likely.

5. "immediately cleared dame Marcella's doubts": "la Dame Marcelle prit son parti" (63).

6. "grey beard": "barbe blanche" (64).

7. "the only thing . . . this side of time": "C'étoit l'unique chose que je désirois" (65).

8. "Never in his life": "Hélas!" (65).

9. "without going about the bush": "où sans chercher de détours" (66).

10. "ran up to Leonora, and casting himself at her feet": "se montra, & courant se jetter aux pieds de Léonor" (67).

11. "made a sensible impression on the mind of Leonora": "troublérent Léonor" (67).

12. "needs not alarm the most perfect virtue": "ne doit point vous alarmer" (68).

13. "I must own indeed . . . other means to speak with you?": "Vous avez sujet, je vous l'avoüé, de vous revolter contre l'artifice, dont je me sers pour vous entretenir; mais n'ai-je pas jusqu'à ce jour inutilement essayé de vous parler?" (68).

14. "He gave over and pressed Leonora no more": "Il cessa de s'opposer au dessein de Léonor" (70).

15. "a piece is saluted with hisses from the pit and gallery": "une piéce que le parterre a mal reçûë" (71).

16. "all in a flutter": "beaucoup d'agitation" (71).

17. "his ears": "la barbe" (72).

18. "The fidelity of governesses . . . solicit their interest": "S'il y a des Gouvernantes fideles, c'est que les Galans ne sont pas assez riches ou assez libéraux" (73).

19. "she began to open as loud as ten fish-women": "il lui prit une fureur de langue" (74).

20. "lay this storm": "essuïa patiemment cet orage" (74).

21. "yet who knows . . . have upon him?": "votre beauté peut lui avoir fait prendre la résolution de vous épouser" (77).

22. "I have a great mind . . . scold him afresh": "je ne retourne encore sur mes pas pour lui dire de nouvelles injures" (77).

23. "any violence upon . . . made his wife?": "ou auriez-vous de la répugnance à l'épouser?" (78).

24. "young Leonora, whose heart was open, and suspected nothing": "la trop sincére Léonor" (78).

25. "deserves the love of any woman": "m'a paru digne d'être aimé" (79).

26. "pleads in his behalf": "l'excuse" (79).

27. "he will stoop to the daughter of Don Lewis": "il se borne à la fille de Don Luis" (80).

28. "if I should flatter myself . . . making myself more miserable": "il ne cherche qu'à m'offenser" (80).

29. "see to get at the bottom of his intentions": An addition by Smollett.

30. "he could not avoid holding me cheap": "il cesseroit de m'estimer" (81).

31. "that he was not indifferent to Leonora": "qu'il en étoit aimé" (82).

32. "your addresses will not be disagreeable": "Il m'a paru pénétré d'une véritable passion" (84).

33. "to swear an eternal fidelity": "que je ne serai jamais qu'à elle" (85).

34. "but being determined, at all events, to accomplish her designs": "Voulant toutefois en venir à bout, à quelque prix que ce fût" (87).

35. "I inculcated in your mind": "je vous ai données" (87).

36. "A lady may hearken . . . with the purest virtue": "Une fille ne cesse pas d'être vertueuse pour écouter un amant" (87).

37. "to advise you . . . with bad consequence": "pour vous faire un pas qui puisse vous nuire" (87–88).

38. "nor could the consciousness . . . remove her scruples": "La pureté de ses intentions ne la rassuroit point" (90).

39. "without being thoroughly satisfied of the honour of his designs": "dont elle ignoroit même les véritables sentimens" (90).

40. "upon that head": An addition by Smollett.

41. "of continual uneasiness": "des peines" (92).

42. "Had you that regard for me you ought to entertain": "Si vous m'estimiez" (92).

43. "because I have been . . . indifferent in your eyes": "parce que j'ai été assez heureux pour vous rendre favorable á mon amour" (93).

44. "can any thing be more cruel, or more unjust!": "Quelle injustice!" (93).

45. "when I have explained the matter to you": An addition by Smollett.

46. "and that he had this matter much at heart": An addition by Smollett.

47. "upon that head": "de ce côté-là" (95).

48. "the violence of my passion for you": "que je vous aimois depuis long-temps" (96).

49. "he would be prying into every thing we did": "ses yeux seront incessamment ouverts sur toutes nos actions" (98).

50. "I must beg . . . would make me do that": "je suis trop ennemi du mensonge, pour oser soutenir cette feinte. Je ne puis me trahir jusques-là" (100).

51. "but all to no purpose": An addition by Smollett.

52. "I am actually . . . of your conduct": "je ne vous comprends pas" (101).

53. "undermine the virtue of this innocent young lady": "ébranla Léonor" (103).

54. "with some difficulty recovering himself": "qui achevoit de se relever avec beaucoup de peine" (104).

55. "Shocked at this discovery, fatal to his repose": "Troublé de cette fatale vûë" (104).

56. "where has he . . . my daughter?": "Où a-t-il vû ma fille?" (106).

57. "However, as she could not avoid . . . without his privity": "Comme elle ne pouvoit s'écarter de la vérité au dénoüement, elle fut obligée de la dire; mais elle s'étendit sur les raisons que l'on avoit eûës de faire, á son inscu, ce mariage secret" (106–7).

58. "thou knowest . . . to wail and lament": "vous ne sçavez pas toutes les raisons que vous avez de vous affliger" (108).

59. "military order of Calatrava": "Ordre Militaire de Calatrava" (112). The oldest military-religious order in Spain, founded in 1158 to protect the city of Calatrava against the Moors. After the reconquest, Ferdinand and Isabella invested the order in the crown.

Chapter 5

1. "and every thing . . . accomplished lady": "rien ne lui manque" (114).
2. "if I can be . . . in his behalf": "je vous offre tout mon crédit pour lui" (115).
3. "but this is not the affair at present": "mais venons à ce que" (115).
4. "I demand a direct answer": "cessez de me couper la parole" (115).
5. "to deliberate . . . so much delicacy": "roulant dans son esprit mille projets de vengeance" (116).
6. "Marcella tried every method she could think of to comfort her": "Marcella essaya de la consoler" (117).
7. "in the most frightful recesses of a desert": "dans le plus horrible séjour" (119).
8. "from his own mouth": An addition by Smollett.
9. "and, melted by Leonora's tears, when they met together": "pourroit bien être touché des larmes que Léonor répandroit dans cette entrevûë" (121).
10. "would make a common quarrel of it": "songeroient à la venger" (121).
11. "in his breast": An addition by Smollett.
12. "What a scandal . . . my name!": "Quelle ingratitude!" (124).
13. "whom he looked upon as fitter for that purpose": "dont il jugea les coups plus sûrs que les siens" (126).
14. "he is the very hero of the university": "le plus redoutable écolier de l'Université" (127).
15. "to see a lady with whom he had an intrigue": "desir de revoir une Dame qu'il aimoit" (127).
16. "made an elopement up to town": "l'école buissonniere" (128).
17. "but making up to him in a great hurry": "qu'il vint à lui avec précipitation" (129).
18. "nettled at this usage": "choqué de ces paroles" (130).
19. "made appear what he could do": "montra ce qu'il sçavoit faire" (130).
20. "Upon which they both marched . . . they stopped": "Ils marchérent aussi-tôt à grands pas, gagnérent une autre ruë, & quand ils furent loin de celle où s'étoit donné le combat, ils s'arrêtérent" (132).
21. "and getting to the door, which was by that time half open": "s'avança vers la porte qui s'ouvrit" (135).
22. "with fury and indignation": "d'un œil irrité" (138–39).
23. "of the obligation I lie under": "Par-là je m'acquitte envers lui" (139–40).
24. "her tears have removed every remaining obstacle": "ses pleurs viennent d'achever l'ouvrage" (140).
25. "I hope you . . . as a sufficient atonement": "que j'expie en vous l'avoüant" (141).
26. "he would not be quite satisfied with their conduct": "il ne leur sçût mauvais gré de la récidive" (143).
27. "he was confounded and so thunder-struck": "il demeura si troublé" (144).
28. "he was on the point of coming to a rupture": "il alloit se broüiller" (147).
29. "all he said was . . . I should see him": "Il m'a dit seulement, qu'il souhaitoit que je visse le Cavalier auparavant" (150).
30. "gave her a particular account": "lui raconta tout" (153).
31. "as if she had been . . . her brother said to her": "comme si elle l'eût ignoré" (155).
32. "monastery of the *Arrependitas*": "*Monasterio de las Arrepentidas*" (156). A monastery that received women repenting wicked lives and devoting themselves to religion.

Chapter 6

1. "pretty singular": "assez rare" (157).
2. "any man": "un Marchand" (157).
3. "the same precaution Caligula formerly did": "il a pris la précaution que prenoit Caligula" (158). Suetonius reports that Caligula, "disguised in wig and robe, abandoned himself nightly to the pleasures of gluttonous and adulterous living" ("Gaius Caligula," *Lives of the Caesars* 4.1).
4. "ransacking": "entourré" (159).
5. "parlour": "salle basse" (160).
6. "they have had . . . a happy conclusion": "elles partagent en ce moment les fruits d'une avanture qu'elles viennent de mettre à fin" (160).
7. "La Pebrada has the best custom": "La Pébrada est la plus achalandée" (160).
8. "A pretty question truly": "Bon, s'il y en a" (161).
9. "with a sufficient number of these convenient ladies": An addition by Smollett.
10. "ever so plausible arguments": "les plus beaux raisonnemens du monde" (163).
11. "a member of the holy inquisition who lies sick": "un Inquisiteur malade" (164).
12. "slops": "bouillons" (164). Soup, gruel *(OED)*.
13. "over the tops of the houses": "sur les gouttieres" (167).
14. "his blood boiled with rage": "Il fremit de couroux" (167).
15. "as a further incitement to his rage": "Pour surcroît de douleur" (167).
16. "gentlemen of the robe": "Gens de robbe" (168). Lawyers.
17. "I'll immediately sow the seeds of division": "Je vais mettre la division" (168).
18. "excellent sport": "beau vacarme" (168).
19. "I riot in the sweets of full revenge": "j'ai goûté une pleine vengeance" (171).

Chapter 7

1. "in this dreadful place": An addition by Smollett.
2. "and is a moot point": An addition by Smollett.
3. "drank such an unmeasurable quantity": "tant bû" (173).
4. "Bravos": "*Valientes*" (174). Hired soldiers or assassins *(OED)*.
5. "a new way of dancing a minuet": "qui a fait faire un mauvais pas à une de ses écolieres" (174).
6. "to draw himself out of this scrape": An addition by Smollett.
7. "from their credulity . . . a pretty comfortable livelihood": "de vivre commodément de cette opinion" (176).
8. "halbert": "Sergent" (176). Smollett here uses "halbert" interchangeably with "halberdeer," or halberdier, a soldier armed with a halberd, a weapon made of a spearhead mounted on a handle five to seven feet long. Halberd denoted the rank of a sergeant. The first recorded usage in *OED* is from Henry Fielding's *Tom Jones* (1749), bk. 7, chap. 11. A halberdier was usually a member of a civic guard, and carrying a halberd was a sign of office *(OED)*.
9. "give me some wine, with pipes and tobacco": "Donnez-moi de la lumiere, du vin, une pipe, et du tabac" (177). Smollett omitted "de la lumiere" (a lamp or candle) from his translation.
10. "recruiting officer": "Sergent" (177).
11. "saluted him with a damnable rap over the head": "lui en déchargea du plat sur la tête une assez rude coup" (178).
12. "spirit of Jago": "par Saint Jacques" (178–79). Saint James the Greater. In legend the apostle Saint James, between the ascension of Christ and his own death, traveled and preached in

Spain. In the first century his body found its way to Spain and was enshrined at Campostella. James is also celebrated in Spain for his assistance in war: he appeared at the Battle of Clavigo (844), and he performed miracles in battles conducted under Alfonso VI (1084–1134) and Sancho III of Castile (1134–58).

13. "chain of the jack": "chaîne de turne-broche" (180). A kind of chain frequently used in roasting jacks, or turnspits (OED).

14. "fifty millions of devils": "cent mille Diables" (181).

15. "but the force . . . not mind the consequences": "d'une maniere qui m'étourdit sur les conséquences" (182).

16. "Hannibal was as good as his word": "En effet" (182).

17. "I will proceed to extremities and broil and carbonade them in such a manner as they little think of": "Je les tourmenterai, l'un & l'autre d'une étrange fançon" (183). To carbonade means to cut into small pieces (OED).

18. "holy office": "Saint Office" (185). Office of the Inquisition.

19. "the moment they . . . the smallest advantage": "Si-tôt qu'elle voit le moindre jour à tirer quelque profit" (185).

20. "Enchiridion": A non-Christian collection of magical prescriptions and incantations for protection against illness and misfortune, dating from the ninth century and first printed in Rome in 1523. See Nevill Drury, Dictionary of Mysticism (Santa Barbara, Calif.: ABC-CLIO, 1992).

21. "Albertus Magnus": "Albert le Grand" (187). Dominican friar and one of the most learned men in thirteenth-century Europe (1200–1280). His immense learning caused numerous miracles to be attributed to him, and many spurious works, including necromantic ones, were similarly ascribed to him. Late in the fifteenth century, when he was considered for canonization, charges of sorcery and magic were raised against him. See Mercia Eliade, ed., The Encyclopedia of Religion (New York: Macmillan, 1987).

22. "the same quantity . . . as was taken from Seneca": "fait à sa femme une saignée comme celle de Senéque" (188). Upon being ordered by Nero, his former student, to do away with himself, Seneca had the veins in his arms opened while he was in a warm bath. Because his blood did not flow easily, he then opened veins in his legs (Tacitus Annals 15.62).

23. "wonderful kind of wash": "eau merveilleuse" (189). A liquid cosmetic for the complexion (OED).

24. "random shot": "d'un coup d'escopete" (190).

25. "sharpers": "Picaros" (191). Rogues or rascals who prey on others (OED); the definition applies as well to picaro (Spanish).

26. "second edition of Gusman de Alfarache": Written by Mateo Alemán (1547–1615), Guzmán de Alfarache (1599, pt. 2, 1604) initiated the vogue for picaresque novels. Related by the repentant Guzmán, who is writing his memoirs from a watchtower, the work interweaves his life of crime, fraud, and deceit with commentary on people's actions that he observes from his elevated position. Its influence on Le Sage, who translated the work in 1732, can be seen in Le Diable boiteux, particularly in the demon's rooftop viewing of Madrid and his discerning knowledge of the people and scenes he views and in the two interpolated romances.

27. "This piece of discipline . . . in his stomach": "Il eut longtemps sur le cœur cette petite correction-là" (192).

28. "Abigail": "suivante" (193). From the name of the "waiting gentlewoman" in Francis Beaumont (1584–1616) and John Fletcher's (1579–1625) The Scornful Ladie (1616).

29. "in the country": "alors absent" (193).

30. "you eclipse all the brilliancy of a birth-day": "je ne vois point à la Cour de Cavalier que vous n'effaciez" (194).

31. "simpering": "soûrit" (194).
32. "The other pricked up his ears . . . heard his cousin say?": "Don Cóme ne manqua pas de demander ce que cette cousine avoir dit" (195).
33. "swallow every thing": "disposé à tout croire" (196–97).
34. "without further preamble": An addition by Smollett.
35. "no ways to your disadvantage": "ne doit pas vous avoir nui" (197).
36. "break my mind": "débuter" (198).
37. "the voice of fame's trumpet": "*que sur la foi de la Renomée*" (199).
38. "broil my vitals": "*je suis la proye*" (199).
39. "by the fate of destiny": "*par une influence de votre astre*" (200).
40. "general officer": "Mestre de Camp" (201).
41. "to make her still more desperately in love with you": "pour achever de la rendre folle de votre Seigneurie" (202).
42. "Luziana was infinitely delighted with . . . reference to herself": "Et à chaque couplet, dont la fille du Mestre de camp se faisoit l'application, elle rioit de tout son cœur" (204).
43. "immolate himself a victim": "sacrifié" (205).
44. "All gentlemen that are . . . to their mistresses": "C'est de vous que les Cavaliers amoureux doivent apprendre à servir leurs Maîtresses" (206).
45. "the eve of St. John, a night so celebrated in this city": "la nuit de la saint Jean, nuit si célébrée dans cette Ville" (207). Smollett omits the next two phrases in Le Sage's text: "aller avec d'autres filles de son espece *à la fiesta del Sotillo*" (207). The infinitive phrase means "to go with other girls like herself"; Le Sage glosses the italicized phrase (literally, "the dance of the Groves") in a footnote: "Sorte de danse particuliere aux Espagnols" (207). The dance celebrates the Eve of Saint John (23 June), commemorating the vigil of the nativity of Saint John the Baptist. The occasion was celebrated in Europe with bonfires and dancing.
46. "to make use of such an opportunity": "prendre la balle au bond" (208). The French phrase is idiomatic, meaning "to catch the ball on the bounce."
47. "pad": "haquenée des écuries" (209). Either a road-horse or a horse that moves along at an easy pace *(OED)*.
48. "consoled for the illness of his mistress from the occasion of it": "consolé d'un accident qui venoit d'une si belle cause" (210).
49. "It happened when these things were thus in agitation": "Dans ce temps-là" (210).
50. "basket-woman": "demeure volé" (212). A woman who peddles her wares in baskets, suggesting a vendor of the lower classes *(OED)*.
51. "Pedro . . . the cruel": "Don Pedre I. surnommé le Juste & le Cruel" (213). Pedro I (1320–67), eighth king of Portugal and fourth son of Alfonso IV, fell in love with his wife's waiting woman, dona Inês de Castro, and sparked a bitter conflict between himself and his father, who ordered Inês to be murdered in 1355. Upon his accession, one of his first acts was to avenge himself on her murderers. During his short reign (1357–67) Pedro devoted himself to justice, but his judgments, which he executed himself, were severe and often violent. The story of Inês de Castro became the basis for several Spanish novels and plays.

Chapter 8

1. "unconscionable extortion": "usure" (217).
2. "I must be dispatched immediately": An addition by Smollett.
3. "Jew": "Juif" (219). Pejoratively used, a grasping or extortionate person *(OED)*, which de-

scribes the moneylender. It also could be that the man is Jewish. During the Inquisition in Spain many Jews who did not flee converted to Catholicism, though they retained their faith. Such *converso* Jews practiced a rigorous, if outward, Christianity, much like the moneylender.

4. "Patricio . . . all thought of his poverty": "Patrice devenant plus honnête & plus poli que la necessité" (227).

5. "Bayonne ham": "jambon d'Estramadure" (227). Smollett's sense of French, Spanish, and Portuguese geography seems a bit askew. He substitutes the name of the French town Bayonne, located in extreme southwestern France near the border of Spain, for Extremadura, a region in southwestern Spain that is indeed well known for its hams. Smollett may have believed Le Sage was referring to the Portuguese province of Estremadura; his confusion may have arisen in that directly north of this Portuguese province is Bayona, a small village on the northwestern coast of Spain.

6. "cully": "écot" (228). A simpleton, easily duped or imposed upon, usually by a sharper or a strumpet *(OED)*.

7. "angel and goddess": "d'étoile & de soleil" (228).

8. "but she did not . . . that secret": An addition by Smollett.

9. "I shall look mean and pitiful": "il n'y a pas d'apparence" (232).

10. "having his wishes crowned with success": "tirer bon parti" (233).

11. "bonne bouche": Le Sage's phrase "laisser sur la bonne bouche" (234) freely translates to "save the best for last"; the meaning here, in effect, is "the best, saved for last."

12. "fortifying himself with patience": "prend patience" (234).

13. "Whilst he was thus employed in these reflections": An addition by Smollett.

14. "done duty as a centinel": "fait le pied de grüe" (235).

15. "whose genius was no ways turned to pleasantry": "animal hargneux" (237).

16. "the learned Azero": "du sçavant Azero" (237). Possibly Baltasar Azeredo, a sixteenth-century Portuguese doctor and professor at the University in Lisbon who wrote a treatise on medicine and a eulogy on Philip II and who composed poetry in Latin and Portuguese.

17. "You'll hardly believe . . . reading sometimes has": "En effet, admirez le charme de cette lecture" (238).

18. "Buen-Retiro": "Buen-retiro" (238). An elaborate palace and parklands built by Philip IV in eastern Madrid around the Hieronymite monastery of San Jeronimo.

19. "I know that . . . to get his bread by": "c'est celui qui nourrit le mieux son homme" (239).

20. "docked": "manchot" (239). To deprive of some part or appendage; in this case, an appendage of the body *(OED)*.

21. "backside": "cul-de-jatte" (239). French slang for "anus."

22. "honest cobler": "honnête Capareto" (241). Le Sage uses the Spanish word for "cobbler." Smollett omits a footnote in Le Sage's text, after "honnête," that reads "Savetier" (241).

23. "rush candle": "chandelle" (243). Tallow candle.

24. "The most minute circumstance has to them something interesting": "Il n'y a pas pour eux de circonstance indifferente" (244).

25. "I am determined to stick by my trade": "Je veux vivre de mon métier" (246).

26. "who are now . . . singing and bawling": "Ils s'égosillent à force de crier & de chanter" (247).

Chapter 9

1. "Of the bedlamites": "Des foux enfermés" (248). Literally, "shut-up madmen." This is scarcely less pleasant than Le Sage's first reference to the hospital as "Casas de los Locos" (chap. 8).

Smollett converts the phrase into a topical English reference, "Bedlam" being a common corruption of "Bethlehem," identifying the Hospital of Saint Mary of Bethlehem, the well-known asylum in London.

2. "patriot": "bourgeois" (248).

3. "he has been cringing at court": "il a fait l'hypocrite à la Cour" (249).

4. "seeing himself always forgot": "le désespoir de se voir toujours oublié" (249). Smollett does not translate "dans les Promotions" (roughly, "when it came time for promotions"), which concludes the passage in Le Sage's text (249).

5. "with a turret of woollen night-caps": An addition by Smollett.

6. "who has cracked his brain in researches": "est venu là pour s'être obstiné à vouloir trouver" (250).

7. "*paulo post futurum*": "*Paulo-post-futurum*" (250). The tenses of Greek verbs are notoriously difficult; the schoolmaster has gone mad studying an obscure form of the future tense.

8. "unequally coupled": "mal mariée" (251).

9. "who was a good-natured woman": An addition by Smollett.

10. "how they gnaw the sheets, my heart bleeds for them": "elles ne sont pas fort contentes. J'entre dans leurs peines" (252).

11. "Don Garcia . . . the arrival of Aurora": "Don Garcie passa quelques jours dans cette Terre, fort impatient d'y voir arriver Aurore" (253). Smollett was perhaps baffled by "terre," which in this context means "estate."

12. "attended by her old Argus": "avec son jaloux" (253).

13. "and imagining that . . . one way or other": "il en pourroit tirer pied ou aîle" (254).

14. "calls to mind every day": "rappelle mille fois le jour" (254).

15. "to come about your house": "pour s'introduire chez vous" (257). Smollett does not translate the next phrase in Le Sage's text: "sous quelque déguisement" [in some disguise] (257).

16. "I should know . . . as he deserved": "je sçaurois bien punir son audace" (257).

17. "by putting you into a breathing sweat": "causant un peu de frayeur" (258).

18. "giving one another reciprocal marks of affection and esteem": "se donnoient tous deux" (258).

19. "he pitched upon his head": "Il tombe à la renverse, se blesse la tête" (260).

20. "for which they may thank themselves": "dont on ne doit se prendre qu'à eux" (261).

21. "what disturbed his skull": "Ce qui lui a troublé l'esprit" (262).

22. "his head whirled . . . his reason ever since": "la tête lui tourna" (263).

23. "great tall boy": "grand garçon" (263).

24. "Bedford-head": "*chez Païen*" (265). The Duke of Bedford's Head tavern, Southampton Street, Covent Garden, was noted for its food, its drink, and the gaming proclivities of its patrons. Alexander Pope refers to the tavern in *Sober Advice from Horace* (1734), l. 150, and in *The Second Satire of the Second Book of Horace Imitated* (1734), l. 42.

25. "traiteur": Le Sage uses the word in the first sentence following the song (265); Smollett's translation there is "tavern." "Restaurant" would also be accurate.

26. "brain was cracked": "qui a le timbre fêlé" (266).

27. "seized with a frantick itch": "Il avoit la rage" (267).

28. "why they are here": "la cause de leurs folies" (269).

29. "corregidor": A Spanish magistrate, sometimes the justice or governor of a town (OED). Smollett uses Le Sage's word here.

30. "cit": "Bourgeoise" (269). Short for citizen, but usually applied contemptuously to townsmen or shopkeepers to distinguish them from gentlemen (OED).

31. "council of the Indies": "Conseil des Indes" (269). The supreme governing body of Spain's

American colonies from 1524 to 1834, the council prepared and issued legislation governing the colonies and approved acts and expenditures by the governors of the colonies. By the eighteenth century its power was waning.

32. "three days and three nights without one wink of sleep": "trois jours & trois nuits d'agitation" (273).

33. "but even connived . . . means to speak to her": "elle eut la foiblesse de se prêter aux ruses qu'il employa pour lui parler" (274).

34. "whenever that family happened to be mentioned": "quand on la mettoit devant lui sur le tapis" (275). "Sur le tapis," an idiomatic expression, means to open a subject for discussion.

35. "to take things upon trust": "à pousser la confiance trop loin" (276).

36. "You will better be able to judge . . . when I tell you": "Quel spectacle pour Stephani" (276).

37. "shall be the immediate instrument of your death": "ce fer va t'ôter la vie" (277).

38. "avowed and declared enemy!": "plus grand ennemi" (278).

39. "I'll go . . . where I can see you": "Je vais me cacher dans une endroit de cette chambre, d'où je t'observerai" (280).

40. "crammed a handkerchief into his mouth": "mirent un linge dans la bouche" (281).

41. "remarkable crabbed temper": "rebarbative" (281).

42. "he therefore revolved . . . the most accomplished villain": "Que faire donc pour n'avoir rien à démêler avec la Justice? Il prit son parti en grand scélerat" (283).

43. "to be tortured . . . under strong suspicions lest Julio": "Une nouvelle inquiétude vint l'agiter au bout de trois jours. Il craignoit que Julio" (285).

44. "the holy brotherhood of Hermandad": "la sainte Hermandad" (286). Formed in medieval Castile, the Hermandad (Spanish for "brotherhood") was a municipal force usually employed for police purposes such as fighting banditry and rural crime. After it was finally suppressed in 1476, the Catholic monarchs created the Santa Hermandad, an organized constabulary that deteriorated into an inefficient police organization and finally dissolved in the eighteenth century.

45. "The other": "Le Chef de la sainte Confrairie" (287).

46. "being willing to know the bottom of this affair": "Ce que voulant approfondir" (289).

47. "killing him dead on the spot": "le tuer" (290).

48. "verbal process": "procès verbal" (290). A detailed account or report (OED).

49. "the beautiful Angelica": In this paragraph, Emerenciana refers to characters in Ariosto's great romantic epic Orlando Furioso (1532).

50. "myrmidons": "archers" (293). A faithful follower (OED).

51. "to see his dear mistress . . . gone mad himself": "vivement affligé de voir sa Dame dans une si triste situation pour l'amour de lui" (293).

52. "though naturally rugged as a flint": "quoique très-peu pitoyable de son naturel" (294).

53. "for, after many learned consultations": "car après y avoir perdu leur latin" (297).

54. "my heart bleeds for them": "J'en suis véritablement touché" (297).

Chapter 10

1. "a sufficient competence to live on": "qui a dequoi vivre" (299).

2. "this good lady has seen the last year of her twelfth lustrum": "La bonne Dame a douze lustres accomplis" (299). A lustrum is a period of five years (OED); the woman is therefore above the age of sixty.

3. "I perceive here two virgins of the age of fifty": "Je découvre aussi deux pucelles, ou pour mieux dire deux filles de cinquante ans" (299–300).

4. "girls of fifteen": "comme des mineures" (300).

5. "I have clipt them off a good even score": "J'ai supprimé vingt années à bon compte" (303).

6. "The same, replied miss very smartly": "Qu'appellez-vous de même, répondit la fille, d'un ton brusque?" (303).

7. "his colours are warm": "Il peint à merveille" (304).

8. "*Inter stultos referatur*": "Let him be accounted among the fools" (unidentified).

9. "may not perhaps deserve an apartment in the college?": "à mériter d'être ici?" (306).

10. "gut them of their spirit and energy": "ôtent tout le sel & l'agrément" (307).

11. "prebendary": "Chanoine" (307). The holder of a prebend, which is the portion of the revenues of a cathedral granted to a canon as a stipend *(OED)*.

12. "I suppose he disposes of it to charitable uses": "Qu'en veut il faire, des aumônes?" (307).

13. "his greatest pleasure . . . to sale by auction": "Il se fait un plaisir de penser qu'on admirera son inventaire" (308).

14. "toyman": "marchander" (308). One who sells devices for sports, trinkets, and other fancy goods *(OED)*.

15. "auditor of Manilla": "Auditeur de l'Audience de Manille" (308). An official whose duties included receiving and examining accounts of money in the hands of others and then verifying the accounts by reference to vouchers *(OED)*. Particularly in Spanish colonies such as Manila in the Philippines, such offices were notorious for extortion and graft.

16. "What an original coxcomb this is!": "Le plaisant original" (309).

17. "his whole frame is in ecstasy of rapture": "il lui prend des élans de volupté" (311).

18. "came and dunned him for the money": "vint les lui demander" (315).

19. "auriculas": "fleurs" (316). A species of primula, also called a bear's ear, named for the shape of the petals *(OED)*.

20. "business of the stage": "vie comique" (316).

21. "who now guttles down with an actress": "qui mange avec une femme de theâtre" (318). To "guttle" is to devour greedily *(OED)*.

22. "the Escurial": El Escorial is a village in central Spain twenty-six miles northwest of Madrid. It is the site of the Escorial, which includes the royal monastery of San Lorenzo del Escorial, one of the largest religious establishments in the world. It was founded in 1563 by Philip II, and all Spanish sovereigns, beginning with Emperor Charles V, are interred there.

23. "to give a serenade": "donner une sérénade" (318). Smollett does not translate the rest of Le Sage's sentence: "à la fille d'un Alcalde de Corte" [to a bailiff's daughter] (318).

24. "just as Monsieur Le Sage does here": Smollett's criticism of Le Sage for slavishly following Dacier is largely unfair. Horace, in his poem, is pursued by an annoying man whom he cannot get rid of. He says to himself, "O Bolanus, with your happy temperament [*celebri felicem*]!" implying that Bolanus would somehow avoid suffering the torments that Horace is now undergoing. But the text tells us nothing more about Bolanus. The description of him that Le Sage offers—a person who tells a man to his face what he thinks of him—captures the common understanding of the passage at the time; that is, Bolanus would not be troubled by the annoying man because he would tell him off. Dacier, though, did not introduce this reading; it can be traced back to Horace's earliest commentators, and it appeared in many annotated editions before Dacier's. Nevertheless, Horace never tells us precisely what Bolanus's "happy temperament" consists of, and Smollett considered himself free to offer an alternate interpretation. In Smollett's version, Bolanus is untroubled because he is indifferent to *tacenda* and *loquenda*, that is, "things to keep quiet about" and "things worth saying," or "sense or nonsense" in reverse order. See Horace *Satires* 1.9.

25. "bubble": someone who is cheated, or "bubbled" *(OED)*.

26. "A Frenchman would not at all relish . . . would only excite his laughter": "Les Lecteurs de cette nation n'en approuveroient pas les expressions figurées, & y trouveroient une bizarrerie d'imagination qui les feroit rire" (321). Smollett does not translate Le Sage's next sentence: "Chaque peuple est entêté de son goût & de son génie" [Every nation is stubborn about its taste and its genius] (321).

27. "get off as fast as they can": "disparoissent" (322).

28. "lady": "fille de l'Alcade" (322).

29. "she inwardly rejoices . . . of her charms": "la cruelle s'en applaudit & s'en croit plus aimable" (322).

30. "sun-gate": "porte du Soleil" (324). Puerto del Sol in Plaza Mayor, once an exclusive residence in the center of Madrid.

Chapter 11

1. "The noble and generous heart . . . the utmost agitation": "entraîné par les mouvemens d'une généreuse compassion" (326).

2. "I suppose now . . . the midst of the flames": "Ne seriez-vous pas homme à vous jetter au milieu de ces flames" (327).

3. "Horace is of opinion . . . cursed him for his pains": See *Ars Poetica* 464–69. Smollett elaborates upon Le Sage's original note (328).

4. "I ask or looked for": "me suffit" (330).

5. "I am plotting for you": "J'ai formé un grand dessein" (331).

6. "to take our observations": "pour continuer nos observations" (332). Smollett does not translate the chapter's terminal sentence in Le Sage's text: "A ces mots, il emporta l'écolier sur une haute Eglise remplie de Mausolées" [With these words, he took the student to a great church, full of mausoleums] (332). In the subsequent chapter, Smollett translates "mausolée" as both "mausoleum" and "tomb."

Volume 2

Chapter 1

1. "who departed this life somewhat before his time": "sorti de ce monde assez brusquement" (4).

2. "there morning and evening": "au lever, au dîner, au souper & au coucher du Roi" (4–5).

3. "the subject of an English tragedy": James Thomson's (1700–1748) *Agamemnon: A Tragedy* (1738).

4. "a friar of the order of Merci": "un Religieux de la Merci" (7). The Order of Our Lady of Mercy, a military and later a religious order, was founded by Saint Peter Nolasco in 1218 for the purpose of ransoming Christian captives from the Moors. The order claimed to have freed seventy thousand captives.

5. "cardinal Ximenes": Francisco Jiménez de Cisneros (1436–1517), Franciscan archbishop of Toledo, cardinal, inquisitor general, and governor of Castile. After being appointed confessor to Queen Isabella in 1492, he proved invaluable in reforming religious orders in Spain. Though he ordered thousands of Korans to be burned, he saved Arabic books on medicine, philosophy, and history. He was also successful in politics, social reformation, and agricultural

improvement. He was wealthy from his archbishop's income, but he continued to live the life of a Franciscan friar, using his money to endow monasteries, convents, housing for the poor, and public granaries.

6. "that at last her curiosity got the better of her": "qu'elle ceda enfin à la tentation de le voir" (8).

7. "relished his doctrine": "le goûta" (8).

8. "Well, how did my lady duchess manage the matter, think you?": "Que fit la Duchesse?" (9).

9. "deceived an angel": "à tromper toute la terre" (10).

10. "This man of many plums": "Ce Doyen" (10), signifying advanced age.

11. "he had not slept with his fathers a few days later": "il ne fût pas mort trois jours plus tard" (11).

12. "absolute minister of the Spanish monarchy": "premier Ministre de la Couronne d'Espagne" (11). Possibly Cardinal Jiménez de Cisneros (see n. 5 above), whose vast array of achievements in religious, political, social, and charitable endeavors matches Asmodeus's description.

13. "represent the despairing lovers . . . with themselves": "representent ces trois Galans déses-perés" (13).

14. "dramatic author . . . Almarus": "Auteur Dramatique a que fait construire dans l'Eglise d'un Village, auprès d'Almaraz" (13). Possibly Francisco de Figueroa (1536–1617), who requested that his verses be burnt after his death.

15. "manes": "mânes" (15); see also "nobles mânes" (16). Spirits of the honored dead (OED).

16. "without so much emotion": "assez hardiment" (16).

17. "when the curtain drops": "finit avec la piece" (16).

18. "so merry as we two have been!": "nous ne boirons plus!" (18).

19. "bumpers": "santés" (18). Cups or glasses of wine filled to the brim and drunk as a toast (OED).

20. "other little fluttering thing": "petite & à l'air évaporé" (18).

21. "Origo, Citheris, and Arbuscula": Roman actresses of the second century B.C. "Just as was once said by Marsaeus, Origo's well-known lover, who gave his paternal home and farm to an actress: 'Never may I have dealings with other men's wives!' But you have with actresses and with courtesans, through whom your name loses more than does your estate" (Horace *Satires* 1.2.55–59). For Arbuscula, see Horace *Satires* 1.10.77 and Cicero *Ad Atticus* 4.15.

22. "who, in the twinkling of an eye": "dans un même moment" (20).

23. "perceive him coming": "La voilà qui s'offre à vos yeux" (20).

24. "but a great many of them will be crocodile's tears": "mais il y en aura bien de commande!" (22).

25. "who has been bed-ridden for some time": An addition by Smollett.

26. "one after the other": "l'un après l'autre" (28–29). Smollett does not translate the terminal sentence of Le Sage's chapter: "Alors le Boiteux en commença le recit dans ces terms, après avoir transporté l'écolier sur une des plus hautes maisons de la ruë d'Alcala" [Then the demon began the story in these terms, after having taken the student to one of the tallest houses on the rue d'Alcala] (29).

Chapter 2

1. "What an infatuation is this!": "Quel aveuglement!" (32).

2. "Get the better of the fury that transports you": "Rendez-vous maîtres de vos transports furieux" (32).

3. "must decamp, and leave the coast clear": "lui laisse le champ libre" (33).

4. "I now labour under": "où je suis" (33).

5. "impetuous": "brutal" (35).

6. "to express his gratitude to both": "pour leur marquer toute la reconnoissance dont il se sentoit pénétré" (36).

7. "the only study . . . in all my wishes": "qu'il faisoit son unique étude d'aller au-devant de tout ce que je paroissois souhaiter" (39).

8. "to instil a passion in my breast": "faites ensorte que je vous aime" (40).

9. "this is the greatest balm I could receive to my wounds": "C'est la plus grande consolation que je puisse recevoir" (42).

10. "felt a sudden flow of joy": "j'eus de la joie" (43).

11. "my fortune as sufficient . . . in the choice of a wife": "assez riche pour ne devoir consulter que mon cœur dans le choix que je ferois d'une femme" (44).

12. "Vanity and ambition . . . shone remarkably in her": "L'ambition & la vanité qui sont deux choses si naturelles aux femmes, étoient les plus grands défauts de la mienne" (45).

13. "perfidious wretch": "infidelle épouse" (48).

14. "quiet my thoughts . . . had put me in": "calmer la colere qui m'enflâmoit" (49).

15. "glutting my vengeance on both": "je me promettois une entiere vengeance" (50).

16. "And indeed I was sincere": An addition by Smollett.

17. "she seemed intent . . . I might stand in need of": "elle montroit une extrême attention à courir au-devant de tous les secours d'ont j'avois besoin" (53).

18. "some time or other got the better of": "se laissoient enfin toucher" (59).

19. "Cicero . . . *Pyladean friendship*": See Cicero *On Friendship*.

20. "Orestes . . . upon our stage": See Lewis Theobald, *Orestes: A Dramatic Opera* (1731).

21. "highly injurious": "offensoit" (60).

22. "he had no time to lose": "les momens lui étoient chers" (61).

23. "her reflections became serious, and crouded upon her": "elle tomba dans une profonde rêverie" (62).

24. "she sighed bitterly": An addition by Smollett.

25. "Don Fadrique loves . . . affection towards him": "Je n'aime point Don Fadrique qui m'adore" (62).

26. "I thought myself . . . into their snares": "je les défiois toutes de me jamais surprendre" (65).

27. "eclaircissement": "discours" (66).

28. "No ways touched": "Insensible" (66).

29. "After the lady had expressed herself in this manner": "Après ce discours" (68).

30. "how ill my favours are requited!": "quel étrange effet produisent en vous mes bontés!" (69).

31. "replied Theodora": "dit Dona Théodora" (70). Smollett does not translate Le Sage's next sentence: "Je n'ai rien promis à Don Fadrique" [I have not promised anything to Don Fadrique] (70).

32. "she could not . . . her charms": "elle n'avoit pû retenir" (72).

33. "to give a freer loose to his grief": "s'abandonner en liberté à sa douleur" (73).

34. "Zarates took great care . . . upon this occasion": "Zarate se garda bien de lui dire sur cela sa pensée" (75).

35. "I harbour in my breast": "j'ai conçû" (76).

36. "with a very dissatisfied air": "d'un air chagrin!" (77).

37. "was a man . . . the greatest command of temper": "eût l'esprit du monde le plus doux & le plus raisonnable" (79).

38. "I took you to my heart": An addition by Smollett.

39. "He then gave him a succinct account": "Alors il lui raconta" (80).

40. "how could I imagine it to be otherwise?": An addition by Smollett.

41. "far from cooling in my friendship": "loin de vous haïr" (82).
42. "Leave me . . . a sacrifice for all": "Abandonnez-moi à mon infortune, & ne faites pas trois miserables, lorsqu'un seul peut épuiser toute la rigueur du destin" (83–84).
43. "but at the same time . . . human nature polished to perfection": "mais elle est non seulement dans la nature du Roman, elle est aussi dans la belle nature de l'homme" (84–85).
44. "they came up . . . gate of the castle": "ils la joignirent à la porte du Château & l'arrêtérent" (87).
45. "while the rest . . . castle in play": "les autres faisoient tête aux gens du Château" (87).
46. "sloop": "tartane" (88). A small, one-masted vessel *(OED)*.
47. "they put on with all their might": "ils poussoient leurs chevaux à toute bride" (89).
48. "melancholy mansions": "tristes bords" (90). A closer translation might be "sad shores."

Chapter 3

1. "and kicking desperately": An addition by Smollett.
2. "That I will . . . satisfy your curiosity": "Le Démon qui ne cherchoit qu'à le contenter, lui donna sur le champ cette satisfaction de la maniere suivante" (91).
3. "he exercises her every day, and is eternally composing": "il compose tous les jours" (92).
4. "in a twinkling finished a scene": "Il en a fait une Scéne" (93).
5. "I am just now brought . . . most beautiful couplets": "Je viens d'enfanter des Vers" (93).
6. "were you shrouded . . . dry bones live": "Quand vous seriez mort la scéne que je viens de composer seroit capable de vous rappeller à la vie" (94).
7. "Palatine library": "Bibliotheque Palatine" (95). Perhaps the Palatinate Court Libraries in Heidelberg, Mannheim, and Düsseldorf. Developed through the efforts of the Elector Ottheinrich (d. 1559), the Bibliotheca Palatina was the finest library in Germany from the late sixteenth century to the mid–seventeenth century, when Pope Gregory XV requested the Heidelberg library as a reward for supporting Duke Maximilian I of Bavaria during the Thirty Years' War (1618–48). In 1662 and 1663 the Bibliotheca Palatina was subdivided into papal libraries. See Ladislaus Buzás, *German Library History, 800–1945*, trans. William D. Boyd (Jefferson, N.C.: McFarland & Company, 1986), 164.
8. "as if their heels were tripped up": "elles se laissent tomber sur le théatre" (95).
9. "Let your little geniuses . . . rule and imitation": "Que les petits génies se tiennent dans les bornes étroites de l'imitation" (96). "Gad" is often substituted for "God" in exclamatory phrases such as "by Gad" *(OED)*.
10. "screwing up his face into a satyrical grin": "en soûriant d'un air malin" (98).
11. "I shall not neglect to put the finishing hand to it": "Je ne le ratterai pas sur ma parole" (99).
12. "The comedian had . . . a proper decorum": "A ces mots, quelque envie qu'eût l'Auteur comique de garder son sérieux" (100).
13. "entertainment": "Comedie" (100). It was common in English and French theaters of this time to have both a tragedy and a comedy on the bill, with the comedy considered the "entertainment." In the *Dictionary* (1755) Samuel Johnson defined this kind of entertainment as "lower comedy."
14. "you are sure . . . her ladyship": "vous êtes sûr d'attendrir la Dame" (100).
15. "let all the rest of it be ever such stuff": "quelque imparfait qu'il puisse être d'ailleurs" (101).
16. "ridiculously besotted": "sottement enchanté" (102).
17. "quivering lips": "précipitation" (103).
18. "Sir, you will not . . . distinguish them": "mais il faut plus de gout que vous n'en avez pour faire

un heureux choix de celles qu'on doit emprunter d'eus" (104). "'Otherguise,' a corruption of 'otherguess,' which is a corruption of 'othergates,' meaning 'of another fashion or kind, different'" *(OED)*. Smollett uses "otherguess" in *Roderick Random*, chapters 32 and 47, and "otherguise" in his translation of *Don Quixote*, 2:3.

19. "bambouzle me": "m'ébloüir" (105).

20. "sublimated fustian": "faux brillans" (106). "Fustian" is a strong, plain fabric made of cotton and linen. Figuratively used, it means a pretentious and banal piece of writing *(OED)*.

21. *"Peripetie"*: "la péripetie" (106). In tragic drama a sudden change in the action upon which the plot hinges *(OED)*.

22. "At that instant . . . various and repeated kicks": "En même-temps, ils se sont tous deux pris à la gorge & aux cheveux, & les coups de poing & de pied n'ont pas été épargnés de part & d'autre" (106–7).

Chapter 4

1. "without hoisting any colours": "sans arborer aucun pavillon" (112). "Hoisting colors" signaled the captain's desire to fight.

2. "sided with the corsair . . . laid her between two fires": "Il s'approcha du bâtiment Espagnol à pleines voiles, & le mit entre deux feux" (113).

3. "strike to the Algerine": "à se rendre pour Alger" (113). The French translates "to yield to."

4. "beating him unmercifully": An addition by Smollett.

5. "What we call . . . the *Serail*": "C'est le nom que l'on donne à tous les Sérails des particuliers. Il n'y a que le Sérail du Grand Seigneur qui soit appellé Sérail" (118); Le Sage's note.

6. "gardens of Eram": "jardin d'Eram" (121). Eram is perhaps a variation of Aram, the Hebraic name for northwestern Syria. Muslim scholars regard "Iram Dhāt al-imad" as Damascus. Despite being in the desert, the ancient city was well watered and had beautiful gardens.

7. "becomes extremely uneasy to me": "fatigue ma patience" (122).

8. "depends upon your success in this commission": "est attachée à la fin de mes souffrances" (123).

9. "whispered him softly": "il lui dit tout bas" (124).

10. "sailing full before the wind": "avoit les voiles au vent" (127).

11. "I should have . . . better of it": "je l'aurois vaincuë" (128).

12. "he had offered to vindicate his conduct": "dont il avoit voulu m'ébloüir" (129).

13. "bearing down upon us full sail": "qui venoit fondre sur nous à voiles déployées" (130).

14. *"strike, strike"*: *"Arrive, arrive"* (130). To strike is to haul down a flag as a salute or a sign of surrender *(OED)*.

15. "the complaisant lover will soon assume another character": "Cet amant soumis dépoüillera bien-tôt sa feinte douceur" (135).

16. "would it not be . . . without answering any end?": "n'est-ce pas vous exposer à un péril superflu?" (136).

17. "that the delicacy of his behaviour towards you": "que la conduite qu'il tient avec vous" (137).

18. "What a violence this is committing upon one's self": "Quelle contrainte!" (137).

19. "throw me into an extasy of joy": "peut tout sur moi" (140).

20. "renegade": "renegat" (143). An apostate from any religious faith, but used especially for a Christian who becomes a Mohammedan *(OED)*.

21. "he should better his business": "il deviendroit plus heureux qu'il n'étoit" (143).

22. "his mother to a Moor, and himself to a Turk": "sa mere à un More & lui à un Turc" (144). In the Ottoman Empire Moors and Turks were distinguished from one another racially, nationally, and politically. A Moor was either a native of Morocco or a Muslim who had fled the province of Andalusia in Spain between the eleventh and seventeenth centuries. A Turk, from Anatolia, would be considered a member of the ruling party, the Ottomans.

23. "considerable sum of money": "quatre cens Patagons" (144). "Patagon" is an obsolete form of *patacoon*, a Portuguese or Spanish silver coin *(OED)*.

24. "He made himself a captain": "Il se fit Capitaine" (144). A slave could achieve such position in the Ottoman Empire. According to *The Present State of Tangier* (London, 1671), a Christian slave could be "sent to Sea, according to the professions and qualities of the Patrons . . . by which means many thousands of Captives have obtained their liberty by their own industry" (92–93).

25. "but his good fortune at last forsook him": "mais il cessa d'être heureux" (145).

26. "under pretence of repairing . . . usually meet": "sous prétexte d'aller au Bagne" (146). Smollett incorporates Le Sage's footnote explaining "Bagne" (baths): "Lieu où s'assemblent les Esclaves" (146).

27. "the old women her attendants being busied somewhere else": "la servoient étoient occupées ailleurs" (150).

28. "I tenderly compassionate the disquiet I have caused him": "je ressens vivement les peines que je lui cause" (152).

29. "and she is quite another thing from what she was before": "Qu'elle m'a paru differente de cette personne" (153).

30. "port": "Porte" (154). The Sublime Port in Constantinople; the French version of the Turkish Bâbiâli, or High Gate, which was the official name of the access to the block of buildings housing the principal departments of the Ottoman Empire.

31. "that dangerous precipice of honour": "dangereux honneur" (155). The danger attending the powerful position of the vizirate was evident in the period 1683–1702, during which twelve grand viziers served the Sublime Port. Several of them died violently.

32. "The six days being at last expired": "En effet, les six jours s'étant écoulés" (157).

33. "but fortune . . . quite good friends": "mais la fortune, avec qui ces amans n'étoient pas encore bien reconciliés" (158).

34. "They were now got out of the garden": "Ils étoient déja hors du jardin" (158).

35. "you deserve not . . . laws of honour": "Tu ne mérites point que je t'attaque en brave homme" (159).

36. "her presence would do neither of them any good": "la présence leur pouvoit être nuisible" (167).

37. "which pierce . . . I now endure": "Je la sens plus que la perte de ma vie" (168).

38. "fathers of the redemption": "Peres de la Redemption" (169). See n. 4, chap. 1, vol. 2.

39. "to procure a restitution of his estate": "de faire rentrer dans ses biens" (170).

40. "Upon this my rage became furious": "A cette vûë je devins furieux" (172).

41. "you don't do me justice": "vous faites injure à mon affliction" (173).

42. "Don Francisco de Mendoza . . . gave very sensible proofs": "Pour Don Francisco de Mendoce, il sentit une vive affliction quand il apprit la mort de son neveu" (177).

43. "which otherways . . . to have done": "ce qu'il n'auroit osé faire sans cela" (179).

44. "in his dying agonies": "derniers soûpirs" (180).

Chapter 5

1. "I want you should tell me": "Je voudrois par curiosité que vous me dissiez" (182).

2. "The emperor Augustus . . . respected himself": "L'Empereur Auguste, dont la tête valoit bien celle d'un écolier, ne méprisoit pas les songes dans lesquels il étoit interessé" (183). According to Suetonius, "Warnings conveyed in dreams, either his own or those dreamed by others were not lost on him: for example, before the battle of Philippi, when so ill that he [Augustus] decided not to leave his tent, he changed his mind on account of a friend's dream—most fortunately took, as it proved. For the camp was captured and a party of the enemy, breaking into the tent, plunged their swords through and through his bed under the impression that he was still in it, tearing the bed-clothes to ribbons" ("Augustus," *Lives of the Caesars* 91, 99).

3. "Horace founds his belief . . . after midnight": See Horace *Satires* 1.10.32–35. Smollett added this footnote to Le Sage's text.

4. "moderate interest": "très-honnête profit" (184).

5. "papillotes": Curling papers *(OED)*.

6. "empty-skulled coxcomb": "un esprit vain & fier" (185).

7. "as in France . . . he has condemned": "comme un Lieutenant criminel assiste en France au supplice d'un coupable qu'il a condamné" (186).

8. "greatly smitten with her": "dont elle est obsedée" (187).

9. "Divine Legation of Moses . . . the Eleusinian mysteries": See William Warburton, *The Divine Legation of Moses* (London, 1738), 1:238ff.

10. "These honest gentlemen . . . such points as these": "Je connois Messieurs les Libraires, ils ne se font pas un scrupule de tromper les Auteurs" (190).

11. "It is a brilliant of the first water": "c'est de l'or en barre" (190). The transparency and luster characteristic of a diamond or a pearl. The three highest qualities in diamonds were formally known as the first, second, and third water. "The phrase 'of the first water' survives in popular use as a designation of the finest quality" *(OED)*.

12. "and leaning back": An addition by Smollett.

13. "He has rid post": "qui est venu en poste" (193). To ride or run in haste *(OED)*.

14. "knight of the golden-fleece": "Chevalier de la Toison" (195). The Order of the Golden Fleece was founded in 1430 by Philip III; its original mission was to defend the Roman Catholic religion and to uphold ideals of chivalry. By the eighteenth century the order was still considered the principal order of knighthood and was awarded only to Roman Catholics of the highest nobility.

15. "it is indeed a pretty odd one": "Il a quelque chose en effet de singulier" (195).

16. "ghostly gravity": "la gravité qu'ont tous les défunts" (196).

17. "great boar cat": "beau matou" (198). "Matou" means "tomcat," as does "boar-cat" *(OED)*.

18. "interpreters of dreams": "Interpretes des songes" (198). The *vates* of ancient Rome, their arts bestowed upon them by Apollo, interpreted natural and artificial phenomena.

19. "Cothurnian hero": "Héros de coulisse" (200). The *cothurnus*, the padded, thick-soled boot worn by Greek tragic actors, literally elevated the actor and so became synonymous with a figuratively "elevated" style of acting *(OED)*. Coulisse, as a theatrical term, identifies a side scene or wing, with the figurative meaning of behind the scenes. A hero of the coulisse is a stage hero, that is, a hero by illusion and stagecraft.

20. "to kill the time": "se donnent pendant cette vie" (203).

Chapter 6

1. "A coquette knows not . . . to act their grimaces": "Les coquettes ne sçavent pas mieux s'ajuster pour donner de l'amour" (205).
2. "scald-head": "taigneux" (205). A head diseased with ringworm or a similar affliction *(OED)*.
3. "that does not a little perplex him": An addition by Smollett.
4. "That is a bel esprit . . . a man of quality": "C'est un bel esprit qui fait le Seigneur en dépit de sa basse origine" (209).
5. "with whom he haggles for a farthing": "il va marchander avec eux, sou à sou" (209).
6. "pitiful dog": "grand crasseux" (210).
7. "whom they look . . . she should be": "qu'ils regardent comme un avanturiere" (211).
8. "You have heard of Cynic philosophers . . . there goes one": "Il y a des Philosophes Cyniques en Espagne. En voilà un" (213).
9. "minuting his reflections down in his place-book": "à faire des réfléxions qu'il écrira sur son registre" (213). To "minute" means to record a note *(OED);* a "place-book" is a notebook for recording "places," or short passages of writing bearing upon a particular subject *(OED)*.
10. "Lucian's Timon": Timon of Athens, called "Misanthrope" for his hatred of mankind and society, converses with Lucian in his *Dialogues*.
11. "The moment these sharks . . . found the tables turned": "Dès que les Parasites ont vû sa marmite renversée" (215).
12. "this old sinner": "ce vieux pêcheur" (215). Smollett does not translate the phrase with which Le Sage continues his sentence: "de race More" [of the Moorish race] (215).
13. "fumbler": "soupirant" (216).
14. "rape of her locks": "sacrifice de sa chevelure" (216). Smollett casts his translation as an allusion to Alexander Pope's mock epic *The Rape of the Lock* (1712, 1714).
15. "Escurial": See n. 24, chap. 10, vol. 1.
16. "Carthusian monastery": "Chartreuse de Saragoce" (218). The Order of Carthusians was founded in 1084.
17. "which enables . . . the receipt of custom": "qui lui donne un beau rang dans la societé civile" (220).

Chapter 7

1. "brings him a list . . . of quality": "lui apporte une fausse liste qui contient les noms de plusieurs personnes de qualité" (221).
2. "share their booty": "à frais communs" (222).
3. "Indeed to warn people . . . coming upon the shoals": "Pour avertir du péril que courent les passans, il faudroit faire mettre devant cette maison des balises, comme on en met dans les rivieres, pour marquer les endroits dont il ne faut pas s'approcher" (223).
4. "this distich": "ces deux Vers" (224).
5. *"fatuos sales"*: silly jokes.
6. "most vile dramatic performances . . . danced horn-pipes": "des Drammes, des piéces de Théâtre fades & entremêlées de Ballets, si extravagans, qu'on y voyoit danser jusques aux *Preterits* & aux *Supins*" (225). Beginning in the Middle Ages, students in Spain recited and sometimes performed classical plays, primarily in order to develop their rhetorical skills. Interludes are short pieces that fill the pauses between acts of a play *(OED);* they could be mimic, musical, dramatic, or, as here, balletic. The English hornpipe, the equivalent of the French

matelote (from *matelot*, or sailor), is a single-person dance associated with the festivities of sea-faring men *(OED)*. Smollett sharpens Le Sage's jest about the "dancers" ("preterits and supines") by personifying these technical terms from the study of Latin grammar.

7. "nomenclator": "Nomenclateur" (226). In ancient Rome a servant or dependent who stood by his master to inform him of the names of people meeting him, usually for election purposes *(OED)*.

8. "in giving of which ... these great personages": "mais ce malin esprit y ajoûtoit toûjours quelque trait satyrique. Il leur donnoit à chacun son lardon" (226).

9. "What a pity it is ... what you have said to him": "C'est dommage qu'un homme qui aime tant à faire plaisir, ait la mémoire si courte, qu'un quart-d'heure après que vous lui avez parlé, il oublie ce que vous lui avez dit" (226–27).

10. "chevalier of the order of St. Jago or Calatrava": "Chevalier de saint Jacques ou de Calatrave" (228). See n. 51, chap. 3, vol. 1 and n. 59, chap. 4, vol. 1. The Roman knights, the equestrian order, were a target of Juvenal's satire. The property qualification was 400,000 sesterces, in Juvenal's time a fairly substantial sum. Juvenal finds, however, that ex-slaves and foreigners who earn fortunes either through low forms of trade or through corruption are becoming "knights" (see *Satires* 5.132–39). Perhaps Le Sage is suggesting that since it is so easy in the eighteenth century to become a "chevalier," contemporary society is even more corrupt than Roman society was. The number of Roman knights had reached as many as five thousand by the end of the empire, also suggesting that these knights were common and undistinguished, as they had become in Spain, because of the low cost of becoming a Roman knight.

11. "academy of Toledo": "Académie de Toléde" (230). Perhaps the "school of translators" established by Alfonso X (el Sabio, "the Wise," 1221–84) in Toledo in the thirteenth century.

12. "the stile certainly ... was plausible and florid": "le stile en étoit effectivement réprehensible; & d'autant plus dangereux qu'il étoit plus brillant" (230).

13. "but to make you understand it": "Mais pour l'intelligence de ce bon mot" (232).

14. "extremely smart": "des plus plaisantes" (234).

15. "If a Turk ... very near": "Un Turc qui verroit ce drôle-là dans un état si florissant, ne manqueroit pas de le croire à la veille d'essayer quelque fâcheux revers de fortune" (236).

16. "a poet that I am sure has no business here": "un Poëte qui n'y devroit pas être" (236).

17. "after having lampooned almost all the grandees in Spain?": "après avoir fait des vers qui offensent de Grands Seigneurs Espagnols?" (236).

18. "Don Joseph de Reynaste, and Ayala, grand judge of the police": "Signeur Don Joseph de Reynaste & Ayala, Grand Juge de Police" (237). Perhaps an historical person, but not identified.

19. "He knows too well ... they are": "Il sçait trop bien que ces sortes de gens, pour la plûpart" (237).

20. "I should come but scurvily off": "je ne serois pas le plus fort" (239).

21. "tossed about ... by these devils your brethren": "houspiller par vos confreres" (239).

Chapter 8

1. "I shall be much obliged ... so much satisfaction": "vous me ferez un vrai plaisir de tenir votre promesse" (241–42).

2. "a little village in Arragon": "la petite ville de Velilla, en Aragon" (243).

3. "he huggs himself": "il est charmé" (244).

4. "bastinado": "bastonnade" (244). An Eastern method of corporal punishment by beating the soles of the feet with a stick *(OED)*.

5. "Dulcinea": "Princesse" (245). See n. 46, chap. 3, vol. 1.

6. "clotted, red beard": "barbe rousse rend effroyable à voir" (246).

7. "Salamanca": "Salamanque" (246). The University of Salamanca, which, from the mid-twelfth century to the end of the sixteenth century, was one of the leading centers of learning in Europe.

8. "whose seat . . . distance from Cinquello": "qui avoit sa chaumiére à deux portées d'Escopette de Cinquello" (247).

9. "it was the rubbish , . . that passed by": "qu'une masure, tant elle menaçoit ruïne de toutes parts" (248).

10. "he frequently could have no idea of a dinner": "il eût de la peine à vivre" (248).

11. "with a suit of crimson velvet . . . sickly yellow": "avec un habit de velours cramoisi tout pelé, & un petit chapeau garni d'un vieux plumet jaune" (248).

12. "he strutted with the utmost insolence": "il tranchoit du Seigneur" (248).

13. "he had a conscience . . . upon such an occasion": "il avoit la conscience d'un dépositaire" (250).

14. "very decently rigged out": "parfaitement bien nippée" (251).

15. "which he looked . . . to his family": "qui réveilla son orgüeil" (253).

16. "Hidalgos": In Spain one of the lower nobility; a gentleman by birth *(OED)*.

17. "all of whom laboured under the disease . . . as himself": "qui tous avoient, comme lui, la rage de la *Hidalguia*" (254).

18. "but to think . . . a lady of Hypolita's quality": "mais pour déliberer de quelle façon il falloit punir ce jeune insolent, qui malgré la bassesse de sa naissance, osoit aspirer à la possession d'une fille de qualité d'Hypolite" (254).

19. "As she therefore . . . her inclinations": "Elle s'abandonna au penchant qui l'entraînoit" (256–57).

20. "called aloud for vengeance": "commencérent à crier: *Vengeance! Don Thomas, vengeance!*" (257).

21. "whose sorrowful looks you take notice of": "dont l'abattement vous a frappé" (260).

22. "when he fell into the hands of the corsair": "Lorsqu'il tomba au pouvoir d'un Corsaire" (261). Smollett does not translate the subsequent phrase in Le Sage's text: "en allant de Valence à l'Isle de Sardaigne" [while going from Valence to Sardinia] (261).

23. "some kind of office": "concierge" (262).

24. "as exactly resembles . . . like another": "deux goutes d'eau à un vieux singe" (262).

Chapter 9

1. "were each fonder than another of his acquaintance": "rechercherent, à l'envi, son amitié" (266).

2. "his purse was eased of its burthen": "l'argent lui manqua" (266).

3. "a bailiff and his followers": "un Alguazil & des Archers" (267).

4. "the trees swelled in all their foliage": "les arbres sont parés de toutes leurs feüilles" (268).

5. "his talents": "son argent" (269). Smollett is perhaps punning here, for a talent is also an ancient unit of money *(OED)*. See Matthew 25:14–30 for the parable of the talents.

6. "at his return": Smollett does not translate the subsequent clause in Le Sage's text: "que l'on n'ignoroit pas pourquoi il s'étoit éclipsé" [that they were not ignorant of his reasons for leaving] (273).

7. "he was again flush of money": "qu'il avoit de l'argent frais" (274).

8. "I found it had been taken from me likewise": "m'a cruellement été ravie" (277).

9. "at least you ought to live in that hope": "Vivez dans cette espérance" (278).

10. "to that end . . . with my friends": "J'y veux employer mon crédit & ma bourse" (279).

11. "at the same time . . . his conscience": "d'une maniere qui conciliât sa réputation avec sa conscience" (280).

12. "The accused person . . . thank his deliverer": "Le coupable sortit donc de certe affaire plus blanc que neige" (283).

13. "I imagine . . . are now quits": "Mais il me semble, dit Don Cléofas, que Bahabon n'en doit plus guére de reste à ce Bourgeois" (287).

Chapter 10

1. "without once sitting down": "sur ses jambes" (291).

2. "you have had a nap of twice twelve hours": "vous avez fait deux fois le tour du cadran" (292).

3. "I choose rather . . . by butchering mutilations": "j'aime mieux le passer sous silence, que de le défigurer" (297).

4. "But one thing . . . for fact": "Je dirai seulement" (297).

5. "to get the better of it": "il faloit vaincre" (299).

6. "A punctilio of honour": "Un sentiment de délicatesse" (302).

Dialogues, Serious and Comic

Dialogue 1

1. "he entertained the public with these flying numbers, at least seven or eight in the year": "il en donnoit sept ou huit au moins par an" (307). "Flying" meaning passing, hasty; in this meaning, rapidly written, therefore ephemeral *(OED)*.

2. "they say . . . mere bagatelle": "On crie qu'on ne s'occupe aujourd'hui qu'à écrire des folies des riens" (307–8).

3. "these broken numbers": "les Brochures à parties" (308).

4. "cold comfort": "foible consolation" (309).

5. "poor chilled author": "pauvre Auteur" (312).

6. "such another brother as mine": "un Financier comme le mien" (312).

Dialogue 2

1. "marriages solemnised . . . the church?": "mariages les plus reguliers?" (314).

2. "in the thoughts . . . will be reduced to": "de la déconsolation de cette pauvre femme" (318).

Dialogue 3

1. "Well, every one to their own taste, I love variety": "le mien est uniquement pour la varieté" (320).

2. "was the younger son . . . being born gentlemen": "étoit un Cadet d'une Province où les

Cadets d'une Province où les Cadets n'ont d'autres patrimoine que leur épée & l'heureuse effronterie de vanter sans cesse leur noblesse" (321).

3. "He must, at that rate, have been always flush of money": "Ainsi il ne manquoit pas d'argent" (322).

4. "Indeed sometimes . . . lasted long": "Il brilloit, c'étoit sa marie, ou plutôt celle de sa nation, mais son fracas ne dura pas long-tems" (322).

5. "phenix of a husband": "mari unique" (323). A person or thing of unequaled excellence; a paragon *(OED)*.

6. "madness, in an English philosopher": "folie pareil dans un Philosophe Anglois" (324). Perhaps a historical person, but not identified.

7. "Not in the least, I assure you": "Nullement" (325).

8. "set off a demi-rep for a pattern of illustrious virtue": "donnoit du lustre à la vertu la plus équivoque" (329). "Demi-rep": a woman whose character is only partly respectable *(OED)*.

9. "people who came from the country . . . as wise as they were before": "des Provinciaux que la curiosité seule amenoit à Paris, & qui s'en retournoient chez eux sans avoir rien vû qu'en perspective" (330).

Receipt for Payment for Correcting the Second Edition of *The Devil upon Crutches*, 5 January 1759. (Bodleian Library, Oxford University.)

TEXTUAL COMMENTARY

PUBLICATION HISTORY

The little that is known of the circumstances surrounding Smollett's translation of Le Sage's *Le Diable boiteux* has been set out in the introduction to this volume.[1] A receipt dated 5 January 1759 acknowledges that he has "Received from Mr. A. Millar Seven Guineas and a half, an Account of Correcting the Devil on Crutches by me Ts. Smollett." This is the one piece of external evidence for attributing *The Devil upon Crutches* to Smollett. Nothing is known of the negotiations for the sale of the translation or the arrangements for its printing, but William Strahan, who printed the first edition of the work for Smollett's usual bookseller, John Osborn, made the following entry in his ledger:

1750
Feby Devil on Crutches 12 ½ Sheets No. 2000
@ £2:13:0 p. sheet   £33:2:6[2]

An edition of two thousand copies is large for the first printing of a translation or for an original novel, but Osborn was willing to take risks, a habit that in a few years would lead to his declaring bankruptcy.[3] That Osborn decided to print such a large number of copies of *The Devil upon Crutches* to be published on 28 February 1750 was related to his success with *The Adventures of Roderick Random* and *The Adventures of Gil Blas*. The first edition of *Roderick Random* was published on 21 January 1748 in an edition of two thousand copies. The second edition was published on 7 April 1748, only eight or nine weeks after the first, in an edition of three thousand copies. The third edition was published on 19 January 1750 in an edition of fifteen hundred copies.[4] The first edition of *Gil Blas* was published on 14 October 1748 in an edition of three thousand copies and a second edition in duodecimo in February 1750 in one thousand copies.[5] Osborn, however, was to be disappointed with the sales of *The Devil upon Crutches*. When he went bankrupt and his stock and copyrights were sold on 14 November 1751, 654 of the 2,000 copies remained.

The remaining copies of the 1750 first edition would satisfy the public demand for the work until 1759, when a second and final edition of Smollett's translation was published. Apart from Smollett's having been paid to revise the 1750 first edition for the 1759 second edition, nothing is known of the arrangements for printing and publishing the work in 1759. It seems not to have been advertised or noticed in the periodical press.

EDITORIAL PRINCIPLES

The first edition of *The Devil upon Crutches* was set from an autograph manuscript or a fair copy made from it, but neither a manuscript nor a marked copy of the first edition from which the second edition was likely printed is extant. In fact, no printer's copy for any of Smollett's works has survived. The nature of the manuscript can only be deduced from letters, never intended for publication, and from an examination of manuscript revisions the author made in a copy of the 1766 first edition of *Travels through France and Italy* for a new edition that did not appear.[6] The revisions for *Travels* include additions, translations of passages in foreign languages, and corrections to the printed text. It might be argued that Smollett, largely free from his numerous editorial tasks by the mid-1760s, had new leisure to correct the *Travels*; but an examination of other works he saw through the press shows much the same care, for he left uncorrected only the kinds of errors that none but the most exacting proofreaders might have caught.[7]

The revisions to the *Travels* are written in Smollett's neat hand, which, after more than two centuries, can be read with ease. A compositor, then, would have had no difficulty reading the author's manuscript of *The Devil upon Crutches* when setting the first edition or the manuscript corrections made by the author in a printed copy of the first edition when setting the second edition. In the process of setting the type, the compositor introduced an overlay of normalization. As John Smith notes in *The Printer's Grammar* (1755), "By the Laws of Printing, indeed a Compositor should abide by his Copy, and not vary from it. . . . But this good law is now looked upon as obsolete, and most Authors expect the Printer to spell, point, and digest their Copy, that it may be intelligible and significant to the Reader; which is what a Compositor and the Corrector jointly have regard to, in Works of their own language." The compositor peruses his copy but, before beginning to compose, "should be informed, either by the Author, or Master, after what manner our work is to be done; whether the old way, with Capitals to Substantives, and Italic to Proper names; or after the more neat practice, all in Roman, and Capitals to Proper names and Emphatical words," and nothing "in Italic but what is underscored in our Copy." When composing from printed copy and "such Manuscripts as are written fair," we "employ our eyes with the same agility as we do our hands; for we cast our eyes upon every letter we aim at, at the same moment we move our hands to take it up; neither do we lose our time in looking at our Copy for every word we compose; but take as many words into our memory as we can retain."[8] Since both editions of *The Devil upon Crutches* and the *Travels* were printed in the new way, numerous changes must have occurred between the manuscripts and the printed books, including some normalization of spelling.

In the lengthy manuscript additions to Letter 11 of the *Travels* (the English translation of a Latin letter to Antoine Fizes and of the professor's reply in French), Smollett followed the old practice, though somewhat inconsistently, of capitalizing nouns and some adjectives. Schooled to capitalize substantives, he continued in his habitual way.[9] But he certainly knew that his capitalization and use of the ampersand for "and" would be brought into conformity with the rest of the book. He seems to have accepted this styling by the printer or at least to have acquiesced. In the printed text of the *Travels* he corrected such small matters as a transposed letter, "muscels" (the bivalve mollusc) to "muscles," and a verb tense "affords" to "afford"; at the same time he allowed to stand such variant spellings as "paltry"—"paultry," "ake"—"ach," and so on. Smollett was not consistent in his spelling, although he did have preferred spellings for most words; but the compositors, by taking as many words into their memories as they could retain, sometimes introduced their preferences. Smollett seems to have been content with the resulting inconsistencies in spelling as long as they were correct, and he did not attempt to restore his capitalization and punctuation.

As noted earlier, *The Devil upon Crutches* was printed in the new way, and thus it likely incorporates a great number of changes from Smollett's manuscript, particularly in spelling and punctuation. It is certain that there are many variations in the use of quotation marks, departing significantly from the practice in most of his works. Usually it is impossible to ascertain if the practice of using quotation marks in a particular way originated with Smollett or the compositor. The French edition of *Le Diable boiteux* used in preparing the translation does not use quotation marks, and it is nearly certain that Smollett likewise omitted them. If he had included them, he is likely to have followed one or perhaps two schemes. The various compositors for both the first and second editions seem to have been baffled about how to proceed with adding quotation marks, and they indicate quotations in a bewildering variety of ways, sometimes using double quotation marks, other times single, sometimes lacing quotation marks down the left margin, other times not, suggesting that they may have been instructed by the overseer of the printing house to add them where needed but were not told what form or principles to follow.

The compositors of the 1750 first edition ceased supplying quotation marks after the opening of the final paragraph at the bottom of H^v (p. 76): "My lord, (says the old gentleman) after such an ingenious confession. . . ." In the second volume they ceased with the beginning of the last sentence of the first paragraph in Chapter III, on $E2^r$ (p. 52): "That I will with pleasure. . . ." The compositors of the 1759 second edition copy-text tried to follow the quotation marks of the first edition, adding occasional quotation marks and omitting others; at the first paragraph on $D10^v$ (p. 68), they began substituting single quotation marks for the double ones in the first edition. The second edition compositors pushed ahead of the first edition compositors by six paragraphs before they abandoned attempts to set quotation marks at the end of sheet F (p. 120). In the second volume the compositors ceased supplying quotation marks at exactly the same place as the first edition compositors had done ($D12^r$, p. 71). Almost certainly the quotation marks were not in the manuscript copy from which the first edition was set. Compositors, paid by the amount of type they set, found determining what kind of quotation marks were needed and where they should be placed too time consuming and simply abandoned the enterprise.

In the Georgia edition of Smollett's *Adventures of Telemachus* the confusion surrounding quotation marks could be remedied by following modern practice, but quotation marks have been eschewed in the present edition as tending to obfuscate rather than to clarify the text.[10] Hence, the inconsistent and infrequent quotation marks added by the compositors have been removed.

The 1759 second edition of *The Devil upon Crutches* has been chosen as copy-text for this edition. Smollett usually took a copy of the last edition of his work and made revisions in it for a revised or corrected edition, as the surviving copy of the *Travels* demonstrates.[11] In the case of *The Devil upon Crutches* he used a copy of the 1750 first edition

and corrected it for the 1759 second edition. As the historical collation indicates, the revisions were detailed and extensive and follow Smollett's known habits found, for example, in his revisions of *Roderick Random*, *Gil Blas*, *Peregrine Pickle*, and *Don Quixote*. As
expected, he corrected errors in the first edition but failed in reading proof to catch
some new errors that crept into the resetting of type for the second edition. An argument might be made for accepting the 1750 first edition as copy-text, retaining its punctuation and spelling as most nearly reflecting Smollett's manuscript and inserting the
1759 verbal changes into this fabric. This editorial procedure has been rejected on several grounds. In the first place, the number of verbal changes and the required punctuation changes to make contextual sense of these changes for the second edition mitigate
against this procedure. In the second place, as the copy of the *Travels* shows, Smollett
accepted the overlay of compositorial changes for the first edition: he corrected none of
them.[12] His manuscript additions also show that he expected the compositors would
normalize his text. All of this suggests that the carefully revised 1759 second edition reflects Smollett's final intentions for this text, inasmuch as this can ever be known.

In the present edition no attempt has been made to achieve a general consistency in
spelling, punctuation, and capitalization, because in the absence of the manuscript and
the copy of the first edition with manuscript corrections one cannot determine whether
Smollett or the compositor was responsible for their variation. Hence the spelling,
punctuation, and capitalization of the 1759 second edition have been retained except
when they are clearly in error or when they obscure meaning or distract the attention
of the reader. All emendations of the copy-text have been made on the authority of the
textual editor. Hyphenated words at a line-end have been adjusted according to the
usual practice of the second edition insofar as that practice can be ascertained from
other appearances or parallels. Only the following changes have been made silently: all
turned letters or wrong fonts have been corrected, the long *s* has been replaced by the
modern letter *s*, and "ae" and "oe" have been treated as digraphs. The abbreviation
"CHAP." has been changed to "CHAPTER" in both the text and the table of contents.
The erratic quotation marks supplied by the compositors have been removed. The dis-
play capitals that begin the first paragraph in each chapter of the work have not been exactly reproduced. The length of dashes and the space around them have also been nor-
malized according to modern practice.

APPARATUS

A basic note in the list of emendations provides the page-line reference and the
emended reading in the present text. Except for the silent alterations described above,
every editorial change in the second edition copy-text has been recorded. Following the
square bracket is the earliest source of the emendation and the history of the copy-text
reading up to the point of emendation. All emendations marked "W" are the responsibility of the present edition. A wavy dash (~) is substituted for a repeated word associated with pointing, and a subscript caret (ˏ) indicates pointing absent in the present text.
The form to the right and left of the bracket conforms to the system of silent alterations,

and there is no record of any variations except for the instance being recorded. When the matter in question is pointing, for example, the wavy dash to the right of the bracket signifies only the substantive form of the variant, and any variation in spelling or capitalization has been ignored. A vertical stroke (|) indicates a line-end.

All hyphenated compounds or possible compounds appearing at line-ends in the copy-text are recorded in the word-division list. The reader should assume that any word hyphenated at a line-end in the present text but not appearing in this list was broken by the modern typesetter.

COLLATION

The present edition has been printed from a photocopy of the 1759 second edition once owned by Lewis M. Knapp, now in Cameron House. This copy was bibliographically collated with copies listed in the bibliographical description of the second edition given below. This photocopy of the 1759 second edition was sight collated against a photocopy of the 1750 first edition once owned by Lewis M. Knapp, now in Cameron House. This copy of the 1750 first edition was bibliographically collated with the copies listed in the bibliographical description of the first edition below.

Notes

1. See pp. xxiv–xxv.
2. BL Add. MS 48800, opening 63.
3. See p. xxv.
4. Albert H. Smith, "The Printing and Publication of Early Editions of the Novels of Tobias George Smollett with Descriptive Bibliographies" (Ph.D. diss., University of London, 1975), 1:4–20.
5. BL Add. MS 48800, opening 63.
6. This copy of the *Travels* is in the British Library, shelf mark C.45.d.20, 21. Apart from the manuscript revisions of the *Travels* and a relatively small number of holograph letters, little survives in Smollett's hand: a one-leaf holograph note on the reign of Edward III in the Berg Collection, New York Public Library, and about a dozen signed receipts and documents. See Lewis M. Knapp, ed., *The Letters of Tobias Smollett* (Oxford: Clarendon Press, 1970), xvi–xvii.
7. Smollett was content to make small changes because the *Travels*, written at a relatively slow pace, did not require the extensive stylistic revisions of the earlier works. In the works of his later career, revision seems to have been carried out before publication; by this time he was a more experienced writer. For discussion of the composition of the *Travels*, see the introduction by Frank Felsenstein, ed., *Travels through France and Italy* (Oxford: Oxford University Press, 1979), xxxv–xli.
8. John Smith, *The Printer's Grammar* (London, 1755), 199, 201–2, 209.
9. Bertrand H. Bronson, *Printing as an Index of Taste in Eighteenth Century England* (New York: New York Public Library, 1958), 17.
10. In the case of *Telemachus* hundreds of hours were spent in an attempt to place quotation marks correctly with no assurance that the placement was correct or represented what Smollett

intended or even might have wished. The "List of Emended Quotation Marks" fills nine pages. Any attempt to place quotation marks according to modern practice in *Devil* would be more baffling still.

11. See also Smollett's letter to William Strahan accompanying a corrected copy of the 1751 first edition of *Peregrine Pickle* to be used in printing the 1758 edition. Smollett also asks to see proofs of the new edition (Knapp, ed., *Letters*, 63–64).

12. Or at least he acquiesced in the compositorial changes; the evidence can no longer be recovered.

LIST OF EMENDATIONS

[The following sigla appear in the textual apparatus of the Georgia Edition: 1 (the first edition; London, 1750); 2 (the second edition; London, 1759); W (the present edition).]

3.3	ILLUSTRIOUS] 1 ILLUSTIOUS 2
3.8	Cojuelo] W Cosuelo 1–2
3.31	They are] W That is 1; There are 2
5.1–4	THE | CONTENTS | OF THE | FIRST VOLUME.] 1 THE | CONTENTS. 2
5.21	*Count Belflor*] 1 *count Belflor* 2
5.31	*Don*] W *om.* 1–2
6.8	*occasion.*] 1 ~ₐ 2
7.34	pats] 1 parts 2
8.25	hips] 1 lips 2
8.42	his guittar] 1 her guittar 2
14.19	then] 1 than 2
14.19	Cleofas).] W ~)ₐ 1–2
14.28	student).] W ~)ₐ 1–2
14.34	other).] 1 ~.) 2
15.8	mine] 1 mind 2
15.17–18	is doubtless] 1 his doubtless 2
15.23	demon).] W ~)ₐ 1; ~.) 2
15.40	faith,] W ~ₐ 1–2
17.12	Cleofas).] 1 ~.) 2
17.30	crutches] 1 Crutches 2
18.15	Asmodeus).] W ~.) 1–2
18.20	was my apartment] 1 was in my apartment 2
18.26	must be!] W ~ ~? 1–2
18.27–28	demon).] W ~)ₐ 1; ~.) 2
19.9	than a litter] 1 than litter 2
19.35	Le Sage] W le Sage 1; la Sage 2
20.17	she has!] W ~ ~? 1–2

21.1	this is!] W ~? 1–2
21.27	Cleofas).] W ~.) 1–2
21.28	Asmodeus).] W ~.) 1–2
21.36	demon).] W ~.) 1–2
22.13	replies] W replied 1–2
22.17	makes!] W ~? 1–2
22.18	walks!] W ~? 1–2
23.14	answers] W answered 1–2
23.19	replies] W replied 1–2
23.19	demon).] W ~.) 1–2
23.24	widow is!] W ~ ~? 1–2
23.35	Leandro).] W ~)ₐ 1–2
23.40	lib.] 1 ~ₐ 2
24.15	Asmodeus).] W ~.) 1–2
25.10	badₐ (replies . . . demon).] W ~. (replied . . . ~)ₐ 1–2
25.25	Leandro).] W ~.) 1–2
25.25–26	ofₐ . . . demon).] W ~, . . . ~)ₐ 1; ~. . . . ~)ₐ 2
25.28	Asmodeus).] W ~ₐ 1–2
26.4	are!] W ~? 1; ~ₐ 2
27.37	affair?] 1 ~. 2
28.9	Count] W count 1–2
30.18	artifice!] ~? 1–2
31.6	Those constant] W That constant 1–2
31.6	have caused] W has caused 1–2
32.4	question),] W ~)ₐ 1; ~,) 2
32.18	sentiments of me?] W ~ ~ ~! 1–2
33.3	what, shall] W ~ₐ ~ 1–2
33.37	says,] 1 ~, 2
35.22	ever?] 1 ~. 2
35.41	tho'] 1 ~ₐ 2
37.9	to believe] 2 (cw) to lieve 2 (text)
39.3	depend] 1 depends 2

39.21	time).] W ~.) 1–2
39.23	rising).] W ~.) 1–2
43.13	Count de Belflor] 1 count de Belflor 2
43.21	present.] 1 ~, 2
43.32	To-night,] 1 ~ₐ 2
44.16	there).] W ~.) 1–2
44.25	arrival!] W ~? 1–2
44.28	amazement?] 1 ~, 2
44.28	Don Lewis.] W ~ ~)ₐ 1; ~ ~? 2
44.28	Are you not] W are you not 1–2
46.24	should,——] 1 ~? 2
46.25	reason] 1 reason's 2
47.27	father!] W ~,1; ~ₐ 2
47.27	Don Lewis);] W ~ ~ₐ; 1; ~ ~)! 2
47.28	we desire.] 2 (cw) we sire. 2 (text)
48.38	intend you for?] W ~ ~ ~, 1–2
48.38	unknown] 1 unkown 2
48.38	lady.] W ~? 1–2
48.41	intend for you?] 1 ~ ~ ~. 2
49.9	husband!] W ~? 1–2
49.10	hatred!] W ~? 1–2
51.6	Asmodeus,] 1 ~ₐ 2
51.11	La Chicona] 1 la Chicona 2
51.17	list? . . . student.] W ~, . . . ~? 1–2
51.33	be? . . . Leandro.] W ~, . . . ~? 1–2
54.3	me!] W ~? 1–2
55.20	Why] W why 1–2
56.34	For the love] W for the love 1–2
58.11–12	you? . . . serjeant.] W ~, . . . ~? 1–2
58.33	Juanella] 1 Juanilla 2
59.12	wants] W want 1–2
59.40	How] W how 1–2

60.24	*quid*] W *qui* 1–2
63.9	reflections),] W ~,) 1–2
64.5	question? . . . voice.] W ~, . . . ~? 1–2
66.18	labourer?] W ~, 1–2
66.18	Zambullo.] 1 ~? 2
66.18	Asmodeus] W Asmodeo 1–2
66.26	Asmodeus] W Asmodeo 1–2
67.2	unconscionable] W unconsciable 1–2
67.38	heartily?] W ~, 1–2
67.39	Cleofas;] 1 ~? 2
68.1	maids,] 1 ~ₐ 2
69.7	beside] W besides 1–2
69.19	have? . . . landlord.] W ~, . . . ~? 1–2
70.43	home!] W ~? 1–2
70.43	Your brother] W your brother 1; you brother 2
72.42	Sunday] W sunday 1–2
75.3	here? . . . him.] W ~, . . . ~? 1–2
75.24–25	see them] W see of them 1–2
77.22	yes,] 1 ~ₐ 2
78.43	God bless me!] W ~ ~ ~, 1–2
78.43	Cleofas,] W ~: 1; ~! 2
79.27	no sighs] 1 not sighs 2
80.21–22	Hidalgo de] W Hidalgo da 1–2
80.32	women than] W women then 1–2
82.13	Guillem] 1 Guillim 2
84.19	gaoler] W goaler 1–2
84.28	into a place] 1 into place 2
84.41	My dear Julio] 1 my dear Julio 2
85.32	gentleman] 1 genleman 2
88.26	cruel] 1 cruelty 2
88.42	doctors] W doctor's 1–2
89.20	convent] 1 concent 2

90.7	twenty-eight] 1 ~ˌ~ 2
90.39	that?] W ~, 1–2
90.40	demon.] W ~; 1; ~? 2
91.44	coxcomb this is!] W ~ ~ ~, 1–2
92.1	laughter;] 1 ~! 2
92.17	ecstasy] 1 ectasy 2
94.25	Le Sage] W le Sage 1–2
96.16	*fire,*] 1 ~; 2
96.18	crying out, water] 1 ~ ~ˌ~ 2
101.1	THE	CONTENTS] 1 CONTENTS 2
103.6	*dead*;] 1 ~, 2
104.12	but pray] 1 put pray 2
104.27–28	mistress of herself] 1 mistress for herself 2
104.38	it? answered she.] W ~, ~~? 1–2
106.16	be? . . . Perez.] W ~, . . . ~? 1–2
106.38	tomb] 1 tombs 2
107.10	illusionary] 1 illusinary 2
109.5	he is gone] 1 it is gone 2
110.6	shrieks?] W ~, 1; skrieks, 2
110.6	demon.] W ~? 1–2
110.21	CHAPTER II.] W *om.* 1–2
111.11	Alvaro] W Alvarez 1–2
111.25	Alvaro] W Alvarez 1–2
111.28	Alvaro] W Alvarez 1–2
111.39	Alvaro] W Alvarez 1–2
112.7	Alvaro] W Alvarez 1–2
112.15	Alvaro] W Alvarez 1–2
112.20	Alvaro] W Alvarez 1–2
112.26	Alvaro] W Alvarez 1–2
114.13	reproach me.] 1 ~ ~ˌ 2
114.27	say? . . . astonishment.] W ~, . . . ~? 1–2
117.6–7	endeavours] 1 endervours 2

118.9	Alvaro] W Alvarez 1–2
118.39	Ægisthus] W Æghistus 1–2
120.15	peace!] W ~? 1–2
122.25	Villareal] W Villa real 1–2
123.24	Theodora‸] W ~. 1–2
123.41	impart to me!] W ~ ~ ~? 1–2
124.36–37	can her repose] 1 can repose 2
124.37	you? . . . Fadrique.] W ~, . . . ~? 1–2
125.18	Villareal] W Villa-| real 1; Vil-| la real 2
126.25–26	Alvaro] W Alvarez 1–2
127.27	charmed with them!] W ~ ~ ~? 1–2
130.17–18	am of opinion] 1 am opinion 2
133.1	Alvaro] W Alvarez 1–2
135.6	asked his name.] 1 ~ ~ ~? 2
136.32	Alvaro] W Alvarez 1–2
136.39	too well] 1 two well 2
137.5	Alvaro] W Alvarez 1–2
137.25	point] W paint 1–2
140.2	occasion] 1 accasion 2
140.29	that? . . . Francisco.] W ~, . . . ~? 1–2
140.34	lady's] W ladies 1–2
141.25	moment's] 1 moments 2
142.40–41	imagination!] W ~? 1–2
143.9	ever be] 1 ever by 2
143.43	honour] 1 hunour 2
145.1	I, your friend] 1 ~‸ ~ ~ 2
145.7	despair);] W ~;) 1–2
145.15	knew that] 1 knew thas 2
146.1	liberty had been] 1 liberty been 2
147.1	Alvaro] W Alvarez 1–2
147.27–28	done, It] W done, it 1–2
153.1	hear!] W ~? 1–2

154.5	through] W thro' 1; though 2
154.16	secret] 1 seceret 2
156.9	vanish!] W ~? 1–2
158.19	street? . . . Cleofas.] W ~, . . . ~? 1–2
159.2	citizen] 1 citizens 2
160.2	have them] W have of them 1–2
160.4	which winds its] W who winds his 1–2
160.39	he knows she] 1 she knows he 2
161.17–18	church? . . . Cleofas.] W ~, . . . ~? 1–2
161.38	alledging] 1 alledg-| 2
163.4	you? . . . Leandro.] W ~, . . . ~? 1–2
163.39	means,] 1 ~. 2
164.24	poor,] W ~ˌ 1–2
164.37	certainly] 1 certainty 2
166.12	Ayala,] 1 ~ˌ 2
167.9	here! . . . Leandro.] W ~, . . . ~? 1–2
168.24–25	long? . . . Leandro.] W ~, . . . ~? 1–2
169.11	pane] 1 pain 2
170.17	gentility] 1 genteelity 2
171.35	begun a conversation] 1 began a conversation 2
173.4	worth had] 1 worth he had 2
173.5	on account] 1 on| on account 2
173.10	reason of it.] 1 reason ofˌ 2
173.16	Castilian] 1 Castillan 2
173.21	who are all dead] 1 who	who are all dead 2
173.24	this! . . . scholar.] W ~, . . . ~? 1–2
173.36	La Merci] W la Merci 1–2
173.42	I am not] 1 I an not 2
174.20	*in what*] 1 *it what* 2
177.8	farther] 1 father 2
177.34	three-fourths] W threeˌfourths 1; three	fourth 2
178.23	hope] W hopes 1–2

179.5   behalf] 1   hehalf 2

181.1   you? . . . student.] W   ~, . . . ~? 1–2

181.1   extraordinary] 1   extrrordinary 2

181.6   I am! . . . concern.] W   ~ ~, . . . ~! 1–2

181.37   has assured] W   have assured 1–2

182.7   this? . . . he.] W   ~, . . . ~? 1–2

183.42   transport of joy] 1   taansport of joy 2

184.4   Zambullo? . . . he.] W   ~, . . . ~? 1–2

185.34   eight. B. Indeed] W   eight. Indeed 1–2

186.21   insult me] 1   insult men 2

187.23   learned you are!] W   ~ ~ ~? 1–2

188.5   *The*] W   *om.* 1–2

188.34   slash] 1   flash 2

189.3   phenix of a husband] 1   phenix of a hus-| hand 2

189.11   simpleton you are!] W   ~ ~ ~? 1–2

190.14   apartment!] W   ~? 1–2

TEXTUAL NOTES

8.25	hips] The first edition reads, "breasts and hips." Smollett decided to substitute the more colloquial "bubbies" for "breasts," but in the process of reading his correction to the small type of the first edition text the compositor, in setting the second edition, reversed the two items and misread "hips" as "lips." The French reads: "qui avec une gorge & des haunches artificielle."
58.14	Annibal] The name appears as "Hannibal" at the beginning of the next paragraph (58.24), then again as "Annibal" (58.40–41), and finally as "Hannibal" (59.5). See also the note on "Asmodeus" (66.18) below.
58.33	Juanella] Here the name appears as "Juanilla," although in the five previous mentions it is "Juanella." In the first edition, only the fifth of the six mentions is "Juanilla" (58.22) and the remainder "Juanella." The text has been emended to conform to what seems to be Smollett's preference.
60.38	Oniate] The name appears below as "Onnate" (63.28). See the note on "Asmodeus" (66.18) below.
66.18	Asmodeus] Only two instances of "Asmodeus" being called "Asmodeo" appear in the entire work. The second instance appears in the next paragraph (66.26), the first paragraph of Chapter VIII. The heading for this chapter, which is between the two instances, has the name in the usual form. Smollett is notoriously inconsistent in spelling characters' names, especially those of minor characters, and they are not emended because there is no clear preference for one spelling over the other. (See *Ferdinand Count Fathom*, p. 455, and *Humphry Clinker*, p. 461.) However, since in all but two instances Smollett spells the demon's name as "Asmodeus," there is no doubt that it was his preferred form. Emending the text avoids the confusion of having one of the principal characters' names spelled two different ways. The usual French spelling is "Asmodée," and this is the reading in the first instance. In the second instance the French has "Démon."
84.19	gaoler] The "goaler" of the copy-text is an acceptable alternate spelling for "gaoler" in the eighteenth century, but since most modern readers would stumble over the word if not be outright puzzled, it has been emended.
111.11	Alvaro] "Alvaro" is the dominant form in "The Power of Friendship," but "Alvarez" appears thirteen more times. For the reason given in 66.18 above, all instances of "Alvarez" have been emended to "Alvaro." The French has "Alvar."
187.1	Lysander] The name appears below as "Lisander" (187.12). See the note on "Asmodeus" (66.18) above.

WORD-DIVISION

1. LINE-END HYPHENATION IN THE GEORGIA EDITION

[The following compounds, hyphenated at a line-end in the Georgia Edition, are hyphenated within the line in the 1759 edition.]

20.11	three-|score		117.13	before-|hand
21.4	billet-|doux		133.13	lye-|by
21.11	bed-|side		138.22	over-|whelmed
21.44	to-|morrow		156.27	well-|made
72.30	coffee-|house		164.1	long-|winded
89.31	three-|score		171.3	waiting-|woman

2. LINE-END HYPHENATION IN THE 1759 SECOND EDITION

[The following compounds or possible compounds are hyphenated at a line-end in the second edition. The form in which each has been given in the Georgia Edition, as listed below, represents the usual practice of the 1759 second edition insofar as it may be ascertained from other appearances or parallels.]

3.30	new-modelled		69.5	pink-coloured
8.20	super-annuated		71.34	crimson-sattin
9.38	house-breaker		76.14	country-house
10.12	footman		76.30	good-natured
10.28	master-builder		83.12	night-time
10.32	threescore		90.19	parish-registers
20.31	lath-backed		91.17	hump-backed
21.12	good-nature		114.19	horseback
23.4	cash-monger		162.25	knight-errants
23.34	To-day		190.10	go-between
39.29	to-morrow		190.16	demi-rep
47.13	thunder-struck		190.28	fire-side
56.9	tavern-keepers			

3. SPECIAL CASES

[The following compounds or possible compounds are hyphenated at a line-end in both the Georgia Edition and the 1759 second edition.]

64.35　　sweet-|meats　　　　　　162.26　　syren-|songs

HISTORICAL COLLATION

3.3	ILLUSTRIOUS] ILLUSTIOUS 2
3.8	Cojuelo] Cosuelo 1–2
3.28–29	that they seem] as seem 1
3.31	They are] That is 1; There are 2
3.34	works extend a whole fathom on the shelves of a library] works stretch to the space of a fathom in a library 1
4.3	who‸ when] that, when 1
4.3	arms, that they may vend] arms, to vend 1
4.5	accepted] done 1
4.6	an indulgence which I dare] which I dare 1
5.1–4	THE	CONTENTS	OF THE	FIRST VOLUME.] THE	CONTENTS. 2
5.21	*Count Belflor*] *count Belflor* 2
5.31	*Don*] *om.* 1–2
6.8	*occasion.*] ~‸ 2
7.7	so fondled] made so much of 1
7.15	pleasure] voluptuousness 1
7.18	In other respects] As to other things 1
7.21	discovers] shews 1
7.22	In point] And in point 1
7.24	as much discretion] as much of it 1
7.27	cherished] preserved 1
7.27	This hint leaves] This leaves 1
7.28	an hundred] a hundred 1
7.31	expressed] done 1
7.34	pats] parts 2
7.38	improved] profited 1
8.13	Frenchmen. He certainly] Frenchmen; and it is certain 1
8.17–18	towers of speculation] speculatory towers 1
8.22	with his own hands] himself 1

8.25	hips] lips 2
8.25	bubbies] breasts 1
8.28	undisturbed] tranquil 1
8.30–31	above three times] more than thrice 1
8.34	for his personal] on account of his personal 1
8.39	to have it printed] to have printed 1
8.41	Castilian, shivering] Castilian, when I saw him, shivering 1
8.42	bewails] bewailed 1
8.42	his guittar] her guittar 2
9.1–2	performed this vow, he] performed this, he 1
9.5–6	basons, kettles, and frying-pans] marrow-bones and cleavers 1
9.10	We must] And we must 1
9.16	emotions] movements 1
9.20	Mæcenas. In order to acquire the character] Maecenas, and to procure himself the character 1
9.20–21	learning, he gives] learning, gives 1
9.21	dictionary-maker. Some] dictionary-maker; and some 1
9.24–25	their shape, and complexion] their complexion and make 1
9.28	preparing slops] getting him slops 1
9.29	these two] they two 1
9.31	his own] their own 1
9.32	begs] beg 1
9.36–37	he desired the demon to convey him] made the demon carry him 1
9.37	caught] catch'd 1
9.40–41	find a man in France] find in France a man 1
9.42	stolen] stole 1
9.43–44	but I am] but am 1
10.2	Mentioning] And mentioning 1
10.14	valet upon] valet at 1
10.16	an hospital] a hospital 1
10.20	beaten] beat 1
10.23	ran mad] went mad 1
10.31	last will] latter will 1

10.33	been. I moreover like] been; and I like 1
11.6	actress at] actress on 1
11.29	manner in which it was begun] manner it was begun 1
13.14	the window of a house] a window out of a house 1
13.18	Although] Notwithstanding 1
13.20	tops] ridges 1
13.21	made the best] making the best 1
13.22–23	perilous course. After] perilous course, after 1
13.23	last he got] last got 1
13.25	sail] swim 1
13.27	entered] got into 1
13.27	examination] reconnoitring 1
13.28	cieling, with books] cieling, books 1
13.30–31	his learned observations] his observations 1
14.14	words, not a] words˄ a 1
14.19	then] than 2
14.19	Cleofas).] ~)˄ 1–2
14.21	all scrub] all such scrub 1
14.23	You jest] No, you jest 1
14.28	student).] ~)˄ 1–2
14.34	other).] ~.) 2
14.35–36	counsel] council 1
15.8	mine] mind 2
15.17–18	is doubtless] his doubtless 2
15.22	power to effect such] power of such 1
15.23	demon).] ~)˄ 1; ~.) 2
15.23	broken] broke 1
15.26	imagined] thought of 1
15.40	faith,] ~˄ 1–2
16.7	last declaration: to hasten] last: to hasten 1
16.13	an half] a half 1
16.16	wide was garnished] wide, garnished 1

16.18   crape, crested]   crape, and crested 1

16.28   an hand in the performance]   a hand in it 1

16.31   paints]   paint 1

16.33   might see a set]   saw a set 1

16.35   smells of perfume]   does with perfume 1

16.41   There were]   There was 1

17.11   and beauty]   and my beauty 1

17.12   Cleofas).]   ~.) 2

17.26   an excellent]   a most excellent 1

17.28–29   according to the poets. From]   as poets say; and from 1

17.30   crutches]   Crutches 2

18.3   the book on Restrictions]   Satan's invisible world discovered, by the rev. Mr. Baxter 1

18.9–10   should think proper]   thought proper 1

18.10   inflict on]   inflict upon 1

18.15   Asmodeus).]   ~.) 1–2

18.20   was my apartment]   was in my apartment 2

18.26   must be!]   ~ ~? 1–2

18.27–28   demon).]   ~)ₐ 1; ~.) 2

19.5   church]   temple 1

19.9   than a litter]   than litter 2

19.28   inward and hidden]   hidden and inward 1

19.31   city miser]   miserly citizen 1

19.35   Le Sage]   le Sage 1; la Sage 2

20.7   his spoils]   the spoils 1

20.17   she has!]   ~ ~? 1–2

20.28   the song is]   the song contains 1

20.39   ancient]   auncient 1

21.1   this is!]   ~? 1–2

21.8   the case is not the same]   it is far from being the same 1

21.15   great deal]   good deal 1

21.22   the community]   this community 1

21.23	that congregation] this congregation 1
21.27	Cleofas).] ~.) 1–2
21.28	Asmodeus).] ~.) 1–2
21.36	demon).] ~.) 1–2
22.7	prescribe for him] prescribe to him 1
22.13	replies] replied 1–2
22.17	makes!] ~? 1–2
22.18	walks!] ~? 1–2
22.38	books were writ] books were wrote 1
22.43–44	sent it to the author] sent it the author 1
23.2	You are in the right] You are right 1
23.14	answers] answered 1–2
23.17	act by way of] act in the interim by way of 1
23.19	replies] replied 1–2
23.19	demon).] ~.) 1–2
23.23	man hard by her] man who is by her 1
23.24	widow is!] ~ ~? 1–2
23.35	Leandro).] ~)ᴧ 1–2
23.40	lib.] ~ᴧ 2
24.15	Asmodeus).] ~.) 1–2
24.17	plums] plumbs 1
24.26–27	insinuated herself into the good graces of two] got in with two 1
24.28	says the student] cries the student 1
24.33	Both at this instant] Both of them at this instant 1
24.35–25.1	who now no longer hears him] who cannot now hear him 1
25.10	badᴧ (replies . . . demon).] ~. (replied . . . ~)ᴧ 1–2
25.24	doctor prescribed] doctor prescribed him 1
25.25	Leandro).] ~.) 1–2
25.25–26	ofᴧ . . . demon).] ~, . . . ~)ᴧ 1; ~. . . . ~)ᴧ 2
25.26–27	answer that there] answer there 1
25.28	Asmodeus).] ~ᴧ 1–2
25.29	hear that racket in the other street] hear, in this other street, this racket 1

25.31   a braying concert of basons, kettles, and frying-pans.]   a concert of frying-
             pans, kettles, marrow-bones and cleavers, &c. 1

25.34   been at large]   been so 1

25.40   That other which]   That other one, which 1

25.43   country]   nation 1

26.4   are!]   ~? 1; ~ₐ 2

26.6-7   They want the protection of one]   One of them, they want his
             protection 1

26.14-15   of this other scene I see]   of this I see 1

26.20   began]   begun 1

27.1   but a slow]   but slow 1

27.5-6   smiling countenance]   smiling and pleasant countenance 1

27.33   wished for on this]   wished for this 1

27.34   lest]   least 1

27.37   affair?]   ~. 2

27.38   the widow]   his widow 1

28.9   Count]   count 1-2

28.12   driven]   drove 1

28.17   ran up to]   run up to 1

28.21   on the mind]   upon the mind 1

29.17   what had passed]   what passed 1

29.21-22   forgiven in one]   forgiven one 1

29.30   given up the suit]   given up 1

29.31   allowed]   let 1

29.40   began]   begun 1

30.1   pity on him]   pity upon him 1

30.3   left off scolding]   gave over scolding 1

30.13-14   and with bringing]   and bringing 1

30.18   artifice!]   ~? 1-2

30.40   any violence]   a violence 1

31.6   Those constant]   That constant 1-2

31.6   have caused]   has caused 1-2

32.2   sworn]   swore 1

32.4	question),] ~)ₐ 1; ~,) 2
32.18	sentiments of me?] ~ ~ ~! 1-2
33.3	what, shall] ~ₐ ~ 1-2
33.16	silk cord, the count] silk, the count 1
33.17	her mistress] her young mistress 1
33.29	she said] she told him 1
33.37	says,] ~, 2
33.44-45	you ought to entertain, you] you ought, you 1
34.1	believe they are, you] believe, you 1
34.20	before this interview, had] before this had 1
34.21	expressed] shew'd 1
34.39	sacred force] sacredness 1
34.39-40	By these means I shall be able to extricate myself from] By this means I shall be able to get myself clear of 1
34.41	inform] acquaint 1
35.5	this expedient.] this. 1
35.9	that looks] which looks 1
35.22	ever?] ~. 2
35.24	obtaining his approbation] getting him to approve it 1
35.41	tho'] ~ₐ 2
35.41-42	unwilling] unwillingly 1
36.10	those things] these things 1
36.15-16	his own interest] his interest 1
36.19	who dares] who would dare 1
37.25	bounds of my duty] bounds of duty 1
37.29	my dear child] my child 1
38.6	explanation] eclaircissment 1
38.9	you shall go] you go 1
38.10	So saying, he took] After saying this he took 1
39.3	depend] depends 2
39.21	time).] ~.) 1-2
39.23	rising).] ~.) 1-2

39.25	count, his heart] count, with his heart 1
39.40	sensible of the horror] sensible to the horror 1
40.2	abyss] excess 1
40.11	weak as to] weak to 1
40.14	a punishment, my being] my punishment, being 1
40.25–26	heaven to witness] heaven to be witness of 1
40.28	believe him to be.] believe. 1
40.30–31	this supposition, perhaps] this, perhaps 1
40.35	this expedient; she] this: she 1
40.36	melted by] melt to 1
40.36–37	together, determine] together, and determine 1
40.41	that reflection gave him small] that gave him but small 1
41.14	moved. Reason] moved. He now came to himself. Reason 1
41.21–22	witness my protestations.] witness upon it. 1
41.24	overcome my passion] get the better of my passion 1
41.30–31	made, and keep my faith, which I pledged to her so solemnly.] made her, and fulfil my faith, which I pledged to her. 1
42.3	besides, he] besides that, he 1
42.8	upon. In] upon; and in 1
42.31–32	He never stirred abroad] He never went out of this inn 1
43.13	Count de Belflor] count de Belflor 2
43.20–21	that subject at present] that at present 1
43.21	present.] ~, 2
43.22	this place; for] this, for 1
43.32	To-night,] ~ˏ 2
44.1	this house] this one 1
44.1	a-going] going 1
44.5	introduced] took 1
44.9	passion of Count Belflor] passion of Belflor 1
44.12	employed] taken up 1
44.15	was he that] was him that 1
44.16	there).] ~.) 1–2

44.18	Belflor] him 1
44.25	arrival!] ~? 1–2
44.28	amazement?] ~, 2
44.28	Don Lewis.] ~ ~)‿ 1; ~ ~? 2
44.28	Are you not] are you not 1–2
44.37	night-gown, he was going] night-gown, was going 1
44.44	Father] My father 1
44.44	Far] So far 1
46.1	Belflor, I] Belflor, that I 1
46.6	escape from my resentment] escape my resentment 1
46.24	should‿——] ~?—— 2
46.25	having made such a pretence] having pretended such a thing 1
46.25	reason] reason's 2
46.36	So saying, he] In saying which, he 1
46.44–47.1	mistress's] mistresses 1
47.4	satisfied with] satisfied at 1
47.12–13	Being desperately] As he was desperately 1
47.16–17	thought every moment an age] grudged every moment 1
47.21	that circumstance is sufficient] that is sufficient 1
47.27	father!] ~, 1; ~‿ 2
47.27	Don Lewis);] ~ ~‿; 1; ~ ~)! 2
47.27	we never find our] one never finds their 1
47.44	was there] there was 1
48.4	discovered this circumstance] discovered this 1
48.13	found her] found herself 1
48.16	misfortunes] misfortune 1
48.38	intend you for?] ~ ~ ~, 1–2
48.38	unknown] unkown 2
48.38	lady.] ~? 1–2
48.41	intend for you?] ~ ~ ~. 2
49.4–5	to the most sublime happiness.] to a state of the greatest happiness. 1
49.9	husband!] ~? 1–2

49.10   hatred!]   ~? 1–2

49.23   in which he had spoke]   he had spoke 1

49.38   lest]   least 1

49.42–44   Lewis. The ceremonies were performed this evening, and the rejoicings are
                not yet over. This is the cause of all this mirth and revelry, every one being
                more overjoyed]   Lewis, which was done this evening, and are not yet
                over. This is the reason you perceive such mirth and rejoicing, every one
                more overjoyed 1

50.10   cast our eyes another way]   turn somewhere else 1

50.11   Look into]   Look upon 1

50.27–28   be the better]   be better 1

50.33–34   about that circumstance.]   about that. 1

50.35   masters]   master's 1

51.6   Asmodeus,]   ~ˬ 2

51.7   no other than]   no other then 1

51.9   those two]   these two 1

51.10   looking attentively at the other]   and regards with attention the other 1

51.11   La Chicona]   la Chicona 2

51.12   other's]   others 1

51.17   list? . . . student.]   ~, . . . ~? 1–2

51.19   new men]   new ones 1

51.29–30   these convenient ladies.]   them. 1

51.31–32   working at]   working upon 1

51.33   be? . . . Leandro.]   ~, . . . ~? 1–2

52.5   geniuses]   genius's 1

52.7   I would first entertain]   I want before that to entertain 1

52.14   chamber adjoining to that]   chamber off of that 1

52.17–18   says Zambullo. He]   replied Zambullo: he 1

52.18   head, replied the demon, and]   head, and 1

52.23   colts foot]   colt's foot 1

52.23   syrup of spit-wort]   brings syrup-spit-wort 1

52.31–32   Cleofas. That]   Cleofas; that 1

52.43   incitement]   incentment 1

54.2	O! Scoundrels] O! the scoundrels 1
54.3	sight is this] sight this is 1
54.3	me!] ~? 1–2
54.6	adventures] things 1
54.14	a fire-work] an artificial fire 1
54.36–37	and who were] and were 1
54.41	prison] prisons 1
55.3	the turnkeys] these turnkeys 1
55.15	paultry beds] poor beds 1
55.20	Why] why 1–2
55.28	minuet; and] minuet. And 1
56.2–3	interest; husbands] interest; that husbands 1
56.3	coquettes love] coquetes to love 1
56.14	risen] arose 1
56.17	and insulted such strangers] and very evily intreated such strangers 1
56.20–21	Your spirits know how to respect an old soldier grown weary under the weight of his accoutrements.] What the devil? do you think any ghost would trouble himself with us, who have been used to breakfast upon ball, and dine upon gunpowder. 1
56.22	that declaration, shewed] that, shewed 1
56.29	this apparition: without] this; without 1
56.34	For the love] for the love 1–2
58.10–11	may depend upon it, my gratitude] depend that my gratitude 1
58.11–12	you? . . . serjeant.] ~, . . . ~? 1–2
58.13	How, fright! sblood] How, fright, godswounds 1
58.17	my word and honour] my honour 1
58.18–19	without its costing] without costing 1
58.22	Juanella] Juanilla 1
58.32	nevertheless, I find] notwithstanding of which, I find 1
58.33	Juanella] Juanilla 2
59.11	some money] something 1
59.12	wants] want 1–2
59.27	the thief] a thief 1

59.40	How] how 1–2
59.41	No, indeed] no indeed 1
59.42	that this is beyond] that is beyond 1
60.4	owned] confessed 1
60.15	He depends] And he depends 1
60.24	*quid*] *qui* 1–2
60.30	No] no 1
61.5–6	the neighbourhood] his neighbourhood 1
61.6	need, and] need of, and 1
61.25	ears at this hint, and] ears at this, and 1
61.26	say? Say!] say: say, 1
61.27	diffuses] spreads 1
62.28	letter was writ] letter was wrote 1
63.9	reflections),] ~,) 1–2
63.21	street at midnight] street in the middle of the night 1
63.22	Accordingly] And accordingly 1
64.5	question? . . . voice.] ~, . . . ~? 1–2
65.5	afflicted at this information] afflicted at this 1
65.17	He imparted this scheme to Floretta] He told Floretta this 1
65.23	cat. This] cat: this 1
66.5	explanation] eclaircissement 1
66.18	labourer?] ~, 1–2
66.18	Zambullo.] ~? 2
66.18	Asmodeus] Asmodeo 1–2
66.19	garnish] entrance 1
66.26	Asmodeus] Asmodeo 1–2
66.27	to-day: a detail that] to-day. That 1
66.30	hence.] from this. 1
66.32	quartered.] ordered. 1
66.34	ducats? Upon] ducats: upon 1
67.2	unconscionable] unconsciable 1–2
67.8–9	this argument, went away] this, went away 1

67.17	as to admit] as admit 1
67.30	he said within himself] said within himself 1
67.38	heartily?] ~, 1–2
67.39	Cleofas;] ~? 2
68.1	maids,] ~ˌ 2
68.8–9	has hired furnished] has furnished 1
68.20	gentleman has written] gentleman has wrote 1
68.23	But while] And while 1
68.24	nuptials, she allowed] nuptials, allowed 1
68.26	entered the apartment] entered into the apartment 1
68.40	Patricio, he is] Patricio, and is 1
69.6	garters; a circumstance which] garters; which 1
69.7	beside] besides 1–2
69.17	Patricio] Upon which Patricio 1
69.19	have? . . . landlord.] ~, . . . ~? 1–2
69.28	wine: these] wine; when these 1
69.39–40	a reinforcement, that he might have it more quickly] some more, to have it more quickly 1
69.44–70.1	those pigeons] these pidgeons 1
70.11	politeness. Hearing] politness; and hearing 1
70.11	she put on an air] put on an air 1
70.23	one of them] one of 'em 1
70.43	home!] ~? 1–2
70.43	Your brother] your brother 1; you brother 2
71.14	twelve: at last, he began] twelve. And at last, began 1
71.27	abroad?] ~. 1
71.27–28	this address, and] this, and 1
71.29	word: and] word. And 1
71.30	read a lecture] read him a lecture 1
72.14	get his bread] get bread 1
72.32	kicks on the breech. That] kicks. That 1
72.42	Sunday] sunday 1–2

73.15–16	cast her arms round his neck, and locked him in her embrace. The good] cast herself upon his neck, and lock'd him in her arms; and the good 1
73.16	no less the emotions] no less motions 1
73.22	Then he gave] After this he gave 1
73.32	child] my child 1
73.42	ate a couple of eggs] eat two eggs 1
75.1	having left] after leaving 1
75.3	here? . . . him.] ~, . . . ~? 1–2
75.3	Son] my son 1
75.9	it! replied his son;] it, replied his son? 1
75.19	the different reasons that deprived them of their senses.] the reasons why each of them lost the use of their senses. 1
75.24–25	see them] see of them 1–2
75.31	had been beaten] had been beat 1
75.34	But this disaster has] But this has 1
76.3	that venerable] this venerable 1
76.12	every human creature.] every one. 1
76.19	women's] womens 1
76.21–22	there addressing himself] and addressing himself 1
76.30	gardener's] gardeners 1
76.31	Child] my child 1
76.32	who are married] being married 1
77.1	charmed: he found] charmed, and found 1
77.6	her: to be satisfied] her: and to be satisfied 1
77.7	private, he said to her] private, said to her 1
77.22	yes,] ~ʌ 2
77.26	But in this supposition you] But in this you 1
78.14	there putting off] where putting off 1
78.15	of which] at which 1
78.15	After which precaution] After which 1
78.18	ran up stairs] run up stairs 1
78.25	than his rage] but his rage 1

78.29	immediately rode] immediately rid 1
78.36	than they had him] but they had him 1
78.39	misconduct] conduct 1
78.39–40	thank themselves.] thank only themselves. 1
78.43	God bless me!] ~ ~ ~, 1–2
78.43	Cleofas,] ~: 1; ~! 2
79.5	that explanation clears] that clears 1
79.13	that great] this great 1
79.14	lover, who] lover, whom 1
79.15	confine him.] shut him up. 1
79.27	no sighs] not sighs 2
79.41	In the original *Paien*, a noted traiteur at Paris.] *om.* 1
80.6	adjoining to that] joining that 1
80.21–22	Hidalgo de] Hidalgo da 1–2
80.32	women than] women then 1–2
80.35	here. You] here; you 1
81.1	an expected match] in a marriage she expected 1
81.5	A chevalier] And a chevalier 1
81.5	St. Jago] St. Jaques 1
81.27	has turned her brain.] has occasioned her turning mad. 1
81.35	sensible of the change] sensible to the change 1
81.42	of it is justly] of it justly 1
82.13	Guillem] Guillim 2
82.32	Notwithstanding] Though, notwithstanding 1
82.35	things upon trust] things much upon trust 1
82.42	by which the principal object of his revenge might escape] that might be the occasion of the principal object of his revenge escaping 1
82.43	waiting] waited 1
82.44	morning, entered her apartment] morning, and then entered into her apartment 1
83.10	Kimen] Ximenes 1
83.12	be the person who] be him who 1
83.33	place where] place here where 1

84.5	leagues] leaves 1
84.11	Kimen] Kimem 1
84.19	gaoler] goaler 1–2
84.22	puzzled] difficulted 1
84.25	revolved] resolved 1
84.25–26	upon to escape] upon	escape 1
84.28	into a place] into place 2
84.41	My dear Julio] my dear Julio 2
85.7	pistol: Julio] pistol; and Julio 1
85.32	gentleman] genleman 2
87.14	every thing that] every that 1
87.40–41	was torture equal to ten] was ten 1
88.20	be chained] be laid in chains 1
88.26	cruel] cruelty 2
88.38–39	but appear] not appear 1
88.40	as it happened, he had no] and, as it happened, had no 1
88.42	doctors] doctor's 1–2
89.9–10	any that deserve to have places here] any one that deserves to have a place here 1
89.20	convent] concent 2
89.34	years was written] years was wrote 1
89.36	lady, and] lady, And 1
89.38	affairs, said she] affairs, said he 1
90.7	twenty-eight] ~,~ 2
90.33	to keep his money] to keep money 1
90.39	that?] ~, 1–2
90.40	demon.] ~; 1; ~? 2
91.14	he has caused them to be printed] he has made them be printed 1
91.44	coxcomb this is!] ~ ~ ~, 1–2
92.1	laughter;] ~! 2
92.17	ecstasy] ectasy 2
94.17	Love-Song] love-song 1

94.25	Le Sage] le Sage 1–2
94.30	character,] ~. 1
94.32	*aiebem*] *acebem* 1
94.41	men's] mens 1
95.4	You captivate the gods above] You rapture men and gods above 1
95.33	concert] consort 1
96.16	*fire,*] ~; 2
96.18	crying out, water] ~ ~,~ 2
97.9	you I must] you must 1
101.1–2	THE	CONTENTS] CONTENTS 2.
103.6	*dead;*] ~, 2
103.16	health. But] health, but 1
104.12	but pray] put pray 2
104.27–28	mistress of herself] mistress for herself 2
104.38	it? answered she.] ~, ~ ~? 1–2
106.10	plums] plumbs 1
106.16	be? . . . Perez.] ~, . . . ~? 1–2
106.38	tomb] tombs 2
107.10	illusionary] illusinary 2
108.27–28	conflagrations] burnings 1
108.36–37	persuaded, pass through Madrid, without leaving] persuaded, only pass thro' Madrid, he will leave 1
108.38	for parade only.] only for parade. 1
108.42	crocadile's tears] tears of the crocodile 1
109.5	he is gone] it is gone 2
109.7	bed-ridden for some] bed-ridden some 1
109.8	single] a batchelor 1
109.10	They affected] They appeared in 1
109.12–13	having whimpered in the character of] having affected to appear 1
109.14	other] others 1
109.14–15	What a blessing] what a blessing 1
109.15	who forego all the enjoyments] who will partake of none of the enjoyments 1

109.16   their representatives.]   them. 1

109.17   that most fathers]   that the most of fathers 1

109.22   youth, in spite of]   youth, spite of 1

110.6   shrieks?]   ~, 1; skrieks, 2

110.6   demon.]   ~? 1–2

110.21   CHAPTER II.]   *om.* 1–2

111.11   Alvaro]   Alvarez 1–2

111.18   Does either of you]   Do any of you 1

111.25   Alvaro]   Alvarez 1–2

111.28   Alvaro]   Alvarez 1–2

111.39   Alvaro]   Alvarez 1–2

112.7   Alvaro]   Alvarez 1–2

112.15   Alvaro]   Alvarez 1–2

112.20   Alvaro]   Alvarez 1–2

112.26   Alvaro]   Alvarez 1–2

112.45   anticipate]   prevent 1

114.2–3   that circumstance greatly]   that greatly 1

114.13   reproach me.]   ~ ~ₐ 2

114.27   say? . . . astonishment.]   ~, . . . ~? 1–2

114.39   one, had such an effect that]   one, made me that 1

114.40   and felt]   and I felt 1

115.36   pen, ink, and paper]   paper, pen and ink 1

116.21–22   privately in the twilight]   privately the beginning of the night 1

116.33   tender]   tendre 1

117.6–7   endeavours]   endervours 2

117.10   chanced]   happened 1

117.29   are just.]   were just. 1

117.41   woman's]   women 1

118.9   Alvaro]   Alvarez 1–2

118.39   Ægisthus]   Æghistus 1–2

119.33   That representing]   That represented 1

120.15	peace!] ~? 1-2
120.32-33	killing one another] cutting one another's throats 1
120.41	I tell it you with] I tell you them with 1
121.6	those marks] these marks 1
122.5	captivate by] captivate to 1
122.10	for any lady not] for any one not 1
122.10-11	she earnestly wishes for] they earnestly wish for 1
122.12	retirement] retirements 1
122.25	Villareal] Villa real 1-2
122.27-28	as that] as on account that 1
123.24	Theodora,] ~. 1-2
123.41	impart to me!] ~ ~ ~? 1-2
124.36-37	can her repose] can repose 2
124.37	you? . . . Fadrique.] ~, . . . ~? 1-2
125.10	besides this instance] including this instance 1
125.10-11	known some few examples] known examples 1
125.18	Villareal] Villa-| real 1; Vil-| la real 2
125.33	masks] mask 1
125.40	an end] and end 1
126.20	all their haste] they made such haste 1
126.25-26	Alvaro] Alvarez 1-2
127.19	brother Bard, who] brother, who 1
127.27	charmed with them!] ~ ~ ~? 1-2
127.33-34	answer for your vigilance.] answer for. 1
130.17-18	am of opinion] am opinion 2
130.18	otherguise folks] otherguess sort of folks 1
130.26	replied] replies 1
133.1	Alvaro] Alvarez 1-2
134.17-18	deprived of the unhappiness] deprived the happiness 1
135.6	asked his name.] ~ ~ ~? 2
136.16	heaven] heavens 1

136.29	whither] whether 1
136.32	Alvaro] Alvarez 1–2
136.39	too well] two well 2
137.5	Alvaro] Alvarez 1–2
137.22	She] And she 1
137.23	dispense with marrying] dispense from marrying 1
137.25	point] paint 1–2
137.44	mussulmen] mussulman 1
138.4	seraglio] seralio 1
138.11	horror: empty] horror. Empty 1
138.29	ecchos] eccho's 1
139.35	hope] hopes 1
140.2	occasion] accasion 2
140.6	In our] In her 1
140.15	lose . . . regret] loose . . . regrets 1
140.16	I am rejoiced] I am quite rejoiced 1
140.22	deliver] liberate 1
140.28	Mezomorto to name her ransom] Mezomorto name her ransom 1
140.29	that? . . . Francisco.] ~, . . . ~? 1–2
140.34	lady's] ladies 1–2
141.8	he insinuated himself] he got himself 1
141.25	moment's] moments 2
142.11	embark] come on 1
142.33	being busied] be-| busied 1
142.40	imagination!] ~? 1–2
143.4	affects] affect 1
143.9	ever be] ever by 2
143.43	honour] hunour 2
144.11–12	advice was very judicious.] advice a very judicious one. 1
144.19	acquainted] acquaisited 1
145.1	I, your friend] ~ˌ ~ ~ 2
145.7	despair);] ~;) 1–2

145.15	knew that] knew thas 2
145.27–28	reached the ship] got to the ship 1
145.30	inspire.] inspire into them. 1
146.1	liberty had been] liberty been 2
146.5	this declaration.] this. 1
146.6	she felt for him] she had for him 1
146.10	surgeon] surgeons 1
146.11	turned] turning 1
146.32	Don Fadrique] Don Juan 1
146.35–36	it. Madam] it; Madam 1
146.43	these fatal shores] those fatal shores 1
147.1	Alvaro] Alvarez 1–2
147.6	set us on shore] put us on shore 1
147.17	to Algiers, and begged] there, and begged 1
147.27–28	done, It] done, it 1–2
148.19	lifted] lift 1
150.28	Mendozas] Mendoza's 1
153.1	hear!] ~? 1–2
153.42	Divine Legation] divine legation 1
154.3	printing a second edition] printing another edition 1
154.5	through] thro' 1; though 2
154.16	secret] seceret 2
154.25	to their pockets] in their pockets 1
156.9	vanish!] ~? 1–2
156.29	Metamorphoses] metamorphoses 1
157.4	The demon who was] The demon was 1
157.31	the troop] that troop 1
158.19	street? . . . Cleofas.] ~, . . . ~? 1–2
158.26	Alcmena] Alcmene 1
158.39	in doubt, whether he should] puzzled, whether he shall 1
159.2	citizen] citizens 2
159.8	not sixpence] not a sixpence 1

159.17   that lady] that fine lady 1

159.22   .Though his family is one of the greatest in Spain] Though he is one of
                the greatest families in Spain 1

160.2   have them] have of them 1–2

160.4   which winds its] who winds his 1–2

160.13   and attendant] and | and attendant 1

160.25   rejoicings] rejoicing 1

160.39   he knows she] she knows he 1

161.11   Apropos. Now] Apropos, now 1

161.17–18   church? . . . Cleofas.] ~, . . . ~? 1–2

161.36   that he who wrote] that who wrote 1

161.38   alledging] alledg-| 2

162.17   let pass] let you pass 1

162.24   ladies in] ladies who lived in 1

163.4   you? . . . Leandro.] ~, . . . ~? 1–2

163.39   means,] ~. 2

164.24   poor,] ~ˌ 1–2

164.37   certainly] certainty 2

165.3   academy at Toledo] academy of Toledo 1

166.12   Ayala,] ~ˌ 2

166.41   and I have not it] and I not have it 1

167.9   here! . . . Leandro.] ~, . . . ~? 1–2

168.24–25   long? . . . Leandro.] ~, . . . ~? 1–2

169.11   pane] pain 2

170.17   gentility] genteelity 2

171.35   begun a conversation] began a conversation 2

173.4   captives] captive 1

173.4   worth had] worth he had 2

173.5   on account] on | on account 2

173.10   reason of it.] reason of ˌ 2

173.16   Castilian] Castillan 2

173.21   who are all dead] who | who are all dead 2

173.21	dead, except] dead‸ excepting 1
173.24	this! . . . scholar.] ~, . . . ~? 1–2
173.36	La Merci] la Merci 1–2
173.42	I am not] I an not 2
174.20	*in what*] *it what* 2
174.28	partaking of] partaking in 1
175.8	road to Corita] road of Corita 1
175.41–42	he had not an instrument] had he had no instrument 1
177.8	farther] father 2
177.34	three-fourths] three‸fourths 1; three	fourth 2
178.7	would have] should have 1
178.23	hope] hopes 1–2
178.33	much as in my power] much as is in my power 1
179.5	behalf] hehalf 2
179.18	opportunity to go] opportunity of going 1
181.1	you? . . . student.] ~, . . . ~? 1–2
181.1	extraordinary] extrrordinary 2
181.6	I am! . . . concern.] ~~, . . . ~! 1–2
181.37	has assured] have assured 1–2
182.7	this? . . . he.] ~, . . . ~? 1–2
183.21	Esculano] Esculana 1
183.42	transport of joy] taansport of joy 2
184.4	Zambullo? . . . he.] ~, . . . ~? 1–2
184.36	liberty which he] liberty he 1
185.34	eight. B. Indeed] eight. Indeed 1–2
186.21	insult me] insult men 2
186.29	had been the eternal] had the eternal 1
187.23	learned you are!] ~ ~ ~? 1–2
187.24	had studied] has studied 1
187.26	likewise] likeways 1
188.5	*The*] *om.* 1–2

188.34   slash] flash 2

189.3   phenix of a husband] phenix of a hus-| hand 2

189.11   simpleton you are!]   ~,~ ~? 1–2

190.11–12   Negociators] Negociations 1

190.14   apartment!]   ~? 1–2

BIBLIOGRAPHICAL DESCRIPTIONS

1. THE FIRST EDITION

THE | DEVIL upon CRUTCHES: | FROM THE | DIABLE BOITEUX | OF | Mr. LE SAGE. | A | NEW TRANSLATION. | To which are now first added, | ASMODEUS's CRUTCHES, | a Critical Letter upon the Work; | And DIALOGUES between Two Chimneys | of Madrid. | Adorned with Cuts. | Michael from Adam's Eyes the Film remov'd | —— Then purg'd with Euphrasy and Rue | The visual Nerve, for he had much to see. Milt. | In TWO VOLUMES. | VOL. I. | [printer's ornament] | LONDON: | Printed for J. Osborn, in Paternoster-Row. | M.DCC.L.

Volume 2: Title page as in volume 1 except "VOL. II." substituted for "VOL. I."

Collation: 12° in 6s (125 x 78 mm.). Volume 1:Π⁴ a⁶ B–Q⁶ R⁴ S⁶ T². Pp. *i* title, iii–vi The AUTHOR's | DEDICATION | To the Illustrious | Don Lewis Velez de Guevara., *bis v–vi* THE | CONTENTS | OF THE | FIRST VOLUME., vii–xviii *ASMODEUS's* | CRUTCHES., *1–188* text, *189–200* INDEX | TO THE | FIRST VOLUME., *201–2 blank.* Volume 2: P⁶ A–R⁶. Pp. *i* title, *iii–iv* THE | CONTENTS | OF THE | SECOND VOLUME., *1–192* text, *193–204* INDEX | TO THE | SECOND VOLUME.

Press figures: Volume 1: iii-2 xvii-1 12-1 43-2 44-2 78-3 120-4 138-4 156-1 163-1 187-2. Volume 2: 23-4 48-3 59-4 66-1 68-1 103-5 126-4 139-2 140-1 176-1 199-3.

Typography: Volume 1: Pp. *bis v–vi*, 81 = 1. C2 = B2, C3 = B3, S2 = P3, S3 unsigned. Headline: 95 CRUTC HES. Catchwords: *viii* THE] *ASMODEUS's* 79 her;] her: 156 'self] ‚self. Volume 2: Page 136 = 156, 175 = 176. Catchwords: *1* ‚The] "The.

Copies: Huntington Library (350964); Lewis M. Knapp copy, Cameron House; Newberry Library (Case Y 762 L576); Oxford University, Bodleian Library (Vet.A4f.669–670); Yale University, Sterling Library (Hfd22 290).

2. THE SECOND EDITION

THE | DEVIL upon CRUTCHES: | FROM THE | DIABLE BOITEUX | OF | Mr. LE SAGE. | A | NEW TRANSLATION. | To which are now first added, | ASMODEUS's CRUTCHES, | A Critical Letter upon the Work; | And DIALOGUES between Two Chimneys | of MADRID. | Adorned with CUTS. | Michael from Adam's Eyes the Film remov'd | ——Then purg'd with Euphrasy and Rue | The visual Nerve, for he had much to see. Milt. | The Second Edition, corrected. | IN TWO VOLUMES. | VOL. I. | [two 66 mm. rules] | LONDON: | Printed for T. Osborn, A. Millar, R. Baldwin, | S. Crowder, J. Rivington and J. Fletcher, | and I. Pottinger. | MDCCLIX.

Volume 2: Title page as in volume 1 except "VOL. II." substituted for "VOL. I"; "T. Osborne" substituted for "T. Osborn."

Collation: 12° (165 x 92 mm.). Volume 1: A⁴ B–M¹² N⁸. Pp. *i* title, iii–vi The AUTHOR's | DEDICATION | To the Illustious | Don Lewis Velez de Guevara., *vii–viii* THE |

CONTENTS., *1–15* ASMODEUS's | CRUTCHES., *16* blank, *17–266* text, *267–80* INDEX. Volume 2: A^2 B–M^{12} N^4. Pp. *i* title, *iii–iv* CONTENTS | OF THE | SECOND VOLUME., *1–260* text, *261–72*, INDEX | TO THE | SECOND VOLUME.

Press figures: Volume 1: iv-5 62-5 64-4 85-4 118-6 142-6 158-2 178-2 204-2 226-3 263-6. Volume 2: 12-5 34-1 37-6 61-4 88-5 98-2 108-3 135-5 157-5 167-6 178-1 214-7 239-1 254-2 266-1.

Typography: Volume 1: Pp. 247 = 257, 258 = 238. No page number: v. D6 unsigned. Catchwords: *viii* THE] ASMODEUS's 31 ˌSuppose] "Suppose 46 ˌA-] "A 90 be-] lieve 113 other] ther 120 desire] sire. No catchword: 36, 121, 133, 138, 194, 218, 269, 270, 271, 272. Volume 2: Page 210 = 211, 211 = 210. Catchwords: *1* "The] ˌThe 23 "It] ˌIt. No catchword: 166.

Copies: Cambridge University library (S735.d.75.2–3); William Andrew Clark Library (*PQ1997.D5.2E.1759); Cornell University Library (PQ 1997 D5 E5 1759); Lewis M. Knapp copy, Cameron House; McMaster University Library (B 17993); National Library of Scotland (AB.1.78.6); University of Virginia (PQ1997.D5.E5.1759); Yale University, Sterling Library (Y2 11257–11258).

INDEX

Laufer, Roger, xviii, xix
Le Sage, Alain René: birth, xvii; law, practices,
    xvii; literature, turns to, xvii; popularity in
    France, xvii; Smollett, career compared to,
    xvii; Spanish literature, influence on, xvii
WORKS:
—*Le Diable boiteux*, xv; characterized, xvi, xvii,
    xviii, xix, xx, xxiii–xxiv, 64 (n. 45); Dacier,
    use of, 19–20, 94 (n. 24); English editions,
    xix; gates of sleep, 153; Homer, comments
    on, 153; Horace, 19–20, 94; popularity, xix;
    publication, xii, xvii, xix; revisions, xix;
    typography, 239; Virgil, comments on, 81,
    153
—Other works: *Le Bachelier de Salamanque*,
    xvii; *Crispin, rival de son maître*, xvii; *Don
    Guzman d' Alfarache*, xvii; *Don Quixote*, xvii;
    Estevanille Gonzales, xvii; *Garder et se garder*,
    xvii; *Gil Blas*, xv, xvii; *Le Point d'honneur*, xvii;
    Le Traître puni, xvii; *Turcaret*, xvii
London Magazine, xxi
Lucian, 160 (n. 10)

Macaulay, George, xxvi (n. 10)
Malkin, Henry, xxvii (n. 34)
Manilla, auditor of, 91 (n.15)
Maximilian I (duke of Bavaria), 127 (n. 7)
Michaelis, Sebastien, xviii
Millar, Andrew, xx, 237
Milton, John, 14 (n. 5)
Molière (Jean-Baptiste Poquelin), xviii
Monthly Review, xxvi (n. 8)
Moore, John, xxvi (n. 9)

Nettesheim, Agrippa von, xviii, 15 (n. 11)

Origo, 94, 108 (n. 21)
Osborn, John (the younger), xx, xxii, xxv, 237
Our Lady of Mercy, Order of, 104 (n. 4)

Pedro I (king of Portugal), 65 (n. 51)
Perrault, Charles, xviii
Pharmaceuticals, Guide to, 207–8
Philadelphia Portfolio, xxvii (n. 34)
Phillip III (king of Spain), 155 (n. 14)
Plautus, Titus Maccius, 161
Plutarch, 15 (n. 20), 23 (n. 39)
Pope, Alexander, 160 (n. 14)

"Portal hymns," 24 (n. 51)
Present State of Tangier, The, 141 (n. 24)
Puerto del Sol in Plaza Major, 96 (n. 30)

Rojas Zorrilla, Francisco de, xvii
Rudwin, Maximilian, xix

Saint Jago (Saint James the Greater), 56 (n. 12)
Saint Jago, knight of, 24 (n. 49), 164 (n. 10)
Saint John the Baptist, 64 (n. 45)
Saint Salvador, Church of, 19 (n. 1)
Salamanca, University of, 168 (n. 7)
Sallust (Gaius Sallustius Crispus), 93
Santa Hermandad, 85 (n. 44)
Scarron, Paul, xviii
Scots Magazine, xxi
Seneca (the younger), 60 (n. 22)
Showalter, English, xviii
Sinclair, George, 18 (n. 8)
Smith, John, 238
Smith, Richard, xxvii (nn. 33, 34)
Smollett, Tobias George: early professional
    disappointments, xv; financial needs, xvi;
    French, knowledge of, xxiii; Latinate
    diction, fondness for, xxiii, xxiv; Le Sage,
    career compared to, xvii; medical
    knowledge, xi, xv, xxiii; pride, xv; residences,
    xv; translation, attitude toward, xv, xvi, xxii,
    xxiii; translator, work as, xv, xvi, xxii
WORKS:
—*Devil upon Crutches*: attribution to Smollett,
    xx–xxii; characterized, xi, xvi, xvii, xviii, xix,
    xx; corrections, of Dacier, 19–20, 94;
    corrections, of Le Sage, 19–20, 94 (n. 24),
    153; dating of composition, xvi, xxiv–xxv;
    geography, confusion of, 69 (n. 5); influence
    on later career, xx; payment, xxiii–xxiv;
    publication, xv, xx, xxv, 237; receipt for
    corrections, xx, xxvii (n. 26); reception, xxv,
    237; revisions, xi, xxi, xxii, xxiv, xxv, 240;
    textual commentary, 237–42; translation,
    method of, xxiii–xxiv; translation, signs of
    haste in, xi, xxv; typography, 239
—Comments on: Cicero, 23, 118; Euripides,
    118; Gellius, Aulus, 93; Homer, 153;
    Horace, 19–20, 24, 93, 94, 97, 151, 161;
    Milton, John, 14 (n. 5); Plautus, 161;
    "portal hymns," 24 (n. 51); Sophocles, 118;

The Works of Tobias Smollett

The Adventures of Ferdinand Count Fathom
EDITED BY JERRY C. BEASLEY AND O M BRACK, JR.

The Adventures of Gil Blas of Santillane
BY ALAIN RENÉ LE SAGE; TRANSLATED BY TOBIAS SMOLLETT
EDITED BY O M BRACK, JR., AND LESLIE A. CHILTON

The Adventures of Peregrine Pickle
EDITED BY JOHN P. ZOMCHICK AND GEORGE S. ROUSSEAU

The Adventures of Roderick Random
EDITED BY JAMES G. BASKER, PAUL-GABRIEL BOUCÉ, AND NICOLE A. SEARY

The Adventures of Telemachus, the Son of Ulysses
BY FRANÇOIS DE FÉNELON; TRANSLATED BY TOBIAS SMOLLETT
EDITED BY LESLIE A. CHILTON AND O M BRACK, JR.

The Devil upon Crutches
BY ALAIN RENÉ LE SAGE; TRANSLATED BY TOBIAS SMOLLETT
EDITED BY O M BRACK, JR., AND LESLIE A. CHILTON

The Expedition of Humphry Clinker
EDITED BY THOMAS R. PRESTON AND O M BRACK, JR.

The History and Adventures of an Atom
EDITED BY ROBERT ADAMS DAY AND O M BRACK, JR.

The History and Adventures of the Renowned Don Quixote
BY MIGUEL DE CERVANTES; TRANSLATED BY TOBIAS SMOLLETT
EDITED BY MARTIN C. BATTESTIN AND O M BRACK, JR.

The Life and Adventures of Sir Launcelot Greaves
EDITED BY ROBERT FOLKENFLIK AND BARBARA LANING FITZPATRICK

Poems, Plays, and "The Briton"
EDITED BY BYRON GASSMAN AND O M BRACK, JR.